Best Short Stories 1990

Best Short Stories 1990

EDITED BY GILES GORDON AND DAVID HUGHES

HEINEMANN : LONDON

William Heinemann Ltd
Michelin House
81 Fulham Road
London SW3 6RB

LONDON   MELBOURNE   AUCKLAND

This collection first published 1990
This collection, together with the introduction and notes,
copyright © Giles Gordon and David Hughes 1990

A CIP catalogue record for this book
is available from the British Library

ISBN 0 434 35415 5

Photoset by Deltatype Ltd, Ellesmere Port, Cheshire
Printed in Great Britain by
St Edmundsbury Press, Bury St Edmunds
and bound by Hunter & Foulis Ltd, Edinburgh

Contents

Introduction

THIS IS THE fifth of our annual collections of stories published in English but not – no insular prejudice here, merely trade custom – by Americans. Less than ever is there any shortage of material. We have read widely, from devoted small magazines in New Zealand to Fleet Street's recently acquired appetite for new fiction. Our selection comes from a wide range of media the world over (including the USA, where the British, Irish and Commonwealth command of the art is frequently welcome) and for the first time we have found broadcast stories, often too chatty to make good prose on the page, of a standard to include.

On a critical if not tendentious note, we thought it depressing that stories by lesser-known writers in a variety of little magazines cut less ice with our taste or judgment than in earlier years, though paradoxically, or thanks to the current climate, many of these were of a higher degree of accomplishment than would have been the case a decade ago. We have made our discoveries – we offer first publication in book form by at least three writers – but most of the best finds tend to be by authors of established voice. So many well-considered names were at the peak of their form, from Nadine Gordimer battling with African tensions no less universal in appeal than

Frederic Raphael jousting with Hollywood follies, that we found it less painful to exclude superb work by such masters of their craft as Edna O'Brien and William Trevor. Not on grounds of quality. By hitting a year when each was coming out with a collection, our enthusiastic choice of both fell victim to the accident of publishing schedules. Our policy is to reprint no story already available in a volume when ours comes on the market.

Five years ago at the outset we offered twenty stories, then crept up to twenty-two. Now, with no lowering of criteria or diminution of quality, we present twenty-five authors for your enjoyment. Certain organs require special mention for the continuing encouragement and home they offer the formerly embattled writer of short fiction. This year the *Observer* again assumed a sophistication in its readership unmatched in the Sunday press. BBC Radio as a patron of stories is often not only ignored by readers but forgotten by story-tellers with their hearts set on the printed page; Jane Gardam's contribution is for both ear and eye. It was good to locate no fewer than three excellent tales in the tenth-anniversary edition of *Granta*, a publication we last year mildly reproved for its concentration on the wrong side of the Atlantic. Finally – apart from the *London Magazine* which continues under Alan Ross to feed its readers a rich diet of fiction – let us cheer the Newcastle-based *Stand* magazine presided over by poet Jon Silkin, a consistent editor of fine new work over many decades. Any caringly up-to-date reader of prose or poetry who chooses to be in touch with his times should subscribe to these excellent and inexpensive periodicals. We represent them both here, but not as fully as with more space we might.

Though we try to avoid detecting trends among the stories we pick, it is likely that this volume contains narratives more engaged than usual: politically engaged. Neither of us is interested in sermons or disquisitions. Yet we were moved by several people – Gordimer, Diski, Kureishi, Treitel – who took up political realities around today's world and converted them, with that unsettling eloquence that is fiction's advantage over reportage, into the power that held Homer's hearers round the fire.

Since our last volume this annual has gone into paperback in this country as *The Minerva Book of Short Stories* and is now to be published every year in the United States as *Best English Short Stories*. From our correspondence, always welcome, a widely suggested improvement (thank goodness, there are few such nudges about the contents) is to drop the word 'best' from the title. We are fallible; but we share tastes in common: so we stand by it – and, as ever, by the pleasures crowded between these covers.

Giles Gordon and David Hughes

It Will Grow Again

CECIL BONSTEIN

THE WOMEN WOULD undress in the cold shed. The guards would shout orders; threaten with whips and clubs. The barking, snarling dogs would rise on their hind legs, pulling at their leads.

'Faster! Faster! Yes, yes; clothing later. After the bath. You stink. You must have bath. Hurry! Hurry!'

The women followed each other fearfully. Hands tried to conceal their nakedness. All had long hair because that was the fashion among them. They came to us, the barbers, to have it shorn. Shivering with fear and cold they came, some weeping, some praying, many silent. All were white-faced – in a state of shock. The lewd jokes and gestures sporadically jerking from the mouths and arms of the guards were frightening; hard to bear. But they were a long line of women. The line absorbed the insults. Made them seem less personal; less individually threatening. A few of the silent women, instead of covering themselves, shambled forward, bodies hunched, heads bent, arms dangling. These knew; yes, I am sure they knew that death was very near.

We stood behind the wooden forms. The women had to approach and sit briefly with their backs to us. Our job was to shear their hair, speedily and brutally. No time-wasting was

1

permitted. Anyone who lost his speed was pulled out. Was kicked and clubbed to a dead pulp as an example to the rest. If unlucky he was subjected to a slower death.

So, a fistful of hair and cut, cut; another fistful and cut, cut. Three fistfuls and a few cuts and the long tresses would be on the floor. When I could, when I felt sure the guards would not hear me, I would whisper through the fearful noise – from the women, the guards, the dogs – I would whisper, 'It will grow again. Don't worry. It will grow again.'

It was a suggestion. A merciful lie whispered to give a flush of strength. To imply that there was still a future. That one day, once again, face and flowing hair would reflect back from an appreciative mirror.

In about fifteen minutes all sounds and sights for them would end. I wonder, too often, even now, what they thought, these helpless women to whom I whispered. I imagine they were only capable of one elemental thought as the gas convulsed their bodies. Still I worry about it.

After we sheared their hair they were herded to the gas chamber between two walls of freshly cut branches and leaves. 'It will grow again.' Had I not promised? I, a fellow Jew. Barbed wire supported the foliage and could not easily be seen. But it was not much of a camouflage. All around was the stench of death. The production-line system frequently failed to keep up with the disposal of the bodies by cremation. The bodies would accumulate and putrefy.

So the women and children would reach the murder chamber. Crying, calling to God, screaming for help they would be crammed violently into it – perhaps, some of them, still hoping desperately that they were going to have a shower. That their cropped hair would grow again.

Maybe I should not have whispered. Who knows?

I am not sure that I have anything significant to say but now, after these many years – and because of what happened recently – I want to talk. Thank you for writing it all down for me and for translating it into readable English.

It is the first time I have spoken so freely. People, thankfully, are reluctant to ask me about my experiences but I can sense their questions.

'What happened to his relatives and friends?'

'How did he manage to survive?'

'What did he see? What did he do?'

Well, these and many more are the sort of questions I would expect if I encouraged people to ask them. They would want me to discuss and describe and analyse; but this is something I will not do. When victims, such as we were, are in competition to survive we adapt in whatever way suits our natures. I have seen acts – a few – of such bravery and self-sacrifice . . . you would be amazed. And I have been sickened by acts of brutality and sadism; of deviousness and cowardice and meanness. But why describe it all? We are trained from babyhood to act against our natures. When the restraints go the torturers and murderers are set free. We men are beasts under restraint. This is the way we are. What further analysis is necessary?

I am a Jew who grew up in a Polish ghetto. Like most of my fellow Jews and like most Poles I was poor. My short formal education was narrow and handicapped by religious prejudice and superstition.

I learned to think in a critical way, I suppose, because I read bits of the Talmud and because I was often with my father when, after the synagogue prayers, some of the congregation gathered in groups to talk. They would discuss, and argue and speculate about God and life, about family and food and, of course, about justice and persecution.

This kind of conversation is a legacy of our history. For one thing, however, we have no answer. Why do people hate and persecute us? Why do they tell lies about us? We shrug our shoulders. We spread our arms. We have no answer. Nevertheless we continue to talk and discuss – should we kill ourselves? – because in conversation there is some comfort.

There came the day when all the Jews in our ghetto were assembled and taken in cattle trucks to the concentration camp. There my family and most of the rest of the people I

3

knew were quickly and painfully murdered and I, because I was young and strong and because they needed replacement workers at the time, was spared.

When I first came to England I declined a job as a barber. How could I ever be a barber again?

Even now I can feel the hair I cut from those women and children. Can smell their fear. Shearing, shearing, shearing, it fell about my feet, kept falling until it reached above my ankles and I had to kick it away. The blond hair, so fine and bright, looked too optimistic; the wrong colour in this hideous camp. Dark hair was coarse and strong. Red hair, the most coarse of all to the touch but in certain lights . . . ah, the passion, the warmth it suggested. But I sheared it off like all the other hair. And children's hair, so delicate, so fine – strands of silk. Of course, they did not understand; did not want to have their hair cut. The length of their hair proclaimed they were big girls, grown up, not babies any more. Still, they did not resist. It was plain to see what happened to those who resisted. So they wept, and I wept inside, and they called to their mothers while I bunched their hair in my fist. Just three bunches and a few quick cuts and it was gone.

There was one girl; she was about fourteen. Her hair nearly reached her waist. How she must have washed and combed and groomed that hair. She covered her face with her hands as I gripped.

Some images I can never forget.

No, I could never be a barber again.

I came to live in Whitechapel because there were people in the district who knew my family. It is difficult to know whether it is safer to live in ghettos, or whether it is wiser to merge with the native population – to become green leaves among other green leaves. To disappear as Jews and let some other minority take the strain of Europe's barbarism. Murdering Jews in the pogroms of Poland and Russia was easy, convenient. All the killer bands needed to do was ask the way to the nearest ghetto.

Nevertheless I settled in Whitechapel. I liked the atmosphere. It was good to be among ordinary, unafraid people. In the grocery shop near where I lived I could buy familiar food like salt or pickled herring or pickled cucumbers all stored in open wooden barrels. The smell of the spices and acid sharpened the air and the appetite. I could buy a hot salt-beef sandwich and breads like brown or black rye and chola, and cakes like plava, honey cake and cheese cake . . .

A charity, the Jewish Board of Guardians, gave me a small allowance while I trained to be a tailor. I did not like the work but it paid a small wage and it enabled me to begin, gradually, to adjust to the new, gentle, much more tolerant society where I now found myself.

I rented a room in a street not far from the London Hospital and furnished it with second-hand furniture. However, I bought a new mattress, one of the firm padded type without springs. It was soft compared to the stone floor or the wooden planks of the camp. Later I bought an old bookcase which I gradually filled with second-hand books. Of course I had no photographs. The blank walls and the empty mantelpiece had to serve as my family memorial. Sometimes I would stare at the wall and try to project my memories of home upon it. What else could I do?

I mentioned my firm mattress. Do you know, I never did discover – I did not wish to enquire – what the Germans did with all that hair. Did they use it to pad mattresses and armchairs? The fabric of some of these must have thinned with wear. Some hair must have seeped out – must still be coming out and floating to the floors of their bedrooms and their living rooms. What do they say when this happens? What do they think? Do they recognise it as human hair? The hair of murdered women and children? And wigs! They must have made wigs from some of the hair. I try not to think about it.

I was lonely, of course. Indeed, in those early months I

preferred to be alone. The work did not satisfy me – but how many non-professional people enjoy their work? Men and women hunched forward all day, sewing, machining, snipping, working at speed. The windows frosted with dirt; unshaded dust-coated light bulbs always alight; rough wooden plank floors patterned with discarded bits of material; steam rising from garments being pressed; the smell of new cloth and dust and sweat . . .

Rachel, a seamstress, worked at a table at right-angles to mine. I thought she was different from the other women and girls. When spoken to she always responded with a charming smile and a few words. However, she hardly ever started a conversation. It seemed to me that she was either shy or that she did not want to encourage closer relationships.

We had caught each other's glances – just fleeting moments when our eyes met – and I felt that she might be vaguely interested in me. However, not being confident with women I had never said anything to her other than 'Good morning' or 'Good night' in the English way. Still, these simple words rewarded me with a smile. A small thing, yet it was something to treasure in these surroundings.

On a dull day, grey in the workshop, grey outside, everyone in a grey mood, one of the pressers decided to have fun. He deposited his pressed work and, returning to his table, made a wide detour as he blundered between the close-packed tables. When he reached a position directly behind Rachel he gripped her firmly below the waist. Pressing heavily against her he pretended he was having difficulty getting past.

She struggled to turn; to get away from him, but his weight was too great. After a few seconds he stepped back. ''Scuse me Rachel,' he said, 'you're just a bit too fat for me.'

She swung round, long black hair swinging; small hands pressed flat against his chest, she tried to push him away, but could not budge him. He roared with laughter at her puny efforts.

''Ere Rachel,' he bellowed, 'you've gone all white. What 'ave yer gone all white for?'

There was a break in her voice as she said, 'Keep your hands to yourself.'

'Push 'im 'arder Rachel,' someone shouted. 'Kick 'im in the goolies.'

'Pick on someone yer own bloody size,' one of the women shouted.

'I bet 'e won't touch 'er again.'

The presser roared. 'You're on.' Now that, as he saw it, he had broken the ice with stuck-up Rachel, and the boss was out of the room, he was ready for some real sport.

Rachel, small, slim, powerless against his size and strength, faced him defiantly. I was momentarily reminded of the despair and terror of all those other helpless women. As he teasingly stretched a hand toward her I shouted, 'Leave her alone.'

He swung round, glaring, fists bunched. I grabbed the heavy tailor's scissors and held it point up toward his face.

Someone touched my arm. 'It's just a joke,' he said.

I pushed him away and kept the scissors raised. 'I told you, get away.'

The presser was uncertain. His fists unclenched. ''Ere, look at der brave man wiv der scissors. Can't a man 'ave a joke wiv a girl anymore?' His tone was whiney. A grown-up boy frustrated. He slouched away. Soon his iron was thumping fast and loud – a strong man's punching reply to me and to Rachel and to everyone in the room. I really think – it is terrible to admit this – I think I would have killed him if he had touched her again.

But the presser, I must not be too hard on him, brought Rachel and me together. Later, when it was time to go home, she came over, touched my arm. 'Thanks,' she said. 'You needn't have, really. I can cope with men like him.'

I laughed. She also laughed. I suppose she weighed less than eight stone. Was only a little over five feet tall, while he was at least six feet, and heavy. Her brown eyes gazing gratefully into mine as she spoke in her soft voice did what any attractive woman's grateful eyes and soft voice would do to a susceptible and lonely man.

It is not necessary for me to tell you the details of our subsequent courtship. We began to meet regularly. We talked, we went to the cinema, walked in the country, listened to music – you know how these things go. Gradually images of her began to dispel the awful memories which, when I was alone, had previously dominated my thoughts.

Rachel told me that she had for two years been taking a commercial course at evening class. Her parents were immigrants from Poland. Her father, a tailor, had always hated her going into what he called the Sweatshop. A few months after the incident with the presser I happily celebrated with her and her parents Rachel's appointment as a clerk to an accountancy firm in Holborn. I missed her presence a few feet away from me but I was glad she was out.

The presser never spoke to me again.

Rachel's parents wanted a synagogue wedding and I did not. It was a Friday night. Bella, Rachel's mother, a shawl over her head, had lit the candles and, hands waving over them, had whispered a Sabbath prayer – plus a few quiet words of her own. We had eaten a traditional dinner of chicken soup and boiled chicken.

'So what do you want?' said Rachel's father. 'Do you want my Rachel to marry in a Registry Office? Is that right, do you think?'

Rachel and her mother, unhappy and worried, were sitting in the large, beige armchairs. He turned to them for support. 'A marriage like that. What is it, eh? Tell me is that a proper marriage? What is wrong with the synagogue?' He was a tall, thin man. He gesticulated with extravagant arm movements as he spoke.

'I'll tell you what's wrong,' I said. 'A synagogue is a place where prayers are said and I've heard all the prayers I ever want to hear.'

'All right, all right, I understand. I know. It was terrible. Absolutely terrible what you went through. We all agree. But for this you should pray more than all of us. Don't you see?

For your poor family you should pray. Who will pray for them if you don't? And you should thank God – yes, you should thank God that you came out alive.'

'But why were we there?'

'You ask me why! Am I God? Do I know all the answers?'

'Listen,' I said, 'Let me tell you about prayers and the Golem of our concentration camp.'

He shrugged. 'Now he's going to tell us a story. All right, I'll listen. At least you can't say I don't listen, but I still want my Rachel to have a synagogue wedding.'

I glanced at Rachel and her mother; at the white, flickering candles. I would rather they did not hear what I had to say but I could not very well ask them to leave. So I began: 'When at night we were in our shed trying to sleep – it was cold, very cold. We lay without any covering on wooden platforms. Among us was a bearded, orthodox Jew who, despite all he had seen, still believed, deeply believed, in God. And he also believed the story of the Golem. That the Golem was once sent by God to save the Jews. Maybe you know the story?'

'I have heard of the Golem. Who hasn't? But Rachel and her mother, they may not know.'

'All right,' I said, 'I'll first remind you about the Golem of Prague.

'According to legend, when the Jews were being rounded up in the ghetto of Prague in the seventeenth century for the children to be roasted, the men battered and murdered and the women raped and murdered, a rabbi, Rabbi Judah Lowe, moulded in the street outside his synagogue a clay image. And while all around him Jews were praying and crying for help, he whispered to this image a name. At the sound of the name the image began to move. Its clay chest began to expand. It expanded massively. It seemed that its chest was sucking in all the surrounding air and all the cries and prayers which burdened the air.

'Its limbs began to stretch and went on stretching. Tall and massive the figure grew – legend says it grew as big as a tree – and its blank eyes suddenly focused. That is how the Golem was born.

'While the Jews stayed with the rabbi the Golem, taking slow, determined strides, began to walk. He walked through the narrow streets of Prague and as he walked he killed. The sound of his heavy steps on the cobbled roads brought to the Christian citizens of Prague the kind of terror they had brought to the Jews.

'Few could escape him. His great clay arms smashed through walls, his feet crushed, his head bludgeoned through windows as his eyes searched out hiding Christians. In two days he slaughtered most of the city's Christians.

'He might have gone on killing. He might have killed all the Christians in Europe. But the Sabbath was approaching. The rabbi began to pray. Standing on a chair, surrounded by his people, he sang a Sabbath prayer. On the last note the Golem stopped his killing and with slow, ponderous steps returned to the rabbi. At a word of command he closed his eyes and became once again solid, unmoving clay. That is the legend.'

'Well, this we know, so. . . ?'

'The name Rabbi Lowe spoke to bring the Golem to life is not known but Jews who believe he existed, Jewish history being what it is, have often cried in despair at the loss of this name.

'Now the man in the concentration camp, the orthodox Jew who believed so deeply in a Jewish God and in the Golem, was one of a team of men whose job it was to incinerate the bodies. The guards had specially selected him for this work. They thought it was funny to have a bearded orthodox Jew destroying Jewish bodies.

'So day after day, praying as he did so, he fed bodies to the fire. The fire quickly consumed them; converted them to chimney smoke; to fine dust lifted by the heat and scattered by every breeze. He prayed and fed more bodies to the fire and they too disappeared, but behind him there were always more bodies. He could not reduce the pile. The Germans considered it a measure of their efficiency that the incinerators never ran out of their special fuel.

'He began to fear that soon the day would come when all the Jews had been murdered. That Europe would be without a single Jew. He grew ever more anguished, ever more desperate, worrying about this dreadful possibility. Eventually he decided that only he could save what remained of the Jews of Europe.

'One night he fashioned out of earth a small model of a man – a black shape with a firm closed mouth and heavy feet and long arms. And night after night, squatting on the stone floor, swaying backwards and forwards in front of it, he prayed. Oh, how he prayed. He prayed to God for help, for His intervention, and in between his prayers he recited names.

'The bodies in the daytime would continue to mass behind him and he would continue to push them into the furnace – but there were always fresh consignments. Where did they all come from? It seemed to him that the guards were sporting with him. That he was in a nightmarish game – a competition.

'Nevertheless he thought he had a chance. A good chance if only God would hear him. What was God doing? Yes, he would teach these murderers that the God of the Jews would not permit His people to be treated in this way. So all through the night, every night, he whispered names and prayed and prayed. He kept us awake with his mournful pleading prayers. Think of all those prayers. But the black figure refused to become the avenging Golem.

'He begged us to think of new names so that he could speak them. We tried to convince him that he was using up his meagre strength, and ours, to no purpose, but he would not listen. His misery and despair grew and we could do nothing for him. It was hard enough for us to stay alive.

'One day he refused to go to work. He said that the need to find the name had become too urgent. Soon there would be no more Jews. God must see this and God would help him.

'The guards were amazed that a Jew could refuse to work. After all, work was a privilege. Workers lived – for a time anyway. A group of them, feet astride, stood in front of him and listened for a while to his prayers and chanting of names. A desperate, urgent chanting. First they laughed and joked about it, then they slowly and expertly began to beat him with their clubs and to kick him with their shiny black boots. "Jew god, where are you?'' they shouted. We had to stand in a circle around them and watch.

'His frantic voice weakened to a whisper, became uncertain, incoherent. Frothy blood blew from his mouth and spattered the earth figure and sprayed the shiny black boots. Eventually, mercifully, he died. The guards laughed and ordered us to clean their boots and to take him to the incinerator.'

They sat facing me looking deeply distressed. Rachel's eyes had grown lenses of tears. What could they say?

Eventually, Rachel's father said, 'Now listen, I understand. Believe me I understand. I don't ask you because I am a religious man. Bella, am I a religious man?'

'I sometimes wish you was more religious,' she said. 'He only prays on Yom Kippur.'

'There, you see. And, God forbid, when relatives and friends die.'

'Well, of course, God forbid, he prays when relatives and friends die.'

'And weddings.'

Bella nodded.

'And that's all. Bella says a few words every Friday night when she lights the candles. Who knows what she says. You saw tonight. And that's all. So I am not a religious man. All right, you didn't find God in the concentration camp. What can I say? I don't know the answer, but still . . . that poor man, he had hope. Maybe that's better than no prayers and no hope. All right, I accept you don't believe, but Rachel . . . Can't you do it for Rachel? I won't say for me or for her mother, but for Rachel. A girl should have a good wedding. It's her special day. Since she was a little baby I saved up for this day. Won't you do it for Rachel?'

He persisted. I could see that he had no intention of agreeing to the simple, secular wedding which I would have preferred. I knew that he was unhappy that Rachel had accepted me for her husband. He would have preferred a professional man for a son-in-law. And Rachel? More than anything I wanted to make her happy. So what could I do? I capitulated.

There is no God but I would, nevertheless, marry Rachel in

the traditional way. The two women were immensely grateful. I was kissed and hugged and her father, with tears in his eyes, shook my hand vigorously. 'Everything will be all right,' he said. 'You'll see, everything will be all right.'

Plans immediately began for the wedding. I left them discussing the hall, the caterer, the guest list, the wedding cars and the photographer. I said I would do whatever they wanted and I did not mention God again.

It was a dull day. The street was an avenue of grey brick lining a black asphalt road. Grey pigeons and grey sparrows sat on roof ledges looking down on us. But the surroundings did not matter. Rachel smiling, black hair down to her shoulders, long white dress, a bouquet of red roses held in her small hands, drew all eyes to her. The grey was the background from which her beauty blazed.

I did the expected things at the synagogue. I stood with Rachel beneath the canopy and prayed. I listened to the rabbi and when required to I prayed. I ritually stamped upon and crushed the wine glass and placed the ring on Rachel's finger and prayed. And then Rachel was my wife. And my prayers? By saying them I had pleased Rachel. It was reason enough.

The reception was in the basement of a restaurant in the Whitechapel Road. The men wore hired evening suits and the women long, colourful dresses. 'Mazeltov. Mazeltov. Mazeltov.' The good luck wish was an intermittent call to Rachel, to me, to her parents and to her close relatives. Every now and again nodding, smiling parents would say, 'Please God by your children.' It was a traditional wedding.

After the dinner we danced to a small band. All the men wanted to dance with Rachel. At one point, to clapping and singing, her mother and father danced the Anniversary Waltz. When I took Rachel on to the floor she whispered, 'It will soon be over.'

My dead family would have been so happy. Hard as I tried I had not been able to supplant my sense of loss. The music and the general atmosphere of gaiety and goodwill only served to emphasise it. I had a sudden premonition; – a view of us all as hollow automata; dancing Jews protectively cocooned in this over-warm hall; temporarily heedless of the hatred – of the murderous impulses massing outside. When would the killing start again? Until Rachel intuitively said, 'It will soon be over,' and squeezed my arm and gazed sympathetically into my eyes. I kissed her long and gently. The guests became human again. The laughter and the clapping engulfed us.

A year after we were married and just before our daughter Rivka, named after my mother, was born, I began to sell general toilet goods on a Saturday in the London markets. It was not always easy to book a pitch at first, but I got to know some stallholders. With their advice I quickly learned the essentials of what I needed to know. Eventually, when I felt confident enough, I happily gave up tailoring. Rachel and I celebrated the event with a meal in the Brasserie of the Oxford Street Corner House. For the first time we took a taxi and felt grand and privileged. Well, just for a few hours.

Two years later we had saved enough to put down the deposit on a small house. Its previous owners had been a middle-aged Jewish couple who, like others recently, their circumstances having improved, had moved out of the East End.

There is a small park near our house. It is just a tiny oblong – a green towel surrounded by two-storey grey-brick houses, but it has a few trees and bushes and beds of flowers. Pigeons and sparrows flutter down from the black slate roofs. Periodically, Rivka helps me to throw damp crumbs of old bread. 'Look, Daddy,' she says, pointing, 'birdy eating.'

Her hair is now almost down to her shoulders. The colour is medium blonde but seems so bright against the backdrop of dark green bushes.

★

The nightmares come less frequently. When they occur they are more bearable since I can reach out to Rachel, warm and safe, in the bed beside me.

Certain images of hair, of a permanent pile of naked emaciated bodies; of men, women and children frantic with fear in the power of insatiable murderers; of bloodstained clubs and whips and boots – will always inhabit my brain and may enter my consciousness at any time. But thankfully they stay hidden for ever longer periods.

Many victims who survived were unable to empty their minds, even for a moment, of its store of horrors. They went mad, or killed themselves – are still killing themselves.

Some, having seen what humans can do and fearing them – feeling forever menaced – have become solitary, haunted people shunning all close human contact.

This is why I have decided to talk to you today and because of what happened yesterday. Maybe my story will give a measure of hope to someone who needs it. Who knows?

Yesterday Rivka and I arrived home to the appetising smell of Rachel's cooking and the sound of her slightly off-key singing. Rachel came to greet us as though we had been away for weeks. A kiss for me, a lift and a hug and a kiss for Rivka. For a moment both their faces were curtained by Rachel's black hair and Rivka's blonde.

'Where have you been all this time, Rivka?' she said. 'Your daddy will get tired if you take him out for so long.'

'We give birdy bread, Mummy.'

'Gave, not give.'

'Gave.'

'That's better.'

And then I said, 'Rivka, your hair is not very straight. What do you think?'

She examined herself very carefully in the mirror.

'Dis bit, Daddy?'

'Yes, Rivka. Over there and just a little bit round the corner.'

Again she looked hard at the mirror.

'Shall I just take a little piece off?'

15

'Daddy . . . just . . . dis . . .' She raised her hand, blue eyes examining them and pointed to the tip of her finger.

I gazed at it very earnestly.

Rachel handed me the scissors. 'Be careful, Daddy,' she said.

'Yes, be careful, Daddy,' Rivka said.

'Yes, of course, Rivka. I shall only take off what needs to come off.'

Gravely, calmly, with my left hand resting lightly and reassuringly on her warm round head, 'Close your eyes,' I said. I began to snip, snip, snip. Slowly, carefully, the way a little girl's hair should be cut, I began to trim the ends of Rivka's fine, blonde hair.

Transfigured Night

WILLIAM BOYD

Selbstmord

IN THIS CITY, and at that time, you should understand that suicide was a completely acceptable option, an entirely understandable, rational course of action to take. And I speak as one who knows its temptations intimately: three of my elder brothers took their own lives – Hans, Rudi and Kurt. That left Paul, me and my three older sisters. My sisters, I am sure, were immune to suicide's powerful contagion. I cannot speak for Paul. As for myself, I can say only that its clean resolution of all my problems – intellectual and emotional – was always most appealing.

The Benefactor

I came down from the Hochreith, our house in the country, to Vienna to meet Herr Ficker. The big white villa in the parks of Neuwaldegg was closed up for the summer. I had one of the gardeners prepare my room and make up a bed, and his wife laid the table on the terrace and helped me cook dinner. We were to have *Naturschnitzel* with *Kochsalat* with a cold bottle of Zöbinger. Simple, honest food. I hoped Ficker would notice.

I shaved and dressed and went out on to the terrace to wait for him to arrive. I was wearing a banana-yellow, soft-collared shirt with no tie and a light tweed jacket that I had bought years before in Manchester. Its fraying cuffs had been repaired, in the English way, with a dun green leather. My hair was clean and still damp, my face was cool, scraped smooth. I drank a glass of sherbet water as I waited for Ficker. The evening light was milky and diffused, as if hung with dust. I could hear the faint noise of motors and carriages on the roads of Neuwaldegg and in the gathering dusk I could make out the figure of the gardener moving about in the *Allée* of pleached limes. A fleeting but palpable peace descended on me, and I thought for some minutes of David and our holidays together in Iceland and Norway. I missed him.

Ficker was an earnest young man, taller than me (mind you, I am not particularly tall) with fine, thinning hair brushed back off his brow. He wore spectacles with crooked wire frames, as if he had accidentally sat upon them and had hastily straightened them out himself. He was neatly and soberly dressed, wore no hat and was clean-shaven. His lopsided spectacles suggested a spirit of frivolity and facetiousness which, I soon found out, was entirely inaccurate.

I had already explained to him, by letter, about my father's death, my legacy and how I wished to dispose of a proportion of it. He had agreed to my conditions and promised to respect my demand for total anonymity. We talked, in business-like fashion, about the details, but I could sense, as he expressed his gratitude, strong currents of astonishment and curiosity.

Eventually he had to ask. 'But why me? Why my magazine . . . in particular?'

I shrugged. 'It seems to be exemplary of its sort. I like its attitude, its, its seriousness. And besides, your writers seem the most needy.'

'Yes . . . that's true.' He was none the wiser.

'It's a family trait. My father was a great benefactor – to musicians mainly. We just like to do it.'

Ficker then produced a list of writers and painters he thought were the most deserving. I glanced through it: very few of the names were familiar to me, and beside each one Ficker had written an appropriate sum of money. Two names at the top of the list were to receive by far the largest amounts.

'I know of Rilke, of course,' I said, 'and I'm delighted you chose him. But who's he?' I pointed to the other name. 'Why should he get so much? What does he do?'

'He's a poet,' Ficker said. 'I think . . . well, no man on this list will benefit more from your generosity. To be completely frank, I think it might just save his life.'

Schubert

My brother Hans drowned himself in Chesapeake Bay. He was a musical prodigy who gave his first concert in Vienna at the age of nine. I never really knew him. My surviving brother Paul was also musically gifted, a brilliant pianist who was a pupil of Leschetitzky and made his debut in 1913. I remember Paul saying to me once that of all musical tastes the love of Schubert required the least explanation. When one thinks of the huge misery of his life and sees in his work no trace of it at all – the complete absence of his music of all bitterness.

The Bank

I had arranged with Ficker that I would be in the Öster-reichische Nationalbank on Schwarzspanier Strasse at three o'clock. I was there early and sat down at a writing desk in a far corner. It was quiet and peaceful: the afternoon rush had yet to begin and the occasional sound of heels on the marble floor as clients crossed from the entrance foyer to the rows of counters was soothing, like the background click of ivory dominoes or the ceramic kiss of billiard balls in the gaming room of my favourite café near the art schools.

Ficker was on time and accompanied by our poet. Ficker caught my eye, and I gave a slight nod and then bent my head over the spectral papers on my desk. Ficker went to a teller's *guichet* to inquire about the banker's draft, leaving the poet

19

standing momentarily alone in the middle of the marble floor, gazing around him like a peasant at the high, dim vaults of the ceiling and the play of afternoon sunshine on the ornamental brasswork of the chandeliers.

Georg, as I shall refer to him, was a young man, twenty-seven years old – two years older than me – small and quite sturdily built, and, like many small men, seemed to have been provided with a head designed for a bigger body altogether. His head was crude and heavy-looking, its proportions exaggerated by his bristly, close-cropped hair. He was clean-shaven. He had a weak mouth, the upper lip overhung the bottom one slightly, and a thick triangular nose. He had low brows and slightly oriental-looking, almond-shaped eyes. He was what my mother would have called 'an ugly customer'.

He stood now, looking expressionlessly about him, swaying slightly, as if buffeted by an invisible crowd. He appeared at once ill and strong – pale-faced, ugly, dark-eyed, but there was something about the set of his shoulders, the way his feet were planted on the ground, that suggested reserves of strength. Indeed the year before, Ficker had told me, he had almost died from an overdose of Veronal that should have killed an ordinary man in an hour or two. Since his school-days, it transpired, he had been a compulsive user of narcotic drugs and was also an immoderate drinker. At school he used chloroform to intoxicate himself. He was now a qualified dispensing chemist, a career he had taken up, so Ficker informed me, solely because it gave him access to more effective drugs. I found this single-mindedness oddly impressive. To train for two years at the University of Vienna as a pharmacist and pass the necessary exams to qualify testified to an uncommon dedication. Ficker had given me some of his poems to read. I could not understand them at all; their images for me were strangely haunting and evocative but finally entirely opaque. But I liked their *tone*; their tone seemed to me to be quite remarkable.

I watched him now, discreetly, as Ficker completed the preliminary documentation and signalled him over to endorse the banker's draft. Ficker – I think this was a mistake –

presented the cheque to him with a small flourish and shook
him by the hand, as if he had just won first prize in a lottery. I
could sense that Georg knew very little of what was going on.
I saw him turn the cheque over immediately so as to hide the
amount from his own eyes. He exchanged a few urgent words
with Ficker, who smiled encouragingly and patted him on the
arm. Ficker was very happy, almost gleeful – in his role as the
philanthropist's go-between he was vicariously enjoying what
he imagined would be Georg's astonished surprise. But he was
wrong. I knew it the instant Georg turned over the cheque and
read the amount. Twenty thousand crowns. A thriving
dispensing chemist would have to work six or seven years to
earn a similar sum. I saw the cheque flutter and tremble in his
fingers. I saw Georg blanch and swallow violently several
times. He put the back of his hand to his lips and his shoulders
heaved. He reached out to a pillar for support, bending over
from the waist. His body convulsed in a spasm as he tried to
control his writhing stomach. I knew then that he was an
honest man for he had the honest man's profound fear of
extreme good fortune. Ficker snatched the cheque from his
shaking fingers as Georg appeared to totter. He uttered a faint
cry as warm bile and vomit shot from his mouth to splash and
splatter on the cool marble of the Nationalbank's flagged
floor.

A Good Life, a Good Death

I got to know Ficker quite well over our various meetings
about the division and disposal of my benefaction. Once in our
discussions the subject of suicide came up, and he seemed
genuinely surprised when I told him that scarcely a day went
by when I did not think about it. But I explained to him that if I
could not get along with life and the world then to commit
suicide would be the ultimate admission of failure. I pointed
out that this notion was the very essence of ethics and
morality. For if anything is now to be allowed, then surely
that must be suicide. For if suicide is allowed, then anything is
allowed.

Sometimes I think that a good life should end in a death that one could welcome. Perhaps, even, it is only a good death that allows us to call a life 'good'.

Georg, I believe, has nearly died many times. For example, shortly before the Veronal incident he almost eliminated himself by accident. Georg lived for a time in Innsbruck. One night, after a drinking bout in a small village near the city he decided to walk home. At some stage on his journey back, overcome with tiredness, he decided to lie down in the snow and sleep. When he awoke in the morning the world had been replaced by a white turbid void. For a moment he thought . . . but almost immediately he realised he had been covered in the night by a new fall of snow. In fact it was about forty centimetres deep. He heaved himself to his feet, brushed off his clothes and, with a gonging headache, completed his journey to Innsbruck.

How I wish I had been passing that morning! The first sleepy traveller along that road when Georg awoke. In the still, pale light, that large hump on the verge begins to stir, some cracks and declivities suddenly deform the smooth contours, then a fist punches free and finally that crude ugly face emerges, with its frosty beret of snow, staring stupidly, blinking, spitting.

The War

The war saved my life. I really do not know what I would have done without it. On 7 August, the day war was declared on Russia, I enlisted as a volunteer gunner in the artillery for the duration and was instructed to report to a garrison artillery regiment in Cracow. In my elation I was reluctant to go straight home to pack my bags (my family had by now all returned to Vienna), so I took a taxi to the Café Museum.

I should say that I joined the army because it was my civic duty, yet I was even more glad to enlist because I knew at that time I had to *do* something, I had to subject myself to the rigours of a harsh routine that would divert me from my intellectual work. I had reached an impasse, and the impossibility of ever proceeding further filled me with morbid despair.

By the time I reached the Café Museum it was about six o'clock in the evening (I liked this café because its interior was modern: its square rooms were lined with square honey-coloured oak panelling, hung with prints of the drawings of Charles Dana Gibson). Inside it was busy, the air noisy with speculation about the war. It was humid and hot, the atmosphere suffused with the reek of beer and cigar smoke. The patrons were mostly young men, students from the nearby art schools, clean-shaven, casually and unaffectedly dressed. So I was a little surprised to catch a glimpse in one corner of a uniform. I pushed through the crowd to see who it was.

Georg, it was obvious, was already fairly drunk. He sat strangely hunched over, staring intently at the table-top. His posture and the ferocious concentration of his gaze clearly put people off as the three other seats around his table remained unoccupied. I told a waiter to bring a half litre of *Heuniger Wein* to the table and then sat down opposite him.

Georg was wearing the uniform of an officer, a lieutenant, in the Medical Corps. He looked at me candidly and without resentment and, of course, without recognition. He seemed much the same as the last time I had seen him, at once ill-looking and possessed of a sinewy energy. I introduced myself and told him I was pleased to see a fellow soldier as I myself had just enlisted.

'It's your civic duty,' he said, his voice strong and un-slurred. 'Have a cigar.'

He offered me a Trabuco, those ones that have a straw mouthpiece because they are so strong. I declined – at that time I did not smoke. When the wine arrived he insisted on paying for it.

'I'm a rich man,' he said as he filled our glasses. 'Where're you posted?'

'Galicia.'

'Ah, the Russians are coming.' He paused. 'I want to go

23

somewhere cold and dark. I detest this sun and this city. Why aren't we fighting the Eskimos? I hate daylight. Maybe I could declare war on the Lapps. One-man army.'

'Bit lonely, no?'

'I want to be lonely. All I do is pollute my mind talking to people . . . I want a dark, cold lonely war. Please.'

'People will think you're mad.'

He raised his glass. 'God preserve me from sanity.'

I thought of something Nietzsche had said: 'Our life, our happiness, is beyond the north, beyond ice, beyond death.' I looked into Georg's ugly face, his thin eyes and glossy lips, and felt a kind of love for him and his honesty. I clinked my glass against his and asked God to preserve me from sanity as well.

Tagebuch: 15 August. Cracow.

If your wife, for example, continually puts too much sugar in your tea, it is not because she has too much sugar in her cupboard; it is because she is not educated in the ways of handling sweetness. Similarly, the problem of how to live a good life cannot ever be solved by continually assaulting it with the intellect.

The Searchlight

I enlisted in the artillery to fire howitzers but instead found myself manning a searchlight on a small, heavily armed paddle-steamer called the *Goplana*. We cruised up and down the Vistula, ostensibly looking for Russians but also to provide support for any river crossings by our own forces.

I enjoyed my role in charge of the searchlight. I took its mounting apart and oiled and greased its bearings. Re-assembled, it moved effortlessly under the touch of my fingers. Its strong beam shone straight and true in the blurry semi-darkness of those late summer nights. However, I soon found the living conditions on the *Goplana* intolerable because of the stink, the proximity and the vulgarity of my fellow soldiers. And because we were constantly in motion, life below decks was dominated by the thrum and grind of the *Goplana*'s churning paddles. I spent long hours in my corner of the bridgehouse needlessly overhauling the mechanism of the searchlight – anything to escape the torrent of filth and viciousness that poured from the men. I found my old despair began to creep through me again, like a stain.

One day we disembarked at Sandomierz and were sent to a bath house. As we washed I looked at my naked companions, their brown faces and forearms, their grey-white bodies and dark dripping genitals as they soaped and sluiced themselves with garrulous ostentation. I felt only loathing for them, my fellow men. It was both impossible to work with them and have nothing to do with them. I was glad that I felt no stirrings of sensuality as I contemplated their naked bodies. I saw that they were men but I could not see they were human beings.

Tagebuch: 8 September. Sawichost.

The news is worse. All the talk is of Cracow being besieged. Last night there was an alarm. I ran up on deck to man the searchlight. It was raining and I wore only a shirt and trousers. I played the beam of the searchlight to and fro on the opposite bank of the river for hours, my feet and hands slowly becoming numb. Then we heard the sound of gunfire, and I at once became convinced I was going to die that night. The beam of the searchlight was a lucent arrow pointing directly at me. And for the first time I felt, being face to face with my own death, with possibly only an hour or two of life remaining to me, that I had in those few hours the chance to be a good man, if only because of this uniquely potent conscious-ness of myself. 'I did my duty and stayed at my post.' That is all I can say about that tremendous night.

★

The Amputee

Of course I did not die and of course I fell back into more abject moods of self-disgust and loathing. Perhaps the only consolation was that my enormous fatigue made it impossible for me to think about my work.

It was about this time – in September or October – that I heard the news about my brother Paul. He was a quite different personality from me – fierce and somewhat dominating – and he had tackled his vocation as concert pianist with uncompromising dedication. Since his debut his future seemed assured, an avenue of bright tomorrows. To receive the news, then, that he had been captured by the Russians and had had his right arm amputated at the elbow, as a result of wounds he had sustained, was devastating. For days my thoughts were of Paul and of what I would do in his situation. Poor Paul, I thought, if only there were some other solution than suicide. What philosophy it will take to get over this!

Tagebuch: 13 October. Nadbrzesze.

We have sailed here, waited for twelve hours, and have now been ordered to return to Sawichost. All day we can hear the mumble of artillery in the east. I find myself drawn down into dark depression again, remorselessly. Why? What is the real basis of this malaise? I see one of my fellow soldiers pissing over the side of the boat in full view of the few citizens of Nazbrzesze who have gathered on the quayside to stare at us. The long pale arc of his urine sparkles in the thin autumn sunshine. Another soldier leans on his elbows staring candidly at the man's white flaccid penis, held daintily between two fingers like a titbit. This is shaken, its tip squeezed and then tucked away in the coarse serge of his trousers. I think if I was standing at a machine-gun rather than a searchlight I could kill them both without a qualm . . . Why do I detest these simple foolish men so? Why can I not be impassive? I despise my own weakness, my inability to distance myself from the commonplace.

The Battle of Grodek

On our return from Sawichost I received mail. A long letter from David – I wonder if he thinks of me half as much as I think of him? – and a most distressing communication from Ficker, to whom I had written asking for some books to be sent to me. I quote:

I see from your letter that you are not far from Cracow. I wonder if you get the opportunity you could attempt to find and visit [Georg]. You may have heard of the heavy fighting at Grodek some two weeks ago. Georg was there and, owing to the chaos and disorganisation that prevailed at the time, was mistakenly placed in charge of a field hospital not far behind our lines. Apparently he protested vigorously that he was merely a dispensing chemist and not a doctor, but resources were so stretched he was told to do the best he could.

Thus Georg found himself with two orderlies (Czechs, who spoke little German) in charge of a fifty-bed field hospital. As the battle wore on more than ninety severely wounded casualties were delivered during the day. Repeatedly, Georg signalled for a doctor to be sent as he could do nothing for these men except inject them with morphine and attempt to dress their wounds. In fact it became clear that through some oversight these casualties had been sent to the wrong hospital. The ambulance crews that transported them had been erroneously informed that there was a field surgery and a team of surgeons operating there.

By nine in the evening all of Georg's supplies of morphine were exhausted. Shortly thereafter men began to scream from the resurgent pain. Finally, one officer, who had lost his left leg at the hip, shot himself in the head.

At this point Georg ran away. Two kilometres from the field hospital was a small wood which, at the start of the battle, had been a battalion headquarters. Georg went there for help or at least to report the ghastly condition of the wounded in his charge. When he arrived there he found that an impromptu military tribunal had just executed twenty deserters by hanging.

I do not know exactly what happened next. I believe that at the sight of these fresh corpses Georg tried to seize a revolver from an officer and shoot himself. Whatever happened, he behaved in a demented manner, was subdued and arrested himself for desertion in the face of the enemy. I managed to visit him briefly in the mental hospital at Cracow ten days ago. He is in a very bad way, but at least, thank God, the charges of desertion have been dropped and he is being treated for *dementia praecox*. For some reason Georg is convinced he will be prosecuted for cowardice. He is sure he is going to hang.

The Asylum at Cracow

Georg's cell was very cold and dark, the only illumination coming from an oil lamp in the corridor. Georg needed a shave but otherwise he looked much the same as he had on my two previous encounters with him. He was wearing a curious oatmeal canvas uniform, the jacket secured with strings instead of buttons. With his big head and thin eyes he looked strangely Chinese. There was one other patient in his cell with him, a major in the cavalry who was suffering from *delirium tremens*. This man remained hunched on a truckle bed in the corner of the room, sobbing quietly to himself while Georg and I spoke. He did not recognise me. I merely introduced myself as a friend of Ficker.

'Ludwig asked me to visit you,' I said. 'How are you?'

'Well, I'm . . .' He stopped and gestured at the major. 'I used to think I was a heavy drinker.' He smiled. 'Actually, he's being quite good now.' Georg rubbed his hair with both hands.

'I heard about what happened,' I said. 'It must have been terrible.'

He looked at me intently and then seemed to think for a while.

'Yes,' he said. 'Yes, yes, yes. All that sort of thing.'

'I completely understand.'

He shrugged uselessly. 'You don't have any cigars on you, by any chance? They haven't brought me my kit. One longs for a decent cigar.'

'Let me get some for you.'

'I smoke Trabucos – the ones with the straw holder.'

'They're very strong, I believe. I don't smoke, but I heard they can burn your throat.'

'It's a small price to pay.'

We sat on in silence for a moment, listening to the major's snufflings.

'It's very cold here,' Georg began slowly, 'and very dark, and if they got rid of the major the conditions would be perfect.'

'I know what you mean.'

'Actually, I have several boxes of Trabucos in my kit,' he went on. 'If you could get a message to my orderly perhaps he could bring me a couple.'

'Of course.'

'Oh, and would you ask him to bring me my green leather case.'

'Green leather case.'

'Yes,' he paused. 'That is essential . . .' He rubbed his face, as if his features were tired of being eternally composed.

'I think with a good cigar I could even tolerate the major.'

I found Georg's orderly in the Medical Corps' billet in a small village on the outskirts of Cracow. The city was clearly visible across the flat cropped meadows where a few piebald ponies grazed: a low attenuated silhouette punctuated by a few domes and spires and the odd factory chimney. In the indistinct grainy light of the late afternoon the bulk of the Marienkirche had the look of a vast warehouse. I passed on Georg's instructions: two boxes of Trabuco cigars and his green leather case.

'How is the lieutenant?' the orderly asked.

'He's very well,' I said. 'Considering . . . Very well indeed.'

Georg died that night from a heart seizure brought on by a massive intraveneous injection of cocaine. According to his orderly, who was the last person to speak to him, he was 'in a state of acute distress' and must have misjudged the dose.

Tagebuch: 10 November. Sawichost.

The simplest way to describe the book of moral philosophy that I am writing is that it concerns what can and cannot be said. In fact it will be only half a book. The most interesting half will be the one that I cannot write. That half will be the most eloquent.

Tea at Neuwaldegg

It is springtime. After a shower of rain we take tea on the terrace of the big house at Neuwaldegg. Me, my mother, my sisters Helene and Hermine – and Paul. I am on leave; Paul has just been returned from captivity as part of an exchange of wounded prisoners. He sits with his right sleeve neatly pinned up, awkwardly squeezing lemon into his tea with his left hand. I think of Georg and I look at Paul. His hair is greying; his clothes are immaculate.

Quite suddenly he announces that he is going to continue with his career as a concert pianist and teach himself to play with the left hand only. He proposes to commission pieces for the left hand from Richard Strauss and Ravel. There is silence, and then I say, 'Bravo, Paul. Bravo.' And, spontaneously, we all clap him.

The modest sound of our applause carries out over the huge garden. A faint breeze shifts the new spring foliage of the chestnut trees, glistening after the rain, and the gardener, who has just planted a bed of geraniums, looks up from his work for a moment, smiles bemusedly at us, clambers to his feet and bows.

The Vanishing Princess or The Origins of Cubism

JENNY DISKI

THERE WAS ONCE a Princess who lived in a tower. It is hard to say precisely if she was imprisoned there. Certainly she had always been there, and she had never left the circular room at the top of the long winding staircase. But since she had never tried to leave it, it wouldn't be quite accurate to say that she was imprisoned.

The room had a door, and the door had a keyhole, and there was, on the side of the door that she had never seen, a key that hung from a hook in the lintel. She had been put into the room at birth and a series of people, who called themselves relatives, had come and gone, visiting the turret room, opening and shutting the door from time to time. They maintained the lock on the door very carefully, making sure it was always well oiled, so that the Princess never heard the key turn in the lock, if indeed it did, and therefore never considered the possibility that she was their prisoner.

Since no one ever spoke to her about the world outside the door she came to assume that it was nothing to do with her. She lacked, perhaps, curiosity: but then no one had ever suggested to her that curiosity was a quality to be cultivated. Anyway, she never attempted to open the door from her side, and so never found out if she was a prisoner or not.

After a while the relatives stopped visiting, and there was a long period when no one came to the room at all. The Princess had little sense of time and barely noticed their absence. She spent her days lying on her bed in the circular room reading the books that filled the shelves that covered the walls from floor to ceiling. Apart from the bed and the books there was a narrow window in the room.

Sometimes, when she was replacing a book she had read, or choosing the next, she passed the window. As a child she had seen green fields and woods far off in the distance, and recognised them from the stories she had read. But since her visitors had stopped coming, the land around the tower had grown rampant and it was many years since she had seen anything but vines and creepers covered with briars and merciless thorns. It looked, at the very least, unattractive.

One day, many years after the Princess had been abandoned in the tower, a soldier passed nearby. He was a mercenary returning from the last of many campaigns; world-weary and bored with the sameness of everything. He noticed the tangled growth in the distance and wondered at it, that wild forest in the middle of rolling fields. Pleased to find himself curious about anything after so long a period of lassitude, he decided to investigate, and cutting through the hedges, unworried, soldier that he was, by the merciless thorns, he discovered the tower, and the staircase, and the door to the room where the Princess lay on her bed reading books.

The Princess looked up from her volume as he came through the door, and waited in silence to find out what he wanted. She felt no great excitement at his arrival, for it didn't seem to her that she was lacking anything in her life. She had what she always had, and wanted, so far as she knew, nothing.

The soldier questioned the Princess about her life in the tower and she told him what little there was to tell: about the relatives who had visited but no longer did, about her books, about the view from the window.

'But what about food?' the soldier asked. 'When they stopped coming, what did you do for food?'

'Food?' said the Princess.

Which was how the soldier discovered that by some means or other, the Princess, never having had food, had never learned to need it. This was of particular interest to the soldier, because although he had done everything and seen everything and been everywhere, and was tired of it all, there remained one thing that still gave him special pleasure: the sight of a woman eating excited him as nothing else now could. And though the Princess was neither beautiful nor not beautiful, she did have an exceptionally well-formed mouth.

'I'll be back,' he said, closing the door behind him. And as he found an oil can above the lintel and oiled the lock, the Princess couldn't tell whether the key had been turned or not.

He returned, although the Princess having no way of gauging the passing of time, had no idea how long it had been since he first arrived. He opened the door and saw the Princess on her bed reading. She looked up and smiled. The soldier took the book from her hands and laid a small cloth on the bed, on which he placed the food he had brought. She smiled again, and without having to be told, began to pick up this morsel and that, first savouring the smell, then pressing it gently against her lips, and finally tasting. It pleased her, and it pleased him to watch her eat.

Now, at intervals, the soldier came to her with food. Never too often and never with too much. Food remained a pleasure but never became a necessity. Whenever he tired of his wanderings he would visit the tower with small delicacies wrapped in a white cloth; and she was always willing to exchange the pleasure of her book for the pleasure of food. This went on for many years. The Princess came to expect his visits, although, in her timeless world, it couldn't be said that she actually looked forward to them.

Then, one day, a second soldier passed that way. By now rumours had spread abroad about the strange Princess in the tower and the soldier who visited her from time to time with small quantities of delicious food. The second soldier had heard these stories and, one day, being battle-fatigued and lacking anything better to do, set out to see if he couldn't find the Princess.

He recognised the thicket covering the tower from a good way off and found the small path that the first soldier had worn through the undergrowth. When he entered the room at the top of the tower, he found the Princess in her usual pose on the bed. She looked up from her book expecting to see the first soldier and his small bundle.

'Don't be frightened,' the second soldier said, although such an emotion had not occurred to her before he said it. 'I've been looking for you.'

And now she did begin to feel alarmed. She had never thought of herself as known in the outside world, and felt a strange distress at the thought of existing in someone's mind as something to be found. The second soldier was a clever man, and knowing about the first soldier and the food, he knew he needed an edge. He looked carefully about the room and thought for a long time.

'I'll be back,' he said, as he closed the door behind him and oiled the lock. And the Princess didn't doubt it.

When he returned he brought with him two objects: a mirror and a calendar with all the days of the week, and the months of the year laid out for years to come. He placed the mirror on the wall in front of the Princess' bed, and nailed the calendar to the door.

'Look,' he said, taking the Princess' hand and leading her from the bed to stand in front of the mirror. The second soldier had understood on his first visit that it was not only food the Princess had lacked all her life.

Having no way of seeing herself, she had no precise notion that she existed at all. And having no way to mark the passage of time, lacked any sense of expectation. The first soldier could come and go, but she did not wait or hope that he would come soon, or this week, or tomorrow.

She looked at her reflection in the mirror, and at first it distressed her. She hadn't seen anything quite like it before. But the second soldier stood by her and she watched his reflection standing next to hers and telling her, 'That is you.'

It took some time, but very gradually she started to think. 'Perhaps it is. Perhaps I am here. Perhaps, when people come into this room, they see me.' And she looked sideways, out of the corners of her narrowing eyes at the Princess in the mirror.

'When I come to see you,' the second soldier said, 'that is what I come to see. You.'

'Me,' the Princess repeated, trying to get used to the idea. It was still very disturbing, and yet, there was something about it that she found very pleasant. Strange, but pleasant.

'I will come again next week,' the second soldier said, and led her to the calendar to show her how to mark the days. 'On this day, Friday, next week, I will come back to see you.' And he looked long and hard into her eyes. For this soldier too had something that gave him particular pleasure. He loved to see in women's eyes a look of expectation, a dawning of new possibilities. And the Princess had eyes that enabled this to show to an extraordinary degree. But that was not all; the look of expectation was only a part of his pleasure. To complete it he wanted to see that gleam fade to a subtler tone of disappointment.

He returned on the appointed day and watched as the Princess' eyes began to show she had understood the nature of time. When he left he gave her another day, and came then too. But on the third occasion he did not come when he had said, but two days later, and there in her eyes was the completion of his pleasure. When he left saying he would be back on such a date, he saw hope and anxiety mingle in a way he could never have hoped for.

The first soldier did not make a visit during this time, and the second soldier was careful to check that the Princess was alone when he arrived. But he left the calendar and the mirror in the room, and she let them stay where he had put them.

When the first soldier came again he looked at both the objects, but said nothing. He laid the food before the Princess and watched her lips as she bit off and chewed small mouthfuls. When she had finished he took up the cloth and walked over to the mirror.

'Stand here,' he said, pointing to a spot just in front of it. He looked at her reflection for a moment and then took off a diamond ring he wore and, using the edge of one of its facets he etched the outline of the Princess' reflection on to the glass.

'I'll be back when I can,' he said, glancing at the calendar, and left.

When the second soldier returned, the Princess was pleased to see him as he came through the door, looking, as she had now come to feel, at her. But immediately his gaze fell on the mirror, and the outline etched upon it. He looked first at the Princess and then at the glass.

'Stand here,' he said, pointing to a spot in front of the mirror, and when she did, he moved her slightly until her reflection exactly filled the outline. The Princess looked at herself, and thought, as she always did, when she caught her reflection as she passed by to return or get a book, 'Here I am.'

The second soldier eased a ring from his finger, and with the edge of a facet of the diamond, drew around the reflection of her eyes. First one, then the other. He stepped back to look at it for a moment, then filled in the lids, the pupils and the irises. At last, a pair of eyes stared out from the outline of a woman on the glass, fixed in an expression of longing and alarm so poignant that the Princess gasped. She could no longer see her own eyes when she looked into the mirror.

When the first soldier came back he spent at least as much time looking at the eyes in the glass as he did watching the Princess eat. When she had finished, he had her stand in front of the mirror and drew her mouth; the lips full and open, mobile and beautiful. The Princess could no longer see her lips when she looked into the glass.

Now, on each occasion, the portrait in the mirror was added to. Each soldier examined the work of the other, and then etched a new piece on to the mirror. The outline became no more than a frame, as each man added a feature according to his mood. An elbow was matched with the bridge of a nose; a wrist with a knee; a buttock curved beside an anklebone; one ear rested on a fingernail. Neither man noticed anything that had gone before the other man's last sketch.

Eventually the first soldier stopped bringing food, and the second soldier no longer bothered with the calendar. There came a time when the Princess could no longer see herself at all in the mirror. 'I'm not here,' she said to herself. 'Perhaps I never was.' And she disappeared.

No one knows exactly how it happened. It could have been that she opened the door one day, discovered that the soldiers had long since stopped locking it, and walked down the winding staircase and vanished forever in the dense, impenetrable forest that surrounded the tower. Or it may have been that, finding herself no longer there, she simply wasn't any more. At any rate, she vanished and no one ever saw or heard of her again.

The two soldiers hardly noticed her absence. They continued to visit the tower, turn by turn, and left their messages for each other on the mirror. The years passed, and although they never met, their contentment and affection deepened. Eventually they grew old and died. One day the first soldier arrived and found that nothing had been added to the glass. It was not long after that he stopped coming too.

And the mirror rusted, the silvering began to flake away, leaving only scratches on the glass that were indecipherable. When the tower began to crumble, pieces of stone fell and broke the glass itself until there was nothing left of this earliest of examples of Cubist art except rubble greened over with wild vegetation. It was to be many centuries before the form would be revived, but by then, no one had any notion that it wasn't the first time.

After the Rains

JANICE GALLOWAY

think
it is too warm here and my heart is racing think
where was I
I was
in the bus shelter. Dripping in there with the rest of them out
of the rain. It must have been about twenty-five past ten
because the bus to the Cross had just drawn up and the brakes
were still squealing and when they stopped there was a sound
of nothing. We were all listening, aware of the difference.
Simultaneously, carefully: we were listening silently together,
trying to fathom what it was. That was what began to give it
away: the fact that we could hear ourselves being silent. A
child outside ducked suddenly and looked up, suspicious. One
gesture. Herd realisation fluttered in the shelter like a trapped
bird. We thought, paused and realised afresh in the same single
second. It had stopped raining. It had stopped raining.

after nine solid months it had stopped raining

We peered with all our eyes and curled pieces of ourselves
beyond the perspex. Tentative, testing from under our rain-
mates and over-handing hoods for our various private proofs.

38

For mine, I took the nearest of the currant bushes to the stop, one of a grove planted by the council to represent nature in the concrete island of the estate. It was dripping yet. I watched. It was dripping yet but

but

but I could swear the drops were less assured now, visible seconds lurching between one
drop and the next as I watched.
not all of us had the patience or the time for such nicety, though. There was a muffled grunt that could have been apology as a large woman bulked past on her way out of the shelter and into the middle of the road, her face bravely upturned to the sky to see for herself. She made it sure for all of us.

Then we were all out with her, all over the road, our talk buzzing, strengthening to outright exclamations of surprise and congratulation. In a burst we were new people. It was like Hogmanay: it was better for we didn't need the drink to open to it.

warmth in my chest
like warm soup to remember it

Spontaneously, without the false prop, we were speaking to perfect strangers, smiling and laughing and clapping them on the back. Folk normally so wary, so shy of ridicule it hurt, we blossomed for each other. We marvelled and cracked jokes while the bus sat like a ruin on the road. Its passengers had joined us, helping the older folk down off the platform. Reckless with enjoyment, one man held up a bottle of lemonade and shook it, his thumb over the neck, to splash it about like celebration champagne. There was laughing and cuddling and general pagan revelry.

★

The driver was out with us too. Even given the festival mood, that was remarkable since he was usually such a bloody-minded big bastard. He made a hammy mime of looking at his watch. He had had his look. The rain was off. Now he was finished. He announced it: if anybodys goin to the Cross they better come wi me cos Im away. No one minded. Yes, we would come, goodnatured to spite him. We started to drift back

was it then?
it was then I saw

As I was straggling on, I noticed something in the corner of the shelter: a wee girl, huddling in on herself and keeking out from between her fingers? I craned out from an upstairs seat for another look as the bus started to move off. She was still there, indistinct behind too much hair. I should have been more curious, maybe done something, but the bus took me and my excitement eclipsed her.

The very road was interesting now the rain had stopped. Commonplaces about the weather became significant as we noted with genuine feeling it was turning out nice or drying up. We knew a change

the change

had begun. In places the tarmac was surfacing. Normally, there was a two-inch film over the whole road, but the hydraulic emergency pumps were working away as steadily and greedily as always, noisily swallowing riversful when no more was falling to replace it. Boys were out on the crest of the road, right in the middle of the traffic path, for the novelty of standing on it without the water tugging at their shoes. They were kicking the planks away too. Sometimes people put planks across between pavements to try and get over keeping their feet drier or because they were afraid of the current. The police did what they could, of course: it was selfish, dangerous and illegal. A plank accident on this very stretch of road had killed one person recently, and cost two others at least one necessary limb each. It was like a prayer touching all of us, a thanksgiving ritual to see those boys kicking the planks away. Someone sang a hymn. The rest of us pointed and waved at them, and at everything else newly emerged from behind the veil of drizzle, rubbing with cuffs at the windows streaming with our too close breath and the wet from our clothes. The chatter on the bus seemed abnormally loud: it wasn't just that we had more to say, but that the white noise of the rainfall was no longer fuzzing everything. The extra dimension to sound as well as that to sight must have been too much for some, though. A few around me were in tears and a low whimpering and groaning came up from the lower deck. Maybe they found it too sudden, maybe even painful.

we should have spoken about it questioned more
we were too pleased with ourselves
too smug

Only half an hour after the rain stopped the sky had lightened considerably. At the Cross, almost every office and shop window was framed with workers looking. Looking out to rediscover unfilled spaces between surfaces. I could see rows of them from my bench seat at the corner of the pedestrian precinct. I was

what was I doing?
just looking too just taking it all in
looking up
it was when I was looking up

Then quite suddenly, without warning, the sun came out. It tore a great rip in the cloud curtain and came out in one movement, one flaming presence. Colour flushed back immediately with shocking, breathstopping vividness. With a catch of emotion, we realised how much of it we had forgotten and how ashen everything had been for so long. The low light, the constant smurr – we had encouraged it. Black and white television had enjoyed a revival; there was a fashion for subdued lighting in our homes – as though we were afraid too much brightness would make the continual rainlight more depressing. We had not fought. But now we took the courage to look and everything blazed; the yellow, the green, red and orange glaring noisily and gloriously in our eyes. As one, we made a long intake of it, then sighed. From all over the Cross and all over the town purred a sigh of relief and wonder. The sun had come out.

the sun had come out

Those of us in the street spurred to motion again, some hurrying to see into the window of the television showroom for affirmation. We were only ordinary folk and untrusting of the evidence of our own eyes. For a moment or two, all we could see was a cookery demonstration, then a news flash. It told us the sun had come out. A cheer. The cookery demonstration continued to mix and fold itself behind the printout.

Then it disappeared altogether and a man came on to explain with radiating lines and velcro symbols about the weather. We got another news flash. It said that scientists were confident this was the end of the rain for some considerable time. There would be a full report later. We were satisfied and turned away from the TV to shine our faces upwards, crunching our eyes against the unaccustomed brilliance cracking the sky above our heads.

our scalps began to get warm then

Shop workers clustered in doorways and filled their display windows with faces tilting toward the sunlight. As if it had been waiting for this moment, it appeared then: a massive, seven-coloured arch fanning above us, pouring itself above the buildings and the town, looping and glittering to prickle ready tears. We applauded. We all applauded the rainbow and its promise. We were radiant.

*

By the afternoon it was hot. I hadn't moved much: the length of the street, a little shopping, then back to the bench at the Cross to watch the day unfold along with others who had the time, the reward of the jobless. The streets were misty and dry patches squared out on the paving. None among us could have foreseen such a difference in so short a period. City Bakeries sold out of sandwiches as people lunched al fresco. Bright dots of tee-shirts began to appear among the crowds. Sloughing off rainclothes allowed us to look at ourselves afresh and become dissatisfied with what we saw. Those that could went to change: light trousers, summer dresses, short-sleeved shirts with bleachy angles poking out. Some improvised, rolling up trouser legs as though they were at the beach in a jokey but serviceable imitation of bermuda shorts, fit for the steamy tropic the Cross had become. Almost everyone wore a hat, sunglasses or visor against the glare. It came from more than unaccustomedness, this sharpness against our eyes. More news flashes confirmed the suspicion: it was indeed a freak heatwave and the temperature was rising by the minute. A thermometer in the travel agent's window bled steadily upward and made a talking point for all watchers as we rolled up our sleeves and loosened collar-buttons.

I went to the riverside walkway
cooler there
then it was later did I fall asleep
I must have slept
but I woke and

It was later afternoon when I returned. The Cross was much less crowded; many had drifted off out of the punishing light. There was a crowd under the canopy of the Co-op looking out from its little shade as they waited for their bus home. The newsagent's on the corner shut and the women who worked there walked across the road to join them with keys jangling into the stillness. As I watched them walk across, I saw something pale and puffy billow out from under their feet. It took me a minute to place what it was. It was dust.

43

dust

Dust rising up from gutters that had churned with running water for so long. It was scarcely credible. My head thumped as I thought about it and with the heat and windlessness of the street. Workers who had poked from their doorways earlier to seek the sun now did the same for air. It must have been hell in the shops – all that glass. A very plump woman who owned the flower shop appeared at her open door, wheezing and gasping, the effort of her lungs making her very red about the face and chest in her short summer frock. Some shops were near to closing now and a few individuals were out lowering shutters, keen, I suppose, to get out of the thickening air. Numbers swelled at the bus stop, waiting.

waiting

They sweated and sighed, pearls of their moisture oozing to drip and melt on the slab pavement. It was very still, the absence of the hiss of rain had left a vacuum. The pumps had cut long silence.

no flies there was no thrum of flies

It was sickly quiet and the air seethed with expectation. Something

something was coming
it was coming then

Then there it was. A stretching sound, like a mass intake of breath: a sort of inrush of air that came not from us, the people, but from above our heads. Then that low rumble along the horizon, hollowing the ear across the line of the sky. It was the sound of men clearing their throats. Now an earth-rippling crack: we looked up. Overhead, the rainbow, evanescing more wildly, was criss-crossed by countless others, all arching and diving at crazy angles over and through and around themselves, filling up every corner of the clear blue so none remained as a touchstone for the sky. Immediately, a huge rushing surged in my head, spreading from ear to ear as though some invisible hand were unzipping the hair from the skull. I threw up my hands defensively. I could see others were doing the same and some had fallen down on their knees.

too late
too late for that

A few children danced incongruously about on the pedestrian walk-way, either from stupidity or delight at what they saw and it occurred to me we were not all seeing or hearing the same. It was certain we were all inhabiting something far out with the normal run, but *not the same thing*. The faces around me, behind the glass in doorways and on the road varied so extremely.

high sudden screaming

Then all heads turned from their own pain to find the source of a single shrill scream. It was the florist. She appeared to be trying to pull

a shoot
no
several green shoots

she appeared to be trying to pull several green shoots and leaves from her dress as we watched. More and yet more leaves burst out despite her efforts, and I realised suddenly they were not attached to her dress. They were attached to her elbow, to her arm. I looked harder. They were her arm. *They were her arm.* Greenery surged up her neck and into her hair, buds clustered then filled out and burst into riotous bloom in a pink halo all around her head. Huge roses ripened at her armpits and elbows, camellias and magnolias fanned out of her cleavage.

She had stopped struggling with it now and enough of her face remained to let me see she was smiling. She was welcoming the beauty of the garden, of the flowers she had become, smiling at the perfumed loveliness that was herself. I felt a twinge of outrage, but as I looked again at the woman's smile and at her childish delight I was moved with compassion. I had to admire it too. The scent was overpowering.

it carried all the way from the other side of the road.

Her assistant was next. Formerly a girl of about seventeen, now a living display of hyacinth and spring ferns. The grocer in the next doorway was gazing down affectionately at a cabbage foresting the front of his overall. He saw me gaping over, hesitated then pointed at it shamelessly with his carroting digits. The reaction of the crowd to his bravado was enthusiastic. Some cheered and one old woman tottered over for a closer look, muttering endearments. Another hurtled from the back of the bus crowd to give himself room: a check-out boy I recognised from Tesco's. A pregnant bulge at the front of his coat elongated as he stood, squaring out to make a full-size trolley complete with front wheel to balance the projection from his body. As though pleased to have joined the élite, he lowered his shopping into it with great dignity.

Behind him, the electrical goods manager of the Co-op came out to display a shiny transparent door in the centre of his wide barrel chest, and turned from side to side to show off the gaily coloured washing tumbling inside in graceful whorls, beaming amid the congratulations of his proud neighbours. All the while the sun grew hotter.

it is too warm here

I began to walk the length of the street to find some shade for myself where I could more comfortably continue to watch. I had begun to see a pattern in it and wanted to see it unfold. I thought I knew what would happen, though some might have longer gestation periods than others. Loud snortings and scufflings emitted from the bookies as I went past ducking into the doorway to avoid soft collision with a squashy bundle emerging from the Wool Shop. It was taking off.

too fast
a whisper of warning

mouthing in my head, half-formed. Perhaps I recalled the

child in the shelter from the morning. I was waiting then too. Realisation prickled its beginnings up the back of my neck. I ran round the corner and saw the truth of it.

An enormous pulsating grub writhed reflexively in the gutter, its blind bulbous tips waving in what looked horribly like appeal. Beyond this nerveless thing, the pavement crawled with three-headed phantoms, blocking my progress. Where features should have been was only tight, smooth skin, blanket grey and eyeless. The phantoms hovered helplessly and fell as another of their kind fumbled from the council offices, apparently in an extreme of agony, and would have cried out as it spattered down had it a mouth to scream. I spun back against the wall of the Employment Exchange to get out of its way, then rebounded as quickly at the ripping cold of it against my skin. Even in this heat, frost had feathered the windows and a faint mist of frozen vapour issued from the open gate and its maw of jaggy ice teeth. I knew nothing would come out of there.

It was sure now.
There would be others like this too. Not flowers, not harmless eccentricities, but other things.

terrible other things

A foul, pitiful screeching that pierced to my bowels forced me to turn. I was facing the butchers. The howling and the bloody trail at their doorway
I would not look in there
I did not want to see

I began to run again faster
curiosity pushed my glance down despite the urgings of reason
my hands were very pale and whitening still
they were stark white

I kept on running.

Chinese Funeral

JANE GARDAM

'I COULD DO without the coffin,' said the Englishwoman. 'Going to China with a coffin.'

'It won't be here for long,' said her husband. 'They're taking it off at Lamma Island. We call in there. He's going to be buried at home. We're dropping him off. He died in Hong Kong.'

'How do you know it all?'

'Oh. I do. What's the matter with you? Coffins go all over the place. Aeroplanes. Ships. Cruise ships are full of them – empties for emergencies. I saw three in a stack once in Victoria Station. In Spain they arrange them round the undertakers' offices. On shelves. I've seen them. Wrapped in plastic, like long chocolates.'

'Oh, for heaven's sake,' she said. 'Anyway those aren't full ones. This is a full one.'

'They were full,' he said. 'In Spain. No two ways.'

'Glib. Silly,' she said.

'Anyway,' said the husband, 'this one's out of sight. Below deck. You wouldn't know it was there if you hadn't seen it coming on board.'

'I can see the awful people,' she said.

Near the stern of the boat noisy men with excited eyes

pushed each other about like lads on a treat. They wore sacking robes and their heads and hands were covered by slap-happy blood-stained bandages, loose and trailing. The blood was not blood but vermilion paint. One man held a long trumpet. All had bare feet.

The husband said, 'I wonder if they're the professional mourners?'

She said, 'It's awful. They're enjoying it.'

'Yes,' he said. 'A bit wild. The after-life for them is horrible, you know. The sleep of oblivion. Desolate. Frightening.'

'They're *enjoying* being frightened,' she said. 'They're getting a kick.'

'Yes and no,' said the husband. 'Yes and no. Don't forget they're surrounded by spirits.'

'Brandy.'

'No. Evil spirits. The trumpet is to frighten them away. Hong Kong isn't all computerspeak and banking. Well, Lamma Island isn't anyway. Superstition goes deep, deep.'

'It does with me too,' she said. 'There's something about travelling with a coffin.'

'I'm surprised at you, Ann.'

'Not bad luck exactly,' she said. 'I don't know. Inopportune. Time rolling on. And back.'

'Well so it does,' he said.

When the boat came alongside the sunny island he watched the waiting crowd of mourners on the quay and the bandaged people shouldering the coffin and bearing it away to the sound of the trumpet. The woman stayed in her seat reading the guide book, her hands over her ears.

Fourteen were going on the day trip to China from Hong Kong. One was a Nigerian, the rest British, all unknown to each other. They had met on the Star Ferry waterfront, Kowloon side, before dawn. They were all middle-aged to old, a rather heavy, thoughtful lot, too early awake. As the sun rose and they headed north to the southern tip of China, threading the islands that lay in strings like the humps of sea

49

monsters ('It's where they got the idea of dragons,' said the husband), the Nigerian began to read a copy of *Time* magazine and the others clicked about with cameras. One big old Englishman as they stepped from the boat on to true Chinese soil straightened his shoulders and tightly blinked his eyes. His wife took his hand and they interlaced their fingers. They stood not looking at anything in particular.

At the Customs, a woman in khaki, watching a screen, stretched for Ann's handbag and removed from it two apples that must have shown up on the X-ray. 'I suppose they looked like hand grenades,' said Ann. The unpainted mask-face did not smile but the eyes of soldiers standing by looked sharp. 'I didn't know we couldn't bring them in,' she said. 'Here – we'll eat them. It's a shame to waste them.'

But there was a sudden great flustering and the apples were seized back from her hand and thrown in a bucket with other wicked things – Cadbury's chocolate, sandwiches in foil and a bottle of something. 'I hope they get a pain,' said Ann. 'I suppose they'll eat them the minute we're out of sight.'

'That we do not enquire,' said a voice. Standing by the mini-bus that was to be their home till nightfall was the Chinese guide, brilliant-eyed, happy, young. He ran about laughing and shaking hands with the English group. 'Here you leave Hong Kong behind and give yourselves to me and to our driver here. He is a wonderful driver though he speaks and understands no English. He is my friend. I am a student of a Chinese university and he is uneducated, but he is my friend. For several years now, together in vacations, we have guided western tourists. We ask you to be patient with us. I ask you to ask me any questions you wish. I will answer everything. *Everything*. But we have much to do and far to go and when I say, "Come, hurry up please, no longer", you must obey. Thank you and get in.'

The driver had a long, unsmiling face. A precise and perfect line ran from eye-socket to the point of the jaw. A leaf. A Picasso. His white hands lay for the moment loose on the wheel. The hands of Moiseiwitsch. The guide was jolly, square-faced, amiable, with shaggy fetching hair. Side by side

the two heads turned to the road, giving it all attention. Ann
suddenly saw the driver's hands running with blood and the
guide with upflung arms, facing the dark. She cried out.

'What's the matter?' said the husband. '*What* did you say?
You're shivering. Put your sweater on.'

'It's – .'

'Whatever is it? You look awful. Oh lord, are you car-sick?
The road's going to get much worse than this.'

'No. I saw something. I don't know what – . Something – .'

'Will you forget that coffin?'

'No. Not the coffin. Something coming. Rolling like a sea.'

'They'll give us some tea soon,' he said. 'When we stop to
see the kindergarten show and the market.'

'We got up too soon,' he said in a moment, and put an arm
round her shoulders.

At the kindergarten show the human marionettes danced
and sang and tipped their perfect little heads from side to side.
Afterwards they ran across to the audience to shake every
hand, fixed smile on every blank-eyed face. 'Come now,'
called the guide with his different smile. 'We have much to see
and a hundred miles before lunch.'

'I'll find some tea,' said Ann's husband. 'There's always
tea,' and she stood waiting, watching the children being
marshalled together for the next performance as a new load of
tourists came streaming in. 'Could I see some of the ordinary
children?' she asked, but the guide said 'No, no, no – come.'

She sat in the bus, drank tea, felt better. And soon began to
watch the endless fields on either side of the road. Endless,
endless. Grey. The thin crops, the frail, earth-coloured
houses, here and there a pencilled, fine-leaved tree and a
matchstick-figure in a round hat scratching and chopping at
the dun earth with a hoe. Chop and drag. Chop and drag. For
hours they drove under a rainy sky. 'Time is over,' she said.

'Better?'

'Yes. I don't know what it was. It must have been a dream.
It was a sort of – day-mare.'

'It was a short night,' he said. 'You're tired.'

As the country faded by she began to see beauty in the timelessness and silence and hugeness of the land, the people scarcely touched down on it like specks. At a lay-by worn by other tourists' feet they all got out to take photographs of peasants sowing seed on the plain. One ancient leather face looked up into Ann's camera. Looked away.

'Come now, come,' laughed the young guide. 'The road soon changes. It will become bad. After lunch it may be slow. We are going to a beautiful place for lunch. Well, it is the only place. Here it comes. It is perfectly hygienic. Do not judge by its surroundings.'

They picked their way through filth to the one new building in a sad town. Driver and guide disappeared and the party spinning a turntable of food at two round dining tables loosened up a little. The old Englishman ate sparingly, expert with chopsticks, the rest hungrily with spoons. The Nigerian ate hardly at all. All the food was fawn. 'Not exactly Hong Kong,' said Ann's husband.

'It is *amazingly* good. Amazing,' said the old Englishman. 'Amazing that they can do this. You have no idea.'

'You know China?'

'Oh yes. For twenty years. And we left twenty years ago.' He looked at his wife who had no need to look back at him.

'*And*,' he said, 'we are unlikely to be here again.'

'Oh – don't say that,' said Ann.

'Not because of our age,' he said. 'None of us may come back again.'

'And now we shall hurry on,' said the guide. They noticed under the high electric bulbs of the echoing restaurant that he was rather older than they had thought and that some of the earlier insouciance was gone. Some of the acting. 'I shall warn you,' he said, 'we come soon to a point where it is not impossible that we must turn back. Before we get to the city there is often a huge traffic condition and we stand still a long time. It is known as the Rush Hour. A misnomer. I ask you to be patient if this happens and perhaps read books or sleep. Ask me questions or we perhaps might sing? May I ask you now at this moment, not to look out to the left of the bus please? Look only straight ahead, please, or to the *right*.'

Everyone at once looked out to the left, where a bedraggled and very long string of people dressed in white was moving at an urgent jog-trot over the fields towards the main road. Some wore tall white dunces caps. All had fluttering streamers and dabs of vermilion paint. Four shouldered a skimpy coffin.

'To the right. To the right,' called the guide, 'the *right*. It is a Chinese funeral. Funerals are very important in China. It is not polite to watch them. In East or West it is considered ill-mannered to watch peoples' grief. It is not civilised to watch a Chinese funeral.'

'It is bad luck to watch a Chinese funeral,' said the big old Englishman in Ann's ear – he sat behind her. 'He is being kind to us.'

'It is our second today,' said Ann.

The driver slammed his foot down and they sped on, over a road full of holes and lakes of rain, past a sugar-beet factory red with rust. 'The Russians flogged to us that factory,' the guide announced over his microphone – his lunch and the funeral had excited him. 'The Russians made mugs of us. As usual. Nothing works.'

On they sped, past stagnant black water, ditches crammed with lotus leaves. A village. A temple. A snow-storm of white ducks waiting to be cooked. In a dirty town, pavement-artists gathered round the bus in front of a defunct red-lacquered palace, calling and laughing. 'These are all students,' said the guide. 'These are my tribe. Though they do not speak such good English as I do. I am very good.' He laughed at himself and the bus laughed with him and said he was telling the truth. Someone began to clap. The Nigerian looked loftily out of the window. They flew on, rounded a bend and hit the traffic.

It stood ahead of them as far as they could see. 'And this,' said the guide, 'is where we must put to the test the capacity for patience. At first I suggest we take some sleep.'

Guide and driver, expert as grasshoppers, folded them-selves in their seats and a little of the black cap of hair on each head, one polished, one shaggy, showed above the ramshackle head-rests. The heads leaned together, like babes-in-the-wood. Ann felt her hands ache to stretch and caress.

53

She felt again, darkness round the two young men and turning quickly, frightened, said to the old English woman, 'This can't be much fun for you. This new China. Having lived here before. We thought it was all supposed to be so much better now. Is it just that we've been in Hong Kong for a week? Cloud cuckoo?'

She said, 'Oh no. It is wonderful to be back.'

'Ha,' said the guide, bobbing up, arranging himself on a perch by the dashboard, taking up the mike. 'This it seems is a good opportunity. The driver does not speak English and is in any case asleep. None of you will stay in China for more than a day. I tell you then this. China now looks forward with hope and joy. There is to be a great and glorious transformation. Blood will flow, but we stand to overthrow evil men and we shall win liberty. I ask you to think of me soon. At the time when the world will be watching us. You will remember me and what I say.'

Tottering as the bus jerked forward again, he fell aslant back in to his seat and turned away from them. For perhaps a mile they bowled easily along.

But then – round the next bend – the traffic again before them, ramshackle, dead-still, solid, and more came swinging up behind them, hemming them tight.

'We shall now miss our train to Hong Kong from the city,' said the Nigerian, speaking for the first time.

'There is nothing to be done,' said the old Englishman, and settled back comfortably. His wife smiled.

Ann's husband said, 'Better sleep, Ann. We don't know what the end of this is going to be.'

'No.'

'Don't look so *doom-laden*,' he said. 'It's all education. After all, it's not our country.'

He hoped that she had not seen that the funeral party of an hour ago had caught up with them and was jogging along the side of the bus between it and the oily ditch of lotuses. The mourners' feet were black with dust, faces were hidden by white hoods. The crazed tall hats bobbed up and down as they passed by, and out of sight.

Jump

NADINE GORDIMER

HE IS AWARE of himself in the room, behind the apartment door, at the end of a corridor, within the spaces of this destination that has the name HOTEL LEBUVU in gilt mosaic where he was brought in. The vast lobby where a plastic-upholstered sofa and matching easy chairs are stranded, the waiting elevator in its shaft that goes up floor after floor past empty halls gleaming signs – CONFERENCE CENTRE, TROPICANA BUFFET, THE MERMAID BAR – he is aware of being finally reached within all this as in a film a series of dissolves passes the camera through walls to find a single figure, the hero, the criminal. Himself.

The curtains are open upon the dark, at night. When he gets up in the morning he closes them. By now they are on fire with the sun. The day pressing to enter. But his back is turned; he is an echo in the chamber of what was once the hotel.

The chair faces the windscreen television set they must have installed when they decided where to put him. There is nothing to match its expensive finish – the small deal table and four chairs with hard red plastic-covered seats, the hairy two-division sofa, the formica-topped stool, the burning curtains whose circles and blotches of pattern dazzle like the flicker of flames: these would be standard for a clientele of transients who spend a night, spill beer, and put out cigarettes under a heel. The silvery convex of the screen reflects a dim, ballooned vision of a face, pale and full. He forgets, and passes a hand over cheek and chin, but there is no beard there – it's real that he shaved it off. And they gave him money to fit himself out with the clothes he wears now. The beard (it was dark and vigorous, unlike the fine hair of his head) and the camouflage fatigues tucked into boots that struck authoritatively with each step, the leather-bound beret; took them all off, divested himself of them. There! He must be believed, he was believed. The face pale and sloping away into the pale flesh of the chin: his hidden self produced for them. It's there on the dead screen when he looks up. A child he remembers – himself? – had a dog who, when it was caught and bathed, emerged trembling, ashamed, revealed by the wet fur plastered to its frame to be other than it had appeared in its luxuriant coat.

They supplied a cassette player of good quality as well as the widescreen television set. He is playing, so loudly it fills the room, presses counter to the day pressing against the curtains, the music track from a film about an American soldier who becomes brutalised by the atrocities he is forced to commit in Vietnam. He saw the film long ago, doesn't remember it well, and does not visualise its images. He is not listening: the swell and clash, the tympani of conflict, the brass of glory, the chords of thrilling resolve, the maudlin strings of regret, the pauses of disgust – they come from inside him. They flow from him and he sits on and does not meet the image smeared on the screen. Now and then he sees his hand. It never matched the beard, the fatigues, the beret, the orders it signed. It is a slim, white, hairless hand, almost transparent over fragile bones, as the skeleton of a gecko can be seen within its ghostly skin. The knuckles are delicately pink – clean, clean hand, scrubbed and scrubbed – but along the V between first and third fingers there is the shit-coloured stain of nicotine where the cigarette burns down. They were prepared to spend foreign currency on him. They still supply from somewhere the imported brand he prefers; packets are stacked up amply in their cellophane, within reach. And he can dial room service as indicated on the telephone that stands on the floor, and, after a long wait, someone will come and bring cold beer. He was offered whisky, anything he liked, at the beginning, and he ordered it although he had never been one to drink spirits, had made the choice, in his profession, of commanding the respect accorded the superiorly disciplined personality rather than the kind admiringly given to the hard-living swaggerer. The whisky has stopped coming; when he orders a bottle nothing is said but it is not delivered.

As if it mattered.

Covered by the volume of the music, there is the silence. Nothing said about the house. The deal included a house, he was given to understand it would be one of the fine ones left behind and expropriated by the State in the name of the people, when the colonials fled. A house with a garden and watchman for privacy, security (in his circumstances), one of the houses he used to ride past when he was the schoolboy son of a civil servant living here in a less affluent white quarter. A house and a car. Eventually some sort of decent position. Rehabilitated. He had thought of information, public relations (with his international experience); it was too soon to say, but they didn't say so.

Everything he wanted: that was to be his reward. The television crews came – not merely the tin-pot African ones but the BBC, CBS, Zweites Deutsches Fernsehen – and the foreign correspondents flew in with their tape recorders. He was produced at press conferences in the company of the Commander of the Armed Forces, the Minister of Defence, and their aides elegant as the overthrown colonial ones had been. A flower arrangement among the water carafes. Him displayed in his provided clothes, his thighs, that had been imposing in fatigues, too fleshy when crossed in slightly shiny tropical trousers, his chin white, soft and naked where the beard was gone, his hair barbered neat and flat with the dun fringe above the forehead, clippers run up the nape – on his big hunched body he saw in the newspaper photographs the head of a little boy with round bewildered eyes under brows drawn together and raised. He told his story. For the first few months he told his story again and again, in performance. Everyone has heard it, now. On the table with the four chairs drawn up a cold fried egg waits on a plate covered by another plate. A jug of hot water has grown tepid beside a tin of instant coffee. Someone has brought these things and gone away. Everyone has gone away. The soaring, billowing music in the room is the accompaniment the performance never had. When the tape has ended he depresses the rewind button to play it again.

They never mention the house or the car and he doesn't know how to bring up the subject – they hardly ever come to see him anymore, but maybe that's natural because the debriefing is over, they're satisfied. There's nothing more to tell the television crews and the press. There's nothing more he can think of – think back! think back! – to find to say. They've heard about his childhood in this capital, this country to which he has been returned. That he was an ordinary colonial child of parents who'd come out from Europe to find a better life where it was warm and there were opportunities. That it was warm and there was the sea and tropical fruit, blacks to dig and haul, but the opportunity was nothing grander than the assured tenure of a white man in the lower ranks of the civil service. His parents were not interested in politics, never. They were not interested in the blacks. They didn't think the blacks would ever affect their lives and his. When the colonial war began it was away in the North; troops came from the 'mother' country to deal with it. The boy would perhaps become an accountant, certainly something one rung above his father, because each generation must better itself, as they had done by emigrating. He grew up taking for granted the activities and outlets for adventurous play which had no place in the reality of the blacks' lives, the blacks' war: as an adolescent he bonded with his peers through joining the parachute club, and he jumped – the rite of passage into manhood.

In the capital, the revolution was achieved overnight by a relinquishment of power by Europe, exacted by the indigenous people through years of war in the rural areas. A few statues toppled in the capital's square and some shops were looted in revenge for exploitation. His parents judged their security by the uninterrupted continuance, at first, of the things that mattered to them: the garbage continued to be collected twice a week and there was fish in the market. Their modest lives would surely not be touched by black rule. He was apprenticed as draughtsman to an architect, by then (more prestigious than accountancy) and his weekend hobby, in addition to jumping from the sky, was photography. He even made a bit of pocket money by selling amusing shots of animals and birds to a local paper. Then came the event that – all at once, reeled up as the tape is filling its left cylinder on rewind – the experience that explained everything he had ever done since, everything that he was to confess to, everything he was to inculpate himself of and judge himself on in his performance for the journalists under the monitoring approval of the Commander of the Armed Forces and the Minister of Defence, during the probing of debriefing, the Q and A interviews; and to himself, in fiery dimness behind the curtains' embers, facing the fish-eye of the TV screen, surrounded by the music, alone. He took a photograph of a sea-bird alighting on some sort of tower structure. Soldiers lumbered with sawn-off machine guns seized him, smashed his camera and took him to the police. He was detained for five weeks in a dirty cell the colonial regime had used for blacks. His parents were told he was an imperialist spy – their innocent boy only two years out of school! Of course, this was all in the confusion of the first days of freedom (he would explain to his audience), it was to be expected. And who was that boy to think he could photograph anything he liked, a military installation of interest to the new State's enemies? That white boy.

At this point in the telling came the confession that for the first time in his life he thought about blacks – and hated them. They had smashed his camera and locked him up like a black and he hated them and their government and everything they might do, whether it was good or bad. No – he had not then believed they could ever do anything good for the country where he was born. He was sought out by or he sought out – he was never made to be clear on this small point – white people to whom his parents had successfully appealed to get him released. They soothed him with their indignation over what had happened to him and gave him a substitute for the comradeship of the parachute club (closed down by the blacks' military security) in their secret organisation to restore white rule through compliant black proxies. How it was to be done was not yet formulated, allies from neighbouring cold and hot wars had not yet been found, money from international interests wanting access to oil and mineral finds had not been supplied, sources for material and mercenaries to put together a rebel army in the bush were still to be investigated. He bent quietly over his drawing board and at night he went to clandestine meetings. He felt importantly patriotic; something new, because his parents had abandoned their country, and this country in which he was born had been taken back by the blacks for themselves. His parents thanked God he was safe in good company, white like them but well-off and knowledgeable about how to go on living here where it was warm, trusted to advise one if it were to be time to leave. They were proud when told their son was being sent to Europe to study; an act of philanthropy by compatriots of the country they had all once emigrated from.

Of humble beginnings, he had come into the patrimony of counter-revolution.

The telephone is not only good for house calls that summon the old black man shrunken in khaki who brings the beer, brought the egg and covered it with a second plate. He can phone long distance every day, if he wants to. There is never a bill; they pay. That was the condition understood – they would provide everything. So he phones his mother every third day in the European city to which she and his father returned when the people who knew about these things said it was time to go. He has only to dial, and it's winter there now and the phone will ring on its crocheted mat in the living-room behind double-glazing, discovered to him (so that was where his parents came from!) when he was set up in the same European city. They must have realised soon that he was not studying. At least not in the sense they would understand, of attending an institute and qualifying for a profession you could name. But it was obvious to them he was doing well, he was highly thought of by the people who had recognised the young man's qualities and taken him up after the terrible time when those blacks threw him in prison back where everything was lost, now – the civil servant's pension, the mangoes and passion fruit, the sun. He was involved in the affairs of those people of substance, international business too complicated for him to explain. And confidential. They respected that. A mother and father must never make any move that might jeopardise the opportunities they themselves have not been able to provide. He was always on his way to or from the airport – France, Germany, Switzerland, and other destina-tions he did not specify. Of course his gift for languages must have been invaluable to the people he worked with rather than for – that was clearly his status. He had not an apartment but a whole house purchased for him in the privacy of one of the best quarters, and his study or office there was not only lined with documents and books but equipped with the latest forms of telecommunication. Foreign associates came to stay; he had a full-time maid. His delicate, adolescent's chin disappeared in the soft flesh of good living, and then he grew the beard that came out dark and vigorous giving him the aspect of a man of power. They never saw him wearing the rest of its attributes: the bulky fatigues and the boots and the beret. He visited them in civilian clothes that had come to be his disguise.

The first time he ever used the phone on the floor was when he phoned her, his mother, to tell her he was alive and here. *Where?* How could she ever have supposed it – back, back in this country! The sun, the mangoes (that day there was fruit supplied on the table where the egg congeals, now), the prison a young boy had been thrown into like any black. She wept because she and his father had thought he was dead. He had disappeared two months previously. Without a word; that was one of the conditions he adhered to on his side, he couldn't tell his parents this was not a business trip from which he would return: he was giving up the house, the maid, the first-class air tickets, the important visitors, the book-lined room with the telecommunications system by which was planned the blowing up of trains, the mining of roads, and the massacre of sleeping villagers back there where he was born.

It is the day to phone her. It's more and more difficult to keep up the obligation. There's nothing left to tell her, either. From weeping gratitude that he was alive, as time has gone by she has come to ask why *she* should be punished in this way, why he should have got mixed up in something that ended so badly.

Over the phone she says, Are you all right?

He asks after his father's health. Does it look like being a mild winter?

Already the wind from the mountains has brought a touch of rheumatism.

Do you need anything? (Money is provided for him to send to his parents, deprived of their pension; that's part of the deal.)

Then there's nothing to say. She doesn't ask if he's suffering from the heat back there, although the sun banks up its fire in the closed curtains, although she knows well enough what the climate's like in summer, and he was gone seven years and cannot reacclimatise. She doesn't want to mention the heat because that is to admit he is back there, she and his father will never understand what it was all about, his life; why he got himself into the fine house, the telecommunications system, the international connections, or why he gave it all up. She says little, in a listless voice, over the phone. But she writes. They deliver her letters, pushed under the door. *Why does God punish me? What have your father and I done? It all started long ago. We were too soft with you. With that parachute nonsense. We should never have allowed it. Giving in, letting you run wild with those boys. It started to go wrong then, we should have seen you were going to make a mess of our lives, I don't know why. You had to go jumping from up there. Do you know what I felt, seeing you fall like that, enjoying yourself frightening us to death while you fooled around with killing yourself? We should have known it. Where it would end. Why did you have to be like that? Why? Why?*

First in the weeks of debriefing and then in the press conferences, he had to say.

They demanded again and again. It was their right.

How could you associate yourself with the murderous horde that burns down hospitals, cuts off the ears of villagers, blows up trains full of innocent workers going home to their huts, rapes children and forces women at gunpoint to kill their husbands and eat their flesh?

He sat there before them sane, and was confronted by the madness. As he sits in the red gloom in front of the widescreen television set, the fuse of a cigarette between the fingers of his fine white hand and his pale blue eyes clear under puppy-like brows. Shuddering; they couldn't see it but he shuddered within every time to hear listed by them what he knew had happened. How could they come out with it, just like that?

Because horror comes slowly. It takes weeks and months, trickling, growing, mounting, rolling, swelling from the faxed codes of operation, the triumph of arms deals secretly concluded with countries which publicly condemn such transactions; from the word 'destabilisation' with its image of some faulty piece of mechanism to be rocked from its base so that a sound structure may be put in its place. He sent the fax, he took the flights to campaign for support from multi-national companies interested in access to the oil and minerals the blacks were giving to their rivals, he canvassed Foreign Offices interested in that other term, spheres of influence.

In the fine house where an antique clock played an air over the sudden stutterings of communications installations, the war was intelligence, the miracle of receiving the voice of a general thousands of kilometres away, on the other continent, down there in the bush. When he travelled on his European missions he himself was that fighting man: the beard, the fatigues, the beret. The people he visited saw him as straight from the universal battlefield of right and left; the accoutrements transformed him for himself, so it seemed he was emerged from that generic destiny known as the field of operations.

You mean to say you didn't know?

But nobody talked. A push was achieved or it wasn't. A miniature flag moved on the map. Men lost, and losses imposed on the government forces were recorded. There were some reverses. A huge airlift of supplies and material by the neighbouring African state allied in the cause of destabilisation was successful; the rebel force would fight on for years, village by village, bridge by bridge, power stations and strategic roads gained on the map. There would be victory on the righteous side.

Nobody said how it was being done. The black government spread reports of massacres because it was losing, and of course the leftist and liberal press took up the tales. Intelligence, tuned to the clock with its gilded cupids, filed these: under disinformation about destabilisation.

Here, always, they waited for him to go on. He swallowed continually between phrases and while he was telling, they would watch him swallow. The cold egg won't go down. There is a thin streamer of minute ants who come up six floors through the empty foyer and the closed reception rooms and find their way along the leg of the table to food left there; he knows. And telling, telling – telling over and over to himself, now that no one comes to ask any more, he swallows, while the ants come steadily. Go on, go on.

It wasn't until I went to the neighbouring State that provided the material, planes, intelligence supplied by its agents – it is a white state and very advanced – to the communications centre it set up for us in the house in Europe. There was also a base.

Go on.

A training base for our people. It was secret, no one knew it was there. Hidden in a game reserve. I was very confident – pleased – to find myself sent not only around Europe, but chosen to go to that State. To liaise. To meet the Commander of National Security and Special Services there. See for myself the important extent of co-operation in our mutual dedication to the cause. Report back on the morale of our men being trained there in the use of advanced weapons and strategy.

Yes?

A crescendo comes in great waves from the speaker provided with the tape player: to win the war, stabilise by destabilisation, set up a regime of peace and justice!

During press conferences, at this point an ooze of heat would rise under his skin. Their eyes on him drew it up from his tissues like a blister. And then?

There's no one in the room, the curtains are closed against everyone. Swallow. I saw the male refugees captured at the border brought in starving. I saw how to deal with them. They were made to join our forces or were put back over the border to die. I could see that they would die. Their villages burned, their families hacked to death – you saw in their faces and bodies how it really happened . . . the disinformation. It wasn't talked about at that base, either. Our allies, at the dinners they gave – game dishes and wine, everything of the best provided, treated like a VIP – they didn't talk about these things. Well . . . I was shown around . . . everything. The secret radio station that broadcast the Voice of our organisation. The latest weapons made available to us. The boots and uniforms made in their factories. (That outfit of mine must have come from there.) The planes taking off at night to fly our men, armed and equipped to do what they were trained to do. I knew, now, what that was.

Yes?

Of course, it was war . . .

So?

. . . War isn't pretty. There is brutality on both sides. I had to understand. Tried to. But planes also came back from over the border at night. Not empty. They carried what I thought were refugee children to be saved from the fighting; girls of twelve or thirteen, terrified, they had to be pulled apart from each other to get them to walk. They were brought in for the

men who were receiving their military training. Men who had
been without women; to satisfy them. After dinner, the
Commander offered me one. He had one led in for himself. He
took off her clothes to show me.

So, yes, I knew what happened to those girl children. I
knew that our army had become – maybe always was – yes,
what you say, a murderous horde that burned hospitals, cut
off the ears of villagers, raped, blew up trains full of workers.
Brought to devastation this country where I was born. It's
there, only the glowing curtains keep it out. At night, when
the curtains are drawn back it is still there in the dark with the
blind bulk of buildings, the traces of broken boulevards and
decayed squares marked in feeble lights. Familiar to me, can't
say I don't know it, can't say it doesn't recognise me. It is
there, with the sun pressing against the window, a population
become beggars living in the streets, camping out in what used
to be our – white people's – apartments, no electricity, no
water in the tiled bathrooms, no glass in the windows, and on
the fine balconies facing the sea where we used to take our
aperitifs, those little open fires where they cook their scraps of
food.

And that's the end.

But it's gone over again and again. No end. It's only the tape
that ends. Can't be explained how someone begins really to
know. Instead of having intelligence by fax and satellite.

Back in the room in Europe with its telecommunications there
was on record the whereabouts of this black regime's repre-
sentatives abroad. One day he went there. In the rebel army's
outfit, with the beard, so that they could shoot him if they
wanted; so that they would realise who he was and what he
knew. Not the atrocities. Something else; all that he could
offer to efface the knowledge of the atrocities: complete
information about the rebel army, its leaders, its internal
feuds, its allies, its sources of supply, the exact position and
function of its secret bases. Everything. Everything he was
and had been, right back to the jump with the parachute and

the photograph of the tower. They didn't shoot. They kept him under guard so that the people from the telecommunications headquarters in the room with the antique clock would not kill him before he could tell. They handled him carefully; himself a strange and rare species, kept captured for study. They were aware of its worth, to them.

Debriefing is like destabilisation, the term doesn't describe the method and experience. Day by day, divested of the boots, fatigues, the beret and the beard, first-class flights, the house in Europe, the dinners of honour, the prestige of intelligence – his life. He has been discovered there beneath it, sitting quite still on a chair in a dark room, only a naked full neck pulsating. In the silence after the tape ends it is possible to think there is the distinct sound of ants moving in an unwavering path.

They knew they couldn't have it for nothing – his life. They haven't provided the house with a garden that was part of the deal. Or the car. Of course, he can go out. Go where he likes, it was only for the first six months that he was restricted. Once they know they can trust him, he's not of interest to them any longer. Nothing more, now, to lead them to. Once he's told everything, once he's been displayed, what use is he to them?

They are right. Perhaps they will never come to him again.

The girl emerges from the bedroom, she sleeps late.

There is a girl. They didn't supply her. But they might have; she was there in the waiting room when he went under surveillance to a doctor. He politely let her take her turn with the doctor first, and when she came out they got talking. I don't see how I'm ever supposed to follow this diet, she said, what can you buy if you haven't got foreign currency – you know how it is, living here.

Yes – for the first time he saw it was so: he lives here. Perhaps it was possible for him to get what she needed? She didn't ask questions; access to foreign currency is not a subject to be discussed.

The girl's been in the bedroom all morning, just as if there was no one there. Now the dim room prolongs her lassitude, no break between night and day. Pink feet with hammer toes drag over the floor; she makes tasting sounds with her tongue against her palate. She takes a deep breath, holds then expels it; because he doesn't speak.

So you don't want to eat?

She has lifted the covering plate and touches the yellow mound of the yolk with her forefinger; the congealed surface dents shinily. She wipes her finger on the T-shirt that is her nightgown. A sprig of houseplant she brought and put in a glass, one day, is on the table where she set it down then; in the cloudy water, the darkened room, it has sent out one frail, floating thread of root. Ants are wavering at the rim of the glass. The thin buttermilk smell of her fluids and his semen comes to him as she bends to follow the ants' trail from the floor. After he had finished with her, last night, she said: You don't love me.

He was assailed by the sight of the twelve-year-old child and the Commander.

Then she heard something she couldn't believe. The man weeping. She drew away in fear and repugnance to the side of the bed.

She hangs about the room behind him, this morning, knowing he's not going to speak.

Why don't we go to the beach. Let's have a swim. I'd love to go and eat some prawns. We can take a bus. There's a good place . . . it's cheap. And don't you feel like a swim, I'm dying to get into the water . . . Come on.

She waits patiently.

Has he shaken his head – there was some slight movement. There is nothing in the room she can turn to as a pretext to keep her there, waiting to see if he accepts her forgiveness, her humble understanding of her function. After a few minutes she goes back into the bedroom and comes out dressed.

I'm going. (Qualifies:) Going for a swim.

This time he nods and leans to take a cigarette.

She hasn't opened the door yet. She's hesitating, as if she thinks she ought to make some gesture, doesn't know what, might come over and touch his hair.

She's gone.

After the inhalation of the cigarette has become his breath and body, he gets up and goes to the window. He pulls aside the curtains to left and right. They are parched and faded, burned out. And now he is exposed: there is the bright stare of the beggared city, city turned inside out, no shelter there for life, the old men propped against empty facades to die, the orphaned children running in packs round the rubbish dumps, the men without ears and women with a stump where there was an arm, their clamour rising at him, rising six floors in the sun. He can't go out because they are all around him, the people.

Jump. The stunning blow of the earth as it came up to flexed knees, the parachute sinking silken.

He stands, and then backs into the room.

Not now; not yet.

Company

ROBERT GROSSMITH

EVER SINCE THE old woman, his niece, left the house and joined their vaporous host, he had spent the day idly wandering from room to room in the grip of ancient memories. Here was the room he was born in, here the attic he played in as a lad, the log cabin, crow's nest, castle turret of his solitary, always solitary fantasies; here the bathroom where he passed a guilty adolescence poring over chiaroscuro nudes in fear and circumspection; here the room he died in, not yet a man, lungs full of mustard gas, already turning vaporous. They were all dead now of course, his mother, father, sisters, grandparents, even the old woman, his niece, all together again, though hardly a family. The blood-ties that had seemed to bind them while alive had loosened with the prospect of a common eternity, blood after all proving no thicker than air. No, it was the memories that held him, the memories he subsisted on, like a diet of ersatz foodstuffs, knowing he would never taste real nourishment again.

It was therefore with something resembling a sense of physical pleasure that, sitting one day at the foot of the stairs gazing glumly at the worn patterns on the carpet, his attention was alerted by the bright metallic tinkling of a key in the lock. He looked up, doubting the evidence of his phantom senses,

With an ill-fitting shudder the door burst open to admit a wedge of dusted sunlight and three haloed figures, almost transparent in the light.

The corpulent sales-pitching estate agent – for such he took him to be – led the prospective buyers into the hall, a handsome smiling couple in their thirties. Ignoring the agent's patter, they surveyed the gloomy baroque interior with a sceptical eye, taking in at a single glance the high dust-dark ceiling, the peeling paintwork, antique banister, heavy oak-panelled doors. Of course it needed some work doing on it, the old woman had let it get into a quite a state as you could see, but nothing a good sweep and a few coats of paint wouldn't fix.

He stood up and joined the group in the kitchen, nodding his agreement. As for the structural condition of the building, it was really first-rate – well, the surveyor's report would confirm that – and it couldn't be better situated as far as local services were concerned. He followed the trio from room to room, admiring with them the view of the fens from the upstairs windows, echoing the estate agent's paean to the housebuilders of yore, endorsing his exaggerated claims about the costs of heating and upkeep. It was surprising, they'd find the fuel bills were actually quite low, the walls retained the heat, you see, and –

Well, they'd think about it. It was a bit bigger than they'd had in mind, they only had one child, a little girl (a little girl!), but on the other hand they had to admit they did like it, it had a sort of friendly lived-in feel, didn't it, Clive?

Time passed, the surveyer did his surveying, other viewers came to view, and somewhat to his surprise the couple returned, complete with rubber plants, budgie, colour TV, modern aluminium-frame furniture and their little girl, Angela, four. He took to her instantly, as she took to the house. The bright green, improbably large eyes, the head of dark ringlets that tumbled as she ran, the dimpled cheeks, the freckles, the busy legs pounding the stairs – 'It's like a castle, Mummy!' – there was something in her so saturated with vibrancy, vitality, that one could almost have persuaded oneself that decay was an illusion. Who would dare predict that one day this hair would be white, these gums toothless, this delicate blooming skin as blotched and tough as old shoe leather? As his fondness for her grew and he began to appreciate the depths of emotional attachment of which he was still unexpectedly capable, it struck him that what he was experiencing was a kind of love; a chaste, fraternal or paternal love, as befitted his condition.

At first he was content to remain in the role of onlooker. Settling below the ceiling in the corner of the room where she played, he would gratefully observe her solitary games, eavesdrop shamelessly on her conversations with her dolls, beguiled by her guileless charms. When bedtime came he would follow her upstairs, installing himself on top of her wardrobe or like a dog at the foot of her bed, watching over her through the night. It was as if, through her, he was able to live again, to recover a vicarious existence of his own. He waited impatiently for her return each day from school, cursed the sunshine that took her out to play in the garden, dreaded the inevitable summer holidays and impromptu weekends away that deprived him of her company, leaving him alone in the vast desert empire of his solitude, murdering time till her return. He was happiest when she was sick and forced to keep to her bed; nothing too serious, a chill would do, or a mild lingering tummy upset. Sometimes, when especially lonely and bold, he would sidle in beside her, nestling his formless form against her sleeping curves, enfolding her with his fleshless arms. He managed not to waste time dwelling on the future – her future of course, he had none, or rather too much of it – on what would happen when she grew up and – well, he managed not to think of such things.

The idea took shape slowly. After all, he didn't want to frighten her. Besides, he knew how the others scorned such diversions. Accept the facts, they said or seemed to imply (they seldom spoke), the world of the living is lost to you forever, you have no place there, let it go. Most of the others had made the transition successfully. The earthly world had faded for them, dimmed, dissolved, grown remote and insubstantial, as spectral in their eyes as their world was to the living.

But the idea would not go away, it pursued him, niggled at him, refused to let him rest. If only he could become her friend, her secret friend, no one else need know. They both needed a friend. What possible harm could there be in that?

He chose to materialise one afternoon when her mother was out shopping and her father busy mowing the lawn. Dressed in his old army uniform with his decorations prominently displayed, he looked, he thought, rather handsome, distinguished, even a little dapper. No burglar or child-molester would affect such an elaborate disguise.

'Hello,' he said, standing in the open doorway of the living-room – an apt location for his first appearance, he thought.

She looked up from the floor where she lay mutely mouthing the captions of a brightly coloured comic; studied him with interest and suspicion.

'Who are you?'

'I used to live here.' He took a step into the room, closing the door behind him. 'Just popped in to see what the old place looks like. What's your name? Mine's William. You can call me Billy.'

'How did you get in? My mummy and daddy told me not to speak to strange men.'

'I'm not a strange man. I told you, I used to live here. Do you want to play a game?'

'What sort of game?'

'I don't know, you choose. How about hide-and-seek?'

'My name's Angela,' she said. 'I'm five.'

'Hello, Angela.'

'You look funny. Are you a soldier?'

'Sort of, yes.'

'Mr Green was a soldier. I know because he told me.'

'Who's Mr Green?'

'The man in the sweet shop.' Then, her suspicions aroused again, 'If you used to live here you'd know that.'

'I've been away a long time,' he said. 'In the army. Just got back. Mr Green didn't work in the sweet shop when I lived here. There wasn't a sweet shop.'

They continued to talk. As he felt himself gaining her confidence he advanced slowly into the room, rediscovering the forgotten art of ambulation. With excessive caution he skirted those areas where the sunlight streaming through the French windows threatened to penetrate his disguise, expose him for the shadow he was. He rested against a mahogany table supporting an empty fruit bowl and a red ceramic vase. The polished surface of the table, he noted with the usual regret, disdained to return his reflection.

'Do you have many friends, Angela?'

'Hilary's my friend. Her daddy's a policeman.'

'Can I be your friend, Angela?'

He could only assume she was about to answer in the affirmative because at that moment the door he had closed behind him was flung briskly open – 'I'm back, Popsie!' – and the head of Angela's mother thrust itself into the room. He evaporated instantly but with such precipitateness that the vase on the table against which he had been leaning was sent rocking on its base and crashing to the floor, fracturing into a dozen pieces. Angela's mother turned to the noise with a start. She closed the door and threw it open again, repeating the experiment without success: the fruit bowl refused to budge. Puzzled, she knelt down and began gathering the shards of pottery from the floor.

'It was the man.'

'What man?'

'The man who was here. The soldier. He made himself invisible when you came in.'

'Come and help me unpack the shopping, there's a good girl.'

The next time he visited her he was more careful. Angela was in her bedroom feeding and dressing her dolls, her father in the garage tinkering with his car, her mother in the kitchen with her arms in a sinkful of grey suds – a conventional tripartition of roles he was pleased to see had survived the disastrous changes of modern life.

'Hello, it's me, Billy,' he said, stepping out from behind the wardrobe with a nervous smile meant to deprive his sudden entrance of menace.

She looked up from where she stood by a miniature crib in which a naked pink doll contentedly sucked air from the tiny plastic bottle nuzzled in its face. A slight furrowing of the brow and narrowing of the eyes betokened the tentative shaping of a question.

'Are you a magician? I saw a magician on the telly once who could do that. He could make himself invisible. Pouf,' she went, mimicking with ten tremulous fingers two rising balls of smoke.

'That's right, I'm a magician. I can do lots of tricks.'

'Will you teach me them? I like tricks.'

'Well, I don't know, they're secrets really. I'm not supposed to tell anyone.'

'If you were my friend you'd tell me. Friends aren't supposed to have secrets.'

'Well, we'll see, we'll see. Perhaps when you're a bit older.'

'Grown-ups always say that,' she complained. 'My mummy and daddy don't think you're real. I told them about you but they don't believe me. They think I made you up.'

'You believe I'm real, don't you?' – the note of anxiety in his voice betraying him.

'Of course. I can see you, can't I? And I can touch you if I want.' She took a step towards him.

'No, don't do that!' Backing away towards the wardrobe.

'Why not?'

'Because, because I'm all dirty, my clothes are dirty. You don't want to get your nice clean frock all dirty, do you?'

'Why do you wear those funny army clothes? You don't look like a proper soldier.'

She was asking too many questions, it was time to leave.

'Look, shall I do my trick again? Do you want to see me disappear?'

She shrugged her shoulders. 'If you want.'

'All right, but this time you count to three, all right? Then say the magic word: Alacazam. Got it? Alacazam. Any time you want me to appear, just say the magic word.'

She counted with ponderous deliberation. 'Alka-seltz!'

Running into the space he had vacated, she palpated the air with her fingers as if searching for a hidden crevice, then skipped back with a giggle to her dollies.

Those were the happiest days of his death. He floated freely about the house, born up by a sense of belonging once more to the land of the living, or if not quite belonging then at least being accepted as a sort of naturalised alien, or, more appropriately perhaps, a soldier on furlough, a prisoner on parole.

His euphoria made him reckless. Sliding under the covers that night when he had assured himself she was asleep, he took it into his head to materialise. Using words like 'materialise', or for that matter 'head', in connection with what was at best an ethereal act is liable to be misleading. To materialise, in this context, simply meant that, had she opened her eyes, she would have seen him there beside her, or imagined she did. Unfortunately, this was precisely what happened. He evaporated before the shrill piping scream had time to leave her lungs, scrambling to the top of the wardrobe, curling into a ball, imploring her soundlessly, invisibly, to curb her cries, be quiet, he hadn't meant any harm, he'd just wanted some company, that was all.

'It was the man, the man,' she gave out between huge gulping sobs, burying her face in her mother's shoulder.

'Shh shh, it was just a dream, darling, just a dream, Mummy's here now, it's all right, all right.'

'He was in my bed, the man.'

It irked him that she had reacted in this way. He'd been friendly, after all, he'd been nice to her, what was she afraid of? If only he could talk to her, explain, apologise, he'd never do it again, honestly, not if she didn't want him to, cross his heart and hope to – well, never mind. But to appear before her now, he knew, would only make things worse, increase her fear, alienate her further. Especially as the so-called 'dream' in which he'd entered her bed was succeeded by a series of real (that is to say illusory) nightmares in which he apparently repeated and elaborated on the act. Night after night she would awake in a tangle of sweat-soaked sheets, screaming she'd seen him again. He came to despise his shadowy reflection of his already shadowy self, this imposter, this double, this malevolent twin, spreading a trail of terror and laying it at his door.

There was nothing for it, he had to speak to her again. He waited till she'd been tucked in and read to and was lying awake in the yellow glow of her bedside lamp, now left on all through the night, humming quietly to herself. She halted mid-phrase and looked up at him, lips parted in preparation for the automatic scream.

'Don't cry, Angela, please. I don't want to hurt you, just be your friend.'

'I don't like you,' she said uncertainly. 'You've been scaring me. You're not a nice man. I'm going to call my daddy.'

'Don't, Angela, please. Look, I promise I won't visit you again if you don't want me to. Just say so and I'll go away, I promise.'

'Go away!' she said. 'I don't want to see you ever again.'

He was beginning to lose patience with her. 'Come on now, don't be silly. Look, I told you I'm your friend, didn't I, you can't send me away, I'm your friend for God's sake!'

'Mummy! Daddy! Mummee-ee!'

In a fit of pique he swept a phosphorescent arm across the desktop cluttered with dolls and dolls' clothing, dolls' hair-brushes, dolls' toys, dolls' dolls, sent them clattering to the floor. 'Play with these, don't you? Bloody dolls! Just bits of plastic, dead bloody plastic! What about me, what about me?' The momentum of his anger and frustration, suddenly finding a release after a deathtime of denial, proved impossible to contain. He charged through the room in a swirling vortical haze, upsetting the furniture, ripping the posters from the walls, lifting up a mirror and shattering it against the desk, stamping hysterically on the dolls that littered the floor at his feet, crushing their hollow unfeeling skulls, tearing them limb from limb, flinging the mutilated remains at the walls and windows, howling. He evaporated in a heap as the door flew open behind him.

Everything was going wrong, why was everything going wrong? He hadn't meant to fly off the handle like that, it just happened, ghosts had emotions too, he wasn't perfect. And now he had spoiled everything, everything.

He took once more to roaming the house without aim, borne down by the weight of his solitude and grief. When even movement proved beyond him, he would retire to a dusty corner of the attic or huddle in a foetal ball in the grate of an unlit fireplace, roasting in the cold ashes of self-pity and self-hate. How could he now enjoy watching over her through the night when aware that she might awake at any moment, denouncing him for dream crimes he had had no part in? How could he even enter her room when afraid that the icy draught he bore in his train might alert her to his presence, set into irresistible motion the whole familiar histrionic routine?

Slouched one evening before the television set, watching a daft late-night horror movie with Angela's parents, he heard them talking about him.

'Poltergeist! So the place is haunted, is that it? Bloody ridiculous! What's he want us to do, get in a priest to exorcise it?'

'Please darling, try and stay calm, I'm just telling you what he said, that's all. Apparently it's got nothing to do with ghosts, it's quite a common phenomenon, especially among young girls. Some sort of release of psychic energy or something. They can break things, start fires, you know, cause a lot of damage.'

'But Christ, Shirl, you saw that room. That wasn't just breaking things. She must have done that physically, with her hands. But why, why?'

'I know, I know, I'm just telling you what he said, that's all.'

How endearing the living were with their obstinate refusal to countenance any but the most grossly physical of explanations in their commerce with the spirit, how they feared the intangible, the unknown. Sometimes it seemed to him that for all the arid lunar emptiness of his own existence, the real tragedy was theirs. He at least knew how things stood, he had

had time – so much time! – to adjust, while they still had to live through the monstrous metamorphosis of death, still had to suffer the pain of that fatal wrench. How differently they would treat their bodies, how they would glory and exult in the flesh, how plunder its pleasures, if they knew the hollow ache of facing eternity without it. How they will miss that heavenly machine when it gasps up its infernal ghost.

Things had come to a head, they couldn't go on as they were. It was clear their relationship was fractured beyond repair. It was equally clear that he couldn't continue indefinitely in his present condition, slinking and skulking round the house, wilting under the burden of an oppressive guilt. He must appear before her one final time, explain what had happened, quietly, without rancour, obtain her forgiveness, then vanish forever in the penetralia of the house till nature made them equal again.

He selected for his day of valediction one sultry Sunday afternoon when both parents were in the garden sunbathing; prostrate, beach-clad, toning up their cancerous tans. It was too hot for Angela, who lay on her bed by an open window, listlessly turning the pages of a well-thumbed comic, sipping a glass of orange squash through two thin coloured straws.

The main thing was not to frighten her. He materialised inside the wardrobe – less alarming, he thought, than suddenly appearing unannounced in the middle of the room – and pushed the door gently open with a sly forewarning creak. So innocent and incorruptible she looked, lying there in her red (what was it called?) jumpsuit on the bed. As cherubic as her name. He coughed to signal his presence and assumed a simpering, as he thought disarming, smile.

Instantly she was up on the bed and backing away from him. Her lips parted, breaking not in a cry but in a thin gasp and bubble of saliva like one of the speech-bubbles in the comic she'd been reading.

'It's all right, Angela, it's all right, I've come to say goodbye, don't be frightened, please.'

She had retreated dangerously close to the open window. In a single movement she turned on her heels, thrust her torso over the sill and split the air with a spirit-curdling scream. 'Mummee-ee!'

Her body was extended so far across the sill he was afraid the slightest movement would topple her, send her tumbling, plummeting to the patio below. He rushed towards her to prevent her fall, grab her ankles, hold her down, but even as his ghostly fingers grazed the fabric of her trouser-leg he knew he was too late, she had gone, overbalanced, was already somersaulting through the air like one of her own dolls, swooping to embrace the geometric grid of flagstones flying up to meet her. He could only look on with her parents in mute helpless horror as the implacable laws of gravity were fatally confirmed.

He didn't wait to see if she was dead. Dead or alive, what was the difference? Either way he had to leave. If alive, she would never want to see him again. If dead, he would be haunted by the ghost of her memory, by the permanent presence of her absence from the family where she belonged. The thought of all those unlived years, those untasted experiences, would pursue him like a life sentence, a death sentence, through eternity. Besides, how should he explain himself to her newly arrived spirit, how convince her of his thoughtless good intentions, how justify what he had done? No, the crime was clear, parole would be revoked, and escape was the only option. Shimmering through the open window and passing silently over the huddled scene of grief being played out below, he drifted sluggishly towards the whispering fens, then slowly up, up, up, like a child's gas-filled balloon, on his way to heaven knows where.

The Man with the Dagger

RUSSELL HOBAN

THERE IS A short story by Jorge Luis Borges called 'The South'. It is a story full of sharpness, having in it a lance, a sword, the edge of a door, two knives, the strangeness of life and the familiarity of death.

The protagonist of the story is Juan Dahlmann, secretary to a municipal library in Buenos Aires in 1939. His paternal grandfather, a German immigrant, was a minister in the Evangelical Church. His maternal grandfather was 'that Francisco Flores, of the Second Line-Infantry Division, who had died on the frontier of Buenos Aires, run through with a lance by Indians from Catriel . . .' Dahlmann keeps the sword of Francisco Flores and his daguerreotype portrait and has 'at the cost of numerous small privations . . . managed to save the empty shell of a ranch in the South which had belonged to the Flores family.' He has never lived on this ranch; year after year it waits for him.

Hurrying up the library stairs one day, Dahlmann strikes his head against the edge of a freshly painted door and comes away with a bloody wound. The next morning 'the savour of all things was atrociously poignant. Fever wasted him . . .' He nearly dies of septicaemia, and after a long stay in a sanatorium he leaves the city to go to his ranch for his convalescence.

On his arrival in the South he has a meal at a general store near the railway station. Three men are drinking at another table; one of them has a Chinese look. This man provokes Dahlmann by throwing breadcrumb spitballs at him, then challenges him to a knife fight. Dahlmann knows nothing of knife-play and is unarmed but an old gaucho throws him a naked dagger which lands at his feet. 'It was as if the South had resolved that Dahlmann should accept the duel. Dahlmann bent over to pick up the dagger and felt two things. The first, that this almost instinctive act bound him to fight. The second, that the weapon, in his torpid hand, was no defence at all, but would merely serve to justify his murder.'

Dahlmann picks up the dagger and goes out into the plain to fight. 'Without hope, he was also without fear . . . He felt that if he had been able to choose, then, or to dream his death, this would have been the death he would have chosen or dreamt.'

With the dagger Dahlmann has seized the critical moment that defines . . . what? The right time to die? No use to attempt an analysis of Borges's intention – by the time Dahlmann picks up the dagger he is a fiction of his own making.

Now for as long as there will be print on paper, even longer – for as long as there will be one rememberer to pass this story on to another, even longer, even when all the rememberers are dead, Dahlmann, with his being vibrating between the strangeness of life and the familiarity of death, will live in this moment of unknown definition that he has seized. I wanted to talk to him.

The White Street

I thought the story would be the most likely place to look for Dahlmann, so I went there. I found it in a quiet street where the trees made little black shadows in a dazzling whiteness; it was an old rose-coloured house with iron grille windows, a brass knocker and an arched door. Beside the door was a brass plaque; engraved on it in copperplate script: *The South*.

I knocked, and after a time I heard slow footsteps within and the thud of bolts being drawn back. The door opened slowly and in a very narrow aperture there appeared a vertical fraction of an old woman's face at the top of a blackness of clothing. Her one visible eye was black and difficult to meet.

'Good afternoon,' I said (my watch had stopped but the street was white with heat and light and the sun seemed almost directly overhead). 'Is Señor Dahlmann at home?'

'There's no one here,' she said. 'We're closed.' The aperture and her face became narrower and disappeared with a click. There was the sound of bolts thudding home; her footsteps receded. Behind me the white street shimmered in the heat; far away a dog barked. I didn't want to turn around and see that white street again; I felt myself to be a prism through which the white light would reveal its full spectrum of terror.

I stood facing the centuries-darkened door until I felt myself flickering into black-and-white, then I turned back to the street. It too was flickering in black-and-white like an old film in which nothing had yet happened.

There was a boy flickering in front of me. His head was bent so that his straw sombrero concealed his face, his hands were behind his back. I didn't notice his feet.

'Where's Dahlmann?' I said.

'New in town?'

'Yes.'

'Do they have discretion where you come from?'

'Some do.'

'But not you.'

'I'm a writer, I need to know things.'

'What you need is not to be in too much of a hurry. I'll take you to the hotel.'

His manner was that of one who has seen everything. 'I bet the stories you could tell would make a hell of a book,' I said, 'if only you knew how to get them down on paper.'

He shrugged. 'Not everything needs to be written down.'

We walked without speaking past many churches and past many squares with fountains. Everything continued black-and-white, the streets gradually becoming populous with voices and footsteps and people. Eventually there appeared, not in the most expensive part of town, a small hotel with its name in unlit neon tubing: HOTEL DEATH. On its glass doors were the emblems of American Express, Diners Club and Visa. Opposite was a square with a fountain; on the far side of the square was a church.

'I'll see you later,' said the boy, and wasn't there any more.

Hotel Death

'What can I do for you?' said the skeleton at the desk. He was wearing a garish print shirt outside his trousers, he had a bottle of whisky and a glass and he was smoking an inexpensive cigar. The black-and-white was holding steady. A slowly turning fan in the ceiling stirred the grey shadows and the drifting dust motes in the lobby.

'Have you got a Señor Dahlmann registered here?' I said.

He blew out a big cloud of inexpensive-smelling smoke. It came out of his mouth in the usual way. 'No.'

'You haven't looked.'

'I don't need to.' He poured himself a whisky and lifted his glass. 'Here's looking at you.'

I looked into the hollows where his eyes would have been; the shadows were not unfriendly. The whisky didn't run out of the back of his jaw, it just disappeared. He noticed my staring.

'It didn't bother you that I can talk without a tongue but you draw the line at drinking without a throat, is that it?'

'Not at all,' I lied.

'You want to check in?'

'No.'

'You look pretty old. Why not do it now and beat the rush? We got TV in every room and if you get lonesome I can send somebody around.'

'Skeleton whores?'

'Don't knock it till you've tried it.'

'Later,' I said. 'I've still got things to do.'

'Like what?'

'Like finding Dahlmann.'

'Are you sure you want to?'

'That's what I came here for.'

'Are you sure?'

'Look, let's not turn this into a philosophical exercise. I'll see you later.'

'You know it.'

I went outside and stood by the doors and stared at the flickering black-and-white of the church and the square and the fountain and the dusty street through which passed mules and ox-carts and dark people with sandalled feet and white cotton clothing. There was a smell of faeces and rotting fruit; there was the tolling of a bell and the buzzing of flies. From an upstairs window came the sound of a guitar.

There was a little whiff of lemony fragrance. 'Hi,' said a soft voice next to me. I turned and saw a really stunning skeleton with just the faintest touch of grey on her cheekbones; I recognised it as blusher. No eye shadow, her eyes were nothing but shadows. She was wearing a black poncho, a shiny black Rudolph Valentino hat with a flat top and a broad brim, and black boots. She was shapely in a way that made flesh seem vulgar.

'Why the blusher?' I said.

'I've seen things. Why are you looking for Dahlmann?'

'I think he may have something to tell me.'

'Perhaps I too have something to tell you.'

Together we walked off into the sunlight that would have made a blackness before my eyes if we had been in colour.

Noir's Room

I thought she would rattle but she didn't. What happened was that after the first few moments she stopped being a skeleton for me and simply became who she was, clean and elegant and more naked than I should have thought possible. With her lemony fragrance and that improbable blush on her cheek-

85

bones she was utterly girlish in my arms while there echoed in my mind an ancient scream of desolation and all sweetness gone, gone, gone with her clean white feet running and her black poncho, flapping down endless corridors of neverness.

'What's your name?' I said.

'Noir.'

'How much do I owe you, Noir?'

'Nothing, I'm not working now.'

'Why aren't you working now?'

'Sometimes I make love for money and sometimes I do it for me. This one was for me.'

'How come?'

'You ever do it with a skeleton before?'

'No.'

'I wanted your skeleton cherry,' she said, and kissed me. The room was a subtle composition of grey and black shadows with lines of brilliant white between the slats of the blinds. Through the front window came the sounds of a street market. On a table there were white lemons in a basket, there was a bottle of gin. I could feel colour impending but I held on to the black-and-white. Across the patio someone with a guitar was playing and singing a tango. The shadowy guitar and the quiet husky male voice made the gin seem miraculous.

'What do the words mean?' I asked her.

She listened for a moment, then she whispered in my ear:

> *Such a little, such a little, such a little*
> *difference, my heart —*
> *such a little difference between the one*
> *and the other.*

'Is it really such a little difference?' I said.

'Listen,' she said with her mouth still close to my ear, 'I'll sing you a verse of my own:

> *You were with me, with me, with me, my heart —*
> *you were naked in my arms, to you*
> *I gave my naked self, my onliness.*

Was it less than you've had from others?

I kissed her delicate ivory face. Her mouth was sweet.

'Don't go looking for Dahlmann,' she said. 'What can he tell you that I can't?'

'I don't know. I don't even know what I'm going to ask him.' I got out of bed and put my clothes on. I didn't look back at her as I opened the door and went out.

'It could have been good,' she said.

Sidekick

Again I was hearing the buzzing of flies in a street that smelled of faeces and rotting fruit. Here also there were a square and a fountain and a church; the market stalls clustered under awnings along the near side of the square. The flickering seemed a little less steady than before.

There was a skeleton boy with his hat over his eyes, he was sitting on the ground leaning against the house I'd just come out of. He pushed the hat back and looked up at me as if expecting something.

'What is it?' I said.

'Don't you recognise me?'

'No.'

'I'm the kid that took you to the hotel.'

'Funny, I never noticed you were so bony. This place is full of regular people; why am I always talking to skeletons?'

'Maybe you speak our language.'

'Why is that? Am I dead?'

'What a question! You don't ask questions like that around here, it isn't that kind of a place, there's nothing that simple.'

'All right, then, I'll ask you something else: what's your interest in me? Why did you take me to that hotel and why have you been waiting for me here?'

'What's the matter with you? Don't you go to the movies? I'm the clever little street kid who helps you out; I'm your sidekick, I'm the only one on your side.'

'What's your name?'

'Whitey.'

'What about Noir? Isn't she on my side?'

'Shit. Women!'

'Well, is she or isn't she?'

'She's my sister but she hasn't got much sense and she gets mixed up with all kinds of people.'

'Like me.'

'And others.'

'What others?'

'All kinds. You see that big guy in the rumpled white suit down at the end of the square?'

I looked. The man was over six and a half feet tall, weighed about 300 pounds, and appeared to be the standard sort of henchman or subordinate villain one sees in films. He had nothing of a Chinese look about him and he was not entirely unfamiliar to me but I seemed not to remember who he was. 'Who's he?' I said.

'Don't you know?'

'Why should I know?'

'Because this is that kind of place, some of us are skeletons and some are extras but anybody else with any real action in the story is somebody you know.'

'Maybe I'll know him later but I don't know him now. You say he's one of the people Noir's mixed up with?'

'I'm not sure.'

'Never mind him for now. What about Dahlmann?'

'What?'

'Do you know where he is?'

'I don't exactly know where he is but I think I know when you can find him.'

'When will that be?'

'Later. Have another look around the square.'

I had another look. There was a second big man more or less the same as the first one. Now I seemed to be remembering these men from times when they were less big and I was much younger: the first one would be . . . John? John Something. Tumteetum. De Grassi? Bonanno? 'We'll settle this after school down by the boathouse,' he'd said. I'd preferred not to.

Long, long ago. Some things you walk away from and they
walk after you. I'd fought Joe Higgins and I'd lost but that had
never bothered me. The second one, was he Sergeant Somebody from my army days whose offer to take off his stripes
and step outside I'd declined? Matson? Mason?

'. . . around the square,' said Whitey.

'What did you say?'

'Have another look around the square.'

There was a third big man in a rumpled white suit. He was
from no more than fifteen years ago, this one. I'd never known
his name; he had been a stranger in a bar, another of my
backdowns. 'What's happening?' I said. 'Is this the day when
all my cowardice falls due?'

'What can I tell you? Every day has in it all your days. The
past is something that sticks to your shoes like cowshit. If
Yesterday had kept his pants on Tomorrow wouldn't have a
big belly. Run is a good dog but Fight is a better one.'

'O God, skeleton aphorisms.'

'When I first saw you, you were knocking at the door of
The South. Why were you knocking at that door?'

'I wanted to ask Dahlmann what happened when he picked
up the knife.'

'Why?'

'It's something I've thought about for a long time.'

'Why?'

'Various reasons.'

'Maybe because there were so many knives you didn't pick
up?'

'What are you, the skeleton of Sigmund Freud as a boy?'

'No, I'm your sidekick. I'm the clever little street kid who
helps you and I'd like to know how many big guys in rumpled
white suits we're talking about. How many are there altogether?'

'More than one would like, I suppose.'

'Then let's get out of here before more of them turn up. One
thing . . .'

'What?'

'What you're doing now, keep it going as long as you can
until you're ready for the other.'

'You mean keep the black-and . . .'

'Discretion.'

'And the other?'

'Is what you think it is.'

It was night. Flickering steadily, I moved the slats of the blind apart and looked down into a deserted black-and-white square with a ruined fountain. 'I'm tired of running,' I said.

'I love it when you talk discreet,' said Whitey.

Night Run

We were in the deserted square. The street lamps offered only a feeble and hopeless glimmer that seemed continually to be swallowed up in obscurity. Dim lights punctuated the darkness at odd intervals. Whitey and I stood listening to footsteps that never receded into the distance quite as they should have done.

'Let's get ourselves a car,' he said. We crossed to the far side of the square and he slipped along silently trying doors until an infirm pick-up truck opened for us. We climbed in, Whitey was busy with his hands under the dashboard, there were sparks, the motor started with a roar and we were off.

'Turn on the headlamps for Christ's sake,' I said.

'It's better that you don't see too much, you'll lose your nerve.' Rattling and roaring, we disappeared into the obscurity that had swallowed up the feeble glimmer of the street lamps.

John Kobassa & Co

There was a van blocking the road. In the beams of its headlamps I saw Noir struggling in the grip of one of the big men in rumpled white suits. Whitey braked hard and we jolted to a stop in a cloud of dust. The other two big men were there as well.

'I knew this was going to happen,' I said.

'What did you expect?' said Whitey, 'Cucumber sandwiches?'

'I guess not. But really . . .'

'What?'

'What can they do to her? She's already a skeleton.'

'What a gringo you are.'

'What do you mean by that?'

'Honour is nothing to you, eh? Do you want to watch all three of them having my sister here in front of you? Is that the sort of thing you like?'

'No, I shouldn't like that at all.'

' "No, I shouldn't like that at all," ' he mocked. 'What are you going to do about it? Have you got balls or are you a miserable capon?'

'Aren't you going to help? She's your sister.'

'I'll do sidekick things, like stand on the bonnet and hit them with the starting handle if they get close enough.'

I got out of the truck. Now I remembered them clearly: John Kobassa; Sergeant Moxon; Nameless Stranger.

'You remember us, do you?' said John. He was the one holding Noir.

'Don't worry about me,' Noir said. 'There's nothing they can do to me that hasn't been done before.'

'They're not going to do anything to you,' I said. 'It's me they want. Let her go,' I said to John. 'Here I am.'

'It's about time,' said John.

'Hello, chicken,' said Sergeant Moxon. 'I've been waiting for you for forty-three years.'

'I'm here now. How come all of you are so much bigger than I remember and nobody's old except me?'

'That's how it goes when you put things off too long,' said Nameless Stranger. 'Now if you're ready, we'll do what we didn't do that other time.'

So we did it. When I came to, the pick-up's headlamps were on, the three big men and the van had gone, and Noir was kissing me. I'd been very wise to keep it black-and-white; if it had been full colour they might well have finished me off altogether. As it was, I doubted that my injuries were any worse than if I'd been run over by a medium-sized car: seven or eight of my ribs were broken along with one or two limbs, my head and my dentures; also there seemed to be a fair amount of bleeding both external and internal. All in all I thought it best not to try anything too active for a while so I stayed where I was and looked at Noir out of my one working eye.

'How are you?' she said.

'Terrific,' I mumbled toothlessly. 'If I'd known how good I was going to feel afterwards I'd have looked them up sooner.' It was then that I noticed that the blusher on her cheekbones was pink and not grey and things weren't flickering any more. 'Where's Whitey?' I said.

'Here I am.' He was climbing down from the top of the pick-up.

'Did you stand on the bonnet and hit them with the starting handle?'

'Nobody came close enough.'

'Can we find Dahlmann now?'

'You don't have to find me,' said a new voice. 'I've found you.'

'You're Dahlmann?'

'I'm Dahlmann.'

Without ever having seen a photograph of Borges that indicated his height, I'd always thought of him as a short man and I'd assumed that Dahlmann would be short as well, so I was surprised to see that he was a tall thin man of forty or so, wearing a rumpled white suit but none the less elegant and soldierly in his bearing. His face was long and narrow, with the watchful eyes and cultivated blankness of a man of action; his hair was very black and he had just such a daguerreotypical beard as Francisco Flores must have worn.

'Why were you looking for me?' he said in a perfectly flat and uninflected voice.

Had I expected friendliness? I couldn't remember. I tried to scramble to my feet but one of my legs gave way. Noir came to me and effortlessly lifted me up, then drew back and stood watching me intently. Before the unforeseen actuality of Dahlmann I tried to be as dignified as possible. I no longer wanted to speak the words that I had planned to say but I spoke them as if damned and preordained to do so: 'I wanted to talk to you about what you did, I wanted to know what happened and how it was when you took the dagger in your hand and went out into the plain.' What I said sounded wet and stupid and it was a lie: I no longer wanted to know what had happened and how it had been; I just wanted to go home. I looked at Noir and she blew me a kiss.

'You mean this dagger?' he said. He threw it into the air, the blade flashed in the light of the headlamps as it went end over end and the dagger returned haft-first to his hand. With his face still blank he said, 'What do you think happened?'

'I think you were killed.'

'That's your opinion, is it?'

'Yes.'

'Would you care to back that opinion?'

'How do you mean?'

'Would you like to try me?'

Inwardly I sighed but I said nothing aloud. It was night, the darkness was full of the many and mysterious colours of black. In the light of the headlamps there seemed to be a genuine blush on Noir's painted cheekbones; the shadowy hollows of her eyes sparkled with tenderness. It was night, it was dark, but in my mind a vast and tawny plain opened before me under the sun of the South as Whitey threw me a long knife that made a small hiss as it stuck into the ground at my feet.

An Affair

DESMOND HOGAN

IT BEGAN A few years before they met, like most affairs. On a train from Dublin West they were seated near one another. Carl got involved in conversation with some of her companions. He was on his way from Dublin, having received a prize for a painting that day. She was on her way back to the convent school after a day's outing. Some girls sidled towards Carl and imprisoned him. He told them he was English. Elizabeth was on the other aisle, in her Cadbury's chocolate blue blazer, blonde curls hemming in a smile. She saw him. She witnessed the scene. She forgot it. Carl too had been in a navy school blazer that day, though a day pupil, bearing the regalia of his school in the Gresham Hotel, Dublin. Feet had reluctantly dragged away from Carl in Athlone as a bevy of eyes still lingered on him. The girls had to get another train on to Mayo. Carl had peace for the rest of his journey home. There was a smile on his lips as the train made its way through the bogs full of white hawthorn, still lit by the May evening. Elizabeth in her school on a peninsula in Mayo straddled into a chapel for some reason and, though lately having become somewhat negligent for her devotions, paused briefly before the red light in the dark.

They both happened to be in Paris that summer, students of

French, she an au pair girl, the pastel shades of the revolution washed into a sombre and feckless August. Carl was staying in the suburbs, sleeping under the watch of gigantic factory chimneys. Flames coughed into an iron sky. Among the bulbous chimney bellies Carl walked along the edge of a sky that annihilated the frail stem of his being. This was not Paris. This was the girdles of a Hell first recognised in dreams in County Galway. Elizabeth lost her virginity on a couch to the hairy, late-thirtyish father of the children she was guarding. The spectacle was completed when he, trousers still half down, began crawling on the carpet for something he'd lost. Carl on the steps of Sacré Coeur looked down on Paris and rhetorically told himself there must be someone there who would understand him. The mauve ice-creams had turned sour. Elizabeth brushed down Boulevard Saint Michel, past galleries of laughing books, and perceived the first chestnuts in the Luxembourg Gardens. Carl before leaving Paris glimpsed the same chestnuts.

At eighteen years, his last year at secondary school, cycling to school by oblique birch trees, the hospital sinking into mud distantly, Carl had a desire to live in a tree. There was one tree, easier to see when you were walking, on the way to school, by a red-roofed bungalow, he had chosen as a possible residence. The grey skies had a dignity though. Elizabeth, after completing her intermediate certificate, had abandoned the school in Mayo which she'd reached by reason of a quirky scholarship and was living again at home, in Dublin, attending a convent school in Rathmines. You could walk to the centre of town both from her home and from school, and in the late afternoons she cascaded with other blue-garbed schoolgirls into Bewleys', poured into the cellar café and there, before the eyes of a generation of boys, performed feats with cigarettes in her fingers. Laughter gushed with a certain accent from Dublin middle-class Catholic girls. There was seduction and snobbishness in the laughter and also ripples of self-mockery. No one needed to be persuaded by them. Little groups of boys joined them and middle-class Catholic Dublin accents mingled. The waitresses in Bewleys' wore crimson and tremblingly carried plates of white frothed cakes to the young people.

Carl got a lift to Dublin with the dentist's son in order to begin studying in the College of Art in Kildare Street. The Volkswagen crawled with evening through the Midlands. Elizabeth's father lectured in the College of Art but Carl only brushed past him on a wide stairway. Carl's mother had arranged he live with a family in the suburbs and he cycled into town, sometimes passing the American embassy outside which Elizabeth often protested in late afternoons with the young man she was in love with. First she'd speed home to change into a jaundiced anorak and then join Bartholomew Macnamara under placards that avowed such statements as 'For Christ's sake stop the child murder'. Bartholomew Macnamara had a black falling moustache and he was the son of a professed millionaire and he occupied a little flat on Clyde Road and after following one another around in circles for an hour or two Elizabeth would go to Bartholomew's flat to be made love to on an Indian bedspread. Then she'd creep home, walking or getting the 84 bus to Rathmines where her parents had a house and her father stored seascape paintings in the attic, often little girls in those West of Ireland seascapes – Elizabeth ensnared on childhood holidays.

Batholomew Macnamara absconded to a flat of his father's in London the summer after Elizabeth did her Leaving Certificate and she followed him, bringing his washing to a launderette despite the fact there was a washing machine in the flat. She liked the presence of black women in the white, desolate, peeling enclave. She'd recline there, on her own, the woes of her life in her forehead. Bartholomew was Dublin's most charmed and widely known young radical and here she was taking his washing to a launderette, pushing ten p's systematically into a slot. But he slipped away from her, staying in Richmond with another love, and she got a train on the trailing route to Dublin. Starting at University College Dublin she realised she was pregnant and rapidly journeyed back to London to get rid of the child. She was eighteen. Carl was nineteen, a melancholic, slightly humped art student. Dublin patted their cheeks with the same November chill.

The first time they spoke was in the Country Shop off the Green, midpoint between the University College buildings at Earlsfort Terrace and the College of Art in Kildare Street, over lemon iced cake. Little bunches of primroses were bestowed on the tables and Elizabeth's hair shone as did her face. Elizabeth and Carl had a brief conversation. Elizabeth's face was still pale despite its red clown smile. Carl and she spoke of countries where vulnerable tribes and castes were being massacred. They did not meet again for over a year and that was at a party in Carl's first flat – he finally having got away from his affectionate family – by the sea. She turned up with a caravan of theology students, not properly invited but half-invited, having encountered someone in a pub in Lower Leeson Street who was going.

There was a revelry under the May moon; a girl swam around in the sea in a long black coat, moving her hands as though it was a lethargic day on the Mediterranean; Elizabeth went to piddle under a Martello tower, her piddle a rosette on the clean cement. Afterwards, drunk, swaying, on a rock she threatened to throw herself into the sea. 'My daughter,' she cried, 'my daughter.' A ship was passing the Hill of Howth. Carl stepped over rocks and took her as she bent towards the water, ripples of orange greeting one of her fingers. Afterwards in bed – someone asleep in an enormous bath under an Edwardian ceiling next door – Elizabeth told Carl she was going to call her daughter Christina. It was Carl's first time making love, other than to a young Northern male Protestant. In the morning Elizabeth made porridge. A theology student ambled from the bathroom. It never occurred to Carl to wonder how she knew her baby would have been a girl, fit to be called after the poetess Christina Rossetti.

The following autumn – early, glistening September – they moved in together, in another flat, this time in Rathgar; part of a Victorian cottage. Her parents lived nearby but they were neither obtrusive nor admonitory. Her father was a quiet man, the lazy, Bohemian forties in his eyes and her mother her

father's protector. Her parents' love affair was still in motion.
Carl wore clean white shirts now and his steps were unfalter-
ing. Elizabeth appeared outside the house in kimonos and
scarlet petticoat-like skirts. The angelic-looking students of
Dublin were invited to the house. Theosophany was pursued
on the carpet. Elizabeth and Carl would go seeking wood in a
nearby estate, clouds smoking down around frightened-
looking, frail branches. Carl's mother came once or twice
from the country, her face worn away like an old penny.
Handbag over her wrist she harangued Carl for his lack of
morality. But Carl could proceed without being disorientated
by her onslaughts. Carl's mother did not like Elizabeth. 'A
wench' and 'a wretch' she called her alternatively. In Ranelagh
an old man toasted chestnuts and Elizabeth slipped by her, a
birthday cake from McCambridges' for Carl under her arm.

They caught trains to Galway and to Kerry; they returned
again and again to a cottage on a peninsula in County Kerry;
Elizabeth turned over an old copy of Lawrence's *The Rainbow*
she found there. Visitors from another time or maybe some
old schoolmistress fond of wayward reads. Seals tumbled on
the beach in March esctasy; nuns whispered along it; Pablo
Picasso died and Carl wrote an obituary to him on the sand.
The tip of one peninsula looked to the tip of another and often
you met old men there, by deserted Famine villages, who had
not ever been as far as the next peninsula in their lives. Both
Elizabeth and Carl were doing examinations at the end of the
school year. Elizabeth trembled a little as, in a scarf and her
mother's short woollen coat, she looked to America.

Carl won an award for a painting, and being at a loss decided
on living in Paris for a few months. Elizabeth joined him
there, demurely at first, arriving in the little courtyard off the
Rue des Boulangers a few weeks after he'd set up. They were
back in a city together they'd once sojourned in at the same
time – separately. Trouble was difficult to define; Carl had
been authoritarian in his treatment of Elizabeth; she was made
to run in and out purchasing vegetables, cheese, and bread
from the fiery grottos of vegetables, cheese, and bread
outside. Elizabeth over the late spring and over the summer in

Dublin had begun sleeping with other people; trespassing into other people's big beds; Bartholomew Macnamara returned and she ended up with him, on a floor, after a party in Dalkey she'd attended without Carl. Carl had worn a red jersey as if to show his anger. In Paris she brought a Moroccan aristocrat home one night and Carl – his mother had ingrained him with politeness – had to endure their making love in the next room. A slap on Elizabeth's blanching cheek sent her home; she seized up her bags – a bright new deer-hide bag among them – and muttered angry and nearly incoherent slogans. 'Male chauvinist. Bourgeois brat,' and began the journey home to Dublin where she started studying music. Carl turned up at Christmas. He got a job teaching. They were reconciled – for a while.

The school he was teaching in was in the back streets of Dublin; it was a urinal-red place of exile. The corridors rang with retribution for the working classes. Despite his qualifications and awards it was the best Carl could get or perhaps he was too lazy to try very hard for another post: which he was never sure and afterwards he never teased over this ignominious time, putting paintings on the wall that were likely to be splayed with nests of blue ink. There was one little boy in that school, forever being domiciled on the corridor, who, on hearing that Carl was 'queer', followed him everywhere, up the laneway by Marsh's library, to Bewleys', his jersey red as a fire brigade, and eventually just behind Carl as Carl made his way through the blossoms of the Green, hand in hand with Elizabeth, the little boy undaunted by this manifestation of heterosexuality. In an all-boys' school the little boy himself was known as 'the queer' and he was solicitous about his reputation. Afterwards this mouse-faced boy, with his black stripes of hair and his lips patented with good looks, suggested both an omen and a symbol of luck for Carl. An omen because on May 17th just as Carl and Elizabeth were closer than ever before, taking the labyrinthine ways of Dublin in summer clothes, Elizabeth walked into the Dublin car bombings and witnessed death, carnage and the mutilation of shop windows and babies. A symbol of luck because later on, in demesnes of exile,

Carl knew that the image of a little boy was still unresolved to him.

Elizabeth changed after the bombing; she was desolate; she wanted to go away – by herself. In the late May sun she had slung her mother's fur coat on her and she looked older, those lines in her forehead becoming abysmal.

Her way out was to get a student place to San Francisco. She was departing for the summer. Carl resided in Maida Vale in London, awaiting her return, painting bigger pictures, determined never to sacrifice his work to any – to him – demeaning again. He waited in vain. He rang from a red kiosk outside capsizing Edwardian façades in September evenings. Drunks clattered Guinness bottles into bins. She was not returning.

Arriving in San Francisco, before presenting herself at her friend's flat in Clay Street, Elizabeth threw a penny into the Pacific for Carl. It was one of the last coins from the old world. She laboured over the summer, a house painter, saving up money to send to Carl for his fare over. But Carl did not want to come and she did not want to return. In September alone in San Francisco she started breaking down. Near the flat in Clay Street was a Catholic church – an architectural mixture from the thirties – and she often went there in the evenings when her friends were interminably and silently passing around marijuana and she tried to pray but she felt as empty inside as this blank and mundane-looking building. On a rainy evening on a notice board in a launderette – near the flat – her eye seized on a notice for a mystical group. Anything would have done. She went along and change, begun in May, happened completely; there was an earthquake in her personality; nothing was left standing. She wrote to Carl that she was moving north in California and that she wanted to be left alone now with her life and its makings. Before leaving San Francisco at Hallowe'en she bought roses and arranged them in a bowl by a rainy window in memory of Carl. The cardigan garbing her breasts was pink. She reached to a rose but before she touched it it trembled and annihilated itself in a few dozen pink petals.

Without her Carl was weaker and he looked more like the

person he was before they became lovers, a little humped, but he could not entirely revert to that person and he held on to his resolution not to sacrifice his painting again to untoward ends for mere survival, and so back in Dublin he painted backdrops and made props and costumes for a children's theatre company and he gave art workshops to young people in community halls. Gradually, through his work, he held himself straighter again, albeit in more ragged clothes, and under Liberty Hall, Dublin's only skyscraper, he associated himself with Dublin's poor. By staying in the mendicant arts, a little recognition was meted out to his groups by the peers of Irish society and with a little money he was able to purchase a ticket to San Francisco in the late summer of 1976. The children of Ballyfermot were said goodbye to, the piebald ponies tossing their manes among stone walls and among derelict estates. The Aer Lingus plane lifted itself into the grey sky over another estate on which Carl had prised the talents of children, Ballymun, a slum among the North Dublin verdure.

Years of exile, years of meditation, had made Elizabeth almost forget. Two years only really, but those two years seemed much longer. The Pacific waves royally moved in on a beach and on rocks under a benevolent community of white houses. They were more like New England houses, those white houses, built by migrating New Englanders once. Whales went south in winter and spirited her emotionally to a convent on a peninsula in Mayo. She wore a black blazer now. She cut her hair short. To survive financially she worked as a waitress in a roadside café ten miles away, giving most of her earnings to her group. She had become calm now, paid the price of a giddy part of her personality. The knowledge that Carl was coming drifted lazily to her but at the airport in San Francisco she realised, through the haze of her philosophies, that she'd rendered this person totally vulnerable, that she'd sent him out, mindful of a Shakespeare sonnet taught by a nun at school, 'without his cloak'. Carl trod towards her, a smile on a face in a body that had become visibly pained.

In one another's arms at the airport his vulnerability became hers, she was grasped up in it, she gave herself to it, her hair, which had become more gold, grasping for a tear on his neck.

The question in the next few weeks was marriage; everything in their lives and personalities seemed to bring them together; she had the use of a friend's house in Carmel-by-the-Sea, the amber wooded house of an old Hungarian emigré, a man who covered his baldness and contrasted his thick, white, side hair with a black cap, and she and Carl sojourned there, mainly reclining on the floor, watching the Pacific distantly washing in on Point Lobos, a peninsula of wood and seals and elk and blue and flashing species of birds. The sole book the old man had brought from Hungary at the age of twenty-six was left in state on a table. Elizabeth and Carl, on the carpet, on the floorboards, looked to the sea, the white, easy, unhurried waves, and knew their identities had merged in a mutual recognition, that life is sacred and that the mundane human being is capable of excellence, of mystery, of glamour. One afternoon swimming at Point Lobos Carl met a seal who rose from the waves, looked at him, seemed to wonder at this Irishman swimming in November, then disappeared into the grey and turbulent waves which could have been grey waves off Mayo. The old man returned from a retreat at Elizabeth's community and, in a yellow ochre and black check shirt, sitting on the floor, he drank white wine with them, made at Elizabeth's community, and opened the book on the table which revealed poems about journeys and mental imprisonment and spiritual escape. In San Francisco before Carl left he and Elizabeth stayed in a little hotel above a striptease bar on North Beach, the lurid incessant night lights a long way from the style of Elizabeth's northern Californian community. The lucid mornings, recollected by the old man, of Budapest threw a shade into the lucid mornings on North Beach, the hair of Chinese men whipping by the ocean which looked icier. There were no embargoes now. They were closer than ever before. Her frail fist reached for the steadiness of his grasp. She was going to see him in Ireland soon to declare herself and the possibilities of the last few weeks to him.

But over the following few months – intimacy with another

body having changed her – she became close in her community with a young man, another refugee, the son of an actor in Los Angeles who'd frequently ridden across screens as a cowboy. The young man, James, was polite, blond, and in many ways opposite to Carl – he was glacial, contained. They became lovers. Spring came to the beach and she prepared for Ireland, packing clothes already seamed by another affair.

Bringing back the pale autumnal Californian sun to Dublin proved impossible for Carl; the blanched Californian morning mists followed behind him at Dublin airport on a dirtily grey December morning. He returned in a blue denim jacket, blue jeans; this had been his customary attire. But something in him had radicalised, some perception. He'd found his own anchorages again. The sullen façades of Dublin swelled against him. No one took much notice of his raptured accounts of his journey. He laboured on with his painting for the theatre company. Then Elizabeth arrived and in May in Dublin, a picture of James Joyce and Nora Barnacle everywhere to denote the event of a production of James Joyce's *Exiles*, they took to the streets, to the squares; lovers. The green squareside trees, the Georgian pavements loved them. But they were given little love elsewhere. The Liffey stormed against a Neptune-face by the arch of a bridge. They got on a red and dust-lacquered bus to the country and spent a few weeks in Kerry; Elizabeth's arrival had coincided with an award for Carl for a painting and this time the financial endowment was handsome. He wore white shirts that had tiny white chrysalises in them and his face urged against the May lambency. In Kerry there was a cottage near a beach but they had to return to Dublin; Dublin was the testing point, Dublin was the previous nightmare, Dublin was the site of the bombings, the memory of a repairment. There was a party in Elizabeth's house and a congregation of artists, artistes at the party and one young nun, standing nervously in her short black ecumenical garb, a liqueur-glass of white wine in her right hand.

Now it happened there had been a girl in Carl's life for years, as obsessed with him as the little boy in the red jersey at the school, but in a negative capacity; she'd been alongside him his first year at the art school. She'd failed, dropped out, turned up in the vicinity of Elizabeth's second year at the university. She'd ingratiated herself with Elizabeth. She'd had brown thread-like hair and wore blue denim suits herself; her face always looked worried and in recent years it had become more thickly freckled and more worried. Having failed at the College of Art, having failed at University College she'd become a connoisseur of other people's pain and inabilities. When Elizabeth was in the United States Carl had lived in a house in Mountjoy Square with her for a while and in this time, he having the basement, he took a girl home and tried to make love to her. But confronted by pale and heavy thighs which were not Elizabeth's he found he was impotent; he was lapsed. Next morning by some means the news had reached a sphere over cherry buns in Bewleys'. Carl had forgotten about this incident and its import for his sexuality; he'd submerged it. But at the party in Elizabeth's house this girl, having found her way there, resurrected it, somehow affronted by Carl and Elizabeth's show of sexuality, taken aback by the fact that the status quo of pain in Dublin was ruffled. Standing, a pint glass of claret in her hand, she made announcements about it; her face, pale as cold porridge, coming precipitously close to Carl's, she leered, 'You've got medical problems. You're impotent. Everybody knows. The whole of Dublin knows. You're not a man. You couldn't make it. You couldn't do it.' Afterwards the same creature of the blue denim sat by the wainscot weeping, but her tears were too late; when the guests had gone, her parents asleep upstairs, Elizabeth had drawn Carl to her. This time he failed with her. She totally gave herself to him and he could not make love, his sense of manhood still suffering from its attack. In that sliver of a moment their relationship ended. Elizabeth could not understand, Carl could not explain; a detail of his life in Dublin lost to her and its suppression now turning up as a distortion on their worlds, as a weapon of annihilation. Elizabeth left a few days later. James was waiting for an answer from her. A sexual life, which had always been easy, unconsidered, was now blown to a million shaking pieces.

Taking a train to his home on the day of her departure Carl ventured to stroll on a country platform after the train had been to a halt for more than ten minutes; it was evening, he still wore a white shirt speckled with chrysalises, there were two rectangular beds of marigolds on the platform, a little man wheeled on a sack of mail, voices were subdued though, a plane glided West in the sky, its scintillating ermine digging into the deepening blue. This was Midland Ireland, home of little uneventful Protestant spires; the land Carl's mother came from and her dead sisters, her sisters who had all espoused death. Carl held himself very straight for fear if he stopped even a little his whole physique would crumble. The plane in the sky made a discreet rumbling. On its way through Ireland the train had run alongside a canal, waterlilies in abundant sheets on the surface and the odd swan in among the glimmers of light. There was a smell of departing purple lilac in the air. Carl said goodbye to her then. The sound of the plane had died out; it had disappeared from the sky. Carl tried to make some mental statement to her but he found it better to blank out his mind like the light that was weighing into the trees.

A letter he posted at his home told her he was leaving Ireland; a letter in a brown envelope with a mauve stamp on it. Carl left Dublin a week after Elizabeth had gone, telling the city stones that he would never come back, impeaching them for their contribution to the destruction of his relationship.

On a wall on Portobello Road the week he arrived in London there was a slogan near a cartoon showing children playing under an emerald-foliaged tree – 'We teach all hearts to break'. Carl settled with friends in a block of flats on the Ladbroke Grove edge of Portobello Road.

As Carl's emotional life was in a state of post-war annihilation, his career as a painter continued to take rapid steps for the better; nine months after leaving Ireland he was notified by the arts establishment in Ireland – as if they were aware of his absence and as if by way of a consolation prize for the problems which elements of Dublin's art community had given him – that he was being bestowed a substantial travelling scholarship. News turned a grey morning on Ladbroke Grove into a jingle of colours. He'd go to New Mexico, Mexico in search of the light of some of his favourite painters; Lawrence, Georgia O'Keeffe, Rivera. The ticket he purchased was one from London to San Francisco – non-stop.

The flat in Clay Street was still available for staying in; a young man, ruminating over a Berkeley thesis on Swedenborg and a host of angels reclined by the washing machine, silently inhaling marijuana. In fact there was a lot of silence, much toing and froing to Berkeley. The emerald lawns of Berkeley rushed at him, weary students on the lawns. The ex-Dublin theology students were dressing better. They brought Carl on his first Sunday in San Francisco to a nude swimming place, a lake in the country north of San Francisco. Genitals and pubic hair sailed around. It was not until his second week in San Francisco, before he'd rung Elizabeth, that, on a hill under Golden Gate Bridge, looking towards Sausalito, after getting out for a few minutes from a car, the night lights of Sausalito just reaching the tip of the water on the other shore, the student who was driving Carl, in a profusely floral speckled, long-sleeved shirt, laconically mentioned to Carl, just in passing, 'Oh by the way. Did you hear? Elizabeth Murphy is to be married.' Carl did not wait for details; he took a greyhound bus south-east to New Mexico, to the sun and to the light of places where he could stride, holding himself very straight; and where the sun and the light were so intense that they absorbed memory.

Elizabeth's marriage in Dublin turned out to be a kind of festival. She wore pink. A pink suit. Pink roses in her hair. There were roses in Rathgar church. In fact on the way from Dublin airport with James she'd perceived a scarlet flag, hanging from a grey North Dublin council house as if it boded merriment for her wedding. James's many-times-divorced parents attended the wedding. A Dublin Sunday newspaper interviewed James's father. He had blue hair now – the colour of twilight in Hollywood cowboy films of the forties. He wore a white suit – like his son, the groom at the reception in

Rathmines. He stood in the middle of the Edwardian carpet and excited lifetime-celibate aunts of Elizabeth. The young lady who'd challenged Carl's manhood was present. She had achieved something. The destruction of a relationship. The making of another. She looked pleased, in neater, more comely clothes. She drank less. Her face was less porridge-coloured under a little brown and white hat. But before the finale of the reception, an aunt of Elizabeth, injured in a car accident, in a wheelchair, her gnarled, thin, many-ringed fingers on the sides, a woman from Mayo herself, drunk, started shouting, 'Where's that nice boy? Where's Carl Fogarthy?'

Carl Fogarthy was in London; living in Hampstead. He strolled up Keats' Grove that evening. The October twilight tumbled into the last roses. A red telephone kiosk opened and an Indian woman stepped out in long, light, interwoven clothes. A plane submerged into the sky. Carl hugged himself into a donkey jacket and wondered how he should dress, what sort of tie he should wear, at the opening of his first London exhibition in January.

Elizabeth returned to Dublin four years later for her father's funeral. He'd had a heart attack on the wide, winding stairway of the College of Art and had collapsed and died there. In the previous four years Elizabeth's parents had visited her often in Los Angeles. She had not returned their visits. She'd contributed largely to their fares, though. After her wedding she'd absconded with James from the community. He'd taken up his birthright, wealth, status, clothes in Los Angeles, a house in the San Fernando Valley. Elizabeth dressed in clothes from New York, Florence, London now. A handbag was en-wrapped on her wrist. She strode around Dublin after the funeral in formal clothes with a formal gait. Brown Thomas', Switzers' were the places she visited and turned over the china clocks. She sat regally in Bewleys'. It had changed; all self-service now. She waited for the inrushing school girls in uniforms but there were none because it was summer; the uniforms of her convents still splashed like blue ink between her and the other customers. This place would always have the ghosts of uniforms hovering around the white iced, walnut cakes for her. She did not choose a cake. She looked severely ahead of her. Light awakened her through a Harry Clarke stained glass window. She was one of the world's fortunate now. She commanded the international airway paths. She could use these paths at any moment of her choosing; instead she spent most of her time in Los Angeles, journeying sometimes to the community in northern California, spending weeks of retreat there, assisting in the making of wine. Sometimes there, in a white blouse, her pale skin aggravatingly browned, over the vine, on the beach, she'd think of him; he'd make a foray on her mind. He'd never really left her mind, the imprint of his personality still on her personality, his engaging, child's lips, the locks of black hair on his forehead. She was aware that something – beyond them possibly – had obliterated their union. She identified that something with the extraneous evil of the world and particularly with the bombs and the killings of Northern Ireland. She lived in another country now; the Ecclesiastes were usually closer to her than the newspaper. But she could still connect the obliteration of her relationship with Carl to the niggling heads of funerals in Belfast. In some obscure way politics, the infringement of society on the individual, suggested itself as a cause for the end of her relationship with Carl. In a country so prejudiced by the past her closeness with Carl – because of its simplicity – could not survive the thickets, the loathsomeness of bigotry. But then she did not really want to think of politics; that might make her consider Guatemala and El Salvador and she did not want to see the pain of these countries. So she allowed thoughts of Carl to drift with thoughts of suffering Indians in Guatemala or hysterically frightened peasants in El Salvador. But in Dublin, after her father's death, remembering the white skin of her father's chest as he hugged her in his bed when she was a child, she was engrossed by a new and pungent shade of memory of Carl. There had been a sincerity in him which she had not encountered in her husband or friends. She wanted to contact him but she had no idea of his address; save that he lived in London. But in her meanderings in Dublin she discovered one small painting of his in a gallery – a gallery tucked away between the Green and Capel Street – and she was able to get his address there. She got a plane to London after spending three weeks in Dublin. Aer Lingus whirred through the clouds. Her mother had said goodbye to her at the airport and told her, uncharacteristically, that she hoped she was saying her prayers.

One exhibition gave way to another; the lean times to days of plenty. Carl inhabited part of a warehouse in East London. He had sanded the floorboards and he painted there. Very often there were parties in his place. He was woken early one morning by a phone call. Elizabeth had not rung until she'd reached London airport. Perhaps in a way she had hoped he would not be there and that she would not have to go through this encounter. He told her how to come over and what bell to ring.

She, as usual, late, arrived at midday, ringing a bell among a spiral of bells, by a door, near Wapping tube station. Carl led her up a staircase to his floor. An Alsatian barked in the cellars of the house. In his place they drank tea and looked down on the Thames through the huge windows as though it was being shown in a film. They both looked slightly away from one another. Signs of ageing in both their faces. He was thirty-one. She was thirty. But still an obdurate youthfulness. After supper – one or two friends of his calling, surprised to see her there, going away – she stayed the night. She slept on a mattress near his mattress, a river of distance between them. She slept curled towards him. Once in the night he touched her, her legs just below her little knickers. Maybe fatter than before. Then he abandoned her physically and curled up in his own bed. In the morning light they had turned towards one another again, that distance of sanded shining floor still between them.

After descending the depths into Wapping Station as he said goodbye to her, the thought occurred to him: 'Well, now it's over for good and all.' Maybe they'd meet in old age, after a nuclear catastrophe or some such thing. History would certainly have unfolded itself before their next meeting, history with a capital c as it had been tucked into 'Waterloo Bridge' which Carl had seen with his mother as a child on one of his father's nights out in the pub. Bidding goodbye to her he recalled how he'd been christened Carl, because it had been snowing, a polite tumble of snow, and there'd been carol singers outside the hospital after he'd been born. He recalled words of his bitter mother when he'd been a child before she'd become bitter. Words issued beside the wireless with its constant outpourings of ceilidh music. 'Better to have loved and lost than never to have loved at all.' He saw again the picture in their flat in Rathgar, a pair of near naked Olympian lovers flying above a Victorian forest. Yes, this would be the last time; well nearly the last time. Perhaps, as he'd considered, fate still had a meeting arranged for them in their old age. Elizabeth got into the tube crying.

The following evening driving from San Francisco to the community where James had been submerged in retreat for the weeks of her absence and for some weeks before – she'd heard news of her father's death while there – Elizabeth got out of the car, which a friend was driving, as they stopped among vineyards in the Napa Valley. Evening sun trembled on a few sluggardly grape gatherers. A white house distantly was lit up for a few moments. Beethoven's Violin Concerto drifted out from P.B.S. on the radio in the car. The white house – relic of pioneering days – faded into dimness. A tractor was then caught up by the sun. Elizabeth walked from her friends and strolled among the grapes, a pink cardigan falling from the flowers of her dress at her shoulders. She walked for a little, then paused, stooped and picked a green grape from its growth, remembered that she had refrained from telling Carl that she was three months pregnant.

There was a party in Carl's place that night. All kinds of people rushed in after a certain hour, a menagerie of people, punks, post-punks, hippies, journalists, painters, actors, even a woman in boots that looked like a teddybear's feet. Music – brought from upstairs – beat. Stiff Little Fingers. A Belfast group. They sang about soldiers, all kinds of soldiers, hoping they'd go away. Carl, laden with drink, hope, curled up in a corner, slept, dreamt of a world without soldiers, without soldiers who kill the vulnerable, without soldiers who snipe at the child in the womb. In the morning when he woke the party-goers had gone, a piece of lipstick-pink paper was left, and he went to the window, looked to the Thames, and remembered he'd met a child-faced teenager at an exhibition a few days before whom he'd arranged to meet for afternoon tea in Soho that day.

The Loss of Faith

JANETTE TURNER HOSPITAL

HIS FIRST WIFE was living in Sydney when she died, and on that
very day Adam saw her on the subway in New York. He was
just getting off the Broadway Local at Times Square, and
trying to find the place where you go down the stairs for the
crosstown shuttle to Grand Central, when they collided.

'My God,' he said 'Faith!'

For whole seconds he felt his waking vertigo (Adam's dreams
wore bells and motley, they were extravagant, their sense of
humour was decidedly off-kilter) and dizziness nipped at his
brain like a terrier. He thought he could hear a phone ringing;
yes, he definitely heard the descant 'pips' that signal a long-
distance call in Australia. The conviction that he must have been
changing trains at Circular Quay instead of in Manhattan was so
intense that he saw the Sydney sky, very blue, and the Harbour
Bridge, right there against the subway pillars. There was, in fact,
a travel poster (Paul Hogan grinning, the bridge, the opera
house, *G'day, mate, come and see us Down Under for the
Bicentennial*); and so later he thought that this was the
explanation; until later again when his daughter Robbie (the
eldest of his three children, the one who forgave him least)
phoned with the news of Faith's death. But for twenty-four
hours or so he thought the travel poster was the explanation.

'Faith,' he murmured, dazed, unable to move, while Paul Hogan smirked in peripheral vision and Times Square seethed above their heads.

Faith looked young and quite lovely – the way she had looked in their halcyon years – but very pale.

'Keep your hands to yourself, mister,' she said in a flat Bronx accent, and someone shoved him aside and next thing he knew he was in the vast rococo barn of Grand Central Terminal with thousands of people milling around and a horrible sensation – a sort of rising fog of queasiness moving on up from his ankles – that he was going to faint. Air, he thought, *air*, trying to grope his way out to Forty-Second Street but getting lost in the tunnels and turning into the Oyster Bar instead.

'Table, sir?' A waitress laid her hand lightly on Adam's arm and he nodded. She was blonde and mechanically flirtatious. 'Will anyone be joining you, sir? No? This way then.'

It was murky as sin in the Oyster Bar, and he tripped over several pairs of feet. On his table a feeble glow of candle was drowning itself, swamped in paraffin. He gulped down two beers (Foster's, thanks to the ubiquitous Mr Hogan) and told himself: *It doesn't mean anything, seeing Faith's double. It doesn't mean anything at all.* But the trouble with a Marist Brothers education – Sydney, circa late '40s, early '50s – was that the world was always thick with symbol. You could never escape it.

'It means something,' he told the blonde waitress lugubriously.

'It's just the wax,' she said. 'See, if you tip it, you can free the wick again.'

'What?'

'See? I've relit your candle.'

Fat chance, Adam thought. 'My first two wives,' he said solemnly, 'were Australian.' He studied the palms of his hands, seeking clues to a mystery. He raised his head and listened to something far away. 'Is that a telephone ringing?'

She smiled. 'Would you care to order now?'

'And so am I,' he said. 'Australian. Still.' He frowned and added: 'I think.'

'I recommend the Oysters Florentine.'

'If I'm anything,' he amended, taking hold of her wrist and mournfully running an index finger up and down the soft inner skin of her forearm. 'I'm not from New York.'

'Who is?'

'I get down from Northampton – Northampton, Mass. – once or twice a – '

'Don't tell me.' The waitress rolled up her eyes in mock despair. 'You teach at Smith.'

'Well yes, as a matter of . . . How'd you – ?'

'I'm a Smithie. Class of '84. But you weren't . . .'

'No. I went there in '85. What's a nice Smithie girl doing – '

'Working her way through grad school. Columbia.'

'Columbia.' He sighed heavily and rested his hands, palms up, on the table. 'I was at Columbia when . . .' He pondered the zigzag of his marriage line, hanging onto the trail of a thought. 'I'll tell you something weird: I only get down to the Big Apple once or twice a year, but something bloody strange happens every time. I think it's because – '

'Listen,' she said awkwardly. 'I'll come back in – '

' – I associate New York with guilt. That's why it happens.'

' – back in ten minutes, okay? When you're ready to order.'

'What's your name?' he asked, pulling the inside of her wrist to his lips.

'Sandra,' she said. Oh damn, she thought. She was an absolute sucker for a man with tears in his eyes. This was on account, so sundry therapists assured, of her feckless father who'd moved on and moved on, as one day Sandra herself might be able to do. But for now she was stuck (though improving). For now, she would go as far as drinks and sex (provided he was willing to play safe) but not in her apartment, and not more than once, because she knew him already. He'd had a sad life, he favoured clingy and insecure women, she was not – she refused to be – his type.

'I've had a sad life,' Adam sighed.

I am not I am not thank God his type, Sandra told herself, running through her therapist's catechism. I will not be a breast for one more child-man to suck, I am cured of

congenital soft-heartedness, I am definitely learning not to
. . . 'I get off in two hours,' she said. 'If you want to talk.'

'My third wife,' Adam told her as they lay side by side in his
hotel bed, 'well not wife, strictly speaking, we never married
. . . but she was American, a therapist.'

A therapist, Sandra thought. It figures.

'We met on my sabbatical here in New York.'

'At Columbia,' she said.

'Right. Columbia.' Nineteen seventy-six, that year of flags
and tall ships, of academic excitement, marital chaos, erotic
trysts, the smell of hotel sheets – it came back to him with the
faint sweetness of perfume left on a sweater. 'My second wife
was dreadfully unhappy,' he sighed. 'In New York, I mean.
It's very difficult to live with someone as unhappy as that,
someone who is so *desperately* . . . who is I suppose you would
have to say incurably . . . And then Robin, my daughter back
in Australia, my daughter from my first marriage, Robbie got
into trouble in school, well she got herself expelled to tell you
the truth, and Faith, my first wife, the one I saw . . . the one I
thought I saw today . . . Faith called.'

And Carolyn, his second wife, had thrown a tantrum. 'Faith
just never gives up, does she?' she'd stormed.

'But it's Robbie,' he's said bewildered, preoccupied with his
daughter, furious with her, sick with anxiety.

'Hah!' Carolyn had shouted. '*Hah!*'

'What do you mean, *hah?*'

'Hah!' Carolyn screamed. Then she burst into tears. 'Can't
you *see*,' she demanded, 'why she puts Robin up to these
things? Can't you *see?*'

He could see that Carolyn's knuckles were white with
strain. Sometimes it seemed to him that her body was covered
with small sharp spikes.

'It's so obvious,' Carolyn's voice was climbing higher,
higher. 'First the broken ribs, then the stealing, and now this
. . . this *perversion*. She only puts Robin up to it to get your
attention.'

He was frightened for Carolyn sometimes, though Carolyn
seemed to glide protected on the slipstream of her own

incommensurate furies. She scooped up the twins and swept out of the apartment and slammed the door with such force that his University of Sydney beer mug fell off his desk – a theatrical statement that was rather spoiled for Carolyn by her having to return for the children's snowsuits.

'I could never make head or tail of it,' Adam sighed. 'She just packed up and went home to her mother in Perth. Took the children with her.'

'What did you do?'

'Me? Well, nothing.' He had been so *relieved*. 'Of course it was distressing but what could I possibly. . . ? I had to finish my year, I was on a Fulbright. And Rhoda was very helpful – '

'The therapist.'

'Yes. And then my book came out, and Cal State offered me a visiting appointment, and then San Diego, and then Smith. I never got around to going back.'

Sandra lay watching the ceiling. She composed a letter to her old room-mate: *Oh these predictable Smith professors. It's talk, not sex, that turns them on.* Her room-mate was back-packing up the Himalayas in quest of Tantric eroticism and other highs of a spiritual nature. *The love life of male intellectuals,* Sandra telegraphed to her, *continues to be a quest for the perfect listener. There are times when I believe myself doomed to the role of intelligent voluptuous ear. But then, in these days of wine and AIDS, who am I to complain?*

'And Rhoda-the-therapist?' she prompted, to set Adam's quest back in motion.

'Well actually, that didn't last very long,' he said – for Rhoda, who was and always would be in aggressive good health, world without end, amen, Rhoda believed they should all be *friends*, he and she and Faith and Carolyn and all the children and God knew who else. She tried to get him, for example, to telephone his wives on their birthdays. Of course he would not. If you reopen Pandora's box, you deserve what you get. 'So *she* wrote letters,' he groaned, 'to Faith and Carolyn. She actually wrote letters to them.' Of course, neither Faith nor Carolyn ever replied.

'Rhoda's so American. She never understood about

Australian women.' Nor about Australian men. For Rhoda still sent him care packages and birthday wines and invitations to dinner parties that she and her new husband were hosting. She never gave him a moment to mourn for her, the way he did for his first two wives.

For sorrow, that sweet poetic enduring emotion, Rhoda had not the slightest knack.

He frowned, and stared at the night table beside the bed. 'I keep thinking I hear a phone ringing,' he said. 'I keep thinking I hear the long-distance pips.'

In Sydney, Robin pictures Northampton, Massachusetts, and the small postcard-pretty faculty house with sash windows that stick. She pictures the ill-fitting storm frames that let in the draft. She and Natalie visited last year, a mistake. She pictures the phone in the empty living-room. She pictures the hundred-year-old windows rattling softly as the phone rings and rings and rings.

'Ten,' Robin counts. 'Eleven. Twelve rings. The bastard. Always unreachable when needed, how does he do it?'

'Why don't you hang up?' Natalie asks. 'What's the point of letting it go on ringing?'

'Cheap satisfaction,' Robin smiles. 'Thirteen. Fourteen. I like to think of it jarring his house, and it's free.' She looks out the window, past several tacky high rises, towards the strip of Cronulla beach. Some things replay themselves, though she lives resolutely in the present. Still, from the look of her shirred bathing suit, yes she must be nine or ten years old. Eighteen years ago if you keep that kind of score.

'It's still yesterday there, right?' Natalie says. 'It's still yesterday afternoon. He's probably at his office.'

Robin cradles the receiver against her neck and hoists herself onto the windowsill. It's hot outside, a steamy January day. 'Snowing where you are?' she asked the house in Northampton. She can see unemployed Sydney teenagers cruising the beachfront in battered cars, looking for a safe spot to dope up. She can see mothers assembling clusters of children with buckets and spades, rubber floats, towels tied around their necks like Superman capes. She sees her mother a little apart from the other mums, never quite one of the group. Her father is still inside the rented holiday flat, possibly reading a book, possibly watching the footie ('Aussie Rules is football for intellectuals,' he says.) He is cavalier about when he joins them on the beach. Sometimes when she is just getting ready for bed he insists that they all go for a moonlight romp in the waves. Sometimes at low tide he announces, 'Footie time!' and practises his drop kicks on the hard wet sand and makes Robin chase the football and bring it back.

Today he is staying inside the flat.

Robin and her mother spread their towels on the sand, and Faith rubs suntan oil on the child's shoulders and back. They spread white zinc ointment on each other's noses, and make white clown lips, and wrinkle up their faces and laugh, though it seems to Robin that there is always something small and sad, like a ship's bell in fog, deep down in the well of her mother's laughter. Robin looks down the golden slope toward the ocean and jiggles from one foot to the other with impatience; her mother is kneeling, the tube of zinc ointment in her hands, facing back toward the houses.

A change happens. First it touches Faith's hands which tremble for an instant and then turn softer and gentler on Robin's skin. Robin watches the change move across her mother the way a wave moves up the sand. It spreads a *shining*. And the child laughs with sheer happiness because a weight has been taken off her chest. 'Oh Mummy!' she says, locking her arms around Faith's neck, happy, happy.

The mother strokes the child's hair and nuzzles the crook of her neck and looks at the houses. The child turns. Her father is crossing the road, waving, jogging toward them. Against her cheek the child feels the breath of her mother, how it has turned fast and sweet. It reminds the child of something, it smells like . . . like. . . ? like grass after mowing; like the moment when her father puts the mower in the shed and flops down in the shade and reaches up to take the beer from her mother's hand. Her father, zigzagging between traffic, waves and calls out. He flashes his white teeth at them.

The sun is up, everything is different. But then . . .

But then a stray football passes through the air between them and without a thought her father leaps and catches. It is beautiful, Robin thinks, the way he moves. There are shrieks. Giggles. A knot of teenage girls, brown thighs flashing, jumps, laughs, entices, moves in a million directions, clutching for the football, waiting for his pass. He runs, he is engulfed, he makes his pass. And Robin can feel how cold it is on the towels where a shadow has fallen.

Faith looks away, tents a hand over her eyes and scans the empty Pacific. She holds herself very still. She smiles very brightly. 'Go and swim, darling,' she says, with only the slightest tremor in her voice. 'I'll join you in a minute.'

Robin puts her head down and runs straight for the core of the football mêlée. 'Daddy, Daddy!' she calls, and yes somewhere in all those limbs she finds his hand, she extracts him, she tacks up the beach with him.

'Come on then,' he laughs, and the three of them run down the beach and into the surf. The three of them. Robin is in the middle, her mother on one side, her father on the other.

'Bastard,' she murmurs, letting the phone rattle his windows in Northampton, Massachusetts. She hangs up and buries her face in her hands. 'Bastard!' she calls out the window. Natalie goes to her, holds her. 'Daddy!' Robin sobs. 'Daddy, *please*.' She cannot stop sobbing.

In his haste, Adam fumbles the keys and drops them in snow. He can hear the phone ringing inside. Damn. He brushes at several inches of white powder on his doorstep. Damn. Where the bloody hell are the keys?

The phone stops ringing.

He gropes around in the dark with a gloved hand, hears the clink of metal, closes his clumsy fingers around the keys, lets himself in. The house is deafeningly horribly quiet. Against the great sludge of silence he pushes his shoulder and stumbles into his kitchen. He feels ill with anxiety. Lights, music, *the king rises!* Lights, lights, lights!

He turns on the television. 'You cannot *create* faith,' a midnight preacher says earnestly. His certainties coat him like a slick of suntan oil. *Cronulla*, Adam thinks for no reason. The word falls out of nowhere, a black spider of sound, a little leggy knob at the end of a swaying thought. 'Faith is a gift,' the TV evangelist says. 'It is a letting go.'

'Oh shut up!' Adam snarls and snaps off the set. Pouring Scotch, his hands shake so much that an amber spill licks at his table like a wave on a Sydney beach. He holds the glass up to the light. 'I made the TV say those words,' he tells it. 'I put those words in the box. Bloody amazing what the mind will do. A bloody amazing machine.' He drinks the Scotch neat. 'I'm spooked,' he tells the carpet, pouring himself another drink.

'What time is it there now?' Natalie asks.

'Middle of the night,' Robin says. 'There's no point trying again. He must be away.'

'Maybe you should call Carolyn. Doesn't she always keep tabs on exactly where he is because of the child support?'

'I'd rather die,' Robin says. 'She'd accuse Mum of staging her death to get attention.'

Natalie says nothing.

'I'll try one more time,' Robin says. 'For the heck of it.'

'Robin!' Adam lurches into the night table. 'My god, *Robbie!*' Something shifts inside his body. *Yes*, his body says, *this is it.* This is what we have been dreading. The phone clatters to the floor, the knocked-over bottle of Scotch glugs all over it.

'Oh Daddy,' she says. She cannot speak.

Robbie? he asks, tries to ask, but no sound will come to his aid. In any case, to what point? Because he knows, he knows. 'Robbie,' he whispers gruffly. He could be spitting his way through gravel. 'I saw her. I saw her yesterday in New York. She looked so beautiful, Robbie. I did love her, you know.'

Yes, he realises now, he did. He does. *He does*. Something tears away from inside him. A miscarriage, he thinks in vague pain. A hysterectomy. He could be bleeding, he could be wetting himself.

'Oh Daddy,' Robin sobs. 'Right to the end, she believed, you'd visit before she – She kept on making allowances.'

There's so much white noise, it roars in his ears.

'Robbie,' he asks. 'What's that smell? I smell – ' he sniffs; a bubble of something, of anguish, of laughter, gurgles up – 'I smell salt, I smell surf.'

'It's the beach,' Robin says. 'We're in a flat at Cronulla.'

We. Robbie and . . . He feels the mule-kick of anger and revulsion but bites his lip hard.

'I'll get a flight tomorrow, Robbie,' he says.

He finishes the bottle of Scotch and falls asleep on his living-room carpet. He dreams.

On the hard sand, the wet sand, the line of foam licks around his ankles. His back is wonderfully arched, he's on the World's Most Sensuous deck chair, the Great Australian Bight, the famous Bighter, he is cradled by the map of Australia. Silly blighter, Australia teases. Her Queensland finger tickles him. Victoria cushions his feet, a wave catches him by the perthy regions and he floats eastward into the Pacific. This is warm, this is womb fluid, Robin is just being born, not a thing has gone wrong yet, time itself is barely beginning.

Amazing visions come and go in the glass-green walls of the waves, the white crests are creamed with prophecy, a row of little fishes pauses and stares, and Faith, Faith with her sweet bride's face, is coming at him with the speed of light. Effortlessly he turns, he reaches, a perfect catch. It's a gift, it's a gift, laughs Robin, capering on the golden sands of Cronulla.

The Goose Path

ELIZABETH JOLLEY

Along the ridge ran a faint foot-track . . . Those who knew it well called it a path; and while a mere visitor would have passed it unnoticed even by day, the regular haunters of the heath were at no loss for it at midnight. The whole secret of following these incipient paths, when there was not light enough in the atmosphere to show a turn-pike road, lay in the development of the sense of touch in the feet, which comes with years of night rambling in little trodden spots. To a walker practised in such places a difference between impact on maiden herbage, and on the crippled stalks of a slight footway, is perceptible through the thickest boot or shoe.

Thomas Hardy, THE RETURN OF THE NATIVE

THREE PEOPLE, AFTER giving me good advice, died. I don't mean that they dropped dead in front of me as soon as their wisdom fell from their lips. But it seemed as if death followed soon after their parting with certain useful suggestions. Of course other people, now dead, have uttered warnings and promises of conditional success, my father and mother, for example and a succession of governesses and, later, teachers.

Mrs Morton, I always think of her when I'm walking up

this part of the firebreak on the Morton's side of the property
–Mrs Morton, who was always watching to see what I was
doing, told me to burn the broken handle of the mattock.

'Throw it on the fire and burn it out,' she said. I would never
have thought to do this and would have worked a long time at
the split wood trying to cut it away. It's when I come
alongside her old duck pens that I always think of her and how
she used to appear at the fence. She was already sick then. Her
kidneys were all shrivelled up, she often told me. As she
became more seriously ill her face, normally gaunt, looked
round. Puffed with fluid, I suppose. The roundness made me
see something of the child she must have been, and I
remember this too and feel sorry. To be reminded that there
was once a child, with all the shy hopes of childhood, and who
is still a part of the adult, is sad.

The second person was an old woman, a long time ago, a
patient in a hospital in Glasgow. She said to tap a tin all round,
tap tap tap on its sides, on the edge of a table – the sort of tin
with a screw lid – and then it would unscrew easily. Vaseline
or boot polish, she said, that sort of tin. She died the night she
told me this. I, as the recipient of the advice, did not die. I do
not remember now what sort of tin it was I was trying to open,
certainly not boot polish. Vaseline perhaps. It used to be in
tins.

The third person I am not able to remember at all, who it
was and what sort of advice. And every time, going uphill on
this soft ploughed earth of the firebreak, on a level with the
empty Morton duck pens, I try to remember what this third
piece of good advice was, who gave it to me, and the
subsequent death of the person giving it. All I can think of just
here is that when Mr Morton told me that Mrs Morton had
died he could hardly speak for his grief. His eyes were red and
swollen and weeping and I understood that I was face to face at
this fence with someone who really loved another person and
that he would never get over something which is often
brushed aside in the word bereavement. Sometimes now,
after all this time, he speaks about Mrs Morton and the tears
well up in his innocent elderly eyes and it is as if she has just

died all over again and left him alone in his paddocks here at the edge of the bush for ever. Because of this it is possible to know that love exists where the idea of it may be overlooked. Love is not just something for the beautiful and the rich, or between the intellectually refined or the more poetic people.

It does not matter not remembering the third piece of advice, for if I did I should not tell it here as I am of the opinion that something should always be held in reserve. Everything should not be told, it is better to keep some things to yourself. It might be too that one day, on this soft warm earth, I shall recall the third wise remark and, forgetting the habit of secrecy, perhaps tell it to someone right here by the duck pens . . .

This bit of fence is made like a kind of gate. The wire can be unhooked to let a fire truck or a flock through if necessary. Looking at it you would not see straight away that it can be opened to make a way through. Once a ram, belonging to Mr Morton, was caught by the horns in the ringlock. I tried to get the ram off. He was angry at being caught and kept pushing against the fence. His pushing and his horns being so curled made his freedom impossible. I kept going away, trying to forget him and trying to get on with some work but all the time wondering how to get him free. In the end I thought the only way would be to cut the ringlock and ruin the fence. I came back up here with the wire cutters to find that, by some miracle, the ram had freed his own horns and had gone right away across the Mortons' paddock.

When walking I seem to stop by this bit of fence, inadvertently recalling these same random events rather like the recollecting of a sequence of unrelated thoughts and experiences in the ritual of falling asleep. Mrs Morton fell through here once when she was trying to bring me a gift – a cake smothered in cream which, having to be held carefully, caused her to lose her balance. I was all morning painting her wounds with a yellow antiseptic and bandaging the worst ones. The cake, lying where it fell, was an intrusion.

The bleached long grass of my orchard pursues me as if on fire already as I make my way up the slope. I often stop by this particular part of the fence because part of the orchard is up here. My plum trees are here on the left and often I am doing things to them, the things with a sharp pruning knife, which are supposed to be done for fruit trees at different times of the year. The plum trees are Satsuma, President, Golden Drop and the Blue Prune plum. There are peaches and nectarines in this part too. The long grass from the cultivated places spreads a little more, every year, into the bush, and the bush invades the orchard. Some of the fruit trees have grass trees, or black-boys as they are called, growing close to them without harm to either.

Perhaps, really, it is better to take a walk in a place where there is no responsibility. To keep on up the fire-break, which is what I usually do, is to be concerned about the places where it is not of the regulation width, though in a real fire even the correct width is of little use. A bush fire, rampant, leaps across the tops of trees, across roads and rivers and it races over the baldest paddocks. It is usually a sudden change in the direction of the wind which is the saving thing.

To stop here between the Morton duck pens and my fruit trees is to see again the extraordinary fairy-tale, picture-book loveliness of the intense blue of the prune plums hanging secretly in the deep green of the leaves. An enticing and surprising mixture of blue and green reminding of the extravagant colours in the feathers of some exotic bird. The bloom on these small, vividly coloured plums gives the impression of a delicate mist hovering about the trees.

Higher up the slope here, where there is no orchard, there is the bush. The bush grows quickly across a fire-break if it is not freshly ploughed every year. From up here I can look all the way down and across the shallow ravine to a horse stud. I used to call it the Tolstoy country because, across here, they have hayfields and a long paddock fenced with round poles for horses. I like to watch the horses running and not have to worry about the things they can have wrong with them.

The most lovely wildflowers, in their season, appear unexpectedly up here in this part of the bush. I won't list them all as in a catalogue or as in some footage for a film on Western Australia. It is enough to mention the red and green kangaroo paws, at their best when the sun shines through them, and the china-blue leschenaultia, the strong but fragile blue like the clear blue of the eyes of a white goose. There are flowers as if enamelled on the prickly undergrowth, some in clusters and some in wreaths, and this last year the surprise of some delicate orchids in the hollow of the burned-out tree where the fire-break turns and the descent begins.

To follow the fence is to discover where it has been damaged, either pressed down from above or humped up from underneath by kangaroos making their way down to the dam.

To take this walk is to reflect upon time passing and on time standing still. There are places in the bush which seem as if there has been no change over a great many years. The constant changing of the seasons is a relentless movement of time, and the silence seems to make the pause. In the still silence and the great heat of summer, in this remote place, it is easy to forget where you came from, where you are going and, in a moment of remembering, to wonder why you are here at all. There is too the strange hope, at times, that out of the hot dry fragrance and the stillness some wisdom will come. This hope during the walk, over the years, has not faded.

The way down on this far side of the bush is rougher and often there are fallen branches on the fire-break. I try to move a branch but it has embedded itself in the hard ground. It has fallen from a great height. Branches fall, not in a gale as would be expected, but during the stillness of a very hot day like this day. The leaves of the eucalyptus fall all the year round. The fresh green new leaves often glow with a sort of golden red colour and this makes them look as if they are made of a very thin, beaten metal.

It is on the way down that the unwanted thoughts of

inability rise to the surface. Walking is a time for thinking. It is as Hamlet says: *For there is nothing either good or bad but thinking makes it so . . .* A fallen branch too heavy to move and the memory, the thought, which is accompanying the walk is the realisation of the ways in which, after tremendous hopes and activity, life in the little cottage and in the orchard seems to have come to a standstill. In the cottage there are a dozen or more Christmas cards all from Mr Morton, curling up, crammed along the kitchen mantelpiece; on the walls are a series of calendars, one year after another, with pictures of poultry feed and farm machinery. There is a heap of out-of-date telephone directories; there are newspapers lining cupboards and shelves with dates too far back for cleanliness, all with pages of impossibly cheap 'specials'. In the orchard several trees have not had nets put over them, others have not been pruned and yet others have reverted. The place is a paradise for parrots and crows. There are rats in the shed. I have put rat poison in the sprawl of rosemary round the poultry pens . . .

From this part of the fire-break I can look down to the dam. To have this ugly dam the Winter Nelis pears had to be sacrificed. Well, not a sacrifice really, that is just a way of complaining. The Winter Nelis, the trees (small sweet russet pears), travelling from South Australia had to be fumigated and the white ants, finding moribund roots, were soon inside every tree. The Winter Nelis were simply an unsuccessful part of the dream.

Instead of keeping to the fire-break there is a wild place which can be crossed. It is rough and suggests the wilderness. *There is a path which no fowl knoweth and which the vulture's eye hath not seen.* It is here that I remember Mrs Morton's speech of welcome on the day, all those years ago, when I took possession and wandered across the warm fragrant earth hardly daring to step one step after another, not believing that land could really belong to anyone. Mrs Morton, appearing suddenly, said the rabbits would eat everything I tried to grow.

She went on with frightening fire-talk, snake-talk, dried-up-creek-talk, dead-calf and still-born-lamb-talk, poison-weed-killing-sheep-talk, crows stealing eggs, salt in the ground and in the water. All the same I planted tomatoes and seed potatoes, melons and pumpkins. Of course Mrs Morton knew what she was talking about. She was even correct about kangaroos not eating sweet corn but liking to roll in it so that the whole crop could be crushed in one night.

From this wild place there is a track through to the poultry pens. I shall not gather up the dead rats. I have discovered that, in the heat, they disappear quickly. It is here that I think of the word Islam, a foreign word to me. I did not know what the word meant but I understand now that the word means to resign oneself, to submit to something which is greater, is beyond oneself. To bring the wider philosophical belief down to a tiny scratched-out place where I am walking, the submission can be applied to egg-stealing rats and snakes, to a heap of wood which should have been stacked, to a broken old chair propped against a collapsing shed, to the passion vines and the honeysuckle which, growing wild and entangled, have wrapped round the bamboo.

There is a staircase here for the fox. The fox – a vixen, I feel sure – will have climbed up here using the vine as a sort of ladder. The goose-pen fence is smothered in the flowers of the passion vine. The vixen, it must have been a vixen who, leaving her cubs briefly, bit off the heads of all the geese. She, in her raid, took all the goslings and the unhatched eggs, undermining the nests with her industrious digging. This morning the gander stood perplexed in the unnatural silence. All round him the geese lay in a wide semi-circle, their white feathered wings and bodies spread like ballet dancers in formal attitudes of contrition pressed to the ground. Their stage had no proscenium and there was, for their finale, no music. A fox hunts alone like this and this one probably made her visit, single-mouthed, in the moonlight shortly before dawn.

Resignation is powerful but perhaps optimism is the stronger power. Can a person be both resigned and submissive and an optimist as well? I think so. I have already arranged to buy some more geese later on today to start the flock once more.

The gander, unslaughtered, left out by some vixenish oversight, calls out occasionally and holds himself in an alert position, very still, waiting for the once familiar reply. It is clear he has lost his sense of direction and has no idea where to go. He has lost the goose path.

This morning early, in that uncanny silence which seemed to hang over the land in the wake of the dead geese, I burned them all. The cremation used all the dry firewood and the kindling stored for next winter. And a great deal of precious water had to be poured to prevent the funeral pyre from being another kind of fire. And now I stop during the walk and begin, too late, the work of searching out the thick coils of the vines. I spoil the pruning knife hacking at these fleshy ropes. The giant reeds (bamboo) in places are strangled and dead, and have to be cut and broken off and dragged out. It is a terrible tangled mass, this staircase for the fox. The long leaves rustle, sounding like a stream running in a place where water never flows. This is one of the deceitful things like the unhurried whispering of human voices as the wind moves through certain parts of the bush in places where there are no people. Perhaps these sounds belong to mysterious rites taking place in these small hollows of the land some centuries earlier.

It has been said that poetry that sings of 'the enshrined past' cannot answer the demands of the new age. It feels a little bit like this to walk in the bush being deeply attached to something which has existed for a timeless time and at the same time to have to plough up parts of it and to cut other parts of it away. The passion vine is not really a part of the bush, it has been brought here. Some of it must be cut away. It curls snake-like round boots and it springs into the small of the back as if to fell an intruder. It gives the uncanny feeling that someone, not a friend, is hidden close by.

To pause and to look down and across the varying light and shade, down and across the slope of the land, is to see each

ELIZABETH JOLLEY

time, with a fresh clarity, the different shades of green from the translucent pearl green to a deep purple green. To stand in this place at a certain time of the afternoon is to feel the slight change in the air, the *feeling* of the air. Sometimes the gulley winds race in from the east and at other times there is a west wind with its caressing coolness. Thinking about this place when I am not able to be here brings a consolation. Perhaps Thomas Mann felt this same sense of solace when he wrote about the misty edges of the blue green sea at that magic place, Travemünde. The solace and the consolation can never be entirely pure. The magic is often injected with the tincture of human suffering and anxiety. Travemünde, the place for youthful joy and freedom, has its row of old men worrying whether they will be able to rid themselves satisfactorily of the food eaten the previous day . . .

Like a novel, a certain kind of novel, which is a storehouse of observation and experience, thought and feeling, this walk becomes a meditation on human wishes. This meditation is a part of imaginative creation and, to me, is necessary for living and for writing. During the walk the realisation of this, like a prayer against despair, outweighs any sense of inability and failure.

> . . . *The whole secret of following these incipient paths . . . lay in the development of the sense of touch in the feet, which comes with years of night ramblings in little trodden spots. To a walker practised in such places a difference between impact on maiden herbage, and on the crippled stalks of a slight footway, is perceptible through the thickest boot or shoe.*

The goose path. It is about the width of one boot. The thin bleached grass is pressed lightly down between the stretches of tall pale grass. When I first saw this tiny track I could not think who could have made it. It is made by the firm flat treading of geese, one goose following one after another, single file, in a long line as they make their way across the meadow at the bottom of the slope to the dam.

130

To go on with the walk I take the heavy-handled rake and, holding it out horizontally with the shadow of it over the perplexed gander, I walk him down the winding path, down the slope between the orchard trees to the meadow. It is here that he will need to be guided on to the goose path. (An aside: cows and geese walk downhill when they are not sure of the way. To find lost cows and geese it is best to go as far downhill as possible before beginning the search.)

The gander, under the shadow of the rake handle, sets off along the goose path in the direction of the dam. Carefully placing one booted foot after the other, I follow him on the fragile path. The walk here must be serene and unhurried.

The apple trees and the pears and quince are down here. The clay soil of the meadow is salt and is flooded in winter. It is a good thing for pears to have their feet in water sometimes and these trees can tolerate a fair amount of salt. Early in the morning and again at the end of the afternoon flocks of rosy-breasted pink and grey parrots fly across here. At other times the screaming black cockatoos swoop and pause and fly on in their marauding search. Just now it is quiet and in the silence the crows cry loneliness along the narrow valley.

The gander, in the shadow of the rake handle, walks obediently, placing one sensitive foot in front of the other. His clear blue eyes seem to take in the familiar surroundings. If I remove the shadow of the rake he pauses and does not know which way to go. I guide him on towards the dam. Further down the meadow the creek bed is dry except for one or two oily pools. It was always the custom for the geese to pause and sample this water which lies in the cracks of the clay. The goose path has, for this purpose, a well-defined loop which we follow before making for the final straight track which climbs the white clay slopes of the dam wall.

I watch the gander take to the water. He slides in silently and moves as if without any effort out across the unrippled surface. A few slowly widening rings spread round his gliding movement. I walk round the edge of the dam as if to encourage him but instead of diving and flapping his wings, beating them hard on the water, showing himself off as he has been doing before when courting one or more of the geese, he simply makes for the far side and clambers out. He stands on the slope just above the water and makes no attempt to preen his feathers. No sound comes from him. As a rule his voice is the kind of cello with organ-like qualities in the full orchestration of the flock. The geese use their voices like instruments in a well-trained orchestra and without them he seems to have no voice.

It is clear that when the new geese arrive I shall have to help the gander to lead them to the goose path. Perhaps for a few times and then he will lead his small new flock himself. First he will have to wait till they have done gossiping and whispering among themselves. They will preen themselves, pirouetting, stretching out first one leg and then the other. They will taste the water, drinking daintily from the bowls in the goose pen. His flock will be small for the whole year, for geese only lay eggs and nest at a particular time. Meanwhile the never-ending walk must end here for me. The fox's staircase must be demolished before nightfall. After her hunt the golden eyes of the vixen will be bright still and cunning. They hold in their glassiness a knowledge of things not understood but which have to be forgiven. It is as though the ways of the vixen, her energy, her swift stealthy movements, her thoughts and her freedom are still sewn into the tangled vines of her staircase. She is ancient and thin from her nightly expeditions and she will never lie on the creamy neck and plump shoulders of a concert-going woman. Her rough red-gold pelt will not be stroked lovingly by a child allowed to dress up, fondling the pretty but useless little feet of the fox fur lovingly, in her mother's finery before being sent to bed . . .

The unmistakable perfume, the scent of fox, hangs in silence. It is heavy and aromatic, recalling something predatory and womanly with the rich overpowering sweetness of an older charm, an experienced passion accompanying the strength and the determination of the ageing huntress.

I guide the gander back along the goose path. He walks delicately and is unhurried, perplexed still. I keep the shadow of the rake above him and under this protection he continues up the slope between the fruit trees and across to the goose pen.

I have written 'I' throughout. This land in the bush with its tiny area scraped and conquered for cultivation does not belong entirely to me. It belongs to both of us. While writing I found it difficult to say 'we'. It is because of a certain smugness contained in the pronoun 'we'. I once visited some people who kept on, '*We* do this', '*We* have this',' '*We* like it this way', '*We* like it here' – it seemed to me to be an impregnable wall of we and us. 'I' seems more vulnerable and so is more in keeping with how I feel in the bush. I work alone in the orchard and I walk alone in the bush. I am temporary here and vulnerable and in this must speak only for myself.

Goldberg

GABRIEL JOSIPOVICI

WE ARRIVED AT nightfall. Mr Hammond dropped me off at the manor and drove on to see his son. Mr Westfield was expecting me. His manservant showed me to my room. It is larger than our living-room and has a small bathroom attached to it, the whole elegantly panelled and painted white. The windows are large and give on to the kitchen garden, but the big oak and elm trees of the park are visible beyond. It is altogether very pleasant and peaceful, and I am sure I will be able to do very good work here. There is a desk in one corner, and Mr Westfield has provided me with every kind of paper, pencil, pen and ink.

I was given supper in a little room adjoining the main dining-room. It was very abundant and well-cooked, with a pitcher of excellent wine to go with it, and coffee to follow. This I declined, and asked instead for a cup of lemon verbena tea, but that the maid could not produce. She promised, however, to fetch in a supply on the morrow, and provided me instead with a cup of rosehip tea, pleasant to the taste though a little tart.

At nine o'clock I was ushered into Mr Westfield's rooms. He was lying on a chaise-longue, drinking coffee. I did not like to tell him at this juncture that his problems might be eased if he did not drink coffee after six o'clock in the evening. He has presumably already been told this by his physician and chosen to disregard it.

I am to read to him till dawn or else till I am sure he is asleep, whichever is the first. I am to sit in the room adjacent to the bedroom, the very room where I had my first interview with him, in a chair close to the door leading into the bedroom, which will be open. Only when he begins to snore am I to stop. Steady, heavy breathing does not mean that he is asleep. Indeed, he points out that this would be the very worst moment to stop, and the sudden silence would immediately catapult him into wakefulness, even if he had been on the point of falling asleep.

I asked him if he wished to hear me read, but he said he had made enquiries and had every confidence in my abilities. The last man to be employed in this enterprise, he told me, was liable to get carried away and dramatise too much. He wants an even tone of voice but not monotonous. Do not try to read as though you were soothing me to sleep, he told me. I cannot abide that. Read in your normal manner, only do not let yourself get carried away by what you are reading. Only if I am compelled to attend to you will I be able to forget my own thoughts for long enough to fall asleep.

What that he dismissed me, instructing me to return with my book at midnight. I asked him if I should knock and he pondered a moment, and then said that I should. However, he will not reply. Knock merely and then let yourself in. The door will not be locked.

His room was in darkness when I returned, but he called out to me from the bed, and when I answered he asked me to be seated and to begin when I was ready. I settled myself in the chair, adjusted the lamp, and began. But after a while he called out to me again and asked me to enter the bedroom. The light from the lamp allowed me to make out the large four-poster in which I presumed he lay. I stood at the door, but his voice, coming from the recesses of the bed, asked me to come forward and to sit at his bed's side. When I had done so he lay for so long in silence that I thought my simple presence there

135

beside him had been enough to do what all the skills of my delivery had so far failed to do. But eventually he spoke, very softly, and asked me about you and the children. I answered all his questions as simply and clearly as I was able. He asked me then whether I myself had anything written I might choose to read from instead of the books I had brought with me. I answered that I had much, but not with me. I wondered whether he would suggest sending a servant to fetch these the next day, but he lay in silence for a long while, and then asked whether I would be prepared to write some special thing to read to him, night after night.

– What kind of thing did you have in mind? I asked him.

He laughed at that, and said he was not himself a writer, and that he would leave such things to me. I understood then the reason for the desk under the window and the different kinds of paper and pen laid out upon it. I said I would try.

– I will not have anything other than a new composition of your own, he said.

He was silent again then and I wondered what I should do. Did he wish me to return to the other room and take up my reading again, or leave him altogether, or else to sit there in case he had another question for me to answer. I was debating these different possibilities when he said:

– I have read all the books that have ever been written, and it makes me melancholy. A terrible tedium comes upon me whenever I open again one of these volumes, or even when another voice renders me their contents.

– But would not a new book arouse your interest? I asked him. Would it not have the effect of keeping you awake rather than the desired one of sending you to sleep?

– My friend, he said, you speak without thought. A new story, a story which is really new and really a story, will give the person who reads or hears it the sense that the world has come alive again for him. The world will start to breathe for him where before it had seemed to be made of ice or rock. And it is only in the arms of that which breathes that we can fall asleep, for only then are we confident that we will ourselves wake up alive. Am I not right?

I agreed with him straight away. I told him I had not thought in those terms before, but that now he had put it this way I could see the rightness of his proposition.

– My friend, he said, you had no need to see it in these terms. You are a writer, not a thinker. I, alas, am a thinker. That is why you can sleep but I cannot.

After that he was silent again, and for so long that I made a movement to get up from the chair. But as I did so he spoke again.

– No, he said. Stay where you are. Tonight we will talk. Tomorrow you will read to me from your new work.

I wondered then at the boldness of his assumption that I could in a day produce enough matter to read the following night from midnight to the coming of the dawn. I did not like to raise false expectations in his breast, but likewise I did not, at that moment, wish to rouse him by challenging his assumptions. He spoke quietly, and was clearly in a kind of half-sleep, from which it was my duty to lead him rather in the direction of sleep than to arouse him to full consciousness.

He asked me then again about you and whether we minded being thus kept apart for a period of days if not weeks. A poor writer, sir, I said to him, cannot always do what he and his family would like. But if you had to choose, he pressed me, between spending the night at your desk or in your bed, which would you choose? I mean, he added, sensing that I had not perhaps wholly understood him, if you had no other time to write but at night?

I pondered this question, for it seemed to me that he was the sort of man who did not care for an unconsidered reply. And as long as he knew that a reply would in fact be forthcoming he was in no hurry to have it, but would let me take my time, sitting there beside him in the quiet room, with only the light on the desk in the adjoining room keeping the dark at bay.

Eventually I told him what I consider to be the truth, which is that if the choice were for one night there would be no question of my deciding to spend it in bed with you, but that if he was talking about a permanent state of affairs the choice became more difficult.

– Let us say, my friend, he said, that financial considerations do not enter into the equation.

– You are, sir, I said, asking a philosopher's question.

– My friend, he said, what else can a philosopher ask?

– My answer would still be the same, I said. I trust though, I added, that it will not come to such a choice.

– But if it were to? he pressed me.

– Not to lie in bed next to the wife I love would make my life hardly worth living, I said to him. Not to write as I wish would have the same effect. You would condemn me by your insistence that I choose.

– Could you not lie with her and compose as you do so? he asked me.

I told him that the difference between composing in your head and on paper was like that between embracing a ghost and a person of flesh and blood. He seemed to understand, for he was silent then. Once again I felt that he had perhaps finally succumbed to sleep, but once again, as I moved in my chair, his voice came to me out of the recesses of the bed.

– Perhaps, he said, that is the difference between a philosopher and a composer.

I waited for him to continue but he was silent again for a long while. Eventually though he continued:

– It is only ghosts we philosophers ever embrace, he said. That is why so many of us suffer from insomnia.

I waited again and again he continued, after a lengthy pause:

– We need to rediscover the living body, he said.

He seemed happy now to talk to himself. He said:

– But even if we did so it would straightaway die in our embrace.

I did not think he wanted me to talk, but suddenly he asked me:

– What do you think of us philosophers, my friend?

I told him that I did not normally think of them, but that I imagined they were engaged in answering the most important questions of existence.

– Do not stop there, my friend, he said. There is no need to spare me.

I told him I did not understand what he was trying to say.

– We can indeed answer all the central questions of existence, he said. But that is not to say that we have answered anything at all.

– How so? I asked him.

– What is truly central to existence is never a question, he said. That, he added, is why we philosophers lie awake in our beds.

I was silent then, not wishing to agree or disagree with him. Perhaps sensing my dilemma he changed the subject somewhat.

– Why do you think, my friend, he asked me, that your race has produced so few philosophers?

– We have produced more than people imagine, I said.

– Is it, he said, because it is a race which relies for its self-definition so much upon memory?

I was impressed by the acuteness of his understanding.

– Do you know much about our race? I asked him.

– Only what I read, he said. There is precious little opportunity to study the matter at first hand.

– There is more now, I ventured, than in earlier ages.

– Indeed, he said. And we owe this good fortune to what? To nothing other than the bigotry of Oliver Cromwell, who, upon being told that the millenium would not arrive till the conversion of the Jews, on finding that there were no Jews in the Kingdom to be converted, promptly insisted that they be invited back for that very purpose.

I was silent.

– Some might say, he ventured, that God works in mysterious ways.

– Memory, he said, is what separates us from the beasts. How wise then of your people to place memory at the centre of their faith.

– As you know sir, I said, it only acquired that position when we found ourselves deprived of both land and power.

– The reasons are of little import, he said. What matters are the facts.

– There is, I ventured, such a thing as too much memory. To cling too wilfully to memory can lead to the inability to adapt to what is new and changing.

– True, he said, yet of too much memory we can recover, but of none at all?

– We philosophers, he said, tend to act as though memory did not exist.

He was silent again, and for a long time. The house was quite still around us. The heavy curtains on the windows kept out the least hint of light. I heard him sigh, deep in the recesses of the bed.

– My friend, he said. Everything you need is provided you. Should you require anything else you have only to ring. You will come back here tomorrow evening and read to me from a work of your own making.

– Sir, I said.

– You will read until you hear the first birds of dawn, or till my snores are such as to make it quite certain that I am asleep. Is that understood?

I said that it was.

He was silent again. Then he said:

– It is the silence I cannot bear. When the birds start to sing I know there is a world out there and sleep at once opens its arms to receive me.

I would have suggested to him that overmuch coffee might have rather more to do with his insomnia than any metaphysical doubts concerning the existence of the world, and that a bed less bounded by canopies and curtains might also help him breathe more easily and so bring him on the road towards sleep, but I did not feel it was my place. Besides, we need the fee he is offering if we are to pay for the physician and for the men to mend the roof.

– Soon they will begin, he said. Soon the air will be full of the sounds of birds.

He was silent now for such a time that I finally ventured to ask him:

– Do you wish me to go now sir?

– No, he said. Stay till we may hear them.

I waited then again for him to speak, and eventually he said:

– Are you fond of your little ones?

– Indeed, I said to him, most fond.

– I have two sons, he said. One of them is an idiot and the other is a fool.

I was silent, not knowing how to respond to this.

– Their mother was a fool, he added.

I did not know how to interpret his tone, so kept my peace.

– Fortunately, he said, I have the means to keep them from my presence. For the sight of the one fills me with despair and that of the other with horror.

He was silent for such a time now that I thought he had verily gone to sleep, but finally he asked me:

– Describe the method by which you compose.

– Sir, I said, I am ever at your worships's service, but you must allow me to retain the secrets of my profession.

– I feared you would say that, he said. Will you not tell me about the methods you employ?

– I must beg you sir, I said, to leave off such questionings.

– I understand, he said, but there was disappointment in his voice. You may go now.

The lamp was still burning in the drawing-room. I went to the window and drew aside the curtains. A faint glimmer of light rendered visible the lawns, with a thin film of mist lying atop of them. The trees of the park loomed in the distance, indistinct grey shapes, like nothing so much as chairs and tables when they are covered over to protect them from dust when the owner has closed up the house.

I thought that if the curtains in the corridors were not drawn I would be able to find my way to my room. And indeed they were not, and a few minutes later I was in my bedroom, and had thrown off my clothes and fallen on the bed to sleep through the remaining hours of the night.

The less said about the following day the better. I sat at the elegant desk with the paper and pens within my reach. Again and again I started to compose, but nothing came of these beginnings. I pushed back the chair and walked up and down the room before sitting down again and once more picking up the pen. The result was the same. I took myself into the grounds of the manor and walked, my hands clasped behind my back, my notebook in my pocket, waiting for that little nudge from the gods which would set me going, but, alas, it did not come.

You can imagine that my appetite was not of the best. A most delicious breakfast was served me at nine, and an equally good lunch and supper at one and at eight, but in my anxiety I could do little more than nibble. Oh how I wish you had been there! You would have eaten for the two of us. For my one thought throughout the day was that if I could not satisfy Mr Westfield that evening he would be as likely as not to send me packing the next day, and then we would once again have to ask the doctor to be patient and the roofer to wait awhile before he began his repairs. And the thought of all these things, which should have acted as a spur to my invention worked on me instead in the opposite way, and I had, by nightfall, not only not succeeded in finishing anything, I had not even been able to start.

After supper I sat at the desk and wrote. Alas, I no longer even tried to fulfil my obligations to my employer, but instead I wrote – to you.

I knew of course what he would say. He would call me in and sit me again by his bed, as he had on the previous night.

– Well, my friend, he would say. Why do you sit there in silence when you are acquainted with my wishes?

– Alas, sir, I would say, you asked me to read from a composition of my own, and I have to confess that I have none.

– But you knew my wishes, my friend, when you left me last night?

– Indeed I did sir.

– Are you a composer, my friend?

– I am, sir.

– Then why have you not composed?

– One single day, sir, to prepare for a whole night's reading, appears to have been beyond my powers.

– You have enough then for half the night?

– No, sir.

– For a quarter then?

– No, sir.

– For an hour perhaps?

– Alas, sir, no.

– How can you explain that, my friend?

– It is not a question, sir, of beginning at the top left-hand corner, as with the painting of a wall, and proceeding to the bottom right-hand corner. It is rather a question of finding what I call the thread. With that found, the composition can unwind. But the finding is not easy, nor can a set portion of time be allotted to it. It happens sometimes almost at once. At other times many days pass and there is nothing to show for them.

– Mr Goldberg, you were recommended to me as a man in a thousand. As a thoroughly original as well as a thoroughly professional man of letters. Are you telling me that neither you nor your colleagues could fulfil the simple commission I offered you?

– I cannot speak for my colleagues, sir. I can speak only for myself.

– Speak then, my friend, and defend yourself.

– It may be the case, sir, that in the time of Greece and Rome, and even in the time of our glorious Shakespeare, a man of letters could have fulfilled your commission. The writers of those times might in a day have produced for you a dazzling series of variations on any theme of your choice. But, alas, our own age is grown altogether less inventive and more melancholic, and few can now find it in their hearts to 'take a point at pleasure and wrest and turn it as he list, making either much or little of it, according as shall seem best in his own conceit', as an ancient writer on the arts of music puts it. For what we list has grown obscure and difficult to define.

– That is all very well, Mr Goldberg, but you accepted my commission. Is it not unprofessional of you not to stick to your word?

– I did not say, sir, that I had been unable to stick to my word.

– You did not? I thought I had heard you say most clearly, Mr Goldberg, that you had.

– May I explain, sir?

– Mr Goldberg, you had better.

– I cannot of course speak for my colleagues, sir, but only for myself. I have invariably found that when I am at a loss for a subject, when the elusive thread of which I was talking remains resolutely hidden from sight, then there is one way in which I can perhaps call it into being.

– And that way, Mr Goldberg?

– That way is to cease to search for themes or for subjects, but to start from the position I am in. If that happens to be inside a labyrinth from which there seems to be no exit, then this will itself become my theme. I thus sat down after sampling the delights of the supper with which you had so generously provided me, with my mind made up. I would write the composition you asked for in the form of a letter to my wife. Not any letter, you understand sir, but a letter telling her of my visit here and of the circumstances in which I find myself. In that way, if I do not cover myself with the glory that would accrue to the great writers of the past, I at least do not cover myself with total shame, and fulfil, in my own way, the commission you have given me.

In the letter then, I tell my wife of my arrival at your house, of my first meeting with you, and of the first night, in which you so kindly consented to share your thoughts with a mere composer like myself. I tell her about your instructions to me, and about my inability to carry them out, and my final solution to the problem. It is not perhaps the most elegant solution, and I would, I assure you, have produced a more elegant, had I been able. But we, today, can do only what we can, not what we would wish, and this was a solution of sorts, not perhaps without its own kind of elegance. May it at least have the desired effect.

Vibrations

FRANCIS KING

PEOPLE WHO HAVE little in common sometimes, paradoxically, also have too much. Such was certainly the case with Martin, a successful stockbroker, and Luke, an unsuccessful schoolmaster. What they had in common, in a past now almost forty years behind them, was some flurried groping at the minor public school they had attended, Martin with so much distinction and Luke with so little.

The head prefect of Luke's house had sent him, then only fourteen, with a letter to Martin, the head prefect of another house. The letter, about a cricket fixture, had carried the postscript, half-jocular and half-serious, 'Use the bearer kindly.' For two terms, before he had moved on to Cambridge, Martin had used Luke more kindly than he was ever to use him again.

Now Luke telephoned to invite Martin to a small dinner-party to celebrate his fifty-fifth birthday. 'Do you have to ask him?' Huang, Luke's Hong Kong lover, had queried, to be told, 'Oh, yes, I must. After all, he *is* my oldest friend.'

'Yes, I think I could manage that,' Martin drawled, in a tone which suggested that Luke had badgered him for some tiresome favour. 'There's only one little problem, though.'

'Yes?'

'I have this – friend.' Martin always had a friend, but the friend tended to vary from month to month and even, sometimes, from week to week. 'Gino. Italian,' he added.

'Oh, Italian.' There had been other Italians.

'I don't really like to leave him to his own devices. And I know that you'll adore him. He's so full of life, so intelligent, so funny. So I wonder – might I bring him along too?'

'Yes, of course! Of course! Yes, do bring him along!'

Luke sounded more enthusiastic than he felt. In his two-room flat the dining-table, usually half-masked by the television set, stood at the far end of a living-room so narrow that Martin had once unkindly compared it to a railway carriage.

'How can we seat everyone?' Huang asked.

It was a question that Luke had already put to himself. 'Yes, I know, it's a nuisance. Eight we can just manage at the table, but nine . . . We'll just have to divide up and have four in the kitchen.'

'Is it necessary to have this friend of Martin?'

'Yes, I'm afraid it is.' Luke spoke from experience. On a previous occasion, many years before, when he had been less accommodating about an extra guest, Martin had snapped back: 'Well, in that case, my dear, I'm afraid I'm not going to be able to be with you either.'

'It is not good to divide up a party,' Huang said.

'Yes, I know, I know. But there it is.'

Declaring that they had come on from another 'do', Martin and Gino arrived so late that the Chinese dinner, over which Huang had slaved all through that day and half the previous one, failed to reach his usual standard. 'Delicious!' 'Marvellous!' 'Huang, you really have excelled yourself!' But to such compliments Huang remained indifferent, his round, plump face sagging with despair at what he knew to be a failure.

Gino, who worked in a Mayfair hairdressing salon, asked if the food contained any monosodium glutamate. 'I have to be very careful,' he explained. 'I suffer from Chinese restaurant syndrome.' Even when Huang had assured him that there was no monosodium glutamate, he only picked at his food.

Luke had attempted to separate Martin and his friend – 'I want to keep couples apart,' he had said – but Gino would have none of that, insisting not merely on remaining at the table in the living-room with Martin but on seating himself beside him. In this proximity, he and Martin would often converse with each other in an undertone in Italian even when other people were speaking.

Martin always wished to show off his friend of the moment, much as he showed off this or that pair of elaborate, expensive cufflinks by constantly shooting his cuffs, and he showed off Gino now. To this showing-off Gino responded now with pleasure, now with petulance, and now with boredom. Martin told the other guests how Gino came from one of the oldest families in Calabria; how he numbered among his clients film-stars, television personalities and members of the aristocracy; how he had 'this absolutely unerring taste', so that as soon as he had moved in, he had insisted on doing up the Knightsbridge house from top to bottom. Finally he had talked of Gino's clairvoyant powers – 'really spooky', he said of them more than once.

At the mention of the clairvoyant powers, Gino shook his head and then, as though to smoothe away an ache caused by that sudden movement, put a delicate hand to his forehead, rubbing at it with his finger-tips. 'No, no, Martin, this is not the time or the place to talk of such things.'

But clearly, despite his protests, Gino wished to talk of them and was delighted when one of the other guests, an actor, urged: 'Oh, do tell us what form this gift takes!'

Gino held out his glass to Huang who, pale and sweating from his constant to-ing and fro-ing between living-room and kitchen, was stooping over one of the other guests, a vast platter of duck extended in both his small, plump hands. 'When you can spare a moment, may I have some of the red? In a clean glass. I have been drinking the white.' The tone implied both that the white had not come up to scratch and that Huang was a hired waiter.

Having received the red, Gino sipped at it and then smiled over the rim of the glass at the actor, who was both youthful and handsome. 'I get vibrations,' he said. 'It is almost something physical. As though an electric current were passing through me. Or as though an engine had started up. My grandmother had the same gift. I think that maybe she passes on this gift to me. Sometimes I do not wish to get these vibrations. They are difficult, embarrassing. I have vibrations from you,' he added with a mysterious smile.

'Oh, yes?' The actor now sounded nervous.

'You wish you were somewhere else – with someone else. You have come here only because you think that maybe this someone else will also be invited, but now you are disappointed because this someone else is not here.' Again he gave the mysterious smile. 'Am I right? I think that I am right.'

Both the rigidity of Luke's face and the colour mounting up from the actor's throat to his cheeks suggested that Gino had indeed been right.

Gino turned to the frail, elderly man on his left. 'You are not well.'

'I am perfectly well,' the man replied, in a voice at once apprehensive and peevish.

'You *think* that you are perfectly well,' Gino said. 'That is different. Soon you will find that I am right and you are wrong. You will be in hospital – an operation. I am sorry,' he added, a perfunctory afterthought.

Next Gino turned to Luke. 'You are worried, Luke,' he told him.

'Am I? Why should I be worried – on my birthday, with so many good friends around me?'

'A birthday means that one is older. You are worried because you think that maybe you lose your job. Redundant, yes? I have vibrations that Luke is worried. Luke is afraid to lose his job. Am I right? I think that I am right.'

Martin chortled with pleasure. 'What did I tell you? He's brilliant, absolutely brilliant!'

Luke rose hurriedly from his chair. 'Let me see if the others have finished in the kitchen. If they have, we can all sit together for our coffee.'

He massaged one of his hands with the other, his face contorted. Gino might just have slammed a door on his fingers.

'What a terrible evening!' Gino exclaimed, as he climbed into Martin's Porsche. 'After that hell – let us go to Heaven!'

'Oh, I'm far too tired.'

'Nonsense. We will go to Heaven.'

Martin began to drive to the disco. He was always perversely happy to do what Gino told him, abasing his own steely will to one even steelier.

'How can Luke bear to live with that Chinaman? He is so old and so ugly.'

'And so dim.'

'A real dim-sum! A Chinese dumpling!' Gino laughed in delight at his joke. 'Such boring people, all of them,' he went on, a moment later.

'Well, you worked hard to entertain them. I will say that for you.'

'I tried. I tried. But imagine putting some guests to eat in the kitchen! I know that Luke wished me to go to the kitchen. To eat there with that Chinese dumpling! Crazy! I am not a servant. I do not eat in kitchens.'

'What a terrible evening!' Huang sighed, as he carefully stacked the plates in the dishwasher.

'Not terrible at all.' But Luke was lying.

'The food was spoiled.'

'It was delicious.' Two sleepy pears colliding with each other, Luke gave Huang a hug.

'Dry. All dry.' With a deep sigh, Huang disengaged himself and began to range some glasses along the top shelf of the dishwasher. 'Luke, I am sorry, I do not like that Gino.'

'Oh, he's all right. He could be much worse.'

Through the years, Luke had met all Martin's friends, and so many of them had been much worse.

It was not until shortly before Christmas that the invitation was returned.

Gino, not Martin, rang. 'Oh, Luke . . . Martin and I are giving a little cocktail party on Christmas Eve. It is partly for Christmas and partly because my old friend Mimi Livornese –the Contessa Livornese – will be here at the Claridge's and we wish to give her a welcome. You can come?'

'Thank you, yes, that sounds wonderful.' In fact, to Luke, who had reached an age when he hated standing and crowds, it sounded far from wonderful. 'The only thing is . . . Would you mind if Huang came along too?'

There was a silence at the other end of the line. Then in a high-pitched, over-articulated voice, Gino said: 'May I take – how do you say? – a rain check? With Martin. Martin is out right now. We have so many guests already, I am not sure about numbers. We must ask this person, that person. You know how it is. There are Mimi's friends, Martin's friends, my friends. So many – too many people. I will ring you, yes?'

The next day, Martin said to Gino over breakfast: 'What an extraordinary Christmas card!' He did not mean that it was extraordinary because, so small and so obviously cheap, it was not the sort of card that he himself would ever send. He passed the card across to Gino.

On the right side it was inscribed: 'To Martin . . . From Luke and Huang.' On the left side, Luke had written: 'Thank you so much for the invitation to the Christmas Eve party. Perhaps, after all, it would be better to give it a miss. On the one hand, I don't want to leave Huang alone on Christmas Eve, and on the other hand, I'd hate to spoil your numbers. Let's meet early in the New Year, when I hope that both you and Gino will be able to come here again to dinner.'

Having tossed the card negligently back across the table to Martin with a small pout, Gino said: 'I did not tell you this at the time, Martin, but at that terrible Chinese dinner Luke gave me other vibrations. Bad, bad, vibrations.'

'Bad vibrations? What do you mean?'

'I felt sure that this strange friendship between you and him was about to come to an end.' He looked across at Martin with that smile, mysterious and mocking, which people found irresistible, disturbing or both of those things together. 'I felt sure that – how you say? – a chapter is ended. A chapter which has already gone on far too long. Am I right? I think that I am right.'

He was right.

Esther

HANIF KUREISHI

'YOU ARE OBVIOUSLY a sensitive man.' She came to see him for the first time one afternoon to discuss the possibility of taking a master's degree under his supervision, and this is what she said to him. Turning Esther Wilson down was not really an option, his department head implied. So Ray Ford simply turned, in his mind, against her. He would be cool with her. And why not? She was clearly well connected; her husband gave generously to the university, or something in that line. Dinner parties had to be involved – they always were. Privilege had not passed her by; surely she didn't require being liked by him as well?

Esther was in her middle fifties, but now, when women in their sixties were wearing track-suits and taking up wind-surfing, she seemed older. She wore the sort of shoes women pruned roses in, and blouses, cardigans, and tweed skirts, all expensive, well made, and exquisitely undistinguished. Her clothes didn't seem to agree with her; they misrepresented her. They looked as if, in a shop, she didn't quite know what to buy, perhaps because she didn't know who she was. He laughed at this projection; he was like this, he knew.

She was alert, she spoke quietly, she was self-deprecating. Off she went, feeling her way into understanding, leaning forward, fist clenched, and then she withdrew, just in case. 'But perhaps I'm wrong, perhaps I'm hopelessly off the mark.'

'Perhaps you are.'

'Yes, I'm sure I am.'

This was her manner, not her character. Still, it irritated him: he wondered if older women developed this trait of caution so as not to seem too irritatingly certain of things. Certainty would be the domain of their husbands.

But in Esther self-doubt and self-questioning were not a weakness; they were a passion, they distinguished her. Ray preferred this to the behaviour of middle-aged, middle-class women who returned to university when their children left home and who shouted out self-important questions at his lectures and went to dances as if they were eighteen.

Ray was in his early forties and immature. How could he not be if he couldn't get his hands and feelings to stick to any woman, even though he'd advertised in *Time Out*? He'd begun to think women were shallow to set such store by appearances. He'd arranged to meet one woman in a pub he knew to be badly lit. He arrived early, bought a bottle of wine, and set down two glasses, so that she didn't have to see him walk to the bar. As they drank, they fed each other questions on the mutual interests they'd corresponded about, the theatre and Graham Greene. And he wondered if this was the woman he'd spend the rest of his life with – until she excused herself and never returned. The other women had been lacking in the mental area. Young women students turned him into a lecher. As they fled, he pursued, all hands, until he hated them.

But at least with the young women undergraduates he could flirt; he could patronise and show off. He could sit smoking in his airless, modern college room, looking out on the London traffic, his poor feet up on a chair, *Blonde on Blonde* playing as he lectured on American literature of the 1960s. They had to call him Doctor. But Esther called him Ray from the beginning. To contain her growing interest in him, he needed to be formal. She wanted to be easy.

Esther wasn't discouraged by Ray's polite indifference. She began to go to his undergraduate lectures on Lawrence and

Joyce and even Orton, writers not on the syllabus when she'd been at Oxford. After the lecture, as he crookedly propelled himself on crutches to the lift (he'd had arthritis as a child, which had slowed his growing as well as hampering his walking), she would accompany him, but diffidently, making gentle jokes, holding her books and papers in her arms, and carrying his lecture notes, too, as he swung and grunted in effort, a real Gregor Samsa. And the young students rushed off past them to the bar, to the common rooms, to take drugs and have sex, which is what he wished he were doing.

Over the years he had heard students calling him Quasimodo, and the Cripple, and he laughed at their innocent cruelty. Esther's sympathy was far worse. Esther, with inquiring kind eyes that rarely left his swollen face, saw the physical pain that never, for a minute, left him alone. He had reason to suspect that she saw the need and longing, the distorted emotional life, vitiated by shame and rejection and physical isolation. She would know, surely, exactly how much people need to be touched!

Soon she was always in his room, making him tea properly in a pot, buying him a tea strainer and two pretty bone-china cups. She brought florentines from a bakery in South Kensington, and he ate them eagerly, like a schoolboy, two or three in a session. She had come to university to talk, to inquire into every damn thing, to know other people – him! – intensely, intimately again.

'Tell me . . . do you – it may be an impertinent question – '

'No, no, I'm sure it's not. Please – '

'All right, Ray . . .' She sipped her tea, put her head to one side. She was small and delicate and determined to know and feel.

'Have your feelings towards your students changed over the years?'

'Yes.'

'Is it confusing?'

How could he explain? She always asked the right and yet wrong questions, the most tormenting. In the old days he provided the dope the students smoked; they came to his flat, they watched movies together. Once he'd been in a porno-graphic film some of them had shot, a sub-Warhol effort called *Camden Girls*, in which he played a naked dwarf who carried drinks on a silver tray to the young copulating students. But slowly they'd come to bore him. Esther Wilson, virtually an old woman, was informed about theatre, film, television, ideas. If he mentioned that a certain newspaper had deteri-orated, she would know how this had happened. 'Oh, yes, terrible, and the editor, Jonathan – we do know him a bit – is very much aware of the proprietor. Thinks he can resist him. Can you imagine?'

Esther read Ray's essay on Wilkie Collins, published in an academic journal. One afternoon, on an impulse, as she sat opposite him in his room and showed no sign of wanting to leave, he gave her the first draft of his book on Dickens, which she immediately took to the library. She knew how to read, which was a rare talent, as difficult as carpentry. He waited nervously for two days. On her triumphant return she gave him line-by-line criticism. The early evening they spent together in a wine bar nearby. He told her about his illness, how very sick he'd been for so long at school, and how hard he'd worked to develop his mind (he was proud of his head, he told her), and how the library was his gymnasium until he'd been adjudged brilliant and awarded the first job he applied for.

After this, when they parted regretfully, with volumes still to say, he didn't want to be alone, so he drove to south London, where he visited his parents, who still lived in the terraced house he had been brought up in. He and his father discussed horse racing, and Trollope. His mother, wearing a pink housecoat, did his washing. They were cheerful but seemed old. They worried too much, and seeing them living a life of total habit made him long for more life.

He went round the corner in the rain and had fish and chips for supper, not wanting to ask his mother to cook him something. At ten he visited a prostitute, a fleshy, hippy woman who imagined he liked listening to Leonard Cohen when they had sex. She was right in one sense: the music did delay his climax. Unfortunately, her bed, a mattress, was on the floor, and once he got down on to it, he couldn't get up again. When she returned from the bathroom, expecting to see him ready to leave, he was flailing on his back like an overturned beetle, still in his shirt, for he refused to let her see his body.

He went home and sat in his room, memorising his daily poem. Loneliness washed over him like a freezing sea. Must he always suffer this disjunction between mind and body, intellect and feeling?

One day Esther invited him to a matinee of *The Beggar's Opera*, at the National Theatre. He couldn't think of any reason not to go, but he knew that somehow the invitation would lead to trouble. Esther told him about herself for the first time. Her husband, she said hesitantly, was the Conservative MP Walter Wilson, a junior minister in the Thatcher government, a handsome, clever man on his way up, known for his glamour and his right-wing views. Thatcher liked him, he would go far. Wilson wasn't in the suburban wing of the party either, among the sort who read Wilbur Smith novels on holiday. He was cultured, witty. At one time, in the sixties, he'd been a journalist in Washington.

Esther was grander than Ray had thought. Why hadn't she told him all this before? Did she think he'd be repelled by it? Or did she want to be seen, quite rightly, as completely separate from her husband?

Whatever the reason, Ray reminded himself, you shouldn't personalise politics. Yet on the way home, after she'd told him about her husband, he repeated to himself a phrase often used at Cambridge in the sixties: 'objective class enemy'.

'Although Walter is a politician,' Esther said, as they walked slowly along the Embankment, 'he knows a lot of people in other fields. He loathes talking politics; it bores him stiff.' Then she stopped and said, 'We thought you might like to come and have dinner one evening. Would you?' She paused again, as if she understood how complicated this could be for him. 'Don't reply now. Just let me know on Monday. But I would like it very much if you did come.' Ray was flattered by the invitation. He wanted to pursue this; he was excited. But he didn't want to conceal his views for the sake of a meal and a glimpse at people he'd only read about.

That weekend he felt he should discuss it with two ex-students. They were among his closest friends. One lived in a filthy studio and worked in a bookshop; he was unambitious and contemptuous of the straight world. The other was a drug dealer to the rich who wanted only enough money to build a gargantuan record collection. Ray had taught them both; they still read (Hunter S Thompson and Coleridge), but they did nothing. 'You're just élitist drifters!' he said, losing his temper. They couldn't see his dilemma over Esther's dinner invitation. All those people were 'boring, fascist, decadent'. He should, they said, go to the Wilsons' house and crap in their beds – maybe then they'd see what it is to be hated.

Ray had a bath, which was a considerable effort, and put himself into his beige Yves Saint Laurent suit, the only decent clothes he had. He hoped the evening would be worth the supreme effort.

The Wilsons' flat was in a quiet street off the King's Road; they also had a house outside Cambridge. At the door Esther kissed Ray and patted his hand. This was the first time they had touched. He noticed she was wearing scent, and pearl earrings. Her arms were bare, thin and veined, almost transparent. The flat was full of old things: the books were leather-bound, and there were rugs and antique tables and candlesticks. It was a gloomy place. He hated ornaments. Naturally he was the first to arrive, being stupid enough to get there on time. Then Esther disappeared for ages and Ray heard the clock ticking as he sat there on the hard chair she had provided. Otherwise all was silent. Noise and other people were what money sealed you off from.

Walter Wilson burst in with one arm outstretched, as if the arm were pulling him along. He was a large, confident, powerful man, who quickly poured drinks and said how pleased he was – and he looked pleased. He said he liked Wilkie

Collins, education was better appreciated when you were older, and not to worry if he suddenly left the flat – he might have to go and vote in the House of Commons. Ray saw how much more energy Wilson had than anyone else he knew; this man was like an athlete among weekend exercisers.

Other people arrived, four couples in all, including a journalist called Robert Mansfield whom Ray had once admired so much that he bought a weekly paper just to read his column. Mansfield had turned to the right in the late seventies and repudiated his former opinions. Now he was pompous and had a face the colour of boiled ham. Ray began to panic. He kept spilling things in his lap. He didn't want to speak to this man, whatever happened.

At dinner Esther placed Ray between herself and a fair-haired gay man of about his age, a Ronald Firbank enthusiast who worked for a literary paper. Pierre Carter was obviously more Esther's friend than Walter's. Ray wondered if she unconsciously chose male friends who couldn't threaten Walter. 'Walter's always trying to introduce me to girls,' Carter said. 'Walter can't believe that everyone can't be like him. By the way, Esther, I met an estate agent today who made me realise exactly what Proudhon meant when he wrote "property is theft". In Vietnam it's the Year of the Cat, or Earwig, or whatever. Here it's the Year of the Estate Agent, isn't it?'

Ray enjoyed himself listening to Pierre. At the university he didn't run up against much charm, not this effort to entertain, not these wild stories about people he'd heard of – publishers and writers. He could cheerfully have listened for hours, even though things he considered valuable were mocked and he kept being made to feel that nothing mattered, not literature, not ideas, not objectivity, only jokes and the saying of clever things.

Still the evening would soon be over, time was passing without mishap. Or at least it seemed to be, until Ray noticed a disturbance at the othe end of the table. Robert Mansfield – a man who'd excoriated Harold Wilson over Vietnam and ripped into Alec Douglas-Home and then later claimed that the day Margaret Thatcher became Prime Minister was the happiest day of his life – was having a vociferous conversation with Walter Wilson, and the discussion was rolling down the table like a storm, blowing the heads of the guests from side to side.

'Now, take the sixties, if you want to take the blasted sixties,' Mansfield was saying. 'They were the truly wasted years, weren't they? What an age of puerile and harmful illusions! What utter idiots and vapid cranks the ordure of "liberation" fertilised. Buckminster Fuller, Marshall McLuhan – '

Wilson intervened. 'Fanon,' he said firmly. 'Marcuse. Malcolm X – '

'R D Laing.'

'R D Laing, exactly. Szasz. Schumacher.' It became a game. They searched out the names of fools and spat them out and laughed. 'And who reads them now?' Mansfield said. 'What have they contributed?'

'Nothing,' Wilson agreed. 'Bloody fools.'

'If these people were such fools, why was their influence so deeply felt?' Pierre asked.

'Sartre,' Mansfield added.

'A mind like an African desert,' Wilson said.

Esther nodded at Pierre and then looked at her husband for the first time that evening. Ray noticed that her colour was high: she was defiant, hopeful, pleased. Walter must have made her very angry over the years. Then Ray saw that Walter was staring at him.

'What's your view?' Wilson asked, challenging. Perhaps it was like this in the House of Commons. People asked you simple questions that required complicated replies and then glared at you as if your life depended on the answer. 'You must have been around then, Ray,' Wilson said.

'Yes, I was at Cambridge in '68.'

Robert Mansfield was watching him too. 'In the eye of the storm, eh?' Mansfield said. 'So tell us – tell us what you think now.'

Ray stopped eating. He wasn't enjoying the food as he thought he would; he couldn't concentrate on it.

'Things needed shaking up,' he said. 'They really did.' The table fell silent. Plainly, this wasn't enough. Even Esther expected more. Given his education, his position, his being here at the table at all, surely he could come up with more than, 'Things needed shaking up.'

'The times were more exciting then, intellectually, than they are now. The thinkers you mentioned – disparaged – they were opening up new areas of inquiry.'

'Rubbish,' Mansfield said. 'Thank God we've flung out those cranks and redefined freedom. As if freedom were licence and emotion and something called self-expression.'

'It was a romantic time – '

'Don't – '

'But – '

'Don't, I said, don't you dare insult Wordsworth!' Mansfield shouted. 'You should know better, Doctor!'

The conversation turned to the topic of freedom. Ray's opinion was not sought on this subject.

The next time he saw Esther, she said, 'I hope it wasn't too awful.'

'No, it wasn't,' he said. It was true. That day, directing the students in an Ionesco play, he'd walked out, bored by them.

The conversation at Esther's that night had stimulated him. How long was it since he'd examined his beliefs? What was socialism to him? Did he still believe in equality? What was the relation between his ideas and the way he behaved? He spent several evenings writing down only what he honestly thought and felt. He told Esther this, and she seemed pleased. Still, the two of them had never discussed politics, and she changed the subject.

'By the way, Pierre wants to know if you'd review a book for them.'

'Yes, of course,' Ray said immediately. 'It'll be an honour.' This thrilled him more than he could say. He liked being an academic, but more than anything, he'd wanted to be part of the London literary world, writing reviews and articles and perhaps one day having a column of his own. Maybe now, with Esther's help, he was on his way. He wrote the review immediately – they were surprised by his speed – and within a few weeks it was published and he was asked to do another. To thank Esther he took her out to dinner.

He started to talk about how much difficulty he had meeting women of his 'age, size, and sensibility'. This was the hardest thing in his concealed life to talk about, and he'd longed to broach it, but now, just when he got started, Esther interrupted.

'Ray, I shouldn't be talking about this. I haven't told anyone, but you're a friend, I know. Walter has been having an affair with the woman who's been his assistant for some years. It is a common occurrence; many MPs, many men of his age, do the same, and normally I wouldn't bore you with it. But now he tells me he wants to part from the woman. Only she is threatening suicide. He spends hours speaking to her on the phone every night. He really wants to disengage himself, but the conversation always returns to one thing. He goes back to her or she ends her life.'

Ray took Esther home and went in for a whisky. At eleven o'clock Walter came home, and he sat with Ray. Esther left them to talk. Walter was gentler tonight, and attentive. He talked about the Tory Party and how it worked; he asked Ray questions about structuralism – what it was, exactly – and pondered the replies. With an expensive mechanical pencil he made a note of books Ray recommended. Ray felt himself being seduced by this important, thinking man. Walter now wasn't just another man who picked women up and threw them down when he'd finished with them: he was tragic, he followed his impulses to the end, he had much to give and a hunger for life. The telephone rang. Esther came in to the room to tell Walter it was for him, and Ray went home.

A few days later Esther missed Ray's lecture but came to see him after, in his room. 'I went to see Walter's mistress, Kate,' she said. 'Well. She was wearing a dressing gown. She'd been drinking. She was in a state. She told me that during the five years of their affair Walter promised on several occasions to divorce me and marry her. She became pregnant last year, and Walter insisted she have an abortion, saying the time wasn't right for them to have children. Now she is forty and wonders if the time may have passed. I think she is a decent woman, kind and sensitive.'

'She will eventually recover, don't you think?' Ray said. 'Not that I'd know anything about it. But I've read that people do, eventually, pull through.'

Esther wasn't listening. 'Walter has led her a dance. She was of use to him when he was writing his book. She supported him when he lost his nerve as a politician – something that happens frequently, I can tell you. She has obviously given him her heart and he has shown her the door.'

'Esther, are you going to be all right?'

'Meeting her distressed me. It has made Walter seem callous, hard, distant. When someone tells you they love you, they must, I think, open their heart, and he has often said he loved me. The word *love* implies an absolute giving, doesn't it? And when you find they have not given you their heart but concealed a large part of their life from you, you feel pitied.' Esther sobbed. Ray felt useless and irritated. How had he got dragged into all this? What could he be expected to do or say?

Esther got up. But as soon as she was on her feet, her legs went and she fell over, there in his small room with the windows you couldn't open. She fell on to her knees, her hand snatching down photographs and postcards he had stuck to the wall. Then she went forward on to her face.

Ray, on one crutch, went to her as she lay there shaking. Loosen the clothing, he thought. He fiddled with the top of Esther's cardigan. 'Nothing human is alien to me,' he repeated. To get away while seeming to be effective, he hurried up the deserted corridor to the water fountain. When he returned, Esther had moved; she was trying to sit up. As she did so, she waved at something across the room. Yes, she was pointing at the wastepaper basket. He handed her the heavy metal bucket as it was, half full of the screwed-up paper he'd been writing his latest review on. She vomited with three involuntary barks, ejecting a rush of thin and surprisingly dark soup that found its way to the bottom of the bucket, where it discovered a hole through which it seeped. He'd have to clean it up. But how? No – he'd leave the bucket outside for the cleaner. Not his job to clean things up. He was employed to think.

'I feel better now.'

He drove Esther home. For three weeks he didn't hear from her. He didn't ring and she didn't appear at tutorials. He imagined that things were sorting themselves out and life would return to normal. All the same, he found himself becoming angry with her. For God's sake, he didn't want his mind full of these people's lives, their genitals, their self-inflicted problems! England was teeming with people suffering because of this government, people in bad housing, the unemployed, children in rotten schools. He started to despise Esther, and resented the weakness of his involvement with her. At the same time, this was something he wanted to discuss with her. It was in the evenings that he missed her the most – not that he had ever seen her often after six. It was that he missed having talked to her during the day, and by evening his mind was crammed with things he felt she should know.

Three weeks later, quite unexpectedly, she came to see him again. She hadn't brought her books with her, nor had she brought cakes; this was a different age. She sat down and looked directly at him. She was in a hurry.

'How are you, Ray?'

'Yes, fine. And you?'

'I'm so ashamed. I haven't done a stroke of work.'

'You have time, Esther. You always tell me to take time with my work.'

'Yes, you should. Some terrible things have happened, you know.'

'Yes?'

But he thought: they are terrible to you, who have nothing more important than the intricacies of human relationships to think about. He didn't say this.

'Walter's friend, Kate – '

'Yes, how is she? Coming round?'

'She died. She committed suicide.'

'She actually did it?' he said stupidly, but she didn't notice his stupidity.

'We heard nothing from her for a few days, which was unusual, since she rang frantically every night. Walter had given her the name of a psychiatrist he thought she might go to. Then her sister rang to say she'd found Kate dead. She'd been dead for thirty-six hours. The family is very bitter. They blame Walter.'

Ray and Esther walked in Green Park until dark. The effort exhausted him. His whole body ached, but he couldn't complain. He thought constantly of the woman Kate and of the difficulty and seriousness of loving.

That night Ray was tired, but he dragged himself to supper with some ex-Cambridge friends. He shouldn't have gone, but how could he have known the day's events would stir him up so much?

He had three friends to whom, along with their three wives and five children, he was always Uncle Ray. The conversation, relaxed but serious, informed, and elliptical, was about books and television and mutual friends, before it moved inevitably to the Labour Party, its present weakness and how they'd all hated it in the late sixties and had wanted it destroyed to allow a revolutionary party of the working class to emerge. Now they wanted the Labour Party back in power in almost any form. They discussed the universities, the cuts in funding, the lack of belief in objective research and scholarship. More rich American students would be treating the universities like finishing schools. Little, it seemed, could be done as the age slipped into philistinism. People like themselves were not required, Ray realised. 'We're misguided jokes,' someone said. 'Highly educated and capable and yet totally irrelevant.' The children slept in the bedrooms; the grown-ups drank cognac. At the weekend they would take the children swimming and have a picnic. You retreated into private satisfactions, into families. What you believed politically was a matter of words, perhaps of feeling – anger – but never of action.

Ray was drunk when he got home, and he knocked a bookcase over with his crutch. Once again he was alone; no one knew where he was or what he was doing. His existence was not recorded in any other human mind, except perhaps Esther's. He sat at his typewriter and inserted four pieces of paper into the machine, with ancient carbon paper between the sheets.

He wrote the letter three times like this, not wanting to risk photocopying. At four in the morning he finished and went out to post the letters. He had to post them immediately: in a few hours his fury, his courage, would evaporate. A policeman asked him if everything was all right. Ray told him he was an insomniac.

The letters were addressed to the prime minister and to the editor of three newspapers. They disclosed the facts about Walter Wilson and the suicide of his mistress. Ray had included a lot of detail, so that they would take him seriously. Here it was, then, a mere letter written by him. How could such a thing damage a government?

But the story did come out. Predictably, the papers were cautious at first. Wilson's 'assistant' had committed suicide. Then, a day later, Kate's family spoke to the press, confirming the affair and revealing Wilson's numerous promises and deceptions. The story got on to the front pages. It would run for a while. Damage would be done.

At college Ray discussed the scandal with friends and colleagues. He wanted to tell people what he'd done, that all this embarrassment was due to his initiative, but he had to suppress this wish.

He read the papers and watched all the television news programmes. After the first few days of revelations and references to 'Wilson's recent suicide love', followed by 'No comment' from the MP, Wilson and his friends fought back, smearing the dead woman. She was promiscuous (a list of boyfriends appeared), perhaps drugs were involved; mental illness was certainly a factor. Wilson, apparently, was going to get away with it; after all, wasn't he just a normal full-blooded man?

Then the sister went on television. Kate's sister was soft-featured, with rosy cheeks; she was nervous and middle-class. Ray knew immediately that the public would believe her before a smooth-chopped politician. Wilson's ease and confidence before the cameras and press didn't help him now; it made him seem shallow and uncaring. The sister read her statement, saying how Kate had loved Wilson, trusted him, been faithful to him, and how he had left her, driving her to despair. She produced a letter from Wilson that confirmed these things. This finished him. He resigned. He went away.

Ray woke up one day six months later to find he'd lost interest in the whole thing. He didn't want to hear another word about it. It had nothing to do with him any more. It wasn't even particularly important. He wanted to write a book.

But one afternoon he heard a tap at his door, and Esther Wilson came in. She'd brought a chocolate cake and she cut him a large piece. He was surprised by how unchanged she seemed, how cheerful she was. They groaned with pleasure over the cake. She asked him how the pain in his leg was, and how the reviewing was going. He concluded that she had no idea of his involvement in the scandal.

'Walter blames me for ruining his life,' she said, 'for visiting Kate and saying that her persisting with him was pointless. I left her bereft of hope, he says. He is a difficult man to live with, Ray, I can tell you.'

Ray felt she was understating.

'Will you take me to the theatre?' she asked.

'Yes.'

'On Thursday?'

He wondered how he'd be able to keep his mouth shut about what he'd done, but he pushed the event into a corner of his mind. After the theatre he went to visit the prostitute again. She was stoned and it was late – no other clients would come tonight and she was in no hurry for him to leave. She kept calling him a friend. 'Now we're friends,' she said, and gave him a thin joint without tobacco. He didn't feel like explaining that that wasn't what friendship was. They lay there on a busted mattress in a shabby south London basement with the sound of footsteps just above their heads, and he thought of death and how, while you were still alive, you had to try to love other people in whatever way you could. He thought of Esther. She'd liked him, she'd listened to him, responded to him, loved him. He supposed they would carry on being friends. He knew he wanted that.

He pulled himself up into a sitting position. The woman stirred but continued to lie there, naked, on her back, staring at the ceiling. The bed stank of cigarettes, and she smelled of petunia.

The Wrong Vocation

MOY McCRORY

'WHEN GOD CALLS you, he is never denied,' Sister Mercy told us with a finality which struck terror into our hearts.

She stood at the front of the room with the window behind her, so we were blinded and could not see her features but we knew she smiled.

'He waits patiently until we hear his voice. When that happens, you are never the same.'

It terrified me when this thing called a vocation might come; any day out of nowhere to drop into my mind and wedge there like a piece of grit.

'God is looking now, seeing who is pure of heart and ready to be offered up.'

Every girl shifted uncomfortably. Sister looked at our upturned faces and seemed pleased with the effect she was having. By way of illustration she told us about a young woman from a rich home who was always laughing, with young men waiting to escort her here, there and everywhere, and a big family house with chandeliers in the rooms and a lake in the garden.

'I've seen it. It was on the telly the other night,' Nancy Lyons whispered to me.

'With all these good things in life, she was spoiled. Her

weathy father indulged his daughter's every wish. And do you think she was happy?'

'She damned well ought to be,' Nancy hissed while around us the more pious members of the form shook their heads.

Sister placed her bony hands across her chest and stood up on her tiptoes as if reaching with her ribcage for something that would constantly evade it.

'Her heart was empty.'

Sister went on to tell us how the young woman resisted the call, but eventually realised she would never be happy until she devoted her life to Christ. Going out beside the lake, she asked him to enter her life.

'She is one of our very own nuns, right here in this convent. Of course I cannot tell you which sister she is, but when you imagine that we were all born as nuns, remember that we were once young girls like yourselves, without a thought in our heads that we should devote our lives to God.'

There was a silence. We all stared out past her head.

'Oh Sister, it's beautiful,' said a voice. Nancy rolled her eyes to heaven. Lumpy, boring Beatrice, who always sat at the front, would like it. She was so slow-witted and so good. She was one of the least popular girls in the class, a reporter of bad news and always the first to give homework in. With miniskirts *de rigueur*, her uniform remained stoically unadapted. She must have been the only girl in the school that did not need to have her hemline checked at the end of the day. While we struggled to turn over our waistbands Beatrice always wore her skirt a good two inches below her plump knees and looked like one of the early photographs, all sepia and foggy, of the old girls in their heyday.

Nancy pulled her face.

'But wasn't her rich father angry?' someone asked, and Sister Mercy nodded.

'Mine would sodding kill me. They don't even want me to stay on at school. Me mother's always reminding me how much money they're losing because I'm not bringing any wages home.'

'Do you have something to say, Nancy Lyons?' Sister's stern voice rapped.

'No Sister, I was just saying what a great sacrifice it was to make.'

'Ah yes, a great sacrifice indeed.'

But the sacrifice was not just on the nun's part. Everyone else was made to suffer. There was a woman in our street who never recovered after her eldest daughter joined the Carmelites. Mrs Roddy's daughter was a teacher in the order. It was not so much that she would never give her mother grandchildren that caused the greatest upset, but the economics of it where all a nun's earnings go straight back into the convent. Mrs Roddy used to wring her hands.

'That money's mine,' she would shout, 'for feeding and clothing her all those years. The church has no right to it!'

Then her daughter went peculiar. We only noticed because they sent her home for a week on holiday, and we thought that was unusual, but it was around the time they were relaxing the rule. Nuns were appearing on the streets with skirts that let them walk easily, skimming their calves instead of the pavement.

During that week she got her cousin to perm her hair, on account of the new headdress. She assured her that it was all right because even nuns had to look groomed now their hair showed at the front, and every night she continued to lead the family in the joyful mysteries.

'I'll tell you Mrs Mac, I'm worn out with all the praying since our Delcia's been back,' her mother would confide to mine as they passed quickly in the street, while her daughter muttered 'God bless you' to no one in particular and with a vague smile into the air.

But indoors, she borrowed her mother's lipstick, deep red because Mrs Roddy still had the same one from before the war. That was when they thought she was going a bit far, when they saw her outmoded, crimson mouth chanting the rosary. She drove her family mad. She had tantrums and kept slamming doors. Then they saw her out in the street asking to be taken for rides on Nessie Moran's motorbike. Everyone said she had taken her vows too young. She crammed all those teenage things she never did into that week. By the end of it they were relieved to send her back.

Her mother hated nuns. She did not mind priests half as much.

'At least they're human,' she would say. 'Well, half human. Nuns aren't people; they're not proper women. They don't know what it is to be a mother and they'll never be high up in the church. They'll never be the next Pope. They can't even say Mass. What good are they? They're stuck in the middle, not one thing or the other. Brides of Christ! They make me sick. Let them try cooking, cleaning and running a home on nothing. It would be a damned easier life I'd have if I'd married Christ, instead of that lazy bugger inside.'

But she was fond of the young priest at her church, a good-looking, fresh-faced man from Antrim who would sit and have a drink with them at the parish club.

'At least you can have a laugh with him,' she'd say, 'but that stuck-up lot, they're all po-faced up at Saint Ursula's. They're no better than any of us. I'm a woman, don't I know what their minds are like. We're no different. Gossipy, unnatural creatures, those ones are. Look what's happened to our poor Delcia after being with them.'

And then the convent sent Delcia home to be looked after by her family. An extended holiday, they called it, on account of her stress and exhaustion.

'They've used her up, now they don't want what's left over, so I've got her again. What good is she to anyone now? She can't look after herself. She can't even make a bloody cup of tea. How will she fend for herself if the order won't have her back? I'm dying, Mrs Mac, I can't be doing with her.'

My mother would tut and nod and shut the door.

'It's a shame. What sort of life has that poor girl had?' she would say indoors, shaking her head at the tragedy.

'I know she's gone soft now, but she was good at school. Her mam and dad thought she'd be something and now she's fit for nothing if the church can't keep her.'

In the evening we would hear Mrs Roddy shouting, 'Get in off the street!'

Finally they took her into a hospice and we heard no more about it, but Mrs Roddy always crossed the road to avoid

nuns. Once outside Lewis's a Poor Clare thrust a collection
box at her and asked for a donation. Mrs Roddy tried to take it
from her and the box was pulled back and forth like a bird
tugging at a worm. It was not the nun's iron grip, but the bit of
elastic which wrapped itself around her wrist that foiled Mrs
Roddy's attempt to redistribute the church's wealth.

'They're just like vultures,' she would say, 'waiting to see
what they can tear from your limbs. They're only happy when
they've picked you clean. Better hide your purse!'

At the collection on Sundays she sat tight-lipped and the
servers knew better than to pass the collecting plate her way.

'A vocation gone wrong' was what my father called Delcia
Roddy. He would shake his head from side to side and
murmur things like 'the shame' or 'the waste'. He had a great
deal of sympathy for her tortured soul. It was about this time
that I became tortured. He had no sympathy for me.

Sister Mercy's words had stung like gravel in a grazed knee.
At night I could hear them as her voice insisted, 'You cannot
fight God's plan,' and I would pray that God keep his plans to
himself.

'You must pray for a vocation,' she told us.

I gritted my teeth and begged his blessed mother to
intervene.

'I'll be worse than the Roddy girl,' I threatened, 'and look
what a disgrace she was.' Then, echoing the epitaph of W. B.
Yeats, I would point in the darkness and urge 'Horseman; Pass
by!'

It was rather the reverse of the chosen people who daubed
their doorposts and let the angel of death pass over, in order to
survive and play out God's plan. I wanted God's plan to pass
over.

'We are instruments in God's will,' Sister Mercy told us and
I did not want to be an instrument.

I knew if God had any sense he would not want me, but
Sister Mercy frightened us. Beatrice was the one headed for a
convent. She had made plain her intentions at the last retreat

when she stood up and announced to the study group that she was thinking of devoting her life to Christ.

'She may as well, there's nothing else down for her,' Nancy commented.

Yet Sister Mercy told us that it was the ones we did not suspect who had vocations, and she had looked around the room like a mind reader scrutinising the audience before pulling out likely candidates.

The convent terrified me; the vocation stalked my shadow like a store detective. One day it would pounce and I would be deadlocked into a religious life, my will subsumed by one greater than I. Up there was a rapacious appetite which consumed whole lives, like chicken legs. I dreaded that I should end up in a place where every day promised the same, the gates locked behind me and all other escape sealed off. It wasn't that I had any ambitions for what I might do, but I could not happily reconcile myself to an existence where the main attraction was death. I dreaded hearing God's call.

'He can spend years. He can wait. God is patient.'

I decided that I would have to exasperate him, and fast.

Down at the Pier Head, pigeons gathered in thousands. The Liver Buildings were obscured by their flight when they all rose in unison like a blanket of grey and down. I never knew where my fear came from, but I was terrified of those birds. Harmless seagulls twice their size flew about me, followed the ferry out across the water to Birkenhead and landed flapping and breathless on the landing plank. Their screech was piercing, and they never disturbed me. Yet when I stepped out into Hamilton Square and saw the tiny cluster of city birds waiting, my heart would beat in panic. City birds who left slime where they went, their excrement the colour of the new granite buildings springing up. They nodded their heads and watched you out of the sides of their eyes. They knocked smaller birds out of the way and I had seen them taking bread away from each other. They were a fighting, quarrelsome brood, an untidy shambling army, with nothing to do all day but walk around the Pier Head or follow me through Princess Park and make my life a misery.

Once I was crossing for a bus just as a streak of them flew up into the air. I put my hands over my head, the worst fear being that one should touch my face, and I could think of nothing more sickening than the feel of one of these ragged creatures, bloated with disease; the flying vermin which flocked around the Life Assurance building, to remind us we were mortal.

A nightmare I had at the time was of being buried alive under thousands of these birds. They would make that strange cooing noise as they slowly suffocated me. Their fat greasy bodies would pulsate and swell as, satiated, they nestled down on to me for the heat my body could provide. Under this sweltering, stinking mass I would be unable to scream. Each time I opened my mouth it filled with dusty feathers.

Then my nightmare changed. Another element crept into my dreams. Alongside the pigeons crept the awful shape that was a vocation. It came in all colours, brown and white, black and white, beige, mottled, grey and sandy, as the different robes of each order clustered around me, knocking pigeons out of the way. They muttered snatches of Latin, bits of psalms, and rubbed their claw-like hands together like bank tellers. The big change in the dream was that they, unlike the pigeons, did not suffocate me, but slowly drew away, leaving me alone in a great empty space, that at first I thought was the bus terminal, but which Nancy Lyons assured me was the image of my life to be.

Her older sister read tea leaves and was very interested in dreams. Nancy borrowed a book from her.

'It says here that dreaming about water means a birth.'

'I was dreaming about pigeons, and then nuns.'

'Yeah, but you said you were down at the Pier Head, didn't you, and that's water.'

'I don't know if I was at the Pier Head.'

'Oh you must have been. Where else would you get all them pigeons?' Nancy was a realist. 'Water means birth,' she repeated firmly. 'I bet your mam gets pregnant.'

I knew she was wrong, I was the last my mother would ever have, she told me often enough. But Nancy would not be put off. The book was lacking on nuns, so she held out for the water and maintained that the big empty space was my future.

'There's nothing down for you unless you go with the sisters,' she said.

It was not because I lacked faith that I dreaded the vocation. I suffered from its excesses; it hung around me, watching every move, and passing judgement. I was a failed miserable sinner and I knew it, but I did not want to atone. I did not want the empty future I was sure it offered. Our interpretation of the dream differed.

Around this time I had a Saturday job in a delicatessen in town. I was on the cold-meat counter. None of the girls were allowed to touch the bacon slicer. Only Mr Calderbraith could do that. He wore a white coat and must have fancied himself as an engineer the way he carried on about the gauge of the blades. He would spend hours unscrewing the metal plates and cleaning out the bolts and screws with a look of extreme concentration upon his face.

His balding head put out a few dark strands of hair which he grew to a ludicrous length and wore combined across his scalp to give the impression of growth. Some of the girls said he wore a toupée after work, and that if we were to meet him on a Sunday we would not know him.

He used to pretend he was the manager. He would come over and ask customers solicitously if everything was all right and remark that if the service was slow, it was because he was breaking in new staff.

'Who does he think he's kidding!' Elsie said after he had leaned across the counter one morning. 'He couldn't break in his shoes.'

Shoes were a problem. I was on my feet all day, and they would ache by the time we came to cash up. I used to catch the bus from the Pier Head at around five-thirty, if I could get the glass of the counter wiped down and the till cashed. The managers and seniors were obsessed with dishonesty. Cashing-up had to be done in strict military formation. None of us were allowed to move until we heard a bell and the assistant manager would take the cash floats from us in silence.

Inside his glass office the manager sat on a high stool with mirrors all around him, surveying us. If any of the girls sneezed, or moved out of synch, another bell would sound and we would all have to instantly shut our tills while the manager shouted over the loudspeaker system, 'Disturbance at counter number four,' or wherever it was. Sometimes it took ages.

They never failed to inform us that staff were all dishonest. Not the manager, Calderbraith nor the senior staff, but the floor workers, and especially the temporary staff, the Saturday workers, because as they told us, we had the least to lose, and we were 'fly by nights' according to the manager, who grinned as he told us that.

I could not imagine anything there worth stealing. It was all continental meats and strange cheese that smelt strongly, the mouldier the better.

'Have you seen that bread they're selling?' Elsie said to me one Saturday.

'The stuff that looks like it's got mouse droppings on top?'

But people came from all over the city and placed orders.

One Saturday evening I was waiting for the next bus, having missed the five-thirty. My feet ached. The managers would not let you sit down. Even when there was not a customer in sight you were supposed to stand to attention. I took it in turns with Elsie to duck beneath the wooden counter supports and sit on the floor when business was slack. Whenever Mr Calderbraith was about, we both stood rigidly. He loathed serving customers.

'See to that Lady,' he would say, if anyone asked him for a quarter of liver sausage.

I had worn the wrong shoes, they had heels. Throughout the week I wore comfortable brown lace-ups, but at the weekend I wanted to wear things that did not scream 'schoolgirl'. But my mother had been right. I was crippled.

After a few minutes I leant back on the rail and kicked one

shoe off. My toes looked puffy and red. I put that one back and kicked off the other. It shot into the gutter. Before I had a chance to hop after it, a pigeon the size of a cat flopped down and stood between it and me. It looked at me, then slowly began to walk around the shoe. I was rigid, gripping the rail and keeping my foot off the pavement. Then the bird hopped up inside the shoe and seemed to settle as a hen might in a nest. It began to coo. I was perspiring. I would never be able to take the shoe from it, and even if I managed to I would not be able to put my foot inside it after that vile creature had sat in it. I was desperate. Suddenly, as if it sensed my fright, it flew up in the air towards me almost brushing my face with its wings, then it circled and landed squarely back inside the shoe. I did not wait. It could have it. I hopped away from the bus stop and limped towards the taxi stand. I reckoned I had just enough money to get a cab home. It would be all my pay for the Saturday, and I would not be able to go out that night, but I did not care. It would take me, shoeless, right to the front door and away from the pigeon.

Then, I thought it was my mind playing tricks, but I saw three shapes blowing in the breeze, veils flapping behind them. The Pier Head was so windy, I thought they might become airborne. They got bigger. I was certain that they flew. Soon they would be right on top of me. God was giving me a sign. The Vocation had decided to swoop after so long pecking into my dreams. Three silent figures, as mysterious as the Trinity, crossed the tarmac of the bus terminal. I could not take my eyes from them. They seemed to swell the way a pigeon puffs out its chest to make itself important. They were getting fatter and rounder like brown and cream balloons. Carmelites. I could not stay where I was, I had to escape. Some people moved to one side as I hobbled to a grass verge. I tripped on the concrete rim of the grassy area and caught my ankle. As I put my hand down to catch myself, several birds pecking on rubbish rose into the air just in front of me, and I thought for one deluded second that I was flying with them as the white sky span and I tumbled over. Only when my head came level with a brown paper carrier bag did I smell the grossly familiar scent of cold meats.

'Young lady, are you in some sort of difficulty?'

The voice of Mr Calderbraith pulled me out of my terrified stupor. I lifted my head and came eye to quizzical eye.

'Whatever is wrong with you? Can't you walk properly? Good heavens, what has happened to your shoe? Have you been in some sort of accident?' He straightened up and looked around desperately.

'Tell me who did it,' he insisted, 'check that you still have your front door keys.'

I raised myself up on one knee and obediently opened my bag. Everything was intact. Mr Calderbraith's eyes opened wide.

'I really don't understand . . .' he began.

Behind him I could see a triangle formation moving against the empty sky. The three sisters seemed to glide inside its rigid outline like characters in the medals people brought back from Fatima. Behind them flapped wings, veils, patches of brown, and feathers. Dark against the white sky they enveloped me, just as my dream had forewarned. I could not speak. My hands shook.

'What is it? Have you seen the culprit?'

I nodded, still struggling to rise.

'They often work in a gang, these hoodlums,' Mr Calderbraith continued. 'Oh, yes. I've watched enough detective programmes to know how they operate.' He glanced from side to side furtively.

'They've probably left their look-out nearby. Acting casual.' He glowered menacingly at any passers-by.

They were closing in behind Mr Calderbraith. They peered over his shoulder. Inhuman, they cheeped and shrieked. I could not understand a thing. Mr Calderbraith was nodding at me, his head pecked up and down. I reached out and pointed and a dreadful magnetic force pulled me towards them. I was on my feet in seconds.

Mr Calderbraith turned round and saw the three. He shrank away from them.

'You don't mean these, surely?' he said. 'That is stretching it. Have you been drinking? Tell me, were you on relief at the spirit counter?'

'She's had a bit of a fall,' a passer-by said.

'I think she fell on her head,' Mr Calderbraith nodded.

Then turning to the spectators who had crossed from the bus shelter, he reassured them that everything was all right.

'She is one of my staff members, it's all under control, I know this young lady. Let me deal with it.'

The smallest nun, a tiny frail sparrow, hopped lightly towards me, concern marked by the way she held her head on one side. Her scrawny hand scratched at the ground and she caught up a carrier bag that lay askew on the grass verge. The others clucked solicitously. Then there was a stillness. All fluttering seemed to stop. She handed the bag to me and I took it as my voice returned to tumble out in hopeless apologies while my face burned. Hugging the carrier bag to me, I stumbled towards a taxi which pulled up. I fell inside and slammed the door. I breathed deeply, thinking that I was going to cry from embarrassment. Out of the back window I could see the nuns standing with Mr Calderbraith who was looking about as if he had lost something.

'Where to, love?' the driver asked.

My voice was thin and wavery as I told him. I put my head back and sighed. Only when we were half-way along the Dock Road did I realise that I was still hugging the bag. I peered inside. It was stuffed with pieces of meat, slivers of pork and the ends of joints, all wrapped up in Mr Calderbraith's sandwich papers. There was a great big knuckle of honey roast ham. It would be a sin to waste it.

Then I started to laugh. I couldn't stop. Tears ran down my face. Sister Mercy had told us that we had to be spotless, our souls bleached in God's grace. We had to repent our past and ask Him to take up residence in our hearts. I put my hand into the bag and drew out a piece of meat. I crammed it into my mouth. I swallowed my guilt, ate it whole and let it fill my body. As I chewed I wondered at how I still felt the same. I was no different, only I had become the receiver of stolen goods. I wondered if Mr Calderbraith would be nicer to me? I would not be surprised if he let me have a go on the bacon slicer next weekend.

'Are you all right love?' the driver asked.

I was choking on a piece of meat.

'I'm fine,' I coughed, scarcely waiting long enough before I stuffed another bit into my mouth. I ate with frenzied gulping sounds. When I looked up I saw the driver watching me in his mirror.

'God but you must be starving,' he said.

I nodded.

'Well you're a growing girl. You don't know how lucky you are to have all your life in front of you.'

'I do, I really do,' I told him as I pulled another bit of meat off a bone with my teeth. Between mouthfuls I laughed. My one regret was that it wasn't a Friday – I could have doubled my sin without any effort. Then I realised that I had subverted three nuns into being accomplices. What more did I need?

I slapped my knees and howled. God would have to be desperate to want me now.

As the taxi pulled up outside the house I saw the curtains twitch. I did not know how I was going to explain losing my shoe, but nothing could lower my spirits, not even hiccups.

Geology

STEVE McGIFFEN

YES, I LEFT him after we been married thirty-two years and raised four children. We have a boy over to Atlanta is in the fire service another one got a farm machinery business right by here and the youngest one at school studying for a lawyer. They all done alright when you think of what we come from. Our folks, neither mine nor Cal's, didn't have nothing, they was dirt farmers really but won't hear me say it to just anyone, and I will say Cal's folks did have more learnin about them than most of our kind, of the kind we come from. But I was talkin about the children and I didn't say about our baby, little Susie who is just seventeen years old and of course still workin hard at High School and wantin to make somethin of herself in the world and like Cal says not just some dumb wife for some dumb farmer. Cal always was strong on that and now I think, whatever happens now, Susie will want to please her Pa more than ever. She was always for pleasin him, though, and wouldn't come and see me or speak to me when I tracked her down after I left. Course, I never did mean to leave permanent.

I could not stand any more his awful moods. I swear he would go for a week without speaking and he would just set, by the fire sometimes if it was winter and cold out, or in front of the TV, you know but not watching it and just starin and starin. It was like living with a ghost. Sometimes he would go out down to the lake there and just kind of set and watch it. He wouldn't speak to a soul and everyone felt just the same, he was just like a ghost. Except Susie didn't seem to mind, not that he spoke to her more than anyone else, but sometimes he wouldn't've spoke all day, or longer than that, yes, much longer than that. And Susie would put away her books or she would come in from a night out if it was weekend and she would say 'Goodnight, Pa' and lean over him and kiss his forehead and he would reach out and take her hand, give it a little squeeze and off she would go, not a word, but that taking her hand – the rest of the world, including his wife of thirty-two years could 'Goodnight Pa' him until Hell freezes and we wouldn't get nothin, only Susie. I ain't sayin that he shouldn't have given her no favourin, you understand, I was pleased he could see his way to steppin out of it a little for her, because she couldn't have taken him ignoring her and just starin past her like his wife and sons and friends had to take it or shove it. Then he would just come out of it, he didn't exactly start to act like he was runnin for Santa Claus, but he would speak and put down the paper and even smile when he saw Susie come in from school.

Yes, sir, all this time he kept on with his job and so far as I know he would speak to people there, you can't hardly be sheriff and not speak to anyone now can you? But he wouldn't never let me near his office even when we was like two lovebirds, which we always was, and that always seemed to me right and proper for a man so I wasn't about to barge in on him now.

I could've spoken to someone down there and I think I would've if things had just carried on gettin worse, but it would've taken a lot. I'd've felt kind of mean going behind his back and then what was there to say? If he was doing the job alright why should they care how he treats his wife and children? Well, it wasn't as if he ever raised a hand to me though I swear some nights I would've been glad to see him do it, to show he knew I was there.

Yes, sir, these are some of his rocks here but the best ones he drove over to the County Museum on the day he tried to take his own life. I suppose he wanted them to be kept for other folks to see and learn from, but it isn't as if I wouldn't have taken care of them and I guess I would've given them to the museum myself after a while, but I might've kept some just to remind me of him. Yes, sir. I know you're too polite to ask outright but I did love him ever since I was a young girl of maybe fourteen and I love him still and I'm sorry to cry 'n all but I wish I hadn't walked out on him like that and I'm sure Susie hates me for it and I don't blame her but I just want him back now and don't care if he never says another word so long as he gets well and comes back to us all and I wish you'd tell him so because I don't know if he really can't hear or if he's just that way because it's me that's talkin.

You a policeman? Will Sheriff Smith get well? Well I sure hope so. No, sir, that day we was fishin down at the water, me an a couple of other boys. You must know who they was. Then why you askin? Yes, just the three of us, and they was the other boys. Well Marty is older than us, nearly eighteen, but George the same age. Fifteen day before Christmas. George about the same, yeah. We was fishin about quarter of a mile from the Sheriff's cabin. We always used to fish there and if we knew the Sheriff was around we used to one of us go up to there an take a can an ask him for a drink o water. No, we wasn't scared of askin the Sheriff, he always treated us good. Yes, white boys liked the Sheriff too and some white boys, boy called John Marner an his friends, they had a fishin spot the other side of the cabin an used to pull the same trick on the Sheriff as we was always doin, but I didn't see any sign of those boys that mornin.

Well it wasn't really like you say trick an it's a bad thing you doin to somebody. We wouldn't do nothin bad at the Sheriff. I suppose because we liked him but, well, he was the Sheriff, he wasn't somebody you'd choose to sass or nothin. Only reason I say trick is because we always done it the same way an everybody knew what was goin on. We always asked Sheriff Smith for a can of water but he never did give us no water. Sometimes he'd give us coffee an if the other boys weren't with you you'd run back down to the lake with that can of coffee so's it didn't get cold. But mostly he'd give us juice or lemonade. And everyone knew because well, if we'd really wanted water we could just've drunk it straight out of the lake.

It was real hot, yes. I don't know the time, sir, but it weren't that early but not yet time to go to get somethin to eat. No, we'd go back to George's house because that was nearest an our Mas don't like us to stay down there all day without hearin from us, so we'd go up to George's an George's Ma or his growed up sister would fix us somethin to eat and then we'd go back to the lake or maybe do somethin else but I would call my Ma from George's let her know I ain't fallen in the lake, course Marty didn't have to bother 'cos he's nearly growed up too but he used to come anyway cos he had the hots for George's sister. Sorry, Ma. No, Ma.

We saw the Sheriff's car come down the road to his cabin an Marty said to me to get a drink. But I wouldn't go at first cos it always seemed to be me that had to go and it was so hot I was happy just lyin there in the shade with my line in the lake an if I was thirsty just to take a drink from the lake. But the others are both bigger than me. Yes, sir, I did, but George ain't older'n me, just bigger. So it ended with me havin to go up to the Sheriff's cabin. Maybe a half-hour or a little more. Oh, it don't take any time to walk or run up to the cabin but cos I didn't want to go an it was hot'n all I guess I went about as slow as I could. Maybe an hour altogether from when we saw his car to when I got to the cabin. I have to guess that because not one of us didn't have a wristwatch.

Well, I walked right up to the cabin door an I knocked just like I always do but they weren't no reply. No, sir, I wouldn't say it surprised me none cos he could've been out back or somethin. But I knocked again an that's when I heard the noise. Sure, it was a strange noise an it frightened me, sir, I ain't never gonna forget it. Well, first there was a crash which is I guess when he kicked that chair over, then a kind of a yell

– like he was surprised but that don't seem right cos it ain't as if he didn't know what he was goin to do. No, sir.

Yes, sir, I sure was scared, I knew somethin funny was goin on in there but I didn't know what to do. I couldn't hardly go bargin in to the Sheriff's cabin but I didn't want to just walk away.

Sure, I wanted to help him if he was in some kinda trouble, but I don't know if I could say that was what I was mostly thinkin. Well, I guess I was kinda curious about what was happenin in there. No, sir, and I didn't want to go back without nothin cos I knew George an Marty would be mad at me.

No, sir, I don't know if I could describe the sound any better than that. Anyways, I went to look through the window of the cabin and there's the Sheriff hanging there from that rope, an then I didn't think at all, but I just ran to that door an kicked it down – yes, sir, it was bolted but it weren't locked properly, and I just kicked it down. An then I ran in there an didn't hardly know what to do but I just grabbed the Sheriff and tried to kind of hold him up.

No, sir, I don't think he was tryin to kick me away cos he took hold of my shoulders and he held on tight, but I don't think he hardly knew what he was doing, and I didn't know what the hell to do. Sorry, Ma.

The thing was I was holding him up there with all my strength so's the rope wouldn't cut into his neck or break it, I guess. I needed both arms an all my strength just to hang on to him. No, like I said, he weren't strugglin but he didn't hardly know what he was doin far as I could see an I'm standin there tryin to hold him up holding him right around the waist an Ma says to her friends the Sheriff ain't such a big man an if he had been a big man I wouldn't't've been able to hold him there and he would be dead now but he seemed big to me when I was standin there holding him up. And then Marty came.

Sure, Ma, yes, sir, Ma says the Lord made Marty do that so the Sheriff wouldn't die. Well, Marty an George was foolin around with the knife we keep down there – no sir, just for cleanin the fish when we catch 'em. They been foolin around with it an Marty got a bad cut on his arm, come up to the cabin cos he figured the Sheriff would know what to do or maybe he would take him up to the hospital. It weren't that bad though. Anyways, Marty's standin there in that doorway where I run in an left the door open and his arm's bleedin but when he sees me and the Sheriff he forgets all about that an runs in an takes that fishin knife an cuts right through the rope while I carry on holdin him up there. Yes, sir, that was the blood they found on the Sheriff's clothes. Weren't his blood, was Marty's blood. Marty tried to ask the Sheriff where were the keys of his car, but he couldn't get no answer made any sense.

Well, sure, I can remember it all right, he just kept makin this gurgling noise but I thought he was tryin to say, sorry boys, like he was sorry he done tried to do that while we was around to see it. Yes, sir, it sure was awful, an if I live to a hundred I hope I never see an awfuller thing.

No, that was OK, because the keys was in the car all the time, an so we carried him out there an laid him on the back seat an Marty drove him down to the hospital an told them what happened. No, Marty wouldn't let me go along because somebody had to go tell George an so I don't know what happened at the hospital.

I had the knife for the fishin is all. They ain't much I can tell you Bobby ain't already told you. Well, sure, I went up to the cabin get a bandage for my arm an there it was, the door open an the Sheriff hangin there rope aroun his neck an little Bobby holdin on to him like it was his life not the Sheriff's was on the line. So I run up there took out the knife cut the rope got my hands inside the rope around his neck an kinda loosened it, but I couldn't get it off so when I carried him out to the car the rope was still on there. Then I drove him down the hospital an then I guess you know what happened. No sir, I didn't speak to nobody bout it until I seen Officer MacKenzie down there when he ast me a lot of questions about what happened. No, sir.

★

Yes, Pa's been awful depressed about something now for around two years, but I really don't know what, because he would never speak to any of us about it. The final straw, I think, must've been when Ma left him. Well, I don't think she knew of anything else she could do. You see, he just would never speak about what was getting him down. He would either say nothing to anyone for maybe weeks, no one at home that is, or he would be something like back to normal. No, we were all strictly forbidden to go down to his work and one time when my brother Clifford went down there he just told him he was too busy to speak with him. Cliff said he all but had him thrown out of the office.

Sure we were close, he was my Pa, wasn't he? Well, I wish he had spoken to me about what was getting him down, but I don't really think he knew what it was himself. When I was a little girl he was so, well, he was such fun. I was awful spoiled having three big brothers but Pa spoiled me most of all of them. So I guess there must just be some illness in his mind. No, sir, Miss Evans one of my teachers, she was awful kind about it and she says sometimes people try to do that it isn't really that they want to die at all but kind of they're asking for help. I don't see he'd try to hang himself out there miles from town or that he could've known those boys were around, but I know I want to help my Pa and we'll all be doing our best for him.

Yes, thinking about it there is one other thing. A couple of years ago, I know just when it was because it wasn't long after my fifteenth birthday, I got an obscene letter sent to me through the mail. It was pretty horrible and I decided I ought to tell Pa about it, more because he was the Sheriff than because he was my father. Well I sure regretted it. I mean, it was a horrible letter but the way Pa reacted, he went white as a ghost and started to kind of shake all over. I said it's OK Pa, it don't mean anything, just some poor guy with a sick mind who gets his kicks writing dirty letters to girls. Anyway, Pa calmed down pretty quick but I've thought about it since he done what he done and I think it wasn't long after that he started to have his times when he just would not speak.

187

Well, sir, it's kind of embarrassing. No, we burnt it. No, it didn't threaten me at all, it just said stuff that he would like to do to me, I'm sure you can imagine. Well, yes, I guess that kind of letter is always threatening but like I said, you got the idea the guy had gotten his kicks just by writing the stuff. No, Pa certainly took it more seriously than that and he wouldn't let me anywhere on my own, even to school and back for a few weeks after that. Then he suddenly seemed to forget all about it and things just got back to normal. For me, that is, but then like I said the trouble started for Pa.

No, Ma's crazy to say that. I was angry with her when she left him but I always understood why she felt she had to do that and well, that's all in the past now. Family's got to stick together to help Pa.

Cal Smith was the last person you'd expect to do anything like this. I mean, I worked with him for thirty-five years, yes, thirty-five years, since he moved up here from Mississippi and took the job with the Police Department. Sure, he's been down for a while now and I knew things weren't right at home, but, hell, he was doing his job as well as ever and I didn't want to pry into things was none o my business.

Sure, that election they was all the trouble did kind of get Cal down, but I don't see that can have had anything to do with this, it seems a long way back. Well, no, I reckon things at home was getting to him, maybe all his kids being more or less grown made him feel old. Well, no sir that don't make a man want to end his life, but I guess they must've been some sickness in Cal's mind made him get things all out of proportion.

Well, sure, I'll answer any questions you like, but I really don't see what this has to do with what you've come here to find out about. Folks round here won't like it if you go dragging up things most of us would rather forget.

Fact was we hadn't had a murder in this county for five years until about three years ago they was a coloured boy, Ronald Gillespie, popular kind of boy they all used to call him Gillie, they just found him dead down by the roadside, just outside town. They is a closed-down old gas station out there and they found that boy, boy of about twenty-one, strong as an ox and fastest runner in the county, they found him all cut to pieces with an axe. It weren't pretty. They was talk some of the boys hadn't taken to Gillie because he had a mouth too big. But I couldn't ever see it. Some coloured folks said they'd seen Gillie get into a car with some white boys earlier that day, but they couldn't identify them and all they could say bout the car was it had South Carolina plates so we figured it must've been someone from out of town, someone didn't know Gillie, maybe just maniacs done that murder for the hell of it. That would've been the last of it but Cal had to come up for re-election and one of those loudmouth types, one of these negro clergymen in town here name of Billington, he tries to stir people up against Cal, saying he didn't do nothin to find the murderers cos he knew who they were and they was sons of rich white folks. Now, I know this kind of thing used to happen but it just ain't the case any more. Cal's had more trouble from whites saying he's soft on them . . . well, sir, you know he's been called a nigger-lover and all, but he's always had most white votes and he's had most coloured folks' votes too.

No, I don't believe they was any truth in any of these allegations. And neither did the coloured folks because Billington could only get a few hundred of them not to vote for Cal and he won the election easy enough, even if a little less easy than he'd done in previous years. Yes, I believe they was some names mentioned as suspects but there weren't no evidence. Yes, I believe they was Alan Millett and Charlie Page, but like I say, they both had water-tight alibis and the case against them is closed. I don't see it's got anything to do with Cal trying to kill hisself. What the hell could it have to do with that?

Yes, I do. Cal was here all night and, apart from one or two officers coming in and out he would've been the only person here apart from the prisoner. I'm sorry to laugh, but I sure do remember the prisoner. Least, I never saw him but I

189

remember what Cal said to me bout him fore he went off duty that morning. He was a coloured boy from out of town and an educated boy too, studying up at UPenn I believe, and it turns out he's on a trip down to Florida to see his folks and he decides to spend the night here camping out down by the lake. Well, when he is setting up for the night two officers is passing and they spot him from the road and they go down to investigate and he starts sassing them so they haul him in for vagrancy and suspicious behaviour. But the Sheriff decides it's all been a little over-reaction all round and next morning, real early, he lets the boy drive on out of town.

Well, no, I don't suppose the officers were too pleased about any of it, but they probably never should've hauled that boy in. They ain't no law in this state against camping out over night. Thing is, why I laugh, turns out this boy's got just the same interest as Cal, that is what he is studying at school is all about rocks and Cal sure did love to collect rocks.

Who the hell are you anyway? Yeah, well let's see your badge.

OK, but I don't see why I have to answer questions about something I already answered more questions on than I can count. I was home having dinner with my folks and some of their friends at the time the coroner says Gillespie died. There were two state congressmen there and a number of businessmen and their wives. They were all respectable people and they all vouched for me and Alan too.

Well, yes, there was some question at the inquest what time we arrived home but in the end we established to the satisfaction of the jury that we were home well before the incident could've take place. Well, people like Billington will always cause trouble. He had us tried and hung in his own mind. It was not either of our cars he got into. It had out of state plates. We both had solid alibis. I don't know anything about that. You'd better ask Billington.

No, sir, I did not say that Millett and Page killed Gillespie, only that the inquest did not establish that this was not the case. Firstly, the jury was all white and so of course was the coroner. This was the subject of considerable protest at the time. Secondly, and more importantly, crucial pieces of evidence were left out of consideration. The fact that Millet and Page had an alibi, even accepting its legitimacy, for the time of death does not prove that they were not instrumental in that death. It can take a man an awful long time to bleed to death. It was accepted that Gillie had been dumped in a nearby wood and had dragged himself to where he was found. No one understands why he didn't make it that extra few yards to the roadside, but maybe his strength just gave out. In any case, he was attacked in the wood and may have taken several hours to get to the gas station where he died. This is a blindingly obvious fact but one which was not adequately addressed at the hearing. Millett and Page had no adequate alibi for earlier in the day, only saying that they were driving around in Page's car, that they visited various places, all of which admittedly they can verify, but none of which proved that they were not also in that wood at the time Gillie was brutally attacked. Yes, sir, I am bitter about it. I've lived to see a time when the Negro can stand up for himself in this country and I want to see our young men and women, fine young men like Ronald Gillespie, being able to take their rightful place in the world without falling foul of some bloodthirsty lynch-mob.

That's what we're talking about here, a lynch-mob taking revenge on an uppity nigger had the effrontery to run faster than they could, a man who could've been anything in this world he wanted to be. I guess it will be a long time still in this country before coloured people get justice. I don't care if that sound like tub-thumping, it doesn't make it any less true. No, I don't say Sheriff Smith knows who killed Ronald, I only say he didn't do enough to find out. Yes, sir, it was a terrible tragedy and you can tell the Sheriff he has my best wishes and I hope the Lord will go with him. It wouldn't be decent or Christian at this time not to say to you, sir, the Sheriff and I have had our differences but I believe for all that and without taking back a word of what I said when I opposed his re-

191

election, that Sheriff Smith is a good man who tries to be fair
and righteous but what he's asked to do maybe isn't always
fair or righteous. As to that, I guess the Lord will have the last
word on all of us.

Yes, sir, I did. I was driving down from here to Florida where I
have a married sister. It was the beginning of the vacation and I
wanted to take a couple of weeks out before I started this job. It
was coming dark and I saw that lake. I figured I would be safe
enough, didn't even know there was a town nearby. I had a
small tent with me. I got right down by the lakeside and set
myself up for the night, but of course my car was much nearer
to the road. I tried to drive it as far down the track as I could
but the officers must've spotted it anyway. No, I wasn't too
concerned, you don't hardly think of that as redneck country.
Tell you the truth I was quite glad it was cops, it might've been
something worse. But I could see they didn't like the looks of
me and it didn't take a lot of guessing why. Anyway the papers
were all in order for the car, I knew I wasn't breaking any laws,
but something about the way they treated me really pissed me
off. I knew I should be as nice as pie but I guess I was a little
sarcastic with them. I can't remember just what it was I said,
but I know by the time I stopped being real polite I already felt
they'd decided they didn't want no nigger sleeping by their
lake. They searched me in a real aggressive way, then they sat
in their car, made me sit in the back, radioed to see if my car
was stolen or if they had anything else on me, and then told me
they were taking me in for vagrancy. Well, I was mad but I
knew better than to say anything impolite to those officers. I
did ask them when camping in the woods had become an
offence in that state and they said that they considered I was
behaving in a suspect manner and wanted to detain me until
they could establish the veracity of my documents. Well, no,
they didn't quite put it in those words but apart from a little
rough handling, nothing overboard though, they did everything by the book.

Oh, you could see straight away he didn't like it. He looked kind of weary and just told them to put me in a cell. You know it's a real old-fashioned set up down there and when I was sitting in the cell – I think they only had one or maybe two – I could hear everything that went on in the Sheriff's office, though not too clearly and I couldn't see the whole office. One of the officers had driven my car back into town and after a few minutes I heard them come back in and something heavy bang down on the floor or maybe a desktop, and one of the officers says, 'Here, Cal.' Was that the name? Yeah. 'Here, Cal,' he says, 'We found these in that boy's car.' Well, I could guess what they were, then I head the Sheriff say, 'You asshole' –that made me laugh because that was just what I was thinking but I hardly expected the same reaction from the Sheriff. Then he said, 'Get out of here see if you can find someone breaking the law instead of someone trying to get some sleep,' and off they went. I was pretty relieved – obviously the Sheriff wasn't too impressed with his men's work and, well, he'd talked about me, I don't know . . . yeah, he hadn't called me a nigger or even a boy or anything, I was just someone trying to get some sleep. It was like, welcome to the human race. I felt I would get fair treatment from that man, there was just something about him.

Anyway, nothing happened for maybe ten minutes or so then the Sheriff appears around the corner with my tools. Yes, sir, I'm a geology major and, well, I've always been kind of obsessed with the whole subject and if I'm going off for a vacation some place I haven't been before I'm going to take those tools with me and see what I can dig up. Wait a minute, I can show them to you. Here's the same tools here. I suppose the police officers thought they were for burgling or some-thing – in any case they didn't look like the kind of thing a black man from out of state should be driving around in the trunk of his car. But the amazing thing is, and this must have been the best stroke of luck I ever had, is that the Sheriff knew exactly what those tools were. I didn't know that at the time of course, all I saw was the Sheriff appear holding that bag of tools, but I knew he'd seen them and had sent the other officers away with what amounted to a reprimand, so I was feeling a

little more confident. Sheriff didn't sound exactly friendly
though. I suppose he blamed me almost as much as his men for
interrupting his night and then again, he wouldn't want to
give anything away. So he says to me, 'What the hell are
these?' I told him what I just told you, that I was a geologist.
He looked sceptical, but I thought he was kind of putting on an
act. Then he went away again, without saying anything, but
he came back not long afterwards with a wooden box which
was obviously heavy. He opened the box up and says, 'Well
Mr Geology Major, what's that?' I look at it and I say, 'It's a
box crystal of feldspar, the most common mineral in the
earth's crust, known as orthoclase.' He stood there holding
that rock and looking at me and then he broke into a real broad
smile, then he bursts out laughing and I look at him and I laugh
too. He says, 'Had you had any supper when those, when the
officers picked you up?' and I said 'No, sir.' Then he went
away and came back with coffee and sandwiches and apple pie
and we sat up most of the night talking. Well, about rocks of
course. No, nothing else that I recall. Yes, he did seem happy
but then as the night went on he grew very tired and
eventually he said he was going to make some more coffee.
And he didn't come back for maybe two hours. When he came
back he had made some coffee and he said if I wanted I could
go when I'd drunk it or wait another couple hours get some
sleep. Well, I'd dozed off while he'd been away and felt OK so
I said, thanks I'd be on my way.

Well, yes there was. I couldn't identify it at the time but
during some of the time he was gone I could hear this strange
noise. Of course, it was very quiet there in that jail in the
middle of the night and the noise couldn't have been very loud
but I could hear it real clearly. Even so, I just didn't know what
it was, I was drifting in and out of sleep and in any case, it's not
the kind of sound you expect a white sheriff in a small southern
town to be making, but now I know what happened next day
I'd guess that what I heard was that man crying, just crying
quietly to himself out there all alone in his office.

★

I know they all been setting there with their questions they was Elizabeth they was Susie they was even the boys and they was half of the county police and the newspaper man and they was that fella I knowed he was a FBI man or I don't know because I can't think but I want to speak to all of them and I can't say a fucking word I feel my throat been sealed up for ever and now I don't want to die do I fucking Jesus want to die I just want to get well and tell Liza and Susie I'm so fucking sorry and will they ever forgive me and why did I do that when it was all so fucking long ago Jesus forgive me and Liza forgive me and Susie forgive me.

I wish I could tell them what I see an why I sees it but I know I won't ever be able to tell a livin soul an the Lord will know all about it anyhow dammit. They is the field and maybe it's the field where Judas hanged hisself but it ain't Judas swingin there no it ain't an it ain't me neither but I can see the fire too they is this crack in the field and I can see right down into the fire an I see this all the time when I's settin there an they's all sayin Pa, Pa, why won't you say a word just one little goddam word to us but I can only just hear them for the roarin an I can see the rocks an they's red-hot or white-hot flying into the air from the field and right in the middle this fire I can see that boy swinging, swinging just like we left him there with that fire lit under him.

But I can make it go away by thinking about the rocks. A volcano throws out two kinds of rocks, igneous rocks which are what people call lava and agglomerates which are rocks of all different kinds which the eruption has shattered and which are later consolidated. You get fragmentary rocks which people call volcanic ash and some of the lava gets aerated and becomes familiar as pumice. Agglomerates are made up of whatever kind of rocks exist in the area of the volcano prior to its formation and igneous rocks come in many kinds too. In fact nobody really knows how many kinds as there is much disagreement over the classification of these rocks. Alkali basalt, alkali gabbro, alkali dolerite, alkali syenite, then there are the ultrabasic rocks and andesite, anorthosite, trachyte, trachybasals, serpentine, rhyolite, aplite, appinite, basalt and syenite, and the pyroclastic rocks and the monzonites oh there are others I forget but if I concentrate I can see them being thrown up and formed in the fire and then I don't see that boy swingin there by his neck an I don't hear him when the fire gets to his feet an his legs an his balls an I don't hear me laughin an the other white boys laughin at that boy an all his pain an terror but it always comes back. I couldn't leave it behind in Mississippi an I couldn't leave it behind by livin right an I couldn't leave it behind by puttin my mind to those beautiful cold rocks that was made by fire an now they all cold and hard and you can touch them an they ain't got no pain an no hate. I thought I left it behind when I raise a white girl don't hate nor fear no-one least of all cos that person is a coloured person. I couldn't leave it behind by no penance an tellin myself we was just boys an didn't know no better because what do I do make sure my boys an their boys will? And then there it was all happenin again with those fucking crazies an they is got it in for Ronald Gillespie who is worth a hundred of their kind that always shit on my folks as much as they shit on coloured folks and would shit on their own grandmother if it made them think they was better then other people. So they steal or borrow a car an they got a gun and a axe and they make Gillie get in that car with them and they beat the shit out of him with the axe handle and they don't leave it there but one of them takes the axe and buries it in that man's flesh and they leave him there and probably throw the axe way out into the lake and that is the end of one man's life but they ain't no evidence and no chance of finding any because the coroner's court is rigged that way an because I get told by certain parties that my job is on the line and then they know what frightens me so they gets to Susie too. So in the end what can I do to pay that boy back or even to do my fucking job like it should be done? The truth is they ain't nothing and so I could not leave that dying boy hangin back there in Mississippi on that rope in that fire and go to him with my kisses and say now I paid you back cos I ain't paid nothin back. An I could not leave it behind in death because I knew when I hung on the end of that rope that I still hadn't paid my debt to that boy.

I knew I hadn't paid nothin when they brought that boy in that night just fuckin him around and they was dumb assholes didn't know a feldspar from their ass and I held that up an he told me right away what it was.

I can see it right here wherever this is an the faces of Elizabeth and Susie and all the other faces coming and going and them all wantin to know why I tried to take my life and me wantin to know how did he come back from Heaven or Hell to save my life and why did he do that was it forgiveness or was it so's I could go on suffering? I can see his face when we hanged and burnt him and the faces of the other white boys my face reflected in their crazy faces and then thirty-five years on my face in his face my tongue driven out through my lips my eyes bulgin out o my head and then he was there a young black boy looking like an angel an he embraced me like I was a woman like he was lovin me an just held me there an the pain went an I went an I could see the fires an the rocks bein spewed out of the volcano but they weren't no black man hangin there no more in the fire they weren't no rope an no pain an no hate, just the fire an the rocks beginnin their coolin down to those beautiful cold crystals

Baby Clutch

ADAM MARS-JONES

THE HALF-DOZEN Walkmans that used to live on this ward, bought by a charity for the use of the patients, were walked off with in a matter of days. The next batch, if the charity decides to replace them, will have to be chained down, I expect, like books in a medieval library.

At least the television in my lover's room has a remote control; that's something. There used to be a remote for every room on the ward, but one or two have also gone walkies. Replacing them isn't a high medical priority, though perhaps it should be. Life on this ward can seem like one big game of musical chairs, as if death, being spoiled for choice, will come by preference to the person with no flowers by the bed, with no yoghurts stashed away in the communal fridge, the person whose TV has no remote control.

A television looms larger in a hospital room than it could ever do in someone's home. There are so few excuses not to watch it: visitors, coma. Once I came in and was shocked to see a nurse comforting my lover. She was bending over him with a tenderness that displaced me. My lover was sobbing and saying, 'Poor Damon'; it was a while before he could make himself understood. The nurse wasn't amused when she found out Damon was a young man on *Brookside* who'd just been killed.

She'd have been even less amused if she'd known it was the first episode of *Brookside* my lover had ever watched, so he hadn't seen poor Damon alive. But I suppose it was the mother's grief having no actual content for him that let him share it so fully.

There's another television in the day-room, which even has a video recorder and a little shelf of tapes. The day-room also contains an eccentric library, *Ring of Bright Water* rubbing spines with a guide to non-nuclear defence and a fair selection of periodicals. My lover and I find ourselves listing the self-descriptions we find least beguiling in the small ads of the gay press.

'Antibody-negative,' is his first contribution. He resents the assumption that good health is as intrinsic to some people as blue eyes are to others, or the condition, so common on these pages, of being 'considered attractive'.

It's my turn. 'Straight-appearing.'

'Healthy,' is second in my lover's list.

'Discreet.' What kind of boast is that, after all?

'Healthy.' My lover can't seem to get over this little preoccupation of his, so I shut myself up, without even mentioning *non-camp*, *looks younger*, *genuine* or *first-time advertiser*.

Deep down I'm pleased by the silliness of the small ads, pleased to find any evidence that there are still trivial sides to gay life. More than anything, I want there to be disco bunnies out there somewhere, still. But I expect even the disco bunnies arc stoic philosophers these days, if only in their free time. What used to be the verdict on men who loved men – something about being locked in the nursery, wasn't it? There's nothing like being locked in a hospice to make the nursery look good.

We are having a respite between waves of my lover's visitors. Less than half-joking, I suggest that one of the nurses on the ward should function as a secretary, to make appointments and space the visitors out, to avoid these log-jams of well-wishers. I resent the brutal etiquette of hospital visiting, which means that a new visitor tapping hesitantly at the porthole instantly shuts down our intimacy. I try to be tactful, do some shopping in the area or talk to one of the other patients, but I doubt if I manage to be nice about it. Making myself scarce only encourages the other visitors to stay, to cling like leeches. I find the whole business of dealing with the visitors exhausting, and I'm not even ill.

Gently, taking care not to scare off his good fortune, my lover tells me that he is the only patient now on the ward who would benefit from a secretarial service like the one I am proposing. The other inmates have, at the most, two guests at a time. The difference may be one of character (my lover is agreed to be lovable); it may also turn out that the other patients have come back here so many times they have lost the ability to reassure their visitors, after which point the visits tend to dry up.

This is my lover's first major stay in hospital. Transfusions for anaemia don't count, even when he is there overnight. Everybody I come across refers to transfusions in the cheeriest possible terms ('just in for a top-up, are you?' is the standard phrase) though everybody also knows that transfusions can't go on for ever. That's an example of something I've been noticing recently, of how easy it is for people to rise above the fates of third parties.

I'm generally impatient with the visitors, but I make exceptions. I'm always glad to see Armchair, for instance. My lover knows so many Davids and so many Peters he gives them nicknames to tell them apart. Armchair is a Peter; other Peters are Poodle and Ragamuffin.

Armchair is, as advertised, reassuring and cosy, all the more comfortable for having one or two springs broken. Armchair is a fine piece of supportive furniture. When he phones the hospital to leave a message, he doesn't bother any more with his proper name; he just says Armchair. A nurse will come into the room and say, 'Someone called Armchair asks if it's all right to visit,' or, 'Armchair sends his love,' with a faint gathering of the eyebrows, until she's used to these messages.

Armchair is actually, in his way, my lover's deputy lover, or I suppose I mean my deputy. They met a month or two ago, while I was away, and they've slept together once or twice, but it's clear enough that Armchair would like More. It isn't a physical thing between them, exactly – my lover isn't awash with libido at the moment – but Armchair would like my lover to spend nights with him on a more permanent basis. Armchair would like to be a regular fixture at bedtime.

I wouldn't mind. It's my lover who's withdrawn a bit. But Armchair assumes I'm the problem and seems to think he's taking a huge risk by putting his hand on my lover's leg. My lover's arms are sore from the VenFlow, the little porthole the doctors keep open there, and his legs have taken over from them as the major pattable and squeezable parts. My lover's blood, beneath the porthole, is – as we know – full of intercepted messages of healing and distress.

Armchair looks at me with a colossal reproach. But can he really want to sit where I sit? Where I sit is sometimes behind my lover on the bed, wedging him as best I can during a retching fit, so that he is cushioned against the pain of his pleurisy. I hold on to his shoulders, which offer a reasonable guarantee of not hurting him. My medical encyclopaedia tells me that the pleura are 'richly supplied with pain fibres'. My lover has worked this out all by himself.

My lover threatens to give Armchair the yo-heave-ho. I tell him to be gentle, not to dismiss these comforting needs, and not only because Armchair too is richly supplied with pain fibres. I have my own stake in Armchair and Armchair's devotion. If Armchair stops being a fixture, I'll have to think long and hard about my own arrangements and my tender habit of spending as much time away from my lover as I possibly can. I do everything possible to look after him, short of being reliably there.

Whatever it is that ties us to each other, my lover and I, he is much too sensible to tug on it and see, once and for all, how much strain it will take. Much better to stay in doubt.

When I told my lover – he wasn't in hospital at the time – that I was thinking of spending half the week in Cambridge for a few months, he didn't say anything. It took him a while even to ask exactly how far away Cambridge is by train, and he seemed perfectly content when I said an hour and a bit – as if it counted as normal variation in a relationship, for one party to keep himself an hour and a bit away from the other. He didn't ask if I had some grand plan, like writing a textbook, which I think I mentioned once a while back as one of my ambitions. There's something very stubborn about his refusal to call my bluff.

He knows, of course, that part-timers don't have a lot of say in their timetables (part-timers least of all), so if I've managed to fit all my teaching this term into Monday, Tuesday and Wednesday, then I've been setting it up for months.

In Cambridge I stay in the flat of an actress friend who has a short-term contract with the RSC. She's staying with friends in London herself, and all she wants is for the place to be looked after. She warned me that she might come back for the odd weekend, but she hasn't shown up yet and I've stopped expecting her, stopped cleaning madly on a Friday and filling the fridge with fine things. So all I have to do is keep the place reasonably clean, water the plants and listen from time to time to her accounts on the phone of Barbican Depression and of understudy runs that the RSC potentates never stir themselves from the Seventh Floor to see. Her flat is very near the station, which keeps my guilt to a minimum. It's not as if I was holed up in Arbury or somewhere. I'm only an hour and a bit away.

What I do here, mainly, is take driving lessons. In anyone else, learning to drive – especially after thirty – would be a move so sensible no one would notice it. With me it's different. It's a sign of a secret disorder, a malady in its own right, but only I know that.

I've always set my face against learning to drive. I've used public transport as if I'd taken a pledge to do nothing else and have always been careful not to accept lifts unless I have to. You get superstitious about favours when you can't pay them back, not in kind. If someone who has offered me a lift stays on soft drinks, I find myself refusing alcohol as if that was a helpful contribution to the evening. It's probably just irritating. I dare say people think, if he likes his drink so little he'd make a handy chauffeur, why doesn't he get his bloody licence?

I seem to have based a fair bit of my character around not being a driver. Perhaps that's why I was so disoriented when I walked through the door of the driving school that first time. It felt like learning to swim, and this the deep end. But in all fairness, the air in there would give anyone's lungs pause. All the instructors smoke away at their desks when they're on phone-duty or doing paperwork, and there's a back room that's even smokier, with a sink and a dartboard and a little fridge, not to mention a tiny microwave and a miniature snooker table.

I must say I admire the way the driving school draws a new pupil smoothly into apprenticeship. I was given a time for a two-hour consultation with an instructor, who would suggest a test date. I was certainly impressed, and mainly with myself, the competent me they were hypothesising so suavely. It'll take more than suavity to convince me that I'm viable as a driver, but I signed up for my session of consultation just the same, rabbit paralysed by the headlights, unable to disobey the order to climb into the driving seat.

Now that I'm familiar with the place, I can't help thinking that BSM stands for British School of Macho. There's only one woman in the place, who does paperwork the whole time and smiles at me with a forlorn sweetness. The rest of the staff, I imagine, conduct their job interviews in the pub, brusquely screening out non-drinkers, non-smokers, non-eaters of meat, non-players of pool, non-tellers of jokes. I imagine them rolling back with the candidate to the driving school after closing time for some cans of Special Brew, and I imagine them huddled outside the lavatory with their fingers to their lips, when he goes to relieve himself, listening for the clinching chuckle when he sees the HIGH FIRST TIME PASS RATE sign stuck up inside the lid. I imagine them giving each other the thumbs-up sign. And only then, after the candidate emerges from the lavatory, do I imagine them asking, 'By the way . . . can you drive?'

But somehow Keith, my instructor, slipped through their net. He does all the manly things, but he isn't a man in their sense, not at all. He's not a bachelor, but he's not by a long way a family man either, and he moved out of a perfectly nice house to live in a field.

He's a pleasantly runty fellow, brought up in a Barnardo's Home, and he still has a boyish spryness although he's in his late forties. To get from the driving school to the car, or back again at the end of the lesson, he bolts across Bridge Street, whatever the traffic's like, nipping through the smallest gaps between vehicles.

We set off in the driving school's sturdy Metro. It's white, but very dirty, so someone has been able to trace the words ALSO AVAILABLE IN WHITE in dust on the coachwork. The side mirrors are both cracked, and one is even crazed. I promise myself that I'll reward the car, if and when I finally pass, and not the examiner as is customary. I'll splash out on some replacement fixtures.

Towards Keith I have absurdly mixed feelings. I trust him blindly, and have for him the sort of disproportionately solid affection that goes with the analyst's couch more often than the steering-wheel. I admire his self-control. It's not that he doesn't get irritated – when I don't lose enough speed, for instance, approaching a roundabout – but he calms down right away. It's as if he was offering me an example, in terms of temperament, of the use of the gearbox, and how to lose momentum as efficiently as possible. When I stall, he says, 'Never mind, re-start,' without any hint that he's disappointed in me. As with any indulgent parental figure, I have an urge to test his patience to the limit, to make sure that he cares underneath it all.

Once the car ran out of petrol on Queen's Road, but all I could think of when I lost power was that Keith had withdrawn his faith in me, and was overruling my accelerator with the brake on the passenger side. 'Are you braking?' I cried, and he said, 'No, I'm scratching my arse as a matter of fact,' before he realised I wasn't messing him about. We weren't far from the driving school, but he's so little of a walker that he insisted on staying put. We sat there, while his eyes flickered between the windscreen and his multiple mirrors, waiting for one of the other school cars to come by and give him a lift to the petrol station. No one came, and at last, with the night dying, we had to walk after all. But I was so pleased not to have made the mistake myself that I let slip a precious opportunity for mockery – which is pretty much Keith's natural language – and I didn't tease him at all. It was nice to be the one doing the forgiving.

Alongside the exaggerated trust I feel a sharp submerged resentment towards Keith and a desire to do something atrocious, like run someone over on a crossing, while he's taking responsibility for me. In reality, he would put the brake on in a second, but I imagine myself unfastening my seat-belt after the impact and walking away, never traced for some reason though the driving school has my details, and leaving Keith to deal with the consequences.

Sometimes he sets out to provoke me, as if he wanted to bring the crisis on. He murmurs, 'Closer, son, just a little closer, and you're mine,' when a child is playing too close to the road and remarks on the economic advantage to parents of having a child wiped out sooner rather than later, before too much money has been spent on it. But I know this is just his style of cussedness, the same style that makes him answer 'no' in the back room of the driving school to the question, 'Got a light, Keith?' even when he's busy smoking away. It seems to be his solution, as a member of the artificial tribe of driving instructors, to the problem of how to be popular, without being despised for wanting to be liked.

Keith doesn't ask why I want to learn to drive. He takes it for granted, like everybody else, that I should, though in that case he should at least be curious about why it's taken me so long to get round to it. Even if he asked, I don't think I'd tell him my own theory on the subject: that it's to do with control, and also with risk. Anything that gives me the feeling of control is obviously going to come in handy at the moment, whether or not it's a sort of control that I have historically had any use for, but I think I'm also giving myself an education in risk. Being a pedestrian, being a passenger, isn't so very safe – and rattling around on a bicycle, as I do, isn't safe at all – but behind the wheel of a car you have a different relationship with the risks that you take.

I try not to keep secrets from my lover, but I don't talk a lot about what I do in Cambridge. I'm superstitious about that. I seem to think that if I talk to him more than vaguely about Cambridge, the seal will be broken and I'll start talking about him to the people I meet in Cambridge. For the whole cock-eyed arrangement to work, I need to think of the railway line from London to Cambridge as an elaborate valve, which allows me to pass from one place to another but strips me each time of my mental luggage and preoccupations.

The ward is full of its own life and I don't think my silence shows. The patients tend to keep their doors open so as to make the most of whatever passes along the corridors. The staff don't tell you when someone has died, but at least if your door is open someone comes along and says, with an apologetic smile, 'Let's just close this for a moment.' I expect that other people do what I do and peek out of the window in the door, which has horizontal bars of frosting so that I can't be seen, with any luck. I try to work out, from how long it takes for the trolley to make its collection, who it is that's inside it.

I'm sure I'm not the only one making calculations, though it's not a subject that comes up a great deal in conversation at the regular Tuesday tea parties. Then the focus of attention tends to be the chocolate cake brought in every week by an ex-patient, the offering that is richest in symbolism as well as in calories, which somehow always gets finished. Even my lover puts in his few bites' worth.

There's just one man on the ward who's in a different category, a private patient who's recovering from a heart attack in a room that is costing his firm, or BUPA, £210 a day, not including the phone. He takes only short walks as yet, but sooner or later he'll come to the tea party or twig in some other way to what the problem is with everyone else in the ward. Once he asked my lover why he thought he had come down with this particularly nasty pneumonia. My lover just scratched his head, as if it had never occurred to him to wonder. But it's only a matter of time before the cardiac patient or his wife see two men holding hands. They'll be on that expensive telephone to BUPA right away, demanding to know why someone with a bad heart but otherwise good character has been sent to spend his convalescence in Sodom.

The day-room plays host to other events as well as the tea parties. There are the art classes and the Wednesday morning discussion groups. Often there's someone over by the window on these occasions, making faces and emitting harsh sighs, but if so it's just a patient strapped into the emetic aqualung of pentamidine grimacing with controlled disgust as he inhales through a mask filled with bitter gas. Sometimes it's even a discharged patient, coming back for a few lungfuls of fly-killer to keep the bugs at bay.

Through the open doors, at various times of the week, come the visitors who aren't quite friends. There's a manicurist, for one, who asks her clients, when she's finished, if they'd like a dab of nail polish. She quietens any protest by saying brightly, 'Some does and some doesn't, so I always ask.' The first time she offered her services to my lover, she'd broken her wrist and had her arm in a sling. She couldn't work, obviously, so what she was really offering was manicure counselling, rather than manicure as such. My lover said, to comfort her, 'I bite my nails anyway,' and she said, to comfort him, 'Well, you do it very well.'

An aromatherapist comes round from time to time to rub essential oils into people. She doesn't rub very hard, and my lover longs for a real massage, but it isn't easy telling her to be merciless. His pentamidine drip has brought his blood pressure right down, and it's easy to see how she might get the idea he should be handled with care – seeing he needs to be helped if he wants to go as far as the lavatory, which is three steps away.

The aromatherapist takes away the pillows and blankets, and gets my lover to lie face down, with his feet where his head usually goes.

I get a shock every time I visit my lover after she has laid her too-gentle hands on him. It's as if there was some new symptom that could spin him bodily round, from end to end and top to bottom, and cast him down passive and aromatic, his eyes half-closed, on the crumpled sheets.

In the evenings, there are volunteers manning the hot-drinks trolley. They're noticeably more generous with the tea and the coffee than the domestics who push the trolley during the day, who can make visitors feel about as welcome as bedsores. With the evening trolley-pushers, I don't have to pretend that it's my lover who wants the drink if it's me who does really, and we don't scruple to ask for two if we're in the mood. The evening staff don't look right through me if I sit up on the bed next to my lover in my usual slightly infantile posture, facing the other way down the bed and hugging his big feet. This is the arrangement we've evolved now that so much of him is sore that a hug calls for as much careful docking as a refuelling in deep space. For him to see my face has become proportionally more important, as our bodies have had their expressiveness so much restricted.

My lover's soreness is dying down; I can tell because the fidgeting has gone out of his feet. I ask, in an interviewer's tenderly wheedling voice, 'What strikes you most about the whole terrible situation?'

Obligingly he answers, 'It brings out the best in people. And the worst.'

'What, you mean the best *and* the worst?'

'Both. The two.'

He's getting drowsy from the drugs he's on, as the chemical invasions of his body get the better of the surgical ones.

There's a hesitant knock on the door, and when I say to come in, this evening's volunteer stands in the doorway and asks what we want in the way of tea and coffee. I see him flinch when he spots the bag of blood on its wheeled stand, and the tube going into my lover's arm. But I notice too a quickening of interest in my lover, in the few seconds before our volunteer leaves the room to get the drinks from the trolley. Even before my lover murmurs, 'Isn't he gorgeous?' I have realised that the volunteer is very much my lover's type. He bears a passing resemblance to Joy Adamson's husband in the film of *Born Free*, a furry-faced scoutmaster on safari.

But now the volunteer returns with the teas and keeps his eyes turned down from the blood-drip. My lover has noticed his aversion and asks kindly, 'Does the blood bother you?'

'A bit.'

'Just a bit?'

'A lot.' Finally he admits that he sometimes feels faint. My lover looks affectionately at the sump of blood suspended above his arm and drawls, from the drastic languor of his medication, 'Just think of it as a big plastic kidney.' The volunteer resists the cue to look at the blood-bag, with the result that he continues to look deeply into my lover's eyes.

My lover pats the side of the bed. 'Do you have a moment to sit down?' I move over so that my lover can move his legs out of the volunteer's way, but my lover leaves his legs where they are, so the volunteer must make contact or else perch on the very edge of the bed.

The volunteer sits quiet for a moment, then clears his throat. 'Do you mind if I ask you a question?' he asks.

'Feel free,' my lover says. 'You're the guest.'

'Well, you're having a transfusion, and what I can never work out is, what happens to the blood you have extra, when you get somone else's on top of your own?'

'Yes, I used to wonder about that,' admits my lover. 'What happens is, they put another tube in your big toe, and drain the old blood out of there.' He gives the sheet a tug to loosen it from the bottom of the bed. 'Do you want a look?'

For the moment, the volunteer wants to go on looking at my lover's face.

'Don't you think you should?' my lover goes on. 'Shouldn't you try to overcome this silly fear of yours, if you're going to do the sort of work you're doing? Wouldn't that be the responsible thing?'

Mesmerised, the volunteer looks down at my lover's foot under the sheet. My lover pulls the sheet away from his foot. The big toe is pink and normal-looking. My lover looks startled and says, 'Oh, *Christ*, it must have come out, *now* we're in trouble, can you see it anywhere?' The volunteer casts his eyes desperately this way and that.

For some time I have been sending my lover signals of mild reproach about the wind-up job that is giving him so much pleasure; finally he gives in to them. He drapes the sheet over his feet again and says, 'Actually, since you ask, I pee away the surplus.' He smiles at the volunteer, who smiles back, at first incredulously and then with wonder at my lover's healthy sense of mischief.

My lover asks him please to tuck in the sheet round his feet, since it seems to have come adrift.

When the volunteer has gone at last, my lover says again, 'Isn't he gorgeous?' He looks thoughtful. 'But he can't be gay. That's never a gay beard. It's too overgrown.'

'I'm afraid you're right.'

'And you saw those corduroys.'

'Cords are a bad sign. Still . . .'

My lover sighs. 'At least he's not mutton dressed as lamb. He's mutton all right. But he has definite mutton appeal.' It sounds like an advert for stock cubes. 'He just can't be gay, that's all.'

My lover has a fantasy about living in the country with a vet who drives a half-timbered Morris Traveller, and this stranger comes close enough to set it off. A half-timbered Morris Traveller is apparently a car which even animals recognise as the appropriate vehicle for a person who will take care of them, so that they quieten down, even if their injuries are severe – or so my lover says – when they hear its engine note, some time before the car comes into view.

There is something I recognise as authentic in this fantasy of my lover's. It has about it the whiff of self-oppression, which we are as quick to recognise in each other as other couples, I imagine, are at spotting egg-stains on ties or lipstick on collars. The imaginary vet is classified by fantasy as virile and caring, in a way no man could be who loved other men, while my lover enters the picture as a damaged animal, a creature who can't hope to be treated as an equal but who accepts subordinate status as the price of tenderness.

All the same, the volunteer pays a number of return visits. He goes on holiday to Malta for a week and phones the hospital twice, so that the cordless phone – a treat that testifies to the volunteer's special status – is delivered to my lover's room, its aerial extended and gleaming. My lover has exercised once again his knack for being loved. The volunteer out of *Born Free*, meanwhile, is awarded a mark of privilege, a nickname: the Vet. Now my conversations with my lover have an extra layer of mysteriousness to nurses who hear me asking him if he's seen the Vet today. The Vet turns out to be older than he looks, in his mid-forties, so that he could almost be my lover's father. There's certainly something fatherly about the Vet when he sits on the bed and plays absent-mindedly with the hairs on my lover's leg. Sitting there, he might indeed be a father, trying to put off explaining the facts of life to an adolescent son, or a public-school housemaster explaining the meaning of confirmation.

One day I give my lover a bath; feeling clean, after all, is the nearest that people on this ward can come to feeling well. My lover is dizzy and unsteady on his feet, so I use a wheelchair to carry him back along the corridor to his room. I return the wheelchair to the bathroom right away, like a good boy, and the Vet must have arrived just while I was down the corridor, because when I come back I see that the door is closed. I look through the window and see the Vet perched on the bed, conducting his usual earnest conversation with my lover's leg. So I kill time doing a tour of the ward.

I offer to buy the patient in the room next to my lover's some of the ice-lollies he sucks when his mouth flares up, but he's well supplied at the moment, and his thrush doesn't even seem too bad. In fact he's unusually perky altogether. It was his birthday last week, and his ex-lover continued the custom they'd had by bringing him one practical present (a toasted-sandwich-maker) and one pampering present: a big bottle of essence of violets from Jermyn Street. I'm mean enough, by the way, to think that ex-lovers can afford to be generous; I look on them the way lifers in a prison must look on youngsters who are in for a short sharp shock.

The sandwich-maker was taken home, and the essence bottle was wrapped in a flannel and put by the basin, where a cleaner smashed it two days later. She burst into tears, and he told her not to worry about it, but in fact he wants to be reimbursed, and if the hospital doesn't have the relevant insurance he wants it taken out of the cleaner's wages. So now he's unpopular with the staff, but he's sticking to his guns. If dirty looks were radiotherapy he'd have lost a lot of hair by now, but the sense of defending a principle has given his health a definite boost.

When I return to my lover's room and peep through the window, the conversation shows no sign of stopping, so I leave them to it and go back to his neighbour's room, where the basin still smells like a florist's. There was something I glimpsed on the window sill a minute ago that puzzled me, and I summon up the nerve to ask about it.

It's a soft toy in the shape of a fat scheming cat, but a cat that seems to have two tiny hoops of wire fixed high on its stomach.

'That's my hospital Garfield,' explains the neighbour with a little embarrassment. 'I only use it in hospital.'

'No, I don't mean that,' I say, 'I mean, what are those?' I point at the little hoops.

He blushes outright and shyly opens his pyjama jacket. 'What you really mean is, what are these?'

His nipples have little inserted hoops of their own, and the hospital Garfield is indeed, as I thought incredulously at first glance, a soft toy with an erotic piercing.

My lover's neighbour nods at his customised toy. 'The nurses have this great sense of humour,' he says. 'They did that while I was out.'

I am slow to take in the information he is giving me. It is a few moments before I realise that by 'out' he means not just *socially unavailable* but *profoundly unconscious*.

I keep away from my lover as long as I plausibly can. Purely from a medical point of view, flirtation is likely to have a beneficial effect on his low blood pressure. A little teasing romance may actually make him stronger at the knees.

From my own point of view I feel not jealousy, but a definite tremor of worry. My lover's instinct for help is profound and I trust it. If he thinks I'm capable, then I am. But if he enlists the Vet, I lose confidence. It's not that I don't want to share the load. I'd love to. But if my lover is hedging his bets, then I suddenly fear that he has good reason. Perhaps he now realises I will crack up or get ill myself. My equilibrium falters, and the glands of selfish worry, that I have been suppressing for the duration, flare up at once and all together.

On subsequent visits, the Vet consolidates his burly charisma in my lover's eyes by turning out to own the right cars. He doesn't drive a Morris Traveller as such – that would be a little bit spooky. But he does buy glamorous or gloriously dowdy cars cheap in auctions, and garages them with friends or in fields when they need a little more work than he can do, handy though he is. He drives an Alfa that costs him more in insurance every year than he paid in the first place. One of these days he knows that the police will pull him over and ask him ever so nicely not to wear it in public again. Waiting in various locations for a little more cash or an elusive spare part are a Bentley, an Aston Martin and a Wolseley.

My lover has a passion for fast and/or classic cars. Before I knew him he owned an MG – he put an old phone in it in fact, the kind you crank, and used to mime conversations at traffic-lights in summer, with the top down. This was before the days of car phones, let alone the days of commercially made imitation car phones – which I think makes it all right.

I don't follow my lover's car conversations with the Vet. I don't begin to understand what makes one car boxy but lovable, and another one nippy but a little Japanese about the lips.

There must be something about cars that makes people use a

different register, almost a different language. Keith, my instructor, uses a whole mysterious vocabulary of phrases, so that I had to learn to understand his language, if not actually to speak Instructor, before I could really begin learning to drive. He mutters, 'Baby clutch . . . *baby* clutch,' when he wants me to be subtle with my left foot, and, 'Double gas . . . TREBLE gas,' when he wants me to be brash with my right. When I'm fumbling between gears he prompts me ('then three . . . then two'), and when I've finally got it right and married speed to ratio, he says with mild put-on surprise, 'It works!' or else he gives a sort of jeer of approval ('Yeeeeah!'). If I don't need prompting for a minute or so, he'll murmur, 'Looking good,' or, 'I'm almost impressed.' More often he gets me to slow down, with a warning 'Cool it,' or to speed up – for which he mutters, 'It's not happening,' and makes gestures with his hands, sweeping them forwards.

I used to interpret the phrase and the gesture the wrong way, as if what Keith wanted was for the road to be taken away from in front of him, but I suppose that was just my old reluctance surfacing again in the lightest of disguises. I've got it worked out now and give the accelerator a squeeze. If I've been slow to understand him and deliver the speed he requires, Keith gets more direct. The phrases for this are, 'Let's piss off out of here,' or 'Give it a bit of poke.'

If I take my time before changing up, he goes 'mmmm', with a sharp intonation that says what-are-you-waiting-for? If I'm not properly positioned in my lane, he makes a flick of the hand to guide me in the right direction. Often, when I've misjudged a manoeuvre or underestimated a hazard, he says, with a quiet satisfaction, '*Not* a good gear.' To remind me of the mirror he sometimes taps it with his forefinger or mutters – there seems no obvious reason for this choice of language – '*Spiegel.*'

I start to relax in the lesson at the point where Keith lights up his first cigarette. I'm sure he's got enough of a craving that he'd light up sooner or later, whatever sort of idiot I was being, but I become more competent knowing he's felt able to focus his attention on the cigarette packet and the matches for a few seconds. Unless of course it's my terrible driving that makes the comfort of a cigarette so hugely attractive.

Keith opens the window a crack and leans forward to adjust the heating. I take every move he makes as a looming comment on my driving, so I'm absurdly relieved when he's only making adjustments to the car's interior climate. Then Keith talks. It's as if he's trying to simulate the distractions of traffic, when we're on a clear road. There's nothing I find harder than giving talking a low priority; left to my instincts, I'd rather be attentive in the conversation than safe on the road. It's not that I get flustered when he's really trying to put me off my stride – like the time he asked, 'When you going to get married, then?' after he had warned me he was about to request an emergency stop and before he actually smacked the dashboard to give me my cue. That question doesn't faze me, though I gather it's pretty much guaranteed to make the young men botch their manoeuvre. But I'm interested in Keith and what he has to say, and when he stops talking because there's tricky work ahead I can't wait to get the hazards behind me, whatever they are, and go back to what he's saying.

Sometimes Keith talks about nothing, anything, the daily papers, and how he's going to give up the *Sun* when they stop running their Bingo game – unless of course they announce another. He wrote a letter to the *Sun*'s Grouse of the Week column just recently, which they didn't print, complaining about a doctor in the news who'd overturned the car giving his daughter a driving lesson in the grounds of his house. It was taking a living away from driving instructors, that was Keith's Grouse, and served the doctor right, and what would *he* think if people started doing operations on each other in their kitchens?

Sometimes he talks about his history, about Barnardo's and the army and home-ownership.

'I had a lovely house in an acre, lovely car, two-car garage, garden with a rockery and floodlights – spent a grand on landscaping – fruit trees, currant bushes, but it wasn't what I wanted, none of it. I think I worked that out before I finished laying the rockery, but I still installed those bloody flood-lights.'

He moved out from the house he shared with Sue and took up with Olga. Olga is the battered mobile home where he lives, parked in a muddy field a few miles out of town. She's a hulk, but he seems well set up there, in his way. We went out there once, on a lesson; I needed practice, apparently, manoeuvring in muddy conditions, and Keith certainly needed a Calor Gas container picked up and taken for refilling. We had a cup of tea in Olga while we were at it, though his eyes narrowed with distrust at the idea that anyone could drink it without sugar. He takes four spoonfuls and gives the tea-bag a good drubbing with the spoon, as if the point of the procedure was not to infuse a drink but actually to wash the tea-bag free of stains.

Laundry is one of the few services that he's not found a way of doing for himself. He does any telephoning he needs at the driving school, and even brings his electric razor in to work for re-charging with BSM current. He leaves the right change for milk and newspapers in Olga's mighty glove compart-ment and has them delivered right into her cab. But laundry is one thing that's beyond him and so he pops over to Sue's every week or so (and takes a bath while he's at it). He has 'a leg-over' while he's there, but to hear him talk about it, that leg-over isn't the lynch-pin of the arrangement. I imagine Sue in front of her mirror on one of the evenings Keith is expected – he doesn't always turn up, but he knows how to keep just enough on the right side of her that she doesn't come to find him, her horn sounding furiously all the way from the main road as her car crawls into the treacherous field where Olga sits. I imagine her powdering her face and wondering whether she should try some new perfume, not knowing it's Ariel that arouses Keith's senses, not Chanel.

I need a pee after my cup of tea. Keith shows me the lavatory, which is chemical and tucked away in a low cupboard. Keith can stand up in most parts of Olga, but there's nowhere that the roof's high enough to give my head clearance. To use the lavatory, I have to kneel and face forward. Keith gives me a little privacy by going to the cab, where he hasn't bothered to put up cork tiling. He presses a hand to the roof and says, 'Some mornings the condensation's unbelievable in here. It's like Niagara bastard Falls.'

Only when I'm finished with my rather awkward pee does he mention that personally, *personally*, speaking for himself, he finds it more convenient to piss in a bottle and then pour it away, though of course everybody's different, aren't they? There's a coffee jar, scrupulously clean and free of labels, tucked away at the side of the lavatory, which I suspect is his chosen bottle. I wish I'd spotted it earlier, though I doubt if I'd have had the nerve to use it.

Before we leave, Keith shows me his photo album. It's like anybody's photo album – anybody who wasn't thought worthy of a photograph before he joined the army, who built a raft in Malaya based on what people built in films when they were marooned, who had four children by two wives before there was ever a Sue, who kept sheep and chickens for a while in Devon – except that nothing's in order. It's the sort of album where each thick page has a thick sheet of Cellophane to hold the pictures down, no need of photo corners, and Keith seems to like keeping even the past provisional. Perhaps on non-bath evenings he amuses himself by rearranging the photographs, shuffling the blurred sheep and the precise soldiers, the blurred children. In every picture that shows Keith, he is pointing out of the frame, insisting that the real subject is out there somewhere, refusing to be the focus of the composition.

On the way back to town, he gets me to do some emergency stops. If it's at all possible, he synchronises them with young women walking alone. He smacks the dashboard just before we pass. The woman usually glares at us as we stop dead right next to her and then she relaxes into a pitying half-smile when she sees it's only a learner driver, no real threat. Then her face goes half-way back to its original expression, when she sees that Keith is staring at her with a defiant hunger. At times like this, I am able to look at Keith outside the terms of our sealed-in little relationship, outside its flux of resentment and dependence, and he seems, I must admit, like a pretty ordinary little shit.

Even when I have passed my test and put Keith behind me, I can't imagine that I'll do a lot of driving. Pubic transport is enough to get me to the hospital, though I sometimes use my bicycle on a Sunday, partly for the exercise and partly to dramatise my errand, if I'm bringing something for my lover. On the bicycle I can feel like a courier whose package will make a difference to the person waiting for it.

My lover keeps the television on all the time, just turning up the sound when there's something he actually wants to watch. At the moment, a weatherman is standing in front of two maps of the country. I expect they represent the weather tonight and tomorrow. But the weatherman, if he wanted, could also show us the weather of our two healths. His vocabulary of symbols is meagre but it will stretch. My map will be full of smiling suns and light refreshing breezes, a fantasy of summer; my lover's map a nightmare winter, chock-a-block with gales and freezing showers. My lover looks without interest at the screen as it changes. Some of his calm is really exhaustion, but some of his calm is really calm. It helps that he's still in touch socially with the few people he exposed to risk. With a bravery that to me seems insane, they've all taken the test, and they all tested negative.

He keeps a list of his sexual partners, does my lover, though it's not so detailed he could use it to track people down if he'd lost touch. I only found out about it recently. It's at the back of his diary, but then I only found out about the diary recently. Suddenly there was this battered book on the bed, and my lover was saying, oh, yes, he always used to keep a diary, he'd just got out of the habit. He'd just now come across it and was taking a look.

Even my lover had to admit, after a little reading, that his diary-keeping had never been regular; he wrote in his diary only when a relationship was on the rocks. It took tears to get the words flowing and then he would write what were in effect letters to his lovers, full of sombre accusations and depressive spite. He even read me a detailed account of my own selfishness. This was his version of a crisis of which I have no version, since I survived it by not noticing.

I asked if I could look at the diary, and he passed it across. At the back of the book there was a list of numbers and names, starting with '1. John in Toyota Corolla.' Number two was Mark, and number three was Mark and Ben. The list went into the low forties before it met a scrawl, twice underlined: '*Enough of this rubbish.*' The list-making impulse had started to falter even before then. Two numbers in the thirties were entered as 'What was the name?' and 'Macho Letdown'.

My lover gave me a beady look as I read his diary and asked, 'Are you the sort of person who reads people's diaries?'

I didn't know there was any other sort of person, but I avoided the question by holding the book up and waving it. 'The evidence against me is strong.'

'I mean, when the owner's not around?'

'Only if I can find it.' I've only made a couple of searches since then – as much to see if he was bothered enough to hide it as because I'm curious – and I haven't found it, so I suppose the answer to the question is, Yes, he was bothered enough.

The limitations on my lover's future make his past the more precious, and I find that I'm a bit bothered, after all, that I don't know where his diary is.

I bring my lover hot thick soups, in a big old-fashioned vacuum flask with a wide neck. Conventional soups bear the same relationship to my soup as the sun bears to those collapsed stars whose every speck outweighs it. An oxtail is a wispy thing compared to what I make of it with the strong rendering of my pressure cooker. My soups are concentrated expressions of the will to nourish.

But tonight my lover is not to be nourished. 'You know I hate innards,' he says, pushing the plate of soup away almost as soon as I've poured it.

I'm ashamed that I don't know my lover's preferences as well as I should, but I'm also offended and I protest. 'Oxtail isn't innards!'

'It's as good as.'

'Oxtail couldn't be further from innards. Be reasonable. If cows kept their tails on the inside how would they deal with flies?'

Even as I say this, I realise that talk of flies is among the poorer triggers of appetite. The ward is full of tiny insects, as it happens, sustained out of season by the warmth and the abundance of fruit.

Even unmolested, the fruit would look incongruous beside the stack of moulded cardboard vomit-bowls on my lover's bedside table. They look, with their broad rims turned down at one side, like jaunty little hats, as if they were there for use in a big dance production number. We've tried to bring them into our private world by referring to them as 'Berkeleys' or 'Astaires', but the name that has stuck, *vomit-hats*, leaves them uncomfortably real. These homely objects resist the final push into euphemism.

Our little tussle over the soup reminds me of how poorly matched we are in habits and appetites. We don't even have the same taste in bread. I like wholemeal, but his stomach can deal most easily with inflated plastic white, and naturally I give way to him. All the same, I'd have thought somebody could make a killing out of couples like us, by producing a hybrid loaf that combined the two, all the goodness and bran sucked out of each alternate slice and shunted into the next one.

In this way among others, we don't present a united front. Our teamwork seems ragged, while the illness we're fighting is ruthlessly co-ordinated. But then it's only recently, since he came into hospital in fact, that I have though of him, truly, as my lover.

Before then I compared him in my mind – often very flatteringly, it's true – with other men past or possible. But now I compare him only with the world as it will be when he is subtracted from it, not with rival beds but with his bed, empty. That is what locks the phrase in place: my lover.

My lover and I never used pet names or endearments before

his first visit to hospital, but how stupid it sounds when I say so. It's like saying *I never had much use for pot plants and cushions before I came to live in this condemned cell.* Except that the unstoppable progress of medical science has taken our condemned cell and turned it into a whole suite of condemned cells.

Our endearment system is based round the core-word *pie*, derived from the phrase *sweetie-pie* but given its independence in a whole series of verbal caresses. The turning-point in its history was my buying an easter egg with the message piped on it, 'WITH LOVE TO MY SWEET PIE.' This was at a time when a raised patch on the roof of my lover's mouth had been diagnosed as a cancer, a separate sentence on his mouth that his tongue must read and remember every time it makes contact, and I wanted to go to meet him armed with more than a hug. It comforted me to watch the woman at Thorntons in Cambridge – where a free message in icing was a seasonal offer – at work on the egg with her expert nozzle of fondant and her smile of romantic voyeurism, a smile that would have hardened on her lips like painted sugar if she knew she was decorating a sweet to take the bitterness out of a malignancy.

Pie was the word that stuck, the last part of the inscribed egg that my lover would have eaten, I'm sure, if he hadn't kept the whole thing intact, as a totem of chocolate. *Pie* stuck to a number of phrases, private ones at first and then sentences of ordinary conversation, by slip of the tongue to start with and afterwards defiantly, mixing embarrassment and the refusal to be embarrassed. *Pie* functions as pet name (*dear one*), as interrogative (*are you awake?*), as exclamation (*how could you say such a thing!*).

So near have I approached to that which I vowed I would never use, the edged endearment of the grown-up, the *darling* of protest if not yet the *darling* of bitter reproach.

Pie is allied by assonance with *my* (*my Pie*), by alliteration with expressive adjectives: *poor Pie, precious Pie, pretty Pie.*

Occasionally it appears in phrases of estrangement, though its use acts as a guarantee that estrangement is reversible: *crusty Pie, poison Pie, piranha Pie.*

Written down and rationalised as an irrational number – π – it loses a little of its sugar. Transposed into fake Italian *mio Pio* – it acquires a register almost operatic. As a double diminutive – as *pielet* or *pilot* – it brings into play a fresh set of overtones.

Perhaps endearment, verbal sweetness so concentrated nothing else can survive, will prevent infection, the way honey does. Honey yanks the moisture out of bacteria with the violence of its osmosis. Honey has been found uncorrupt in the tombs of the Pharaohs, though it had been left there to be used, after all, to sweeten the darkness of the dead.

Who could have thought when the treasures were laid out in the vault that the bees' modest embalming would last so well, that their glandular syrup of flowers would turn out so nearly eternal?

My lover raises the remote control panel and turns the television off. Late at night, the nurses stop being so demanding, and even Armchair and the Vet can be relied on to stay away. My lover and I don't have to be so guarded in our behaviour.

This is the time we draft our imaginary letters to newspapers and public figures, our radical complaints and proposals. My lover wants to live long enough to be the only survivor of an air crash, so that he can say at the press conference, where he will have an arm in plaster, or perhaps only a finger, 'You see? God doesn't hate me after all, whatever *you* think.' In the meantime he will settle for composing imaginary letters to the papers, setting the record straight day by day.

Sometimes one or the other of us will shed some tears, but we haven't properly settled the agenda of our crying. We're both New Men, I suppose that's what it comes down to, so we have a lot of respect for tears and what they represent. Crying is a piece of expressive behaviour that needs no apology and isn't, absolutely isn't, a demand for attention. We pride ourselves on being able to ask for affection straight out, without needing to break down to do it. There's something a little crass about a hug as a response to tears. A hug can be an act of denial, even, and neither of us is going to make that mistake. We claim the right to cry uncomforted, letting the discharge do its work uninterrupted.

But in practice, I get so distressed by his tears, and he by mine, that we regress just as fast as we possibly can, and smother the expressiveness that we have so much respect for under a ton of hugs.

Endlessly we reformulate our feelings for each other. This is the same superstition that makes people put up bumper stickers – *Keep Your Distance, Baby on Board, I ♥ my π* – to make the roads safe and life go on for ever.

Fate is a dual-control Metro, that much I know, but I'm not clear about who's in which seat. It may be me, or it may be my lover, that squeezes the brake when we approach a bend too fast, or who pops the clutch in to prevent a stall. 'Baby clutch,' I can hear Keith saying in my ear, '*baby*-baby clutch,' as we move off up the hill to where we must go.

Goodness and Mercy

ALICE MUNRO

BUGS SAID SO long to the disappearing land, a dark-blue finger of Labrador. The ship was passing through the Strait of Belle Isle, on its third day out from Montreal.

'Now I've got to make it to the white cliffs of Dover,' she said. She made a face, rounding her eyes and her small, adept mouth, her singer's mouth, as if she had to accept some bad nuisance. 'Else it's over the side and feed the fishes.'

Bugs was dying, but she had been a very slender, white-skinned woman before she started that, so there wasn't a shocking difference. Her bright-silver hair was cut in a clever fluffed-out bob by her daughter, Averill. Her pallor was by no means ghastly, and the loose tops and caftans that Averill had made for her concealed the state of her arms and her upper body. Occasional expressions of fatigue and distress blended in with an old expression she had – a humorous, hardened plaintiveness. She was not looking badly at all, and her coughing was under control.

'That's a joke,' she said to Averill, who was paying for the trip out of some money left to her by the father she had never seen, to remember. When they made the arrangements, they hadn't known what was going to happen – or that it was going to happen as soon as now looked likely.

'Actually, I intend to hang around making your life miserable for years to come,' Bugs said. 'I look better. Don't you think? Anyway, in the morning. I'm eating. I was thinking I'd start taking little walks. I walked to the rail yesterday, when you weren't here.'

They had a cabin on the boat deck, with a chair for Bugs set up outside. There was a bench under the cabin window, occupied now by Averill and in the mornings by the University of Toronto professor whom Bugs called her admirer, or 'that professorial jerk'.

This was happening on a Norwegian passenger-carrying freighter, in the late seventies, in the month of July. All the way across the North Atlantic the weather was sunny, the sea flat and bright as glass.

Bugs' real name, of course, was June. Her real name, and her singing name, was June Rodgers. For the last year and three months she had not sung in public. For the last eight months, she had not gone to the Conservatory to give lessons. She had a few students coming to the apartment on Huron Street, in the evenings and on Saturdays, so that Averill could accompany them on the piano. Averill worked at the Conservatory, in the office. She biked home for lunch every day, to see if Bugs was all right. She didn't say she was doing it for that reason. She had the excuse of her special lunch – skim milk, wheat germ, and a banana mixed up in the blender. Averill was usually trying to lose weight.

Bugs had sung at weddings, she had been the paid soloist with church choirs, she had sung in the 'Messiah' and the St Matthew Passion and in Gilbert and Sullivan. She had sung supporting roles in Toronto productions of operas with famous imported stars. For a while in the fifties she had shared a radio programme with a popular drunken tenor, who had got them both sacked. The name June Rodgers had been well enough known all the time that Averill was growing up. It was well enough known, at least, among the people that Averill usually met. It was a surprise for Averill, more than for Bugs, to run into people now who didn't recognise it.

People on the boat hadn't recognised it. About half of the thirty or so passengers were Canadians, most of them from around Toronto, but they hadn't recognised it. 'My mother sang Zerlina,' Averill said during her first conversation with the professor. 'In *Don Giovanni*, in 1964.' She had been ten at the time and remembered the occasion as one filled with glory. Apprehension, flurry, crisis – a sore throat cured by yoga. A peasant costume with a ruffled pink-and-gold skirt over piles of petticoats. Glory.

'Honey, Zerlina is just not a household word,' Bugs said to her afterwards. 'Also, professors are dumb. They are dumber than ordinary. I could be nice and say they know about things we don't, but as far as I'm concerned they don't know shit.'

But she let the professor sit beside her and tell her things about himself every morning. She told Averill what she'd learned. He walked the deck for one hour before breakfast. At home he walked six miles a day. He had caused a certain amount of scandal at the university a few years ago by marrying his young wife (his dimwit wife, said Bugs), whose name was Leslie. He had made enemies, stirred up envy and discontent among his colleagues with his dalliance, and then by divorcing his wife and marrying this girl who was one year younger than his oldest child. From then on, certain people were out to get him, and they did. He was a biologist, but he had devised a sort of general-science course -- he called it a scientific-literacy course – for students in the humanities: a lively, unalarming course that he hoped would be a modest breakthrough. He got the approval of the higher-ups, but the course was scuttled by members of his own department, who devised all kinds of cumbersome, silly requirements and prerequisites. He retired early.

'I think that was it,' Bugs said. 'I couldn't keep my mind on it. Also, young women can make very frustrating mates for older men. Youth can be boring. Oh, yes. With an older woman a man can relax. The rhythms of her thoughts and memories – yes, the rhythms of her thoughts and memories will be more in harmony with his. What puke!'

Down the deck the young wife, Leslie, sat working on a needlepoint cover for a dining-room chair. This was the third cover she had done. She needed six altogether. The two women she sat with were glad to admire her pattern – it was called Tudor Rose – and they talked about needlepoint covers that they had made. They described how these fitted in with the furnishings of their houses. Leslie sat between them, somewhat protected. She was a soft, pink-skinned brown-haired girl whose youth was draining away. She invited kindness, but Bugs had not been very kind to her when she hauled the needlepoint out of her bag.

'Oh, my,' said Bugs. She threw up her hands and waggled her skinny fingers. 'These hands,' she said, and got the better of a fit of coughing – 'these hands have done plenty of things I am not proud of, but I must say they have never picked up a knitting needle or an embroidery needle or a crochet hook or even sewn on a button if there was a safety pin handy. So I'm hardly the person to appreciate, my dear.'

Leslie's husband laughed.

Averill thought that what Bugs said was not completely true. It was Bugs who had taught her how to sew. Bugs and Averill both took a serious interest in clothes and were attentive to fashion, in a playful, unintimidated way. Some of their best hours together had been spent in cutting up material, pinning it together, getting inspirations.

The caftans, the loose tops that Bugs wore on the boat were patchworks of silk and velvet and brightly patterned cotton and crocheted lace – all from old dresses and curtains and tablecloths that Averill had picked up at second-hand stores. These creations were greatly admired by Jeanine, an American woman on the boat, who was making friends zealously.

'Where did you find those gorgeous things?' said Jeanine, and Bugs said, 'Averill. Averill made them. Isn't she clever?'

'She's a genius,' said Jeanine. 'You're a genius, Averill.'

'She should make theatre costumes,' Bugs said. 'I keep telling her.'

'Yes, why don't you?' said Jeanine.

Averill flushed and could not think of anything to say, anything to placate Bugs and Jeanine, who were smiling at her.

Bugs said, 'I'm just as glad she's not, though. I'm just as glad she's here. Averill is my treasure.'

Walking the deck, away from Bugs, Jeanine asked Averill, 'You mind telling me how old you are?'

Averill said twenty-three, and Jeanine sighed. She said that she was forty-two. She was married, but not accompanied by her husband. She had a long tanned face with glossy pinkish-mauve lips and shoulder-length hair, thick and smooth as an oak plank. She said that people often told her she looked as if she was from California, but actually she was from Wisconsin. She was from a small city in Wisconsin, where she had been the hostess of a radio phone-in show. Her voice was low and persuasive and full of satisfaction, even if she disclosed a problem, grief, shame.

She said, 'Your mother is charming.'

Averill said, 'People either think that or they can't stand her.'

'Has she been ill long?'

'She's recuperating,' said Averill. 'She had pneumonia last spring.' This was what they had agreed to say.

Jeanine was more eager to be friends with Bugs than Bugs was to be friends with her. Nevertheless Bugs slid into her customary half-intimacy, confiding some things about the professor and disclosing the name she had thought up for him: Dr Faustus. His wife's name was Tudor Rose. Jeanine thought these names appropriate and funny. Oh, delightful, she said.

She did not know the name that Bugs had given her. Glamour Puss.

Averill walked around the deck and listened to people talking. She thought about how sea voyages were supposed to be about getting away from it all, and how 'it all' presumably meant your life, the way you lived, the person you were at home. Yet in all the conversations she overheard people were doing just the opposite. They were establishing themselves –

telling about their jobs and their children and their gardens and their dining-rooms. Recipes were offered, for fruitcake and compost heaps. Also ways of dealing with daughters-in-law and investments. Tales of illness, betrayal, real estate. *I said. I did. I always believe. Well, I don't know about you, but I.*

Averill, walking past with her face turned toward the sea, wondered how you got to do this. How did you learn to be so stubborn and insistent and to claim your turn?

I did it all over last fall in blue and oyster.

I'm afraid I have never been able to see the charms of opera.

That last was the professor, imagining that he could put Bugs in her place. And why did he say he was afraid?

Averill didn't get to walk alone for very long. She had her own admirer, who would stalk her and cut her off at the rail. He was an artist, a Canadian artist from Montreal, who sat across from her in the dining-room. When he was asked, at the first meal, what kind of pictures he painted, he had said that his latest work was a figure nine feet high, entirely wrapped in bandages, which bore quotations from the American Declaration of Independence. How interesting, said some polite Americans, and the artist said with a tight sneer, I'm glad you think so.

'But why,' said Jeanine, with her interviewer's adroit response to hostility (a special rich kindness in the voice, a more alert and interested smile), 'why did you not use Canadian quotations of some sort?'

'Yes, I was wondering that, too,' said Averill. Sometimes she tried to get into conversations this way, she tried to echo or expand the things that other people said. Usually it did not work well.

Canadian quotations turned out to be a sore subject with the artist. Critics had taken him to task for that very thing, accusing him of insufficient nationalism, missing the very point that he was trying to make. He ignored Jeanine, but followed Averill from the table and harangued her for what seemed like hours, developing a ferocious crush on her as he did so. Next morning he was waiting to go in to breakfast with her and afterwards he asked her if she had ever done any modelling.

'*Me?*' said Averill. 'I'm way too fat.'

He said he didn't mean with clothes on. If he had been another sort of artist, he said (she gathered that the other sort was the sort he despised), he would have picked her out immediately as a model. Her big golden thighs (she was wearing shorts, which she didn't put on again), her long hair like caramelised sugar, her square shoulders and unindented waist. A goddess colouring, goddess of the harvest. He said she had a pure and childish scowl.

Averill thought that she must remember to keep smiling.

He was a stocky, swarthy, irritable-looking man. Bugs named him Toulouse-Lautrec.

Men had fallen in love with Averill before. Twice she had promised to marry them, then had had to get out of it. She had slept with the ones she was engaged to, and with two or three others. Actually, four others. She had had one abortion. She was not frigid – she did not think so – but there was something about her participation in sex that was polite and appalled, and it was always a relief when they let go of her.

She dealt with the artist by granting him a conversation early in the day, when she felt strong and almost light-hearted. She didn't sit down with him, and during the afternoon and evening she kept him at arm's length. Part of her strategy was to take up with Jeanine. That was all right, as long as Jeanine talked about her own life and didn't move in on Averill's.

'Your mother is a gallant woman and very charming,' Jeanine said. 'But charming people can be very manipulative. You live with her, don't you?'

Averill said yes, and Jeanine said, 'Oh, I'm sorry. I hope I'm not being too intrusive? I hope I haven't offended you?'

Averill was really only puzzled, in a familiar way. Why did people so quickly take for granted that she was stupid?

'You know, I've gotten so used to interviewing people,' Jeanine said. 'I'm actually quite bad at ordinary conversation. I've forgotten how to communicate in a nonprofessional situation. I'm too blunt and I'm too *interested*. I need help with that.'

The whole point about coming on this trip, she said, was to

get herself back to normal reality and find out who she really was when not blatting away into a microphone. And to find out who she was outside of her marriage. It was an agreement between her husband and herself, she said, that every so often they would take these little trips away from each other, they would test the boundaries of the relationship.

Averill could hear what Bugs would have to say about that. 'Test the boundaries of the relationship,' Bugs would say. 'She means get laid aboard ship.'

Jeanine said that she did not rule out a shipboard romance. That is, before she had a look at the available men she had not ruled it out. Once she got a look, she resigned herself. Who could it be? The artist was short and ugly and anti-American. That in itself wouldn't have been entirely off-putting, but he was infatuated with Averill. The professor had a wife on board – Jeanine was not going to scramble around copulating in linen closets. Also he was long-winded, had little grainy warts on his eyelids, and was taken up with Bugs. All the other men were out for one reason or another – they had wives with them, or they were too old to please her or too young for her to please them, or they were chiefly interested in each other or in members of the crew. She would have to use the time to give her skin a good overhaul and to read a book all the way through.

'Who would you pick, though,' she said to Averill, 'if you were picking for me?'

'What about the captain?' said Averill.

'Brilliant,' Jeanine said. 'A long shot, but brilliant.'

She found out that the captain's age was OK – he was fifty-four. He was married, but his wife was back in Bergen. He had three children, grown up or nearly. He himself was not a Norwegian but a Scot, born in Edinburgh. He had gone to sea at sixteen and had captained this freighter for ten years. Jeanine discovered all this by asking him. She told him that she was going to do an article for a magazine, on passenger-carrying freighters. (She might really do this.) He gave her a tour of the ship and included his own cabin. She thought that a good sign.

His cabin was spick-and-span. There was a photograph of a

large, pleasant-looking woman wearing a thick sweater. The book he was reading was by John le Carré.

'He won't give her a tumble,' Bugs said. 'He's too canny for her. A canny Scot.'

Averill had not thought twice about revealing Jeanine's confidences, if they were confidences. She was used to bringing home all information, all enlivening tidbits – home to the apartment on Huron Street, to the cabin on the boat deck, to Bugs. All stirred into the busy pot. Bugs herself was a marvel at egging people on – she got extravagant tangled revelations from unlikely sources. So far as Averill knew she had not kept anything a secret.

Bugs said that Jeanine was a type she had seen before. Glitz on the surface and catastrophe underneath. A mistake to get too chummy with her, she told Averill, but she remained fairly chummy herself. She told Jeanine stories that Averill had heard before.

She told about Averill's father, whom she did not describe as a jerk or an admirer but as a cautious old bugger. Old to her way of thinking – in his forties. He was a doctor, in New York. Bugs was living there; she was a young singer trying to get her start. She went to him for a sore throat, sore throats being the bugbear of her life.

'Eye, ear, nose, and throat man,' Bugs said. 'How was I to know he wouldn't stop there?'

He had a family. Of course. He came to Toronto, once, to a medical conference. He saw Averill.

'She was standing up in her crib, and when she saw him she howled like a banshee. I said to him, Do you think she's got my voice? But he was not in the mood for jokes. She scared him off. Such a cautious old bugger. I think he only slipped up the once.

'I've always used bad language,' Bugs said. 'I like it. I liked it long before it got to be so popular. When Averill had just started to school, the teacher phoned and asked me to come in for a talk. She said she was concerned about some words that Averill was using. When Averill broke her pencil or anything, she said, Oh, shit. Or maybe, Oh, fuck. She said whatever she was used to hearing me say at home. I never warned her. I just thought she'd realise. And how could she? Poor Averill. I was a rotten mother. And that's not the worst part. Do you think I owned up to that teacher and said she got it from me? Indeed not! I behaved like a lady. Oh dear. Oh, I do appreciate you telling me. Oh dear. I'm an awful person. Averill always knew it. Didn't you, Averill?'

Averill said yes.

On the fourth day, Bugs stopped going down to the dining-room for dinner.

'I notice I'm getting a bit gray around the gills by that time,' she said. 'I don't want to turn the professor off. He may not be so stuck on older women as he lets on.'

She said she ate enough at breakfast and lunch. 'Breakfast was always my best meal. And here I eat a huge breakfast.'

Averill came back from dinner with rolls and fruit.

'Lovely,' said Bugs. 'Later.'

She had to sleep propped up.

'Maybe the nurse has oxygen,' Averill said. There was no doctor on the ship, but there was a nurse. Bugs did not want to see her. She did not want oxygen.

'These are not bad,' she said of her coughing fits. 'They are not as bad as they sound. Just little spasms. I've been figuring out – what they are punishment for. Seeing I never smoked. I thought maybe – singing in church and not believing? But no. I think – "Sound of Music." Maria. God hates it.'

Averill and Jeanine played poker in the evenings with the artist and the Norwegian first mate. Averill always went back to the boat deck a few times to check on Bugs. Bugs would be asleep or pretending to be asleep, the fruit and buns by her bed untouched. Averill pulled out of the game early. She did not go to bed immediately, though she had made a great point of being so sleepy that she could not keep her eyes open. She slipped into the cabin to retrieve the uneaten buns, then went out on deck. She sat on the bench beneath the window. The window was always wide open, on the warm, still night. Averill sat there and ate the buns as quietly as she could, biting with care through the crisp, delicious crust. The sea air made her just as hungry as it was supposed to do. Or else it was having somebody in love with her – the tension. Under those circumstances she usually gained weight.

She could listen to Bugs' breathing. Little flurries and halts, ragged accelerations, some snags, snores, and achieved straight runs. She could hear Bugs half-wake, and shift and struggle and prop herself higher up in the bed. And she could watch the captain, when he came out for his walk. She didn't know if he saw her. He never indicated. He never looked her way. He looked straight ahead. He was getting his exercise, at night, when there would be the least chance of having to be sociable. Back and forth, back and forth, close to the rail. Averill stayed still – she felt like a fox in the brush. A night animal, watching him. But she didn't think he would be startled if she should move or call out. He was alert to everything on the ship, surely. He knew she was there but could ignore her, out of courtesy, or his own sense of confidence.

She thought of Jeanine's designs on him, and agreed with Bugs that they were doomed to failure. Averill would be disappointed if they were not doomed to failure. The captain did not seem to her a needy man. He did not need to disturb you, or flatter, or provoke, or waylay you. None of that *look at me, listen to me, admire me, give me.* None of that. He had other things on his mind. The ship, the sea, the weather, the cargo, his crew, his commitments. The passengers must be an old story to him. Cargo of another sort, requiring another sort of attention. Idle or ailing, lustful or grieving, curious, impatient, mischievous, remote – he would have seen them all before. He would know things about them right away, but never more than he needed to know. He would know about Jeanine. An old story.

How did he decide when to go in? Did he time himself, did he count his steps? He was grey-haired and straight-backed, with a thickness of body around the waist and the stomach speaking not of indulgence but of a peaceable authority. Bugs had not thought up any name for him. She had called him a canny Scot, but beyond that she had taken no interest. There were no little tags about him for Bugs to get hold of, no inviting bits of showing-off, no glittery layers ready to flake away. He was a man made long ago, not making himself moment by moment and using whomever he could find in the process.

One night before the captain appeared, Averill heard singing. She heard Bugs singing. She heard Bugs wake and resettle herself and start singing.

Sometimes in the last months Bugs had sung a phrase during a lesson, she had sung under her breath, with great caution, and out of necessity, to demonstrate something. She did not sing like that now. She sang lightly, as she used to do in practice, saving her strength for the performance. But she sang truly and adequately, with unimpaired – or almost unimpaired – sweetness.

'*Vedrai carino*,' Bugs sang, just as she used to sing when setting the table or looking out the rainy window of the apartment, making a light sketch that could be richly filled in if she chose. She might have been waiting for somebody at those times, or wooing an improbable happiness, or just limbering up for a concert.

> *Vedrai carino,*
> *Se sei buonino,*
> *Che bel remedio,*
> *Ti voglio dar*

Averill's head had pulled up when the singing started, her body had tightened, as at a crisis. But there was no call for her; she stayed where she was. After the first moment's alarm, she felt just the same thing, the same thing she always felt, when her mother sang. The doors flew open, effortlessly, there was the lighted space beyond, a revelation of kindness and seriousness. Desirable, blessed joy, and seriousness, a play of kindness that asked nothing of you. Nothing but to set out this bright order. It altered everything, and then the moment Bugs stopped singing it was gone. Gone. It seemed that Bugs herself had taken it away. Bugs could imply that it was just a trick, nothing more. She could imply that you were a bit of a fool to take such notice of it. It was a gift that Bugs was obliged to offer, to everybody.

There. That's all. You're welcome.

Nothing special.

Bugs had that secret, which she openly displayed, then absolutely protected – from Averill, just as from everybody else.

Averill is not particularly musical, thank God.

The captain came on deck just as Bugs finished singing. He might have caught the tail end of it or been waiting decently in the shadows until it was over. He walked, and Averill watched, as usual.

Averill could sing in her head. But even in her head she never sang the songs that she associated with Bugs. None of Zerlina's songs, or the soprano parts of the oratorios, not even 'Farewell to Nova Scotia' or any of the folk songs that Bugs mocked for their sappy sentiments though she sang them angelically. Averill had a hymn that she sang. She hardly knew where it came from. She couldn't have learned it from Bugs. Bugs disliked hymns, generally speaking. Averill must have picked it up at church, when she was a child, and had to go along with Bugs when Bugs was doing a solo.

It was the hymn that starts out, 'The Lord's my Shepherd.' Averill did not know that it came from a psalm – she had not been to church often enough to know about psalms. She did know all the words in the hymn, which she had to admit were full of strenuous egotism, and straightforward triumph, and, particularly in one verse, a childish sort of gloating:

> My table Thou hast furnished,
> In Presence of my Foes

How blithely and securely and irrationally Averill's head-voice sang these words, while she watched the captain pace in front of her, and later, when she herself walked safely down to the rail:

> Goodness and Mercy all my Life
> Shall surely follow me;
> And in God's House forevermore
> My dwelling place shall be.

Her silent singing wrapped around the story she was telling herself, which she extended further every night on the deck. (Averill often told herself stories – the activity seemed to her as unavoidable as dreaming.) Her singing was a barrier set between the world in her head and the world outside, between her body and the onslaught of the stars, the black miror of the North Atlantic.

Bugs stopped going down to lunch. She still went to breakfast, and was lively then, and for an hour or so afterward. She said she didn't feel any worse, she was tired of listening and talking. She didn't sing again, at least not when Averill could hear her.

On the ninth night, which was the last night out, before they were to dock at Tilbury, Jeanine gave a party in her cabin. Jeanine had the largest and best cabin on the boat deck. She provided champagne, which she had brought on board for this purpose, and whisky and wine, along with caviar, grapes, heaps of smoked salmon and steak tartare and cheese and flatbread, from the unsuspected resources of the kitchen. 'I'm squandering,' she said. 'I'm flying high. I'll be wandering around Europe with a knapsack on my back stealing eggs out of henhouses. I don't care. I'll take all your addresses and when I'm utterly broke I'll come and stay wth you. Don't laugh!'

Bugs had meant to go to the party. She had stayed in bed all day, not even going to breakfast, in order to save her strength.

She got up and washed, then propped herself back against the pillows to do her makeup. She did it beautifully, eyes and all. She brushed out and teased and sprayed her hair. She put on her grand soloist's dress, which Averill had made – an almost straight-cut but ample long dress of dark-purple silk, its wide sleeves lined with more silk, of iridescent pink and silver.

'Aubergine,' said Bugs. She turned to make the dress flare out at the hem. The turn made her unsteady, and she had to sit down.

'I should do my nails,' she said. 'I'll wait a little, though. I'm too jittery.'

'I could do them,' Averill said. She was pinning up her hair.

'Could you? But I don't think. I don't think I'll go. After all. I think I'd rather just stay here and rest. Tomorrow I have to be in good shape. Landing.'

Averill helped her take off the dress and wash her face and put her nightgown back on. She helped her into bed.

'It's a crime about the dress,' Bugs said. 'Not to go. It deserves to get out. You should wear it. You wear it. Please.'

Averill did not think that purple suited her, but she ended up discarding her own green dress and putting on Bugs'. She went down the hall to the party, feeling strange, defiant, and absurd. It was all right – everybody had dressed up, some to a remarkable extent. Even the men had decked themselves out somehow. The artist wore an old tuxedo jacket with his jeans, and the professor appeared in a white suit of rather floppy cut, looking like a plantation dandy. Jeanine's dress was black and skimpy, worn with seamed black stockings and big chunks of gold jewellery. Leslie was swathed in taffeta, with red and pink roses on a creamy ground. Over her curvy bum the material was bunched out into one huge rose, whose petals the professor kept patting and tweaking and arranging to best advantage. It would seem that he was newly entranced with her. She was relieved and proud, shyly blooming.

'Your mother is not coming to the party?' said the professor to Averill.

'Parties bore her,' Averill said.

'I get the impression that many things bore her,' the

professor said. 'I have noticed that with performing artists, and it is understandable. They have to concentrate so much on themselves.'

'Who is this – the Statue of Liberty?' said the artist, brushing the silk of Averill's dress. 'Is there a woman inside there at all?'

Averill had heard that he had been discussing her with Jeanine lately, wondering if she was possibly a lesbian, and Bugs was not her mother but her rich and jealous lover.

'Is there a woman or a hunk of concrete?' he said, moulding the silk to her hip.

Averill didn't care. This was the last night that she would have to see him. And she was drinking. She liked to drink. She liked especially to drink champagne. It made her feel not excited but blurry and forgiving.

She talked to the first mate, who was engaged to a girl from the mountains and showed an agreeable lack of love interest in herself.

She talked to the cook, a handsome woman who had formerly taught English in Norwegian high schools and was now intent on a more adventurous life. Jeanine had told Averill that the cook and the artist were believed to be sleeping together, and a certain challenging, ironic edge to the cook's friendliness made Averill think that this might be true.

She talked to Leslie, who said that she had once been a harpist. She had been a young harpist playing dinner music in a hotel, and the professor had spotted her behind the ferns. She had not been a student, as people thought. It was after they became involved that the professor had her enroll in some courses, to develop her mind. She giggled over her champagne and said that it had not worked. She had resisted mind development but had given up the harp.

Jeanine spoke to Averill in a voice as low and confidential as she could make it. 'How will you manage with her?' she said. 'What will you do in England? How can you take her on a train? This is serious.'

'Don't worry,' Averill said.

'I have not been open with you,' said Jeanine. 'I have to go to the bathroom, but I want to tell you something when I come out.'

Averill hoped that Jeanine did not intend to make more disclosures about the artist or give more advice about Bugs. She didn't. When she came out of the bathroom she began to talk about herself. She said that she was not on a little vacation, as she had claimed. She had been turfed out. By her husband, who had left her for a sexpot moron who worked as a receptionist at the station. Being a receptionist involved doing her nails and occasionally answering the telephone. The husband considered that he and Jeanine should still be friends, and he would come to visit, helping himself to the wine and describing the pretty ways of his paramour. How she sat up in bed, naked, doing – what else? – her fingernails. He wanted Jeanine to laugh with him and commiserate with him over his ill-judged and besotted love. And she did – Jeanine did. Time and again she fell in with what he wanted and listened to his tales and watched her wine disappear. He said he loved her – Jeanine – as if she were the sister he'd never had. But now Jeanine meant to pull him out of her life by the roots. She was up and away. She meant to live.

She still had her eye on the captain, though it was the eleventh hour. He had turned down champagne and was drinking whisky.

The cook had brought up a coffee tray for those who did not drink or who wished to sober up early. When somebody finally tried a cup, the cream proved to be on the turn – probably from sitting for a while in the warm room. Unflustered, the cook took it away, promising to bring back fresh. 'It will be good on the pancakes in the morning,' she said. 'With brown sugar, on the pancakes.'

Jeanine said that somebody had told her once that when the milk was sour you could suspect that there was a dead body on the ship.

'I thought it was a kind of superstition,' Jeanine said. 'But he said no, there's a reason. The ice. They have used all the ice to keep the body, so the milk goes sour. He said he had known it to happen, on a ship in the tropics.'

The captain was asked, laughingly, if there was any such problem on board this ship.

He said not that he knew of, no. 'And we have plenty of refrigerator space,' he said.

'Anyway, you bury them at sea, don't you?' said Jeanine. 'You can marry or bury at sea, can't you? Or do you really refrigerate them and send them home?'

'We do as the case dictates,' said the captain.

But had it happened with him, he was asked – were there bodies kept, had there been burials at sea?

'A young chap once, one of the crew, died of appendicitis. He hadn't any family we knew of; we buried him at sea.'

'That's a funny expression, when you think of it,' said Leslie, who was giggling at everything. 'Buried at sea.'

'Another time –' said the captain. 'Another time, it was a lady.'

Then he told Jeanine and Averill and a few others who were standing around a story. (Not Leslie – her husband took her away.)

One time on this ship, the captain said, there were two sisters travelling together. This was on a different run, a few years ago, in the South Atlantic. The sisters looked twenty years apart in age, but that was only because one of them was very sick. She might not have been so much the elder – perhaps she was not the elder at all. Probably they were both in their thirties. Neither one was married. The one who was not sick was very beautiful.

'The most beautiful woman I have ever seen in my life,' said the captain, speaking solemnly, as if describing a view or a building.

She was very beautiful, but she did not pay attention to anybody except her sister, who was laid up in the cabin with what was probably a heart condition. The other one used to go out at night and sit on the bench outside the window of their cabin. She might walk to the rail and back, but she never stirred far from the window. The captain supposed that she was staying within hearing distance, in case her sister needed her. He could see her sitting there when he went out for his late-night walk, but he pretended not to see her, because it seemed to him she didn't want to be seen, or to have to say hello.

But there was a night when he was walking past and he heard her call to him. She called so softly he barely heard her. He went over to the bench, and she said, Captain, I'm sorry, my sister has just died.

I'm sorry, my sister has just died.

She led him into the cabin, and she was absolutely right. Her sister was lying on the bed next to the door. Her eyes were half open, she had just died.

'Things were in a bit of a mess, the way they sometimes are on such occasions,' the captain said. 'And by the way she reacted to that I knew she hadn't been in the cabin when it happened, she'd been outside.'

Neither the captain nor the woman said a word. They set to work together to get things cleaned up, and they washed the body off and straightened it out and closed the eyes. When they were finished, the captain asked whom he should notify. Nobody, the woman said. Nobody. There is nobody but the two of us, she said. Then will you have the body buried at sea, the captain asked her, and she said yes. Tomorrow, he said – tomorrow morning – and she said, Why do we have to wait, couldn't we do it now?

Of course that was a good idea, though the captain wouldn't have urged it on her himself. The less the other passengers, and even the crew, have to be aware of a death on board, the better. And it was hot weather, summer in the South Atlantic. They wrapped the body up in one of the sheets, and between them they put it out through the window, which was wide open for air. The dead sister was light – wasted. They carried her to the rail. Then the captain said that he would just go and get some rope and tie the body up in the sheet so that it wouldn't fall out when they dropped it over. Couldn't we use scarves, she said, and she ran back to the cabin and came out with an assortment of scarves and sashes, very pretty stuff. He bound the body up in the sheet with those and said that he would now go and get his book, to read the service for the dead. The woman laughed and said, What good is your book to you here? It's too dark to read. He saw that she dreaded being left alone with the body. She was right, too, about its being too dark to read. He could have got a flashlight. He didn't know whether he had even thought of that. He really did not want to leave her; he did not like the state she was in.

He asked her what he should say, then. Some prayers?

Say whatever you like, she said, and he said the Lord's Prayer – he did not recall if she joined in – then something like, Lord Jesus Christ, in Thy name we commit this woman to the deep; have mercy on her soul. Something like that. They picked up the body and rolled it over the rail. It hardly made a splash.

She asked if that was all, and he told her yes. He would just have to fill out some papers and make up the death certificate. What did she die of, he asked. Was it a heart attack? He wondered what kind of spell he had been under not to have asked that before.

Oh, she said, I killed her.

'I knew it!' Jeanine cried. 'I knew it was murder!'

The captain walked the woman back to the bench under the window of the cabin – all lit up now like Christmas – and asked her what she meant. She said she had been sitting here, where she was now, and she heard her sister call. She knew her sister was in trouble. She knew what it was – her sister needed an injection. She never moved. She tried to move – that is, she kept thinking of moving: she saw herself going into the cabin and getting out the needle, she saw herself doing that, but she wasn't moving. She strained herself to do it but she didn't. She sat like stone. She could no more move than you can move out of some danger's way in a dream. She sat and listened until she knew that her sister was dead. Then the captain came and she called to him.

The captain told her that she had not killed her sister.

Wouldn't her sister have died anyway, he said. Wouldn't she have died very soon? If not tonight, very soon? Oh, yes, she said. Probably. Not probably, the captain said. Certainly. Not probably – certainly. He would put heart attack on the death certificate, and that would be all there was to it. So now you must calm down, he said. Now you know it will be all right.

He pronounced 'calm' in the Scottish way, to rhyme with 'lamb'.

Yes, the woman said, she knew that part of it would be all right. I'm not sorry, she said. But I think you have to remember what you have done.

'Then she went over to the rail,' the captain said, 'and of course I went along with her, because I couldn't be sure what she meant to do, and she sang a hymn. That was all. I guess it was her contribution to the service. She sang so you could hardly hear her, but the hymn was one I knew. I can't recall it, but I knew it perfectly well.'

'Goodness and Mercy all my Life,' Averill sang then, lightly but surely, so that Jeanine squeezed her around the waist and exclaimed, 'Well! Champagne Sally!'

The captain showed a moment's surprise. Then he said, 'I believe that may have been it.' He might have been relinquishing something – a corner of his story – to Averill. 'That may have been it.'

Averill said, 'That's the only hymn I know.'

'But is that all?' Jeanine said. 'There wasn't any family fortune involved, or they weren't both in love with the same man? No? I guess it wasn't TV.'

The captain said no, it wasn't TV.

Averill believed that she knew the rest of it. How could she help knowing? It was her story. She knew that after the woman sang the hymn, the captain took her hand off the rail. He held her hand to his mouth and kissed it. He kissed the back of it, then the palm-to-rhyme-with-lamb. Her hand, that had lately done its service to the dead.

In some versions of the story that was all he did, that was enough. In other versions, he was not so easily satisfied. Nor was she. She went with him inside, along the corridor into the lighted cabin, and there he made love to her on the very bed that according to him they had just stripped and cleaned, sending its occupant and one of its sheets to the bottom of the ocean. They landed on that bed because they couldn't wait to get to the other bed under the window, they couldn't wait to hurtle into the lovemaking that they kept up till daybreak and that would have to last them the rest of their lives.

Sometimes they turned the light off, sometimes they didn't care.

The captain had told it as if the mother and daughter were sisters and he had transported the boat to the South Atlantic and he had left off the finale – as well as supplying various details of his own – but Averill believed that it was her story he had told. It was the story that she had been telling herself night after night on the deck, her perfectly secret story, delivered back to her. She had made it, and she had to believe now that he had taken it and told it.

Believing that such a thing could happen made her feel weightless and distinct and glowing, like a fish lit up in the water.

Bugs did not die that night. She died two weeks later, in the Royal Infirmary in Edinburgh. She had managed to get that far, on the train.

Averill was not with her when she died. She was a couple of blocks away, eating a baked potato from a takeout shop.

Bugs made one of her last coherent remarks about the Royal Infirmary. She said, 'Doesn't it sound *Old World*?'

Averill, coming out to eat after having been in the hospital room all day, had been surprised to find that there was still so much light in the sky, and that so many lively, brightly dressed people were in the streets, speaking French and German, and probably lots of other languages that she couldn't recognise. Every year at this time, the captain's home town held a festival.

Averill brought Bugs' body home on a plane, to a funeral with fine music, in Toronto. She found herself sitting beside another Canadian returning from Scotland – a young man

245

who had played in a famous amateur golf tournament and had not done as well as he had expected. Failure and loss made these two kind to each other, and they were easily charmed by the other's ignorance of the world of sport and of music. Since he lived in Toronto, it was easy for the young man to show up at the funeral. In a short time he and Averill were married. After a while they were less kind and less charmed, and Averill began to think that she had chosen her husband chiefly because Bugs would have thought the choice preposterous. They were divorced.

But Averill met another man, a good deal older than herself, a high-school drama teacher and play director. His talent was more reliable than his good will – he had an offhand, unsettlingly flippant and ironical manner. He either charmed people or aroused their considerable dislike. He had tried to keep himself free of entanglements.

Averill's pregnancy, however, persuaded them to marry. Both of them hoped for a daughter.

Averill never saw again, or heard from, any of the people who were on the boat.

Averill accepts the captain's offering. She is absolved and fortunate. She glides like the spangled fish, inside her dark silk dress.

She and the captain bid each other good night. They touch hands ceremoniously. The skin of their hands is flickering in the touch.

Arthur Seal and the Hand of Fate

PHILIP OAKES

CIVILISATION CAME TO my part of North Staffordshire in the summer of 1938 when Arthur Seal, a speculative builder whose ambitions went far beyond bricks and mortar, dug an enormous hole in the shale and clay of Mappleton Bank and installed the first-ever open-air swimming-pool in the district. It was a visionary thing to do, although people were slow to give Arthur credit. They pointed to the Midlands' weather which guaranteed rain nine months out of twelve and to the soot which drifted down like a dingy snowfall throughout the year, except for Wakes week when the pot-banks closed down for the annual holidays and the air became suddenly and miraculously clean. But for the most part, they said, it was a waste of time. It was going against nature, besides which there was nothing wrong with the town baths where generations of local children had learned a rudimentary breaststroke or, at least, how to stay afloat before being presented with a swimming certificate, embossed in red, blue and gold on mock vellum.

Arthur saw it differently. 'It's progress,' he said. 'Out of doors is the thing. I mean, it stands to reason. Consider for a moment the beneficial effects of sunlight on the human body. And not only sunlight. The old ultraviolet's coming down as well, whether we can see it or not. We have to open ourselves up to nature. A bit of soot's not going to get in the way. Just look what they're doing in Germany. We could do as much here.' It was not that Arthur was especially pro-German. Even in North Staffordshire there was some slight unease (concern would be putting it too strongly) about the man Hitler and his Brownshirts. But Germany was still the country promoted by the naturist magazines, where bronzed men and sylph-like women posed beside glittering lakes. It was hard to believe that anything evil could emanate from such an heroic setting. What Arthur believed in was the body beautiful and creating the pool was his act of faith.

He lived in a large, detached house at the top of our avenue. His wife, my mother let slip, had gone off with an insurance salesman. It was not Arthur's fault, but his reputation suffered all the same. He was not man enough to keep her, said my friend Gordon Greaves, repeating, word for word, what his father had told him. He was too clever by half, said Miss Parker in the post office. What he needed was someone to give his ideas a dusting of commonsense. Her customers smiled knowingly and egged her on to say more. They saw Arthur about his business. Many of them lived in houses which he had built, but few of them knew much about his private life.

I knew less than most. I was ten years old and, to me, Arthur Seal represented not only money and owning things, but also the kind of glamour which came from a world elsewhere. For a start he was a Londoner and spoke with an accent which those in the know said was Cockney. His sentences seemed to skip, one after the other, like stones skimmed on water, none of them resting long enough to actually sink. And he wore clothes which were equally insubstantial: a jacket the colour of straw, cream tennis flannels, shoes made of plaited leather. Now I realise that his entire wardrobe was conceived as an act of defiance, mostly against the weather, but also against local opinion. He would not stay still long enough to let the grime settle or criticism inflict any lasting wound. In due course he would move on, everyone took that for granted, but first he intended to make his mark.

One weekend when he was trimming his hedge, he gave me sixpence to collect the cuttings and wheel them to the dump on the waste ground where his next lot of houses were going up. Afterwards, he opened a bottle of cream soda and we sat in the garden and drank it as the dusk deepened and midges boiled in the shadows like the bubbles in my glass.

'Are you looking forward to the pool, then?' he asked.

I nodded, my nose full of gas. Usually we drank Tizer or dandelion and burdock, home-brewed by a woman in a back street. But cream soda, or rather American Cream Soda, was a mark of Arthur's sophistication and I was too impressed to even acknowledge the bubbles. 'We'll be opening next month,' he said. 'The mayor's coming. There'll be a brass band and a beauty queen. No expense spared. Everything'll be hotsy-totsy.'

I nodded again. The expression was new to me and I filed it away for future reference. 'How much will it cost to get in?' I asked.

He smiled broadly. 'Nix to you. All the kids in this avenue get in free. I'll give you season tickets.' He put down his glass and leaned forward, as if struck by a sudden thought. 'How many are there of you?'

'Five,' I said. 'Six if you count Kenny Parker at the bottom.' The Parkers' house backed onto the waste patch and officially it was the start of another avenue, as yet unbuilt. Adopting it, we thought, was a neighbourly act.

'Six it is,' said Arthur. 'No more, mind. I wouldn't want to start off broke.'

My mother made a fuss to begin with. 'I suppose he thinks we can't afford it,' she said. Later, though, she changed her mind when Arthur called at the door and made an official presentation of the season ticket. It was in a manila envelope with my name typed in capital letters and she turned it this way and that before unpeeling the flap. 'It's really very kind of you,' she said. 'I'm sure he'll make good use of it.'

'And how about you?' asked Arthur Seal. 'Mothers are welcome too.'

My mother blushed. 'I don't think so,' she said.

'Bear it in mind,' said Arthur and he winked.

It was, I suppose, an automatic response to a situation which came to him as naturally as wearing his cream flannels or his plaited shoes, but it made people regard him as racy, not entirely to be trusted. It was the same waggishness which encouraged me to address him as 'Arthur' and not 'Mr Seal'. Not that he advised me either way. He neither knew nor cared anything about etiquette and his indifference contributed in no small way to his undoing.

The sun shone on the day of the opening of the pool and there was a big turn-out. Arthur had abandoned his Wolseley, a car which smelled thrillingly of leather and petrol, for an open float on which the beauty queen was installed with two attendants. Bracing himself behind the driver's cab, he bowed and bobbed to the crowd, most of them waving free balloons and handkerchief-sized flags, all printed with his trademark, a sleek, black seal, rampant on a tub, with a beach ball balanced on its nose. The same emblem was on the flag which waved high above the pool, coiling and uncoiling against a cobalt sky. Even now when I think of happiness I think of that seal, or rather that occasion. It was such an uncomplicated day; for the spectators, I mean. For Arthur it was less simple. The spec builder had turned entrepreneur. He was selling not only a swimming-pool, but his dream of the future. This I realised, as he saluted his own flag, was what he imagined tomorrow would be like. I shivered with excitement as though someone had walked on my grave.

The entire complex was built like an ocean liner, with a ceramic smoke-stack, blue piping on cream tiles and every window a porthole. There was a poolside café, serving drinks (including American Cream Soda) and toasted snacks. Every table was protected by a striped umbrella. Music seeped from concealed speakers (it could be heard underwater too, Arthur told me later) and there were bathrobes for hire and free paper slippers for the bathers to wear as they reclined on blue canvas loungers.

The real triumph was downstairs where Arthur had installed a milk bar. The stools were uphostered in blue towelling.
The bar top was reinforced blue glass and the windows were
portholes, also tinted blue, through which swimmers could
goggle at their friends only a few inches away.

We could choose from ice-creams coloured green, pink and
purple. A knickerbocker glory, modelled in plaster, stood
beside the till. There were pipes which spat jets of steam and
suds of cream. And everything was spotless. It was more like a
laboratory than somewhere to eat and drink.

'Well, I don't know,' said my mother who had decided at
the last moment to come along and see whether the pool was a
safe place for us to frequent, 'what on earth could it have cost
him?'

The same thought had probably occurred to Arthur, but the
day of reckoning was still several months away. The mayor
made his speech of welcome. Arthur himself said a few
modest words. The beauty queen removed her sash and
crown and, after putting on a rubber bathing cap which
squeezed her face into a grumpy little mask, climbed to the top
board of the diving stand and stood with her arms outstretched like the angel on the dome of the public library. She
remained there for a count of ten, pert in a red one-piece
costume that brandished her body like a fist. Three trumpeters
from the brass band blew a fanfare and in the aching silence
that followed she dived towards the sun, then fell as neatly as a
knife into the pool below.

Arthur watched her head break the surface. 'Right you are
then,' he said. 'Everybody in.'

There was a general scrimmage. Small boys chased each
other up the diving stand and hurled themselves into the pool
like bombs. The band played *Horsie Keep Your Tail Up*. The
mayor accepted a glass of champagne, and as the beauty queen
swam to the side Arthur stooped down and gave her his hand.
He hauled her out to stand beside him and as he did so I saw his
free hand fall, casually but implacably, to rest on her behind. It
was not a calculated act. The chances were he never gave it a
thought; in fact, he said as much later. But for several seconds

his hand lay there like a badge, his fingers cradling her rump, now and then drumming the flesh as if it was the upholstery of a chair.

My mother drew in her breath, a sure sign of disapproval, and the beauty queen, whose name was Edie Collins, the daughter of a pork butcher in Hanley, stepped smartly away from Arthur and dug her elbow in his ribs. He doubled over, hung for a moment in mid-air, then his plaited shoes slipped on the tiles and he plunged in at the deep end. He was a small, dark man with long hair and gypsy sideburns and as he swam towards us it looked as though he was wearing a bonnet, whose ribbons trailed and met beneath his chin. The ribbons dissolved and I realised that Arthur's hair-dye was awash. He clambered out, shedding water like a spaniel, and the assembled visitors drew back. It was probably to avoid being splashed, but it looked as though they were fleeing the devil.

Someone brought towels and Arthur was led away to a changing room. He reappeared ten minutes later, resplendent in a royal blue bathrobe, his hair neatly combed, a glass of champagne in his hand. The band played on. He posed for photographs with the mayor and Edie Collins, whose smile by this time was a mere baring of the teeth, and so the occasion was saved. Not entirely though. There was a report in the local paper as sympathetic as any regular advertiser might expect. Arthur's fall into the pool was treated as a mishap which he had surmounted with style. There were glowing descriptions of the milk bar and the underwater view through the portholes. But beneath the compliments lay the hint, unstated but unmistakable, that a folly had been perpetrated and that it was only a matter of time before its full extent would be revealed.

The summer wore on. There was a heat wave in August and the pool did record business. Arthur took care to remain on dry land, but each day he made an appearance in the café and the milk bar wearing the snappiest of trunks and the brightest of shirts, always with one or two pretty girls in tow. Most of them were blonde and all of them laughed a lot. I could hear them, even from the centre of the pool where I floated on my back staring at the sky and watching the pit wheels spin. It was a strange sensation to lie there and know that on every side the rest of the world was at work. Below us too. We were surrounded by mines and the black pyramids of spoil heaps, and I could never forget that the miners themselves were burrowing beneath me, digging the galleries which shipwrecked houses. It was a thought which sometimes kept me awake at night and I wondered if it had occurred to Arthur too.

Since the opening of the pool his reputation had somehow changed. There were fewer jokes about his wife running away with the insurance salesman. He remained a figure of fun, but at the same time his raciness had intensified. Of course it was absurd that Edie Collins had pushed him into his own pool, but what people remembered was what Arthur had done to deserve the upset. If I closed my eyes I could still see his hand resting on Edie's behind, the fingers splayed against the bright scarlet, the twitch of her rump as she aimed her elbow. It was an image far stronger than the memory of Arthur emerging from the pool. The cause overwhelmed the effect. Arthur was reborn as a ladies' man. He sensed it himself and it became something he felt he had to live up to.

'I don't suppose he does much harm,' said my mother when the latest items of gossip were retailed to her by Miss Parker.

'But those girls are half his age.'

'And twice as wise.' My mother stuck stamps on a letter and gave it to me to post. 'I speak as I find,' she said. 'He's a bit impetuous, I suppose, but I've always found him a perfect gentleman.'

It was not the general opinion. The following week Mr Collins, father of Edie, was charged with assaulting Arthur Seal. He pleaded guilty and explained that the family honour was at stake. Arthur had not only laid hands on Edie. He had further insulted her by sending flowers and invitations to dinner without first consulting the head of the household. 'He said he was trying to apologise,' said Mr Collins. 'And then he smiled. That's when I thumped him.' The chairman of the bench nodded sympathetically and imposed a fine of £5. He understood what Mr Collins meant about Arthur's smile.

Other incidents followed. There was a brawl in the milk bar when Arthur was accused of giving the eye to a girl from the local troop of Guides. An aggrieved husband poured paint stripper over his car. He received letters advising him to go back where he came from. A dead dog was found floating in the pool. Arthur still smiled and more often than not there was a blonde in his passenger seat. But there were rumours of unpaid bills and cheques which had bounced and one day, without warning, work was halted on the new estate that Arthur was building. All was well, said Arthur, everything was hotsy-totsy. But while he bargained with the bank to raise fresh capital, thieves stripped his houses of lead pipes and flashing and a week of thunderstorms turned the site into a quagmire.

'Rotten luck,' I said when I next saw him clipping his hedge.

'Don't give it a thought,' he said. 'Look for the silver lining. That's what you have to keep in mind.'

'Do you want me to pick up the cuttings?'

'If you like,' said Arthur. He fished in his pocket for a coin, but I shook my head.

'For nix,' I said.

He blinked hard and then he smiled. It was a different smile to the one which had so enraged Mr Collins. I was sure of that. The smile which Arthur gave me was both conspiratorial and innocent, but above all it was entirely happy. 'Right you are then,' he said. 'Get on with it before I start cracking the whip.'

I never saw Arthur Seal smile again. The next morning he went to his pool and found it empy. Far below where the miners dug in the dark the earth had shuddered and subsided and a hole like a wound now gaped in the bright blue tiles. No one was especially surprised. Subsidence was a fact of North Staffordshire life and Arthur had been aware of it from the start. Walls cracked, gardens were engulfed. Business went on as usual. Not at the pool though. The police strung up a safety barrier and we filed past it like mourners at a graveside. Arthur's flag hung limply from its mast and, as we watched, it was hauled down and taken inside as though the reminder of good times gone was too painful to bear.

All that winter they tried to repair the damage. In spring a notice went up promising that the pool would reopen shortly, but by then the tiles were grimy, most of the windows had been broken and the hole through which the water had drained away still sat at the centre of the desolation, bottomless and unstaunchable. Arthur filed for bankruptcy. Another firm took over the building of his unfinished houses and one morning I saw him in his garden while two men planted an estate agent's sign beside the rockery.

He beckoned me over. 'Come round to the back door,' he said. 'I've got something for you.'

'What is it?'

'Just a souvenir,' said Arthur and he gave me his flag.

He was not long in selling the house and he had left the district before war was declared in September. Edie Collins was the first of our war brides and the local paper printed a photograph of her clutching the arm of an RAF sergeant whose sideburns were every bit as long as Arthur's. That night I took the flag from my bottom drawer and spread it on my bed. The seal grinned at me, the beach ball glued to its nose, but it no longer seemed to have much to do with the man whose emblem it had been. I remembered Arthur differently. I remembered his cream flannel trousers and his plaited shoes and his unshake-able belief that everything, in due course, would be hotsy-totsy. Best of all, I remembered his hand, pinned like a badge to Edie Collins' behind while the music played and the balloons bobbed and the old ultraviolet poured down. For Arthur it had been the hand of fate, the instrument of his downfall, but he had been too blithe, too busy, too intent on giving and getting pleasure to understand that. As my mother occasionally remarked, he was his own worst enemy and I should bear that fact in mind. 'Hotsy-totsy,' I said aloud and looked through the blackout for the silver lining.

Oranges from Spain

DAVID PARK

IT'S NOT A fruit shop any more. Afterwards, his wife sold it and someone opened up a fast food business. You wouldn't recognise it now – it's all flashing neon, girls in identical uniforms and the type of food that has no taste. Even Gerry Breen wouldn't recognise it. Either consciously or unconsciously, I don't seem to pass that way very often, but when I do I always stop and look at it. The neon brightness burns the senses and sears the memories like a wound being cauterised; but then it all comes back and out flows a flood of memory that nothing can stem.

I was sixteen years old and very young when I went to work for Mr Breen in his fruit shop. It was that summer when it seemed to rain every day and a good day stood out like something special. I got the job through patronage. My father and Gerry Breen went back a long way – that always struck me as strange, because they were so unalike as men. Apparently, they were both born in the same street and grew up together, and even when my father's career as a solicitor took him upmarket, they still got together occasionally. My father collected an order of fruit every Friday night on his way home from work, and as children we always talked about 'Gerry Breen's apples'. It's funny the things you remember, and I can

256

recall very clearly my mother and father having an argument about it one day. She wanted to start getting fruit from the supermarket for some reason, but my father wouldn't hear of it. He got quite agitated about it and almost ended up shouting, which was very unlike him. Maybe he acted out of loyalty, or maybe he owed him some kind of favour, but whatever the reason, the arrangement continued.

If his name is mentioned now they never do it in front of me. It's almost as if he never existed. At first it angered me – it was almost as if they thought I would disintegrate at its sound – but gradually I came to be grateful for it. I didn't even go to the funeral, and from that moment it was obvious my family sought to draw a curtain over the whole event. My mother had taken me away for a week's holiday. We stayed with one of her sisters who lives in Donegal, and I've never had a more miserable time. Inevitably, it rained every day and there was nothing to do but mope around and remember, trapped in a house full of women, where the only sounds were the clink of china cups and the click of knitting needles. It was then the dreams started. The intervening years have lessened their frequency but not their horror. When I woke up screaming for about the tenth time, they took me to a special doctor who reassured them with all the usual platitudes – I'd grow out of it, time was a great healer, and so on. In one sense I did grow out of it – I stopped telling anyone about the nightmares and kept them strictly private. They don't come very often now, but when they do only my wife knows. Sometimes she cradles me in her arms like a child until I fall asleep again.

I hadn't even really wanted a job in the first place. It was all my father's idea. He remembered the long weeks of boredom I had complained about the summer before and probably the nuisance I had been as I lazed about the house. I walked right into his trap. He knew I'd been working up to ask if I could have a motorbike for my next birthday. The signs weren't good, and my mother's instinctive caution would have been as difficult a barrier to surmount as the expense, so it came as a surprise when my father casually enquired if I'd be interested in starting to save for one. I took the bait, and before I knew what was happening, I'd been fixed up with a summer job, working in Gerry Breen's fruit shop.

I didn't like the man much at first. He was rough and ready and he would've walked ten miles on his knees to save a penny. I don't think he liked me much either. The first day he saw me he looked me up and down with unconcealed disappointment, with the expression of someone who'd just bought a horse that wasn't strong enough to do the work he had envisaged for it. He stopped short of feeling my arm muscles, but passed some comment about me needing to fill out a bit. Although he wasn't tall himself, he was squat and had a kind of stocky strength about him that carried him through every physical situation. You knew that when he put his shoulder to the wheel, the chances were the wheel would spin. He wore this green coat as if it was some sort of uniform, and I never saw him in the shop without it. It was shiny at the elbows and collar, but it always looked clean. He had sandy-coloured hair that was slicked back and oiled down in a style that suggested he had once had an affinity with the Teddy boys. The first time I met him I noticed his hands, which were flat and square, and his chisel-shaped fingers. He had this little red pen-knife, and at regular intervals he used it to clean them. The other habit he had was a continual hitching-up of his trousers, even though there was no apparent prospect of them falling down. He was a man who seemed to be in perpetual motion. Even when he was standing talking to someone, there was always some part of him that was moving, whether it was transferring his pencil from one ear to the other, or hoisting up the trousers. It was as if there was a kind of mechanism inside him. Sometimes I saw him shuffle his feet through three hundred and sixty degrees like some kind of clockwork toy. For him sitting still would have been like wearing a strait-jacket, and I don't think any chair, no matter how comfortable, ever held him for more than a few minutes.

On my first morning, after his initial disappointment had worn off and he had obviously resolved to make the best of a bad job, he handed me a green coat, similar to his own but even older. It had a musty smell about it that suggested it had been hanging in a dark cupboard for some considerable time, and although I took it home that first weekend for my mother to wash, I don't think the smell ever left it. The sleeves were too long, so all summer I wore it with the cuffs turned up. My first job was chopping sticks. As well as fruit and vegetables, he sold various other things, including bundles of firewood. Out in the back yard was a mountain of wood, mostly old fruit boxes, and for the rest of that morning I chopped them into sticks and put them in polythene bags. At regular intervals he came out to supervise the work and caution me with monotonous regularity to be careful with the hatchet. It was obvious I wasn't doing it to his satisfaction; his dissatisfaction was communicated by a narrowing of his eyes and a snakelike hiss. As far as I was concerned, there weren't too many ways you could chop sticks, but I was wrong. Unable to restrain his frustration any longer, he took the hatchet and proceeded to instruct me in the correct technique. This involved gently inserting it into the end of the piece of wood and then tapping the other end lightly on the ground so that it split gently along the grain. When he was assured I had mastered the method, he watched critically over my first efforts.

'Too thick, son, too thick. Did your da never teach you how to chop sticks?'

It was only when I had produced a series of the thinnest slivers that he seemed content. I suppose it meant he got more bundles of firewood, but you wouldn't have got much of a fire out of them. It made me feel guilty somehow, like I was an accessory to his stinginess. 'Did your da never teach you how to?' was a phrase I heard repeatedly that summer, and it inevitably prefaced a period of instruction in the correct technique and subsequent supervision.

The rest of my time that first morning was divided between sweeping up and humping bags of spuds from the yard into the store-room. No matter how often I brushed that shop floor, it always seemed to need to be done again. I must have filled a whole dump with cauliflower leaves, and I never stopped hating that smell. Perhaps, if I'm honest, I felt the job was a little beneath me. By the time the day was over, my back was aching and I was still trying to extract splinters from my hands. The prospect of a summer spent working like that filled me with despondency, and the attraction of a motorbike lost some of its appeal. I thought of telling my father I didn't want to go back, but was stopped by the knowledge that I would have to listen to eternal speeches about how soft young people were, and how they wanted everything on a plate. That I didn't need, and so I resolved to grit my teeth and stick it out.

The shop was situated at the bottom of the Antrim Road, and while it wasn't that big, every bit of space was used, either for display or storage. It started outside on the pavement where each morning, after carrying out wooden trestles and resting planks on them, we set out trays of fruit, carefully arranged and hand-picked, designed to attract and entice the passer-by. Above all this stretched a green canvas canopy which was supported by ancient iron stanchions, black with age. When it rained it would drip on to the front displays of fruit and so all that summer I had to carry them in and out of the shop. Inside was a long counter with old-fashioned scales and a till that rang as loudly as church bells. Under the counter were paper bags of every size, miles of string, metal hooks, bamboo canes, withered yellow rubber gloves, weights, elastic bands and a paraphernalia of utensils of unfathomable purpose. On the wall behind the counter was an assortment of glass fronted shelving, sagging under the weight of fruit and vegetables. Above head height, the walls were covered in advertising posters that had obviously arrived free with consignments of fruit and looked like they had been there since the shop opened. On the customer side was more shelving and below it a clutter of wooden and cardboard boxes that seemed designed to ladder tights or catch the wheels of shopping trolleys. If there was any kind of logical system in the layout, I never managed to work it out. I got the impression it had evolved into a sprawling disorder and that so long as everything was close at hand, the owner saw no reason to change it.

In the back of the shop was a store-room where among merchandise and debris stood a wooden table, two chairs, a gas cooker and a sink. The only other room was a small washroom. Beyond this was a small cobbled yard, enclosed by a brick wall topped with broken glass. Over everything hung the sweet, ripe smell of a fruit shop, but in Mr Breen's shop it was mixed with a mildewed mustiness, a strange hybrid that stayed in my senses long after I had left the scene.

I worked my butt off that first day and it was obvious he intended getting value for money out of me. Maybe my father had told him it was what I needed – I don't know. It was nearly time to close and the shop was empty. He was working out some calculations on the back of a brown paper bag and I was moving fruit into the store room, when he glanced up at me with a kind of puzzled look, as if he was trying to work out what I was thinking.

'Sure, son, it's money for old rope. Isn't that right?'

I gave a non-committal nod of my head and kept on working. Then he told me I could go, and I could tell he was wondering whether he would see me the next day. Returning to his calculations again, he licked the stub of the pencil he was using and hitched up his trousers. I said goodbye and just as I was going out the door he called me back.

'Do you want to know something, son?'

I looked at him, unsure of what response he expected. Then, signalling me closer, he whispered loudly, 'My best friends are bananas.' I forced a smile at his joke, then walked out into the street and took a deep breath of fresh air.

The fruit shop did steady business. Most of the trade came from the housewives who lived in the neighbourhood, but there was also a regular source of custom from people who arrived outside the shop in cars, and by their appearance didn't live locally – the type who bought garlic. He knew them all by name and sometimes even had their order already made up, always making a fuss over them and getting me to carry it out to their car. They were obviously long-standing customers, and I suppose they must have stayed loyal to him because they were assured of good quality fruit. He had a way with him – I had to admit that. He called every woman 'madam' for a start, even those who obviously weren't, but when he said it, it didn't sound like flattery, or like he was patronising them. It just sounded polite in an old-fashioned way. He had a great line in chat as well. If he didn't know them it was usually some remark about the weather, but if he did, he would ask about their families or make jokes, always cutting his cloth according to his audience. When a gaggle of local women were in, it was all 'Now, come on, ladies, get your grapes. Sweetest you can taste. Just the thing for putting passion into your marriage', or 'Best bananas – good enough to eat sideways'. They all loved it, and I'm sure it was good for business. Whatever their bills came to, he always gave them back the few odd pence, and I'm sure they thought he was very generous. As far as I was concerned, I thought he was one of the meanest men I'd ever met. For a start, he never threw anything away – that was one of the things that was wrong with the shop. Whether it was a bit of string or a piece of wood, he stored it carefully, and if he saw me about to throw something away, he'd stop me with a 'Never know when it might come in useful, son'. Most of the produce he collected himself from the market early in the morning, but whenever deliveries were made, he inspected each consignment rigorously, with an energy that frequently exasperated the deliverer. If he found a damaged piece of fruit, he would hold it up for mutual observation and, wrestling up his trousers with the other hand, would say something like, 'Now come on George, are you trying to put me out of business?' and he'd haggle anew over already arranged prices. Watching him sniffing out flawed produce would have made you think he'd an in-built radar system. And he was always looking for something for nothing. Sometimes it was embarrassing. If the Antrim Road had still had horses going up and down it, he'd have been out collecting the droppings and selling them for manure.

One day Father Hennessy came into the shop. Mr Breen's face dropped noticeably and about half a dozen parts of his body seemed to fidget all at once.

'Hello, Father. What can I do for you?'

'Hello, Gerry. How's business?'

'Slow, Father, very slow.'

The priest smiled and, lifting an apple, rubbed it on his sleeve, the red bright against the black.

'I'm popping over to the Mater to visit some parishioners. I thought a nice parcel of fruit would cheer them up. Help them to get better.'

He started to eat the apple and his eyes were smiling.

'Of course, Father. A very good idea.'

With well-disguised misery, he parcelled up a variety of fruit and handed it over the counter.

'God bless you, Gerry. Treasure in heaven, treasure in heaven.'

With the package tucked under his arm, and still eating the apple, the priest sauntered out to his car. If he had looked back, he would have seen Mr Breen slumped on the counter, his head resting on both hands.

'The church'll be the ruin of me. He does that about three times a month. Thinks my name's Mr Del Monte, not Gerry Breen. Treasure in heaven's no use to me when I go to pay the bills at the end of the month.'

The frustration poured out of him and I listened in silence, knowing he wasn't really talking to me.

'Does he go up to Michael Devlin in the bank and ask him for some money because he's going to visit the poor? Since when did it become part of my purpose in life to subsidise the National Health system? I pay my taxes like anyone else.'

I think he'd have gone on indefinitely in a similar vein, but for the arrival of a customer, and then it was all smiles and jokes about the rain.

'Do you know, Mrs Caskey, what I and my assistant are building out in the yard?'

Mrs Caskey didn't know but her aroused curiosity was impatient for an answer.

'We're building an ark! And whenever it's finished we're going to load up two of every type of fruit and float away up the road.'

'Get away with you, Gerry. You're a desperate man.'

And then he sold her tomatoes and a lettuce which he

described as 'the best lettuce in the shop'. I'd almost have believed him myself, but for the fact that I'd already heard the same phrase on about three previous occasions that day.

Gerry Breen was very proud of his shop, but he took a special pride in his displays outside, and he did this expert printing with whitening on the front window. Not only did he fancy himself a bit of an artist, but also as a kind of poet laureate among fruiterers. He had all these bits of cardboard – I think they were backing cards out of shirts – and on them he printed, not only the names and prices of the fruit, but also descriptive phrases meant to stimulate the taste buds of the reader. Grapes might be described as 'deliciously sweet' or strawberries as 'the sweet taste of summer' while Comber spuds were always 'balls of flour'. The front window always looked well. Bedded on a gentle slope of simulated grass rested the various sections of produce, complete with printed labels. Each morning when he had arranged it he would go out on the pavement and stand with his hands on his hips, studying it like an art critic viewing a painting. Inside he had other signs saying things like 'Reach for a peach', 'Iceberg lettuce – just a tip of the selection' or 'Fancy an apple – why not eat a pear?'

After the first week or so we started to get on a little better. I think he realised that I was trustworthy and prepared to pull my weight. He probably thought of me as being a bit snobbish, but tolerated it so long as he got good value for his money. I in turn became less critical of what I considered his defects. Gradually, he began to employ more of my time on less menial jobs. After three weeks I had progressed to serving customers and weighing their fruit, and then a week later I was allowed to enter the holy of holies and put my hand in the till. I still had to chop sticks and brush up of course, but whenever the shop was busy I served behind the counter. I almost began to feel part of the business. The continual wet weather stopped me from missing out on the usual activities of summer and I was increasingly optimistic that my father would reward my industry with a motorbike. Mr Breen didn't much like the rain – he was always complaining how bad it was for business.

According to him, it discouraged passing trade, and people didn't buy as much as they did in warm weather. He was probably right. Sometimes, when a lull in trade created boredom, I tried to wind him up a little.

'Mr Breen, do you not think it's wrong to sell South African fruit?'

'Aw, don't be daft, son.'

'But do you not think that by selling their fruit you're supporting apartheid?'

He swopped his pencil from ear to ear and did what looked a bit like a tap dance.

'I'm only supporting myself and the wife. Sure wouldn't the blacks be the first to suffer if I stopped selling it? They'd all end up starving and how would that help them?'

I was about to provoke him further when a customer appeared and I let him have the last word.

'God knows, son, they have my sympathy – don't I work like a black myself?'

The customer turned out to be Mr Breen's wife. She was all dressed up in a blue and white suit and was on her way to some social function. She had one of those golden charm bracelets that clunked so many heavy charms I wondered how her wrist bore the strain, and while she hardly looked sideways at him, she made an embarrassing fuss over me, asking about my parents and school, and gushing on in a slightly artificial way. When she finished whatever business she had, she said goodbye to me and warned Gerald not to work me too hard. I smiled at the name Gerald, and I could see him squirming behind the counter. A heavy shower came on and we both stood in the doorway watching it bounce off the road. He was unusually silent and I glanced at him a few times to see if he was all right. When he spoke, his voice was strangely colourless.

'Never get married, son – it's the end of your happiness.'

I didn't know whether he was joking or not, so I just went on staring at the rain.

'My wife's ashamed of me,' he said in the same lifeless voice.

I uttered some vague and unconvincing disagreement and then turned away in embarrassment. I started to brush the floor, glancing up from time to time as he stood motionless in the doorway. In a minute or so the rain eased and it seemed to break the spell, but for the rest of that afternoon, he was subdued and functioned in a mechanical way. He even closed the shop half an hour early – something he'd never done before.

Nothing like that ever happened again, my first experience of work slipped into an uneventful routine. One day, though, comes clearly to mind. One afternoon when business was slack he asked me to deliver fruit round to a Mrs McCausland. The address was a couple of streets away and I felt a little self-conscious as I set off in my green coat. It wasn't a big order – just a few apples and oranges and things. I followed the directions I had been given and arrived at a terraced house. Unlike most of its neighbours, the front door was closed, and the net curtain in the window offered no glimpse of the interior. At first, it seemed as if no one was in, and I was just about to turn and leave, when there was the slow undrawing of a bolt and the rattle of a chain. The door opened wide enough to allow an old woman's face to peer out at me, suspicion speckling her eyes. I identified myself and showed the fruit to reassure her. Then there was another pause before the door gradually opened to reveal an old woman leaning heavily on a walking stick. Inviting me in, she hobbled off slowly and painfully down the hall and into her tiny living room. She made me sit down and, despite my polite protests, proceeded to make me a cup of tea. The room resembled a kind of grotto, adorned with religious objects and pictures. Her rosary beads hung from the fireplace clock and a black cat slept on the rug-covered sofa. She talked to me from the kitchen as she worked.

'Isn't the weather terrible?'

'Desperate – you'd never think it was the summer,' I replied, smiling as I listened to myself. I had started to sound like Gerry Breen's apprentice.

'Summers never used to be like this. I can remember

summers when the streets were baked hot as an oven and everyone used to sit on their doorsteps for you could hardly get a breath. If you sat on your doorstep these past few days you'd get pneumonia.'

She brought me a cup of tea in a china cup, and a slice of fruit cake, but nothing for herself. She sat down and scrutinised me intently.

'So you're working for Gerry for the summer. I'm sure that's good fun for you. You work hard and maybe he'll keep you on permanent.'

I didn't correct her misunderstanding, but I laughed silently inside.

'He says if it keeps on raining he's going to start building an ark.'

She smiled and rearranged the cushion supporting her back.

'Gerry's the salt of the earth. Do you see that fruit you brought? He's been doing that for the best part of fifteen years and nobody knows but him and me.'

She paused to pour more tea into my cup and I listened with curiosity as she continued, her words making me feel as if I was looking at a familiar object from a new and unexpected perspective.

'I gave him a wee bit of help a long time ago and he's never forgotten it, not through all these years. I don't get out much now, but sometimes I take a walk round to the shop, just to see how he's getting on. He's a great man for the crack, isn't he?'

I smiled in agreement and she shuffled forward in her seat, leaning confidentially towards me.

'Have you met Lady Muck yet? Thon woman's more airs and graces then royalty. She was born and bred a stone's throw from here and to listen to her now you'd think she came from the Malone Road. I knew her family and they didn't have two pennies to rub together between the lot of them. Now she traipses round the town like she was a duchess. You'll never catch her serving behind the counter.'

It was obvious that the woman wanted to talk – she was probably starved of company – and no matter how often I attempted a polite exit, she insisted on my staying a little

267

DAVID PARK

longer, assuring me that Gerry wouldn't mind. I wasn't so sure, but there was no easy escape, as she produced a photograph album and talked me through a maze of memories and mementoes.

Parts of it were interesting and when she told me about the Belfast blitz I learned things I hadn't known before. Before I finally got up to go, she returned to the subject of the weather, her voice serious and solemn.

'This weather's a sign. I've been reading about it in a tract that was sent to me. It's by this holy scholar, very high up in the church, and he says we're living in the last days. All these wars and famines – they're all signs. All this rain – it's a sign too. I believe it.'

When she opened the front door it was still raining and I almost started to believe it too. I ran back quickly, partly to get out of the rain and partly because I anticipated a rebuke about the length of my absence.

There were no customers in the shop when I entered and he merely lifted his head from what he was reading, asked if everything was all right with Mrs McCausland, and returned to his study. It surprised me a little that he said nothing about the time. He was filling in his pools coupon and concentrating on winning a fortune, so perhaps he was distracted by the complexities of the Australian leagues. He had been doing them all summer and his approach never varied. He did two columns every week, the first by studying the form and this forced him to ponder such probabilities as whether Inala City would draw with Slacks Creek, or Altona with Bulleen. For the second column, he selected random numbers, his eyes screwed up and an expression on his face as if he was waiting for some kind of celestial message. On this particular afternoon, reception must have been bad, because he asked me to shout them out. Out of genuine curiosity, I asked him what he would do if he did win a fortune. He looked at me to see if I was winding him up, but must have sensed that I wasn't, because, on a wet and miserable Belfast afternoon, he told me his dream.

'It's all worked out in here,' he said, tapping the side of his

268

head with a chisel-shaped finger. 'I've it all planned out.
Thinking about it keeps you going – makes you feel better on
days like this.'

He paused to check if I was laughing at him, then took a
hand out of his coat pocket and gestured slowly round the
shop.

'Look around you, son. What do you see?'

A still, grey light seemed to have filtered into the shop. The
lights were off and it was quiet in an almost eerie way.
Nothing rustled or stirred, and the only sound was the soft fall
of the rain. In the gloom the bright colours smouldered like
embers; rhubarb like long tongues of flame; red sparks of
apples; peaches, perfect in their velvety softness, yellows and
oranges flickering gently.

'Fruit,' I answered. 'Different kinds of fruit.'

'Now, do you know what I see?'

I shook my head.

'I see places. A hundred different places. Look again.' And
as he spoke he began to point with his finger. 'Oranges from
Spain, apples from New Zealand, cabbages from Holland,
peaches from Italy, grapes from the Cape, bananas from
Ecuador – fruit from all over the world. Crops grown and
harvested by hands I never see, packed and transported by
other hands in a chain that brings them here to me. It's a
miracle if you think about it. When we're sleeping in our beds,
hands all over the world are packing and picking so that Gerry
Breen can sell it here in this shop.'

We both stood and looked, absorbing the magnitude of the
miracle.

'You asked me what I'd do if I won the jackpot – well, I've it
all thought out. I'd go to every country whose fruit I sell, go
and see it grow, right there in the fields and the groves, in the
orchards and the vineyards. All over the world!'

He looked at me out of the corner of his eye to see if I thought
he was crazy, then turned away and began to tidy the counter. I
didn't say anything, but in that moment, if he'd asked me, I
would have gone with him. All these years later, I still regret that
I didn't tell him that. Told him while there was still time.

Four days later, Gerry Breen was dead. A man walked into the shop and shot him twice. He became another bystander, another nobody, sucked into the vortex by a random and malignant fate that marked him out. They needed a Catholic to balance the score – he became a casualty of convenience, a victim of retribution, propitiation of a different god. No one even claimed it. Just one more sectarian murder – unclaimed, unsolved, soon unremembered but by a few. A name lost in the anonymity of a long list. I would forget too, but I can't.

I remember it all. There were no customers when a motorbike stopped outside with two men on it. The engine was still running as the passenger came towards the shop. I was behind the counter looking out. He had one hand inside his black motorcycle tunic and wore a blue crash helmet – the type that encloses the whole head. A green scarf covered the bottom half of his face, so only his eyes were visible. Only his eyes – that's all I ever saw of him. Mr Breen was standing holding a tray of oranges he had just brought from the back.

Suddenly, the man pulled a gun out of his tunic and I thought we were going to be robbed, but he never spoke, and as he raised the gun and pointed at Mr Breen, his hand was shaking so much he had to support it with the other one. It was then I knew he hadn't come for money. The first shot hit Gerry Breen in the chest, spinning him round, and as he slumped to the floor the oranges scattered and rolled in all directions. He lay there, face down, and his body was still moving. Then, as I screamed an appeal for mercy, the man walked forward and, kneeling over the body, shot him in the back of the head. His body kicked and shuddered, and then was suddenly and unnaturally still. I screamed again in fear and anger and then, pointing the gun at me, the man walked slowly backwards to the door of the shop, ran to the waiting bike and was gone. Shaking uncontrollably and stomach heaving with vomit, I tried to turn Mr Breen over on to his back, but he was too heavy for me. Blood splashed his green coat, and flowed from the dark gaping wound, streaming across the floor, mixing with the oranges that were strewn all around us. Oranges from Spain.

They say help arrived almost immediately. I don't know. All I can remember is thinking of the old woman's words and hoping it really was the end of the world, and being glad and asking God to drown the world, wanting it to rain for a thousand years, rain and rain and never stop until all the blood was washed away and every street was washed clean. There were voices then and helping hands trying to lift me away, but no one could move me as I knelt beside him, clutching frantically at his green coat, begging God not to let him die, praying he'd let Gerry Breen live to build his ark and bring aboard the fruit of the world. All the fruit of the world safely stored. Oranges from Spain, apples from the Cape – the sweet taste of summer preserved for ever, eternal and incorruptible.

Skinny Louie

FIONA FARRELL POOLE

The Setting

IMAGINE A SMALL town: along its edges, chaos.

To the east, clinking shelves of shingle and a tearing sea, surging in from South America across thousands of gull-studded white-capped heaving miles.

To the south, the worn hump of a volcano crewcut with pines dark and silent, but dimpled still on the crest where melted rock and fire have spilled to the sea, where they have hissed and set into solid bubbles, black threaded with red.

To the west, a border of hilly terraces, built up from layer upon layer of shells which rose once, dripping, from the sea and could as easily shudder like the fish it is in legend, and dive.

To the north, flat paddocks pockmarked with stone and the river which made them shifting restlessly from channel to channel in its broad braided bed.

Nothing is sure.

The town pretends of course, settled rump-down on the coastal plain with its back to the sea, which creeps up yearly a nibble here a bite there, until a whole football field has gone at the boys' high school and the cliff walkway crumbles and the sea demands propitiation, truckloads of rubble and concrete blocks. And the town inches away in neat rectangular steps up the flanks of the volcano which the council names after an early mayor, a lardy mutton-chop of a man, hoping to tame it as the Greeks thought they'd fool the Furies by calling them the Kindly Ones; inches away across shingle bar and flax swamp to the shell terraces and over where order frays at last into unpaved roads, creeks flowing like black oil beneath willows tangled in convolvulus, and old villa houses, gaptoothed, teetering on saggy piles, with an infestation of hens in the yard and a yellow-toothed dog chained to the water tank.

At the centre, things seem under control. The Post Office is a white wedding cake, scalloped and frilled, and across the road are the banks putting on a responsible Greek front (though ramshackle corrugated iron behind.) At each end of the main street the town mourns its glorious dead with a grieving soldier in puttees to the north and a defiant lion to the south, and in between a cohort of memorial elms was drawn up respectfully until 1952 when it was discovered that down in the dark the trees had broken ranks and were rootling around under the road tearing crevices in the tarmac, and the Council was forced to be stern: tore out the lot and replaced them with plots of more compliant African marigolds. There are shops and petrol stations and churches and flowering cherries for beautification and a little harbour with a tea kiosk in the lee of the volcano. It's as sweet as a nut, as neat as a pie, as a pin.

Imagine it.

Imagine it at night, a print composed of shapes and shadows. Early morning, January 24th 1954. The frilly hands on the Post Office clock show 3.30 so it's 3.25 am, GMT, as everyone knows. (Time is no more thoroughly dependable here than the earth beneath one's feet.) It's unseasonably cold. A breeze noses in over the breakwater in the harbour and in amongst the pottles and wrappers by the tea kiosk, tickling the horses on the merry-go-round in the playground so they tittup tittup and squeak, fingering the bristles on the Cape pines and sighing down their branches into a dark pit of silence. Flower boxes have been hung along the main street

273

and as the wind passes they swing and spill petals, fuchsias and carnations. There are coloured lights and bunting which, if it were only daylight, could be seen to be red white and blue because tomorrow, the Queen is coming. At 3.05 pm the Royal express, a Ja class locomotive (No. 1276) drawing half a dozen refurbished carriages, will arrive at the railway crossing on the main street. Here, Her Majesty Queen Elizabeth II and His Royal Highness Prince Philip will step into a limousine which will carry them up the main street past the Post Office, the banks and the shops which have all had their fronts painted for the occasion (their backs remain as ever, patchy and rusted.) By the grieving soldier the royal couple will turn left towards the park where they will be formally welcomed at 3.20 pm by the mayor and mayoress and shake hands with forty-five prominent citizens. They will be presented with some token of the town's affection. At 3.25 pm they will commence their walk to the train and at 3.40 pm they will depart for the south. The moves are all set out in the Royal Tour Handbook, the stage is set, the lines rehearsed, and the citizens, prominent and otherwise, are tucked under blanket and eiderdown, secure in the knowledge that everything has been properly organised. If they stir a little it is because the wind tugs at curtains, or because through the fog of dreaming they hear some foreign noise outside the windows where their cats and dogs have sloughed off their daytime selves and stalk, predatory, the jungles of rhubarb and blackcurrant. The sea breathes. Whooshaaah. Whooshaaah.

Brian Battersby witnesses a curious phenomenon

Midway up Hull Street on the flanks of the volcano there is one citizen who is not asleep. Brian Battersby is sitting on his garage roof. His legs are wrapped in a tartan rug, his thermos is full of vege soup, and with stiff fingers he is trying to adjust the focus on his new 4-inch Cook refractor. Thousands of miles above his head a civilisation more advanced than any on earth is constructing a canal and by muffled red torchlight Brian is tracing the line of it: from the Nodus Gordii SE in the direction of the Mare Sirenum, at mind-boggling speed: a hundred miles a day? Two hundred perhaps? What machines they must have, what power! Above the Cape a meteor flares, green and white, and Brian pauses, waiting for the shower that will follow, but the meteor grows in brightness. Brighter than Mars. Bigger. A fireball, as large as the full moon! For a moment the whole town is caught in brilliant silhouette and Brian sits motionless on the garage roof, vaguely aware of music, an odd percussive ticktocking. He cannot identify it, but the fact is that every hen in the town is singing. Necks stretched, tiny eyes like amber beads shining in the warm darkness of their fowlruns, they chorus: Wa-a-a-chet auf, ruft uns di-e Stim-mm-e. Awake! Awake! Out on the Awamoa Road a Hereford cow more sensitive than her sisters is levitating above a hedge and cats and dogs have forgotten the jungle and kneel, paws tucked to soft belly. The meteor explodes at last into a sequinned fall of shining particles and the town recovers: hens tuck heads beneath wings, the cow descends with a soft thud and cats and dogs stretch and look uneasily about them into the night, ears flattened. Up on the garage roof Brian is shaking. He knows suddenly and with absolute clarity that those canals are not the work of superior beings who might offer solutions to fallible humanity but are mere ripples of dust blown this way and that by howling wind, and he knows that he, Brian, is a small rather pompous accounts clerk who will spend the next thirty years in the offices of the Power Board, and that his wife wishes now that she'd married Don Barton, former All Black and successful stock and station agent, when he'd asked as a promising junior back in 1948. She stays for the kids and takes out her disappointment in housewifely perfection. It's too much truth to handle all at once. Best not confronted. Brian reaches for his notebook. 'January 24, 1954. 0357 UT.,' he writes with trembling hand. 'Mag. –?? fireball in clear sky. Green and white.' What amazing luck! What a coup! He peers up into the darkness, eyes still dazzled and sparkling and attempts accurate estimation. 'Travelled 30°–35° start 25° altitude 140° azimuth. Approx. 1 min. 58 sec duration.' What a note it will make for Meteor News! 'Accompanying sonic phenomena,' he adds and reaches for his thermos and a shot of hot soup.

Two miles from his garage roof in the Begonia House at the Public Gardens, Louie Symonds, Skinny Louie, aged fifteen, is giving birth.

Skinny Louie has a baby

The Begonia House is warm, steamy, sticky with primeval trickling and the sweet-sour smell of rampant growth. Louie has managed to drag some coconut matting into a corner and squats there, full-bellied and bursting, hands clamped to a water pipe while her body tears in pieces. No one can hear her groan. The Gardens are empty. Only beds of pansies and petunias wheeling away from the glass house along the edges of gravel paths, circling the Peter Pan statue and the Gallipoli fountain and the specimen trees with their identity labels tacked to their trunks. Louie is on her own.

Far away to the south is the dark little warren where she lives with her mum Lill. Lill isn't in tonight either, as it happens. She's been off for three weeks or so on a Korean boat and she won't be back till it leaves for the north with its cargo of snapper and squid, and the girls are put ashore. Lill says she's got a thing for the chinks: she likes them small and smooth and she likes the way they pay her no trouble and she likes the presents: whisky, stockings, a nice jacket. It's better than hanging round the Robbie Burns anyway taking your chances with any poxy john who fancies a bit between jugs. Louie came with her once or twice down the boats, but she gave them all the pip, got on people's nerves being so quiet, hanging around like a fart at a funeral, so Louie stayed home after that while Lill with her Joan Crawford lips and her hair curled went into Port. At this moment she's bobbing about two miles off Kaikoura wondering if she's got enough to go eight no trumps and Louie is in pain. She has walked for days to this place, travelling by night, and by day when the sun slammed down like a pot lid, she has curled round her belly and slept under a bush or a bridge.

She has often done this: got the jumpies, set off walking till she's quiet again, then turned from home. This time she's had them bad. She has walked and slept for days, sucking a stone for spit, following the road up from the city to the hills, past the white rock where she lay once months before to warm herself in the sun. She'd been sprawled, dozing, light tangled in her lashes in tiny scarlet stars, when a shadow fell upon her like a stone. Louie looked up and there was a hawk hovering. She lay very still. The hawk flew closer, settled. She took the weight of him gasping as his talons drove tiny holes in her breast. He dipped his tailfeathers in her open mouth. She smelled the dry bird scent of him. Then he rose wings beating into the sun and she lost him in the glare.

She passed the rock two nights ago. Yesterday morning she stopped near a country store where she got a whole Vienna slipping it quick as winking under her coat while the man was lifting trays from a truck. She'd sat under a hedge in early morning half-light and picked out a hole, chewing slowly, and a plump grey mare had come to her from the mist and stood while she squeezed its titties and took the milk, licking it from her fingers, glutinous, sticky, Highlander Condensed. When the sun was up, she slept. It was wise to hide by day. She didn't trust cars. When she was little, cars came to their house, crawling like grey beetles round the road from Port and when they saw them they'd run away, her and Alamein and Yvonne, because the cars meant questions and picking at their hair for cooties and ice-cream sticks forcing their tongues back and where? And why? And how often? And Lill in a paddy, though she was nice as pie to the lady clearing a space and saying would she care for a cup of tea? But as soon as the car had gone it was bloody cow and why the hell couldn't Louie learn to smile instead of standing there like some mental case because if she didn't they'd have her out to Seacliff, she looked that daft. Lill slammed around them savage, so they learned to scatter when cars came, hiding like the cats in the smooth places beneath the hedge or the washhouse. But once Ally and Yvonne weren't quick enough and the lady got them, took them away somewhere and they were never seen again. So Louie hid from cars. You couldn't trust them.

Tonight, Louie has crossed some paddocks sniffing for the sea and found herself on a hill above a railway line which curved down into a crisscross pattern of light. Her body was heavy and her back ached. She'd been picking at the bread rolling doughballs when she went to the lav suddenly, no warning, right there in her pants, so she peeled them off and stuffed them steaming into a bush. Cough said a sheep. Louie began to walk along the railway towards the town. The pain in her back was growing and another tiny nut of it pressed at the base of her skull.

Clump clump clump sleeper by sleeper careful not to fall between and have bad luck. Around her everything was coming alive: trees tapped her shoulder, fence posts skittered by on the blind side and the grass lined up and waved. The weight in her belly heaved and she had to stop at the bottom of the hill for everything to settle. The railway line crossed a street. Louie stepped from the sleepers onto tarmac and ahead was an arch of flowers, framing black shadow.

Then the pain came up from behind and grabbed her so that she had to cry out as she used to at school when Wayne Norris chinese burned her arms or stuck her with a pen nib saying cowardy custard cry baby cry only this was worse and she tried to run away through the archway into the dark. The pain lost her there for a bit so Louie took her chance, stumbling across a lawn to the shelter of trees and a cage where a bird asked her who was a pretty cocky, along paths frilled with grey rows of flowers to a glass house gleaming when the moon came from behind cloud where Louie hid, sneaking into a corner. But this pain was too smart. It had slipped in beside her already and was squeezing sly, cowardy cowardy custard, driving her into a black hole where there was nothing but a voice groaning over and over and her body ripping and suddenly silence. A slither. And silence.

On the coconut matting between her legs lay a sticky black

thing, wriggling in the sweet stench of blood. Louie crouched waiting for the pain to jump her again but it had gone, sidled off shutting the door silently. Louie wiped some jelly from the black thing and it mewed under her hand. They lay quiet together. Slowly the glass about them turned to grey squares then white and Louie felt her legs twitch. The warm air here settled round her head like a thick blanket and she needed out. She took her cardy and wrapped it round the thing then stood carefully, wobbling a little, and went outside where the grass was shiny and her feet left dark prints as she walked on water past the bird and the flowers to the archway and the street. She moved slowly past houses with their curtains drawn still and the cats coming home to sleep, down a long street to the shore. The sea was stretching and waking too and the clouds as she walked up the beach were golden bars with the sun slipping between. She stopped from time to time to wash blood from her legs. She ate the last of the bread. In a cleft in the low clay cliff were a wheel-less Ford, some mattresses stained and spitting fluff, broken boxes, a pile of rotting plums. Louie was tired. She dragged a mattress into the car, and curled to sleep. On the gear shift a nursery spider had spun its web. Baby spiders jittered under the membrane, hundreds of them. Louie prodded gently at their opaque shell and they scattered at her touch but she was careful not to tear a hole because then the cold could come in and kill them all.

That's the story of how Louie Symonds, daughter of Lilleas Symonds popularly known as Shanghai Lill, gave birth. The paternity of the child is in some doubt. It is possible that the father is Wayne Norris, an acned youth who, since primary school, has paid Louie in bags of lollies for a quick poke in the cemetery on the way home. She's particularly fond of gobstoppers. She likes lying back in the long grass beside the stone IN L VING MORY of Isabella Grant 18 blank blank OH D TH WH IS THY NG while Wayne wiggles his dicky about prodding hopefully, and when she's had enough of that she can say get off, roll over and see how the lolly has changed from red to yellow to blue.

Wayne is a definite possibility.

It is equally probable that the father is a hawk.

The Queen Comes by Train

The Queen was coming. Maura stood with her mother and father and Shona down by the railway crossing at the very end of the route. She would have preferred to be in the Park suffering torments of jealousy while some other little girl with perfect curls and a perfect dress handed the Queen a posy while performing a perfect curtsey, but they'd been late and this was the closest they could get.

Dad hadn't wanted to come at all. 'Load of poppycock,' he'd said. 'Mrs Windsor and that chinless cretin she married riding along waving at the peasants and mad Sid and the rest of them bringing up the rear kowtowing for all they're worth. Lot of nonsense.'

'I think she's pretty,' said Maura, who had a gold Visit medal pinned to her best frock and a scrapbook of pictures cut from Sunny Stories in her bedroom: The Little Princesses at Play with the Royal Corgies on the Lawn at Balmoral, The Little Princesses in their Playhouse which had a proper upstairs and wasn't just a made-over pig pen with ripped sheets and curtains. 'Mrs Barnett says the Queen has a peaches and cream complexion.'

'Peaches and bloody cream!' said their father, thumping the table so his tea spilled. 'There weren't too many peaches around back in 1848 when her lot were gorging themselves in London while our lot ate grass, and don't you forget it.' Dad hated the Queen, Oliver Cromwell and Winston Churchill because of the Troubles and the Famine and because they-came-across-and-tried-to-teach-us-their-ways.

'That's years ago,' said Mum. 'Now turn around Maura so I can brush out the other side.' Maura turned, glad to be relieved of the tight ringlet sausages which had dug into her scalp all night.

'And what about during the war?' said their mother, who was pink-cheeked today and ready for a fight. 'They stayed in London didn't they? They stayed with the people in the East

End right through the Blitz and the Queen Mother even said she was glad the palace got bombed because then she could feel they were sharing the suffering.'

'Suffering?' said Marty. 'What did she know about suffering, one of the richest families in the world and you know how they got there don't you? Murder and betrayal and half of them illegitimate into the bargain, born the wrong side of the . . .'

'Shh,' said their mother, her mouth tightlipped round a blue satin ribbon. 'The children . . . Hold still, Maura, for pity's sake.'

Marty drank his tea morosely. 'Eating grass,' he said. 'Eating dirt, so some English bugger could go in velvet.'

A final tug at the ribbon and Maura was released.

'Well, are you coming or not?' said Mum driving a hat pin into her pink church hat, and Dad said he supposed he would, if she was that set on it, but he was damned if he was going to get dressed up. The Queen would have to take him in his gardening clothes or not at all, and Mum said nonsense, you're not leaving the house in that jersey, so go and get changed, there was still time, but of course there wasn't and they could hear the crowd roar like a wave breaking before they were halfway down the hill and they had to run and push even to find the place to stand by the Gardens gate.

The Pipe Band was wheezing and wailing a few yards away and Maura would have liked to go and stand up close to watch the men's cheeks puff and the rhythmic flap of their white duck feet and to feel her ears buzz with drum roll and drone. But they were inaccessible through a dense forest of legs and bottoms: fat, skinny, trousered, floralled and striped, milling about so that she felt as frightened and inconsequential as she had when she'd opened the gate at Uncle Roy's and the cows had pressed through before she'd been able to jump to one side, buffeting her in their eagerness to get to the paddock. She'd have liked a ride on her father's shoulders, but Shona was already in place looking goofy with her paper flag and her bottle teat clenched between her teeth. Maura tugged at her mother's hand, but knew she was too heavy and that her mother couldn't lift her, not now with the baby inside. Mum looked down and said don't fuss poppet and hang on tight because there's such a crowd. Maura needed no instruction. Around her the huge bodies pressed and she took sticky hold of her mother's skirt. The crowd noise was like static which tuned in snatches into God Save the Queen and cheering. (The Mayor's wife was presenting Her Majesty with a white begonia in a silver casket, Mrs Barnett told them next morning, and the Mayor was giving the Prince a photo of the Begonia House to hang on the wall at Buckingham Palace.) Then the roar built like rain drumming and mum stood tiptoe saying, 'Oh, she's coming! Maura, you must see her properly, this is a Once-in-a-Lifetime Opportunity!' And before Maura could protest she had scooped her up, and was tapping a man's shoulder and asking, 'Could my daughter get down to the front please? She can't see.' Handing her over like a parcel, passed from person to person till she stood at the very edge of the crowd where there was no coach and no horses but an ordinary man and woman walking along the road past the baths, talking sometimes to the crowd or waving, and the woman's face was a bit like the Queen's but not peaches and cream and topped with an ordinary hat, not a crown. People were calling hurrah hurrah and the pipe band shrilled so Maura waved her flag uncertainly as the man and woman passed by and in a very ordinary way, exactly as anyone might, climbed up the stairs onto the train, turned and waved, and the train chugged (whooshaaah whooshaaah) away down the track.

Then the crowd broke. Maura stood with her paper flag but no hand came down out of the press of bodies and no voice said, 'Ah, there you are Maura,' lifting her up to safety. She was pushed and prodded, spun and stepped about until she found herself up against a floral arch and beyond it lay a smooth and empty lawn, so she went there, and once she was there she remembered the parrot and then Peter Pan and then the Begonia House where you could pick up fuchsias from the floor and wear them for ear rings, and that was how she found the baby.

It was like finding the kittens mewing blind and wriggling

in the long grass by the sand pit, except that the baby's eyes were open and it waved its hands sticky and streaked with cream but perfect just the same with proper nails. Maura took her hanky and spat on it as her mother did for a lick and a promise and wiped at the baby's dirty cheek. The baby turned instantly to her finger, opened its pink toothless mouth and sucked. Maura was entranced. She gathered the baby up as she had gathered the kittens, tucked firmly inside the dirty cardigan, and carried her discovery out into the sun.

Peg and Marty are Granted Understanding

They stood by the gate, frantic, pale. 'Bloody irresponsible,' Marty was saying. 'Sending a child her age off on her own in a crowd like this.' He hadn't realised till this minute how much Peg's impulsive optimism, which he loved, also infuriated him and how much he longed to attack and destroy it. Predictably she was refusing to recognise how appalling this situation was. He knew. He'd seen the worst happen. He'd seen a man step on a patch of desert dust and his legs sever, the trunk falling after in a torn and heavy arc. He went to mass, but knew it was useless, that this was simply habit, and that you could pray as Donovan prayed on the truck coming out at Sidi Rezegh and die mouthing Hail Mary in bubbles of blood. He voted Labour, argued with Jansen in the tea room and said that the unions were full of bloody commies and they'd been dead right to send in the troops in '51, but knew that this faith too was illusion, that there was no common cause, that the reality was each man alone, bleating, as the blow fell. And here was Peg with a daft bright desperate smile saying the swings, she'll have gone to play on the swings. And Peg is avoiding Marty's eye but knowing him there beside her, the heavy dark weight of him and his despair which she can't touch, ever, or relieve. She can make him laugh, she can love him, but when they lie together a bleak and faceless nothing sprawls between them grasping at her throat so she wakes, heart beating night after night. She fights against it in Marty, suppressing panic as she does now, refusing to share his vision (Maura face down on the duckpond, dragged into the water lilies by the swans, hand in hand with some enticing nameless terror . . .) But at this moment she knows suddenly that she won't be able to struggle for ever, that her optimism is a frail thing and that in time she will have to choose: leave or give up the fight, let the blackness take her. Love and survival are in opposition. It's appalling. Too big a truth to face all at once. Better encountered bit by bit. But look, there is Maura now, safe and sound after all ('You see?'), her blue nylon dress stained and carrying a grubby bundle. And 'Mum,' Maura is saying. 'I've found us a baby.'

They take the baby along the street to Dr Orbell's surgery and as they pass people draw back on either side like waves parting and quiet for a second with curiosity. But when the family with its grubby bundle has passed, an extraordinary thing happens. People turn to one another and in a sudden rush, earnest and eager, they confess those things that have most oppressed them. They tell one another truths, pleasant and unpleasant. So McLean, most prominent of the prominent citizens, tells Davis the Town Clerk that he bought land on the northern river flats six months before development on a tip-off from a cousin on the council. Jameson, junior partner in Lowe, Stout and Jameson seeks out Lowe and tells him he has invested £5,000 of clients' money in a salmon hatchery which appears certain now to fail. Partner reveals that he has swindled partner, parent has coerced child, friend has failed friend. So the day of the Queen's visit ends for some in scuffling and recrimination, for others in forgiveness and pity. We make what we can of the truth.

What Happened to Louie

When it grew dark, Louie walked along the shingle to the river's mouth. Her legs still ran with blood and her breasts tingled so that she had to lie face down on the cold river sand to soothe their swelling. She followed the bank inland through dank grass willow and blackberry, feeling her body lighten, her feet finding their accustomed rhythm and visible again across the sack of her vacated belly. That night she ate a pie she found in a safe hanging from a tree. Yellow pastry, gravy, meat. On the third night she ate only a handful of leaves so that her mouth ran with a green cud. The norwester blew down the valley, burning the grass to brown crackle and a butter-moon slid across the sky. The river was loud with the sound of stones being dragged to sea. She came to a hall, brightly lit within its rings of cars, and climbed the smooth shoulder of the hill behind. Scraps of music, thump of dancing, laughter, the rattle of sheep running off into tussock and matagouri. Louie stands alone on the crest looking out over the valley. The power lines loop from hill to hill and Louie reaches out to swing down and away with them. Like in the movies. Like Tarzan.

She dazzles in a moment and rises splendid into the night sky.

The Young Farmers' Club Experiences a Blackout

In the valley the Young Farmers' Club summer dance is interrupted by a blackout halfway through the Military Two. Couples stand arm in arm in the dark while Mort Coker tries the switches and the fuse box in the kitchen. Someone has a look outside and shouts that the whole place is black, it must be bird strike or a line down up the valley. In the darkness body blunders against body giggling. Then Ethne Moran finds a torch and the beam of it squiggles over faces caught wide eyed like rabbits on a road. Someone brings in a tilly lamp. The band attempts a few bars, deee dum dee dum who'syerladyfren, but stops because no one seems to be interested. They stand about instead talking, and a few couples are edging away to the dimly lit corners. Then Ethne, who has organised the supper, claps her hands and jumps up onto the stage. 'Come on,' she says, lit by the tilly lamp and holding in her outstretched hands a strawberry-cream sponge. 'No point in letting good food go to waste! Give us a hand, Margie.' Margie Pringle brings out the sausage rolls and finds a bread knife and Ethne kneels by the lamp to cut the cake into triangles, cream spurting beneath the blade. Side on her white dress is transparent and Ross Meikle watching thinks she's a cracker. Big breasts, curving stomach, long in the leg, and good teeth nice and even, with that little gap at the front. Ethne looks up. She hands him a piece of cake, then leans towards him and bites his ear lobe very gently leaving her uneven imprint in soft flesh. 'You do something to me,' she sings in a buzzing whisper, 'that electrifies me.' So they go outside into the warm night where it turns out that she isn't that struck on Bevan Waters after all, that she'd fancied Ross all along. On the back seat of the Holden she proves moreover to be astonishingly inventive, so that together they execute with ease a whole series of manoeuvres which Ross had previously discounted as possibly risky, definitely foreign and perilously close to deviance. Ross thinks as a result that it might be worth dropping Margie Pringle who was getting on his nerves anyway with her lisping sweetness and that he'd be better off with Ethne who was bossy god knows but had a few clues.

Meanwhile, within the hall, Warren Baty is confessing that it was his ram that had got in amongst the Coopers' Corriedale-Romney flock last winter and Jim Cooper, a whole season lost, is saying, never mind, no lasting harm done. And Alasdair McLeod is telling the Paterson brothers that it was him who nicked their chainsaw; he'd come round one afternoon when they were out and borrowed it and he'd meant to give it back but they'd made such a fuss calling in the police and all that he hadn't felt he could face it and he'd be round next day just to get the bloody thing off his conscience. Miria Love is telling Joan Shaw that she doesn't like the way she conducts Women's Division meetings and Pie Fowler is telling anyone who'll listen that she can't stick the valley, they're a bunch of snobs who've never let her forget for one minute that she's a townie and she'll be off back to the city just as soon as she can settle things with Bill.

Around the walls hang the valley teams since 1919, lined up

for the photographer, thighs spread, fists clenched, unamused by the extraordinary goings on in the darkened hall: under the influence of the night, sausage roll in one hand, beer in the other, the young farmers appear to have been overwhelmed by truth. The room is buzzing with honesty and for some the accompaniment is love and forgiveness, for others bitter recrimination. There seems to have been a sudden rise in the temperature. 'Remember the morning after,' the valley teams counsel, stonily. 'In the morning will come the accounting.'

A Power Board gang went to check the lines next day. They found nothing out of place and the power had come back on, of its own accord, at dawn. There was a pair of footprints burned deep in a rock by the pylon; about a size five, they reckoned. That was all.

So, that's the story of how Skinny Louie, daughter of Lilleas Symonds popularly known as Shanghai Lill, gave birth, and walked up the valley and vanished in splendour.

Her baby was taken in care by Marty and Peg Conlan. She'll be grown by now, ready to come into her territory. Any day we could hear of her, storming in from the desert, swooping down from the eye of the sun, casting truth about her like a bright shadow.

And won't we scatter.

The Beverly Hills Snowman

FREDERIC RAPHAEL

I FIRST MET Charlie Lehmann in London in the sixties. He did not, I am pretty sure, come to swing; he came because the dollar was strong and it was cheaper to produce movies in Europe than in California. Swinging could wait; Charlie preferred the roundabouts. He liked the English style altogether: English tailoring and English countryside and English cars. He even liked English weather ('Seasons are nice, we don't have seasons in Los Angeles') and the odd English writer, which was where I came into his life.

I had written a film or two, but I had been warned against Hollywood by a thousand novelists who imagined that they had Gone Wrong because they went Out There. (The sun made them sour.) I wanted to be involved in Cinema, which was a Cause, never in Movies, which were an Industry. When Charlie Lehmann called me, I was properly wary. It took him all of thirty seconds to break down my stubborn resistance to lunch at Les Ambassadeurs. I told him that he was wasting his time if he wanted me to do the kind of Candified Crap with which his name was associated. I had read Lindsay Anderson and I despised Big Stars and sentimental endings. 'Tell me what you want to do,' Charlie Lehmann said, 'and let's do that.'

Strictly on those terms, I went along with plovers' eggs and fresh salmon stuffed with caviare, but I ate them, of course, in a sceptical style, with just a hint of satire in my attitude to the champagne. I was a leather-jacket, no-tie man and I didn't care who knew it. Charlie wore a charcoal-silk suit and a Sulka tie and an off-pink Turnbull and Asser shirt (double-buttoned cuffs? I *think* so) and black Lobb shoes. He was slim and a little sallow and quietly spoken. He was very nice, which was a slight disappointment. Did I want my Hollywood legends to smoke cigars and ask Terrible Things of me? Had I hoped for a loud bastard who would want me to make a musical out of *Crime and Punishment*?

Charlie was no crawler, but he approached intellectuals with respect, as well as money. It was not an unpleasant combination. Having left home when he was sixteen, he had gone from St Jo, Missouri, to New York and worked under Jed Harris in the theatre. He lived in a cold-water rooming-house in a closet he shared with the roaches. Jed Harris yelled at him (Jed Harris yelled at everybody) and one day he yelled back. Jed took him to a farewell lunch and gave him some advice, in lieu of salary: 'Don't work for other people, work for yourself. Be a bastard instead of working for one.'

In his first shot at being a producer, Charlie lost every penny he didn't have (he had found a backer, later his first wife) and then he got luckier. One hit led to another. California was on the line: Darryl wanted to buy the new play. Charlie didn't want to sell. Darryl called back. He was sore, but accommodating: Charlie went to work at Fox. He was there right through the war. An ulcer kept him out of the Service. By 1945, he was Established. He did elegant movies and he ran a tight ship, but being a bastard was never his style. 'You can only be what you are,' he said.

'Bleak news, Charlie,' I said.

He looked at me with the disillusioned appreciation which I found so disarming. 'Not if you're young and talented.'

'You don't look too old to me,' I said.

'When are you going to say something about talented? And what are we going to do together?'

I resisted the idea he first raised as the trolley with the profiteroles and other death-dealing merchandise came to our table – a musical version of *It Happened One Night* – but when I suggested something I *knew* that he would *never* want to do (based on one of my own stories) he said, 'OK, let's do it.' How do you get out of that one?

Business and pleasure should be distinct, wise men say, likewise friends and associates. In Showbiz, however, it is not easy to stay detached. If I preferred, at first, to regard Charlie as a Mythical Figure, he was not eager to remain Olympian. When we began to work together, we met at his Piccadilly office, but quite often we adjourned to his Regent's Park home for lunch.

Lindsay Anderson would not have approved. The food was delicious; the plates were Haddon Hall; the service (maid and butler) discreet. The living-room had been done by David Hicks. It featured Renaissance busts (porphyry-streaked) in niches on either side of the mantelpiece. A display table contained all the Regency snuff boxes it possibly could. It was an enviable apartment (which I tried to despise), but it seemed, except for the servants, a little lonely.

One evening, at the White Elephant, a London American (in a new Douggie Hayward suit), came up to where my wife and I were dining and said, 'So you're working with Charlie! How goes?'

'We have Audrey in a negotiation,' I disclosed.

'Send a gunboat; they'll need one. Have you met *her* yet? The legendary Mireille? Alias Mrs Lehmann?'

'I think she's still in the States. Her mother –'

'That devoted family gal, she doesn't hurry back, does she?' Sam Blitz said. 'How are you, Sylvia?'

'Oh, am I here?' my wife said. 'Hullo, Sam.'

'Aren't you going to say anything about my new suit?' I said.

Sam felt my narrow lapels. 'Why pay more?' he said.

The morning Audrey agreed to do our picture, Charlie looked like a young man. Sallowness purged, the blood shone in his cheeks. I heard him tell Pat to book a table at the

Mirabelle, for three. It was to be the first time I saw Mireille. When she came in, in a little Jean Muir number, all conversation stopped. I am not exaggerating; I am reporting. A movie star, sitting between Spiegel and Preminger, looked at the newcomer as though she were a debt-collector. There is no sense in cataloguing her attributes; Mireille was a beauty, but she made no big deal of herself. She congratulated me on Audrey and apologised for intruding on our celebrations. I forgave her. I would have forgiven her for a selection of Serbian folk songs: she graced the occasion and yet seemed very modest, like a goddess on her day off. Lucky Charlie!

We had to wait quite a while before we could actually shoot the movie. It was a time of luxuriant frustration. I did not want to write another movie, but I found it difficult to settle to a novel. All the best men wanted to work with Audrey, but no one we wanted was available. With Mireille back in town, Charlie had a busy social life. Sylvia and I soon became part of it.

The apartment in Cumberland Terrace was now as crowded as it had previously been depopulated. Mireille's dinner parties were elegant and entertaining. The only bores were millionaires. Charlie always welcomed Sylvia and me as if we were the only people he really wanted to see, but he appeared to have as many friends as fine weather could ever procure.

I must have been a little jealous, because one evening, I said, 'How about a musical of *Timon of Athens*, Charlie, with a happy ending? We can do the whole show right here in the barn!' I indicated that revised Hicks drawing-room, with its Hindu sculptures and the new collection of tin cans. (Sam Blitz said you could tell they were Art, because they had left out the soup.)

Charlie said, 'Happy? *Here*?'

I laughed. In the sixties we laughed at everything, especially after a good dinner. But was I amused? An alarm rang in my head and it did not stop all night. It had been convenient to see Charlie as a father-figure. I wanted to believe him as happy as our children insisted that Sylvia and I were. Charlie's guard had slipped, for a bitter second, and I could not rid myself of the taste. I only hoped that the next day (when we were to talk about the changes Paul wanted before he would consent to do our picture) I should find Charlie in smiling mood.

He was on the telephone, to a Duke. His Grace, it seemed, was not available to dine on a certain day; Charlie begged him to be. He begged like a rich and confident man who did not take no for an answer. When finally he got what he wanted, the face he turned to me was neither smiling nor triumphant. 'See what I mean?' he said. 'Happy ending? Let's talk about Paul.'

'I don't want to do what he wants,' I said.

'Nuts to him. Neither do I. I don't want to do what anybody wants. But I do it. You're lucky. You don't have to.'

'Then why am I here?' I said.

He responded with a look of such anguish that I felt like the shit I was pretending to be. 'Do you mean that?'

'If I meant it, would I say it?'

'England!' he said. It sounded like a resignation speech.

'Let me buy you lunch today, Charlie, will you? Spoil me.'

I wanted and I did not want to hear what Charlie told me in our corner at Scott's (the old, Edwardian place on Leicester Square): 'She doesn't love me. She never did.'

'Why did she marry you?'

'I asked her. A lot.'

'Mireille could marry anybody she wanted.'

'She never wanted anybody. Being wanted is what she wants. And me, I know all there is to know about long-stem roses, and Cartier watches. Oochie-Gucci-Gucci is just the kind of babytalk she liked to hear.' Charlie was funny when he was sad, and he was very sad. 'Know when I realised? She wanted to go to Klosters for our honeymoon. Christmas. The planes were jammed. The hotels too. I said how about Wengen? Wengen they could do. She said Klosters or nothing. Everyone she wanted to see was going to be at Klosters. "I'll be at Wengen, if you will," I said. She gave me a look. "Fix it," she said. I got a flight, through a banker in Zurich, but the best hotel only had a room, no suite. I had to pull strings till my hands were raw. She said, "How can we not have a suite? Fix it." I bought a raft of shares in the company, a week before Christmas, and she had her suite. We had a honeymoon with more people than'll ever come to my funeral. She's a beautiful, beautiful woman, as long as she gets everything she wants. Everything. I'm not on the list. She likes you. A lot.'

I said, 'Don't fix it.'

The parties went on and then, in December, they stopped. Mireille's mother had taken a turn for the worse. Absence made Charlie's heart grow more anxious. He called her a lot. She called him when she needed something, or more of something. Would she be back for Christmas? It was probable, and then it was unlikely and then, the day I stopped by the office with a Matisse drawing (a little one, a little one) for Charlie, it was impossible.

That was how he came to spend Christmas with us in the country. Sylvia was afraid that he would find it primitive. If he did, he also seemed to like it. He brought great presents for the kids (our grand-daughter has the rocking-horse now) and he made great hamburgers. It snowed on Christmas Eve and Charlie rolled the biggest snowball our children had ever seen and turned it into a snowman to remember. He took pictures to prove how big it was. He waited for Mireille to call, but the lines must have been very busy. I wished he would be angry, but he was only hurt. Sylvia and I were very fond of him.

She came back, just when we were thinking that perhaps she was going to put him out of his agony. Our movie got made, and panned (it is now a classic, they tell me). The dollar weakened. The Americans fell out of love with London and with the European talent, which had taken their money with such greedy reluctance. Charlie decided that he would have to go back to California. As soon as he had the right offer for the Cumberland Terrace apartment, with or without the Dukes of her choice, we were no longer a social highlight. We asked Charlie and Mireille to dinner a few times, but they always had something else they had to do. Mireille, Charlie hinted, did not want to be with a happy couple.

Now that they were leaving London, Mireille fell in love

with the Quantocks. Charlie bought a 'cottage' to cheer her up, a place they could always come to, if they felt like flying for eleven hours. He did everything he could to unpurse those lovely lips, but happiness was no longer in London and not even he could fix it otherwise.

I wrote a new screenplay for Charlie (from a novel he had bought for six figures) and it so happened that the final story conference was the following Christmas. We all flew out. Charlie's place on Chevy Chase had a guest wing where we and our children could reach out and pick our own oranges. Mireille was there, and she was very gracious. I knew she was a prize bitch, but I kept liking her. Until Charlie brought out the pictures of our white Christmas. Her face darkened.

'Why can't we have a white Christmas?' she said. 'Here in Beverly Hills.'

Charlie said, 'They don't do them, angel.'

'I want to make a snowman.'

'We'll have to fly somewhere.'

'Here. In the garden.'

I looked at Sylvia.

Charlie said, 'Settle for palm trees.'

I could hear it coming. It came: 'Fix it.'

'You want to skate on the swimming pool too, I suppose?'

'Sure,' she said. 'Why not? You're supposed to be a bigshot.'

'You never swam in the damn thing,' Charlie, 'and now you want to skate on it?'

'Anyone can swim in Beverly Hills.'

'Ice and a snowman, anything else?'

'Anything else, I'll ask Santa.'

We were glad to get into our separate quarters and watch eighteen channels of junk. Charlie and I had conferences with the director (who always wanted to be a writer). Between huddles, Charlie was on the telephone. He had a friend who owned a ski resort and another who owned an ice-hockey team. He was savagely determined to give Mireille exactly what she had asked for. Early on Christmas morning, deadheating with Santa, a very big truck arrived with some loud and ingenious machinery on board. Not long afterwards, they came from the ice-hockey rink. I did not understand how, but by sun-up the palm trees were up to their knees in authentic Hollywood snow. The swimming pool was crusty with greeny-white ice.

Mireille had just one present under the eight-foot spruce in the cathedral-ceilinged living-room: a pair of skates.

Mireille said, 'I haven't skated in years, you know that.'

'You made a deal. Honour it.'

'Don't speak to me like that, Charlie.'

'Now.'

By God, she put on the skates, sitting on the diving board, and – with naked hatred in her exquisite green eyes – she teetered onto the ice.

'Skate,' Charlie said. 'Like you promised Santa you would.'

She skated. She skated pretty well as a matter of fact. She began to enjoy herself. She swooped and span. Attagirl! And then, all of a sudden, the ice creaked; the ice cracked; the ice folded in like Monsieur Hulot's famous canvas canoe and Mireille was not skating any more. She was in the deep end. No, there was no tragedy. But comedy can end in tears too. We hauled her out, shaking with shock and rage, but not before she managed to contract what she swore was pneumonia and certainly turned into a cold bad enough to be grounds for divorce.

She got into her Mercedes, wrapped in yards of towel, and said she was driving straight to her mother's. I hardly knew what to say, but I felt I had to go over to the main house. As I approached I heard a terrible sound. Imagine discovering your father-figure in tears. Charlie was going back and forth in a genuine colonial rocking chair, his hands over his wet cheeks. These choking noises came from his chest. 'Charlie,' I said, 'I'm so sorry . . .'

He took his hands away and I saw not a father but a naughty boy.

'*Charlie!*' I said. 'You didn't . . .'

He nodded. 'I fixed it.'

'About time, I guess.'

'Now let's go and make that snowman.'

We did, and it was as good as the English one. Some said better. But it didn't last, of course. What does, in Beverly Hills?

At Brackus's

D. J. TAYLOR

HIS FATHER, OLD Joe Brackus, had opened the first gas station up on Choctaw the summer after they had built the freeway extension and turned the stony plateau with its view out over Tennessee and the river into a tourist site. He had put in an ice-cream parlour and a kiosk which sold cigarettes and Seven-Up, and for a time the teenagers who drove their girlfriends up there at the weekends and the aged joyriding couples who strayed over the state border by accident would stop and ask him directions or buy guttering tubs of Dixiecup ice-cream which was the parlour's stock-in-trade. But then the ridge had been bought by a real estate company from Memphis who wanted to build a block of timeshare apartments, the teenagers started heading West to Dyersburg where there was a marina complex, and Brackus found himself with an empty forecourt and a ten thousand dollar compensation fee: so he put the money into Brackus's.

It was the sort of place you find occasionally in the South, which is emulative of so many other places in the South that the effect borders on parody. There was a neon sign that said *Brackus's Bar and Diner*, there were menu cards printed in the shape of opening saloon doors and bowls of sawdust for cigarette ends. And because old Brackus was a bluegrass boy whose family had originally come out of Kentucky during the depression, there was a squat, rickety stage where country bands used to play on Saturday nights, and a set of buckskin gear which the waitresses sometimes wore to serve drinks at the bar. 'Pure Annie Oakley,' Barrett the journalist used to say, but on the strength of it Joe Brackus got himself profiled in *Dixie* magazine standing under a Confederate flag on which was printed the slogan 'The South Will Rise'.

The *Dixie* profile was a portent. Unexpectedly, Brackus's had paid its way right from the start. Saturday nights would find a restive, cosmopolitan crowd packed together on the narrow benches or seated raucously around the big pine tables which Joe had got out of an L.L. Bean catalogue. Denimed wiseacres from the farming end of Cook County, seventy miles away, moneyed Nashville brats with their daddies' credit cards, the local lumpenproletariat from the Choctaw sawmills. In its second year of existence Brackus's got a mention in one of the Nashville listings magazines. Not long afterwards the Dixie Dance-Kings played there at the end of their first Southern tour and Joe Brackus added on a children's parlour extension, bought his wife some cosmetic surgery and wondered about sending his kids to college.

There were two children: Scott and an older girl called Elaine. 'Snipped right off the Southern vine,' Barrett sometimes said, in the days when he wrote reviews of the house bands in the local paper and occasionally had dinner at the Brackus bungalow on Sunday nights, but the precision masked an uncharacteristic lack of certainty. Joe Brackus was an easy-going, two hundred pound small-towner who, even after Brackus's got put into all the regional guidebooks and Waylon Jennings turned up unannounced to play at a charity benefit, would still walk into the local drugstore on a Saturday afternoon and treat himself to a family pack of See's chocolates. The kids were different. For a start they were brighter. They were sharper. They weren't your couple of average Southern kids who wonder maybe about going to Nashville and working in real estate but end up settling for a third share each in the old man's timber yard. All through the early years you could see old Joe figuratively scratching his head about Scott and Elaine. They dug around the local schools for a while – finishing up at high school in Jackson, which pleased Brackus – but you could tell that it was all temporary, that they viewed the old man as an embarrassment who happened to be their father. Eventually Elaine married a Florida lawyer she met at a rock concert one Fall in Miami and went to live down in Tampa Bay. She had a job in an architect's office and came home at Christmas, although Barrett used to say that the architect's office was a front and he had seen her once in an X-movie he had got from a video store. Yeah.

That left Scott. Cook County wasn't the easiest place in the world to be Scott Brackus, but he managed it somehow. He played baseball for the local team, the Cook County Pirates, and you saw him occasionally with the busty cheerleaders in the back parlour of Brackus's. When he was nineteen he won a talent contest hosted by the Nashville country station, and the picture of him dressed in his denim cowpoke's outfit shaking hands with some tubby little WA 125 announcer was taped to the wall of Brackus's. Old Joe had hopes for Scott, in that shy, puzzled way which substitutes ambition for understanding. When a second division country band played Brackus's Scott would be there backslapping with the musicians, helping to tune the steel guitars, sometimes bobbing up on stage to take part in an encore or emcee some starry-eyed pack of Louisiana grizzlies who thought Brackus's was the big time. Sometimes he did session work, away in Memphis, with the Dixie Stealers, the Cottonpickers, bands you had heard of. They had a habit of never putting the session players' names on the record sleeves. But he looked the part. He played a big, unwieldy Hofner Les Paul in a laboured style which the oldtimers said reminded them of Roy Orbison. And though the drinks at Brackus's were more expensive than anywhere else in the county, and old Joe wouldn't let him run up a tab, Scott was there drinking most nights of the week.

One Tuesday night when trade was slack and the jukebox was blaring out Allman Brothers records over the empty tables, I met him in the parlour. He looked ghostly, a little out of place amid the solidity of Brackus's cattleprod decor, the steerhorn wall fixtures and the giant bottles of Southern Comfort. There was a rumour going round, I later discovered, that one of the Pirates' cheerleaders had spent the weekend in an abortion clinic at La Grange. But we talked about my job – I had just got Photomax, the big repro business, to give me their local franchise which meant driving round the country with a mobile photo-lab – and after a while I suggested that he ought to be playing more, go into a studio maybe and cut a record.

'I could do worse.' He didn't seem offended at this piece of simpleton's advice, which every bar-propper in Brackus's had been offering him for the last year-and-a-half. 'The old man wants me to get a job.'

'What sort of a job?'

'That depends. If I wrote down my qualifications you'd piss yourself. I was an English major. Subsidiaries in economics and art and design. Round here they want you to chop wood or work at the gas-station carwash.'

The way he said *gas-station* made me think that old Brackus must have had a few words. 'Maybe it doesn't have to be chopping wood,' I told him. 'What did you specialise in on the art and design course?'

'Christ. Ceramics. Expressionism. A little photography.'

I offered him an assistant's job in the lab there and then, which seemed to please him, and said I'd be in touch again after I'd spoken to the Photomax people. 'Here's hoping,' he said, all lazy and wide-eyed, but as if he meant it.

It took a week to get a decision out of Photomax about funding an assistant. In the meantime Barrett filled me in on the pool-table gossip from Brackus's. 'Let me tell you something, my man' – Barrett always talked as if he were some wisecracking negro from an NBC cop serial – 'the word on Scott Brackus isn't good. Sure, Ruthie – the one with the tits and the snaggle teeth – had a hoover job over the weekend. Her pa was down to see me on Monday. Plus the old man finally got to lose his temper.'

'The old man lost his temper with Scott?'

'You got it' – and here Barrett positively bridled, as if he were Huggy Bear sashaying around the set of *Starsky and Hutch*. 'Happened in here, a couple of days ago. Rockin' Dopsie was playing, you know, those zydeco boys from the bayou. The Cajun Twisters. Scott was hanging around with his guitar, the way he does for an encore, when old Joe jumps out from behind the bar and tells him to shift his ass away from the stage. Right there in front of the Twisters' manager. You never saw anything like it.'

'So what did Scott do?'

'What would you do, man?'

I told Barrett about the job with the mobile photolab. 'The South will rise,' he said tolerantly (Barrett had tried and failed to get a job on *Dixie* magazine). 'It's a nice idea.'

I was busy that week, ordering up film from the suppliers in Nashville and checking the insurance for the lab, but it wasn't difficult to go on hearing about Scott. The local Kodak rep had been at Brackus's the night old Joe delivered his grand remonstrance. Ruthie with the tits and the snaggle teeth made a brief, etiolated appearance at the Pirates' midweek game. People in bars and at supermarket checkouts started to talk about 'that mother', and Scott became suddenly that most typical of Southern whipping boys, the privileged kid who goes wrong, the strapping six-footer with the wide smile who breaks his daddy's heart. I saw him a couple of times down at the Stonewall, the gentleman's club where old Brackus had bought him life membership on his eighteenth birthday, and he had that sullen, companionless look of the person who can't find anybody to accept his offers of drinks. Ruthie's father was on the committee of the Stonewall.

Then, when the letter of acceptance came from Photomax, he disappeared. Out East, people said, to see his sister, but Joe Brackus didn't know and none of the bar-proppers at the Stonewall had heard. The Pirates played their Saturday night game against the Johnson City Rednecks, but there was no sign of him down by the coaches' dug-out or swapping backchat with the Redneck supporters along by the burger stands. Midweek, the Atlanta Express were headlining at Brackus's but you looked in vain across the smoky cavern to the bar, past the rows of Choctaw saw boys in their black donkey jackets, for the sight of Scott shouldering his way towards the stage with the Hofner clasped under his arm.

As usual Barrett had the details. At the close of a discussion of the feature which he figured writing about the photolab he said shyly: 'Looks as if Scott finally hit the big time, my man. Tuesday last week, down at the Winnebag. You never saw anything like it.'

I shrugged. The Winnebag was a blues bar on the west side of Cook County which might have held thirty people. Barrett went on in that half sassy, half respectful way he had: 'Sure, I was there, my man. You know the score at the Winnebag. Some Memphis brats down to get a taste of country living, half a dozen niggers hollering for "Dust My Broom", and Scott gets up and does a couple of standards – "D–I–V–O–R–C–E", "Tennessee Slide" – you get the idea? And it's not the blues, but it's kinda tuneful and since he's a local boy and everybody remembers old Joe from way back people start clapping their asses off. Which could have been just fine, just fine, my man. A little novelty. A little *colour*. Yes sir. And it happens, it just so happens that there was a guy from Cherry Red' – Cherry Red was the big Nashville country station – 'up at the bar. Seersucker suit, fancy cane, you know the sort of stuff those candyasses wear when they're out to impress the hicks. Looking at Scott with his tongue hanging down to his chin.'

Barrett flicked me an inscrutable look – the sort of look he gave when the paper sent him to cover an Odd Fellows convention at Lafayette.

'And after that he lit out?'

'And after that he lit out. Nashville. Memphis. One of the Cherry Red studios someplace. But take it from me, my man, you can kiss goodbye to your photolab assistant.'

The crises of Joe Brackus's commercial career had been flagposted by his ability to bury the hatchet. Even when the real estate company had bought him out from the gas-station the old man hitched up his trousers, marched into the Stonewall and stood the company lawyers a four-course dinner. So a week later when Scott got back from Nashville there was a tab at the bar at Brackus's and anyone who could claim the slightest acquaintance with the family was swarming after free beer. I saw him there one evening in the middle of a cloud of hangers-on: local guitarists who figured he might put a word in at Nashville, a flaxen-haired grandmother who had appeared at the Opry in 1957, a couple of the Pirates' cheerleaders. He looked tired and flustered, but when he saw me he prised himself free from the grasp of Ruthie with the tits and the snaggle teeth and came loping over. I told him I'd heard the news.

'It's a break,' he said, a touch sheepishly. 'Too bad about the photo-lab, huh?'

'It doesn't matter,' I told him. 'Congratulations. What's the deal with Cherry Red?'

'The usual thing. A couple of weeks demoing. Some radio work – they got a majority stake in the two Nashville country stations. Maybe a billing at the Opry if I shape up.'

'What does the old man think?'

Scott grinned. 'He's on cloud nine. You know he used to play himself? Bluegrass. Kentucky stomp. I reckon I owed him this. You know,' he went on, 'I've had so many people tell me I've arrived that I might just start believing it.'

The way he said *arrived* made me wish I hadn't written the polite letter to Photomax.

After that you couldn't walk into a bar or diner without hearing about Scott. It wasn't that there hadn't been people like him before – after all, you could hardly throw a stone in Cook County without hitting a pedal steel guitarist or a guy who figured he could write lyrics for Willie Nelson – but somehow they had all faded away, to playing hotel residencies or copier salesmen's conventions. Barrett's favourite story was of a faded family act called the Country Cousins ('Cook County's Finest') whom he had discovered playing in a motel outside Atlanta. The irony, according to Barrett, was that the Country Cousins had actually *improved*. Set against this catalogue of blighted hopes and thwarted ambition, Scott looked a success. There was the letter from Cherry Red. People remembered the talent contest, and the youthful Scott singing at kids' parties and the boy scout barbecues of long ago. Even Barrett unbent sufficiently to write it up for the *Cook County Sentinel* and a second photograph of him, square-jawed and resolute, got taped to the wall of Brackus's.

Not long after the story appeared he was gone again, to Nashville, people said. Taking the photolab out round the county I used to look for mentions of him in the trade papers you found lying around the barbers' shops or pinned to the walls of roadside diners. There was a paragraph or two, early on, listing him among the 'New signings to Cherry Red' but that was all. Somebody came back from Nashville and said they'd seen him on stage at one of the small talent clubs, along with some harmonica players and the Tallahassee Country Gospel Choir. Third on the bill. Old Joe Brackus stopped answering enquiries. People stopped asking.

Maybe six months later I bumped into Barrett at the Stonewall, where he'd been taking the committee's views on the new freeway. 'Scott's back,' he said.

'At Brackus's?'

'You got it, my man.' And Barrett smiled that lazy, mischievous smile that made me think again of Antonio Fargas. 'Prodigal son,' he said.

I stopped off at the bar a couple of nights later when the Dixie Stealers were headlining. It was one of those tense, sultry evenings you got occasionally at the end of summer when the crowd at Brackus's got surly and the sawmill boys threw beer glasses at the microphones. I got there just as the Stealers were finishing their set ('Sweet home Alabama' sung to the accompaniment of lofted Confederate flags) but there was no sign of Scott on the stage or waiting, guitar slung under his arm, over by the PA stacks. At the bar I brushed past Barrett, who had his arm round a cheerleader and his tie yanked down into a low, pendulous knot on his chest.

'You seen Scott?'

Barrett jerked his finger back over the bar, pointing hard at the giant bottles of Southern Comfort and the henge of beer cans. When I saw Scott bending down over the beer pump, straightening up as old Joe snapped an order from the cash register, I realised that none of the carefully chosen phrases of welcome I'd rehearsed would do. 'The South will *rise*,' Barrett said gleefully, loud enough for the bar to hear, and I stayed just long enough for Scott to catch sight of me, sidling off with that sad, resolute feeling you get head on with somebody else's tragedy.

Shaking Hands with Theodor Herzl

JONATHAN TREITEL

ALTHOUGH IT IS November, Jerusalem is hot. There is a white dust on the hills and alleys and the Homburg hat of the notable thinker and writer Dr Theodor Herzl. His black beard is itching. It is 1898. Two minuscule flunkeys in canary-yellow livery lean back on the Byzanto-Romanesque double doors of the Grand Levantine Hotel on Jaffa Road. Herzl enters. The doors swing shut and bang his bottom. 'Ahem,' says Herzl. The clerk at the reception desk says, 'One minute, sir.' The clerk's head is bent over the crossword puzzle in the overseas edition of the *Chicago Clarion and Puzzler*. The clerk considers solutions; he angles his skull; his ultra-straight hair-parting teeters like the needle on a weighing machine. 'And what can I do for you, sir?' 'I have reserved a room. The name is Dr Herzl.' 'It is very difficult. We have little space. The German Kaiser is paying a state visit to the Pasha so most of our suites are –' 'Yes, yes. That in fact is precisely why I myself am in –' 'What was the name, sir?' The clerk glances up; he peers at Herzl's nose through pince-nez, the better to gauge its curvature. 'I am afraid we have nothing suitable, Mr Cohen –' 'Dr Herzl.' 'Perhaps, on some future occasion, Mr Levy –' 'Dr Herzl.' 'Next year, possibly, or in the new century –' 'But I insist!' Herzl drums his fist on the counter. 'I have come all the

way from Vienna to Jerusalem expressly to meet the –!' 7
Down is ORCHESTRA (anag.). Herzl flings up an arm in a
theatrical gesture. The clerk blinks. Herzl orates, 'Do you
expect me to sleep in the gutter?' '*That*,' says the clerk, neatly
pencilling in CARTHORSE, 'is entirely your own decision,
sir.'

Who should Herzl bump into as he stumbles backwards out
of the Grand Levantine Hotel but his old chum Siegfried Perl.
'Good to see you, Tancred!' says Perl, slapping Herzl on the
back. '*Tancred?*' says Herzl, slapping back. 'My name is Dr
Theodor Herzl.' 'Don't you remember? Vienna University?
The Lippizaner Club? Your nickname?' 'Of course I remember . . . er . . . Galahad. But what are you doing in Palestine?'
'I live here. I am a *Zionist*. *Zionism* is the name of a political
movement founded by a certain Dr Theodor . . . Surely not?'
Herzl blushes and nods. Perl says, 'Then you must come
round for pastries and coffee! Where are you staying?' 'Well
actually –' 'Then you must stay at my house. No, I insist!'

Perl guides Herzl through the narrow rutted alleys. 'I live at
19 Mehmet Ali Street,' says Perl. 'It is quite easy to find. You
just follow the Stations of the Via Dolorosa. Here you are
flagellated. Here you slip and fall. Just before you are crucified,
make a sharp left.'

As Herzl follows his friend along the winding route, he
smells an odd, nasty but richly nostalgic smell. He cannot
quite place it.

Herzl is made welcome at 19 Mehmet Ali Street. He likes
the look of the place at once: it has such a reassuringly cluttered
Central European air. Here is a brilliant Turkish carpet on the
floor; here is another one on the table. Here is the mantelpiece,
weighed down with Meissen shepherdesses and Byzantine oil
lamps. The walls are hung with lots of little German oil
paintings in the 'Levantine Mode': an odalisque leans against a
palm tree; a Bedouin warrior sits upright on his camel; a
bejewelled Sultan decapitates a negro slave. 'Which reminds
me,' says Herzl, 'I am to be received by the Kaiser tomorrow. I
must make a good impression. He has influence with the
Ottomans. I will persuade him to favour a Jewish State in

Palestine!' 'Bravo!' says Perl. The other members of Perl's family also express their admiration. Perl introduces them. 'Here is my son, Karl-Heinz.' A thin spotty youth, clapping very softly. 'And this is my daughter, Brunhilde.' An aproned girl with floury fingers; she claps, and the white powder rises in a shaft of sunshine. 'And last but not least, my dear lady wife. Her name is –' A dark plump woman, pearl-earring'd; she pouts at Herzl. '– You may call her Frau Perl.'

So Herzl is settled down, in the master bedroom, of course. Herr and Frau Perl move temporarily into Brunhilde's room. Brunhilde is assigned a camp bed in the kitchen. One effect of these manoeuvrings and shiftings is to displace four chamber-pots; these are lined up against a wall of the sitting-room. At this point, Karl-Heinz, a shy, serious young man, makes the first and only joke of his life. In years to come, at dinner parties and soirées, he will tell of Herzl's visit and repeat this witticism. Since the pun translates poorly from German into Hebrew, he will have to explain the punchline at length. 'Ach,' says Karl-Heinz, 'this house was so *commode* and now it is full of commodes!'

Coffee and cakes are to be served shortly in the sitting-room. Frau Perl grinds the coffee beans in a cylindrical copper device which resembles a land mine. Herzl offers to assist. Frau Perl narrows her eyes at Herzl and says, 'Such a gentleman!' Herzl knocks over the grinder and the beans scatter on the floor. Herzl gets down on hands and knees and retrieves them. Frau Perl joins him, crawling alongside, and panting, 'Such a gentleman! Such a gentleman!' Herzl and Frau Perl simultaneously grab the same bean; their hands touch. 'The Hegelian synthesis of the nation-state, *pace* Zionism, is the instantiation of the *ethnos*, would you not agree, Dr Herzl?' says Perl, who was sitting on the sofa all along. 'Yes,' says Herzl, rising to his feet.

Turkish coffee is ground and percolated and poured into the best Rosenthal china coffee-cups. Brunhilde enters from the kitchen bearing a silver platter loaded with a massive chocolate cake topped with whipped cream. 'Tell me, Dr Herzl,' Brunhilde says, presenting Herzl with a generous slice, 'is my

Sachertorte as scrumptious as the Sachertorte at Sacher in Vienna?' Herzl tastes the offering. He chews a mouthful, slowly. Dark crumbs nest in his beard. Whipped cream whitens his moustache. In his considered opinion, the cake is over-baked and too sweet. 'Certainly, Brunhilde.' Throughout Brunhilde's prolonged old age, whenever she has the opportunity to feed her children and grandchildren her favourite dry sugary Sachertorte, she will mutter: 'So aristocratic! Such *Kultur*! As good as in Sacher, he said, better even!' And her family nod. And she will mumble to herself: '"Delicious, Brunhilde," he said. "Mmm, Brunhilde," he said. "Yum yum, Brunhilde," he said. Nobody calls me *Brunhilde*, now. I have a new Israeli name. I know it begins with B . . . *Bracha*? . . . *Beruria* . . . *Bilha* . . . ? Oh, I'll forget my own name next.' Herzl also samples Linztorte and Apfelstrudel. He makes appropriate comments. Everybody is satisfied.

It is bedtime. Herzl is lying on his back between the sheets of the double bed. His neck is pressing on the hard bolster. He is reviewing his tactics for the forthcoming meeting with the Kaiser. He is sucking his beard. He blows out the candle. He cannot rest comfortably in this strange bed. He turns on his right side; he smells Perl's male odour. He rolls over onto the other half of the bed; he is disturbed by the faintest hint of Frau Perl's *Nuit d'amour*. He falls asleep.

An odalisque, leaning against a palm tree, is waving to a tall turbaned Bedouin seated on a cream-coloured camel on top of a pile of shiny brown camel droppings. The odalisque, who is Brunhilde, assures Herzl the droppings are at least as delicious as those made in Vienna. A Sultan, waving a bloody sword, commands Herzl to eat the stuff. *Delicious*, says Herzl compliantly; though in fact it tastes dry and sugary. The Bedouin, who is Perl, informs Herzl that he will have to stay in this prison forever to demonstrate his Zionist commitment. The camel licks Herzl's beard; the camel is Frau Perl. The camel caresses Herzl's ribcage with a bony ankle; or the Sultan's sword is poking his heart; or the Kaiser himself is posing heroically with his jackboot on the recumbent Herzl.

Herzl awakes. He is lying on the very edge of the double bed. Some complex hard object is digging into his side. He rolls over and pulls back the sheets. He was sleeping on Frau Perl's whalebone corset.

It is morning. A harsh sun angles through a gap in the shutters and hits Herzl's head. A muezzin calls all good men to prayer and awakens Herzl. Herzl arranges himself with care. He brushes his hair, beard, teeth and tailcoat. He fastens his starched collar with a pearl collar stud, and, for double security, holds it in place with a safety pin at the back.

Herzl strolls into the sitting-room. Perl greets him with a firm handshake and a cry of, 'Long live the Zionist Ideal!' Herzl says, 'Ah, good morning.' Frau Perl rises from the sofa; her hair is done up in a chignon and she is wearing a low-cut dress; she looks at Herzl and says nothing. At last, she says, 'Did you sleep well?' Herzl considers how to reply. She says, 'Isn't that muezzin drone simply awful?' Herzl says, 'Very well, thank you. And you?' She says, 'My! you look smart.' Herzl says, 'Yes, quite dreadful.' She says, 'Would you like a little music?' Herzl says, 'You're attractively dressed yourself.' 'A Jewish state or a state of Jews, that is the question, is it not?' says Perl loudly. 'Do you want some coffee?' Herzl nods. Perl shouts at the kitchen door, 'Karl-Heinz! Make the coffee for my old friend. Brunhilde! Bring on the strudel.' Frau Perl repeats, 'Would you like a little music?' Perl says, 'Surely you're not going to the Kaiser without a top hat? He'll have your head chopped off if you don't wear a top hat. Top people are very keen on top hats. Not to worry, I've got a top hat upstairs somewhere. You can borrow mine.' Perl goes in search of his top hat. Whenever the name of Herzl will crop up in political discussions in years to come, Perl will always refer to him as 'Whatshisname-I-lent-my-top-hat-to'.

In contrast, Frau Perl will refuse to mention Herzl. She will say, 'Ach, men, always talking this boring politics.' Now, she is alone in the sitting-room with Herzl. She walks over to a window niche, where there is a high shelf set with Dresden figurines and half a Philistine saucer. Underneath it is Frau Perl's prize possession: the *Symphonium*, a cross between a pianola and a phonograph. Frau Perl turns the handle to crank the machine. She selects a shiny metal disc pierced with slots in a spiral pattern. She places it on the turntable. The *Symphonium* emits a tinny music-box sound; it is playing *Deutschland Über Alles*. Frau Perl turns to face Herzl. She says, 'Ah, music, it is my soul!' She walks towards him. 'There is little good music in Jerusalem. How I miss it. My husband doesn't like music. Have you been to the latest Strauss in Vienna?' 'No,' says Herzl. 'How I envy you! We must talk about music in the twilight.' 'I won't be here this evening. After meeting the Kaiser, I'll have to catch the train to Haifa, and then the boat. Thank you for your kind hospitality.' 'Farewell!' Frau Perl opens her arms wide to embrace Herzl and bursts into tears.

At this point, Karl-Heinz and Brunhilde enter from the kitchen bearing a jug of coffee and a plate of strudel smothered in whipped cream; and Perl comes down the stairs carrying a large candy-striped box which he opens to reveal a dusty, slightly moth-eaten top hat. Herzl smells four smells: the aroma of coffee, the odour of strudel, the stink of mothballs, and *Nuit d'amour*. Herzl will shortly be received by the Kaiser who will listen to Herzl's plea for a Jewish National Home in Palestine and turn the request down flat. And Herzl will deliver a speech at the World Zionist Congress in which he will argue there is nothing special about Palestine and why should the Jews not settle in, oh, say, Uganda. Now Herzl sees the four members of the Perl family advancing on him from every direction. Suddenly, he recognises that strange nostalgic stench which had troubled him earlier. It is the Jewish Smell. He backs towards the door. 'Go away!' he cries. 'Go away, you Jews!'

In the Dark

CHARLES WILKINSON

IT WAS ONLY on the morning of the very day that she'd invited
Melanie to lunch that Joanna suddenly realised what a terrible
state the flat was in. A long time had passed since either Brian
or she had entertained, and somehow she'd grown accustomed to what she always liked to imagine was the cultivated
clutter in which they lived. Now she saw the living-room
through Melanie's eyes: the old newspapers draped over the
sofa; the brown sock that looked as if it had been trodden into
the carpet; and, even worse, the empty bottles, normally so
much a part of living with Brian as to pass unnoticed, perched
on the mantelpiece and packed into the wastepaper basket.

Joanna looked at her watch. She had ten minutes left before
she was due to leave for work – time, at least, to dispose of the
bottles and the sock. She found a black plastic bag in the
kitchen and set about tidying up. On the dusty window sill
was a pile of unopened manila envelopes, a testament to
Brian's waning administrative gifts. She was about to pick up
the bills and fling them into the bag when she remembered
what Melanie had said: 'Try bringing a little order into your
life, Joanna; it can only lead to happiness.' She put the bills
down.

Outside chill sunlight fell on crumbling terraces; horns

sounded; and, just beneath her in the street, she could hear the clicking footsteps of secretaries hurrying to work. Carrying the bag, she went back into the kitchen. The bottles slithered and chinked in the darkness; fear, familiar and unwelcome, began to tingle just beneath the surface of her skin. She let go of the bag and watched it withering shinily on the floor. Such misplaced concentration was a habit she'd have to break if she was to be a success in the office. Yesterday she'd caught herself studying a silver pencil on her desk with the sort of absent-minded vigilance which reminded her of how when she had been possessed by fear, and after Brian had given up being able to help her, she had spent hours pretending to do the washing up, wrists mittened in warm water, eyes attentive only to the tiny, iridescent bubbles dying slowly, until she became still with fascination.

Joanna went out onto the landing and, just as she had done every morning for the past three years, pushed open Brian's door. The curtains were still drawn, and he lay there, the contours of his body scarcely visible beneath an enormous white eiderdown, soft and powdery as a snowfall. She imagined him huddled into the blind hollow of his sheets, dreaming coldly beneath the weight of such enormous softness. What time would he get up? Eleven? Twelve? She closed the door. It was hard to imagine that they had once been able to help each other with logic and laughter.

She ran down the stairs and out into the street. Although the sky was absolutely cloudless, the blue was a shade greyer than seemed possible, as if it were not really a sunny day at all. A fresh wind caught her ankles, reminding her how much she hated wearing a business suit, and for a moment anxiety welled up irrepressibly in her.

It was always the same: the wind itching his naked legs with sand, the brown seaweed crackling beneath his feet and above him fine clouds blown like dust across a hard white sky – everything dry and cold. As he walked slowly across the beach, he heard distant voices, the sound of ropes straining and the excited cries of the gulls. The sea looked perfectly clear, light and saltless, and he thought that if he went on he would leave the horrors of the shore behind and drink the cool blue water.

A silent, minatory tremor: mud and sand curled towards him in eel-like streaks and then expanded slowly until the sea was opaque. Somewhere the ropes still creaked and moaned; the voices became urgent. He waded into the sullied waters until only his thin chest and face were exposed to the raw wind. He began to swim and was only just out of his depth when he noticed it. Tilted like a damaged fin, speckled with greenery, its bows broke the surface. Tiny waves stung his eyes and his mouth filled with grey sand until a sudden swell jolted him almost upright and he saw the great man-of-war, barnacles glinting, its decks starred with light, rise from the sea as smoothly as if it had been greased. As he floundered, he saw it sail far above him into the air. Its decks were streaming, its broken hull rained water. The ropes that held it were only just visible against the parched white sky.

The sea closed over his head. For an instant its surface blazed and then receded from his outstretched hands. Shadows that might have been fish drifted past. He sank deeper, netted in grains of sand. The dark ocean floor waited to receive him. His flesh would part tenderly from his bones . . .

. . . until he was walking down the quay, thinking how fine the day was, how hungry the cries of the gulls and harsh the roar of the traffic. And there was the ship in the dock being pounded by water cannons. He remembered how this was necessary in order to ward off the influences of air and light and prevent the wood from disintegrating. The jets of water sprang so fast as to seem as still as ice; only when they had hit the hull did they join and become liquid, slithering, black-white and glistening. As he walked towards the ship, the sun grew brighter and the heat more intense. The birdsong died away, the water cannons stopped and silence filled the earth and sky. He watched the ship drying and saw how it turned from dark grey to light grey; and then, when it was almost white, the wind blew flakes from its deck and they settled on the quay like snow. But there was no water anywhere. The hulls crumbled, the decks disintegrated and the winds carried them away like dust in the hot, rainless air.

Brian woke up and stretched out his hand for a mug of water. His dehydrated body felt vulnerable under the white sheet. He had foolishly left the curtains slightly apart and a bright column of light had fastened itself to the wall. He winced and turned over. Joanna had asked someone to lunch. Someone she worked with. That meant that she would probably hide the gin and he would have another bad day. Perhaps it would be just as well to ingratiate himself with her by shaving. He got out of bed, opened the bathroom door and immediately cowered away from the brash light that raced at him off the white tiles. The bathroom was normally a dark place, but two weeks previously Joanna had broken the blinds. It was a fact which he kept forgetting. As he picked up his razor his left hand began to shake uncontrollably. Shaving would have to be postponed. Outside the brown-limbed children were rolling in the grass, pushing one another down a slide and hiding in the bushes.

Once he had dressed he went into the living-room. Joanna, tousle-haired and wearing jeans and a sweater that was far too large for her, was sitting cross-legged on the floor. She was looking up at a tall, expensively dressed woman, whose name Brian now remembered was Melanie, and speaking in the urgent, stumbling manner that she unconsciously adopted when too eager to please. With a shock Brian realised that neither of them had noticed him. As he moved forward, Melanie continued to stare at Joanna with the ardent concentration of a portrait painter studying a prospective model.

'What do you do?' said Melanie to Brian.

Melanie and Joanna were perched on the sofa; Brian, pot-bellied and unshaven, was lying on a beanbag, an arrangement that ensured that all the available seating in his flat was occupied. Last week he had sold all the tables and chairs; the week before he had replaced the bookcases with an unsteady-looking structure made out of planks and bricks. There were, however, plenty of books.

'What line are you in?' Melanie persisted.

Brian had been staring out of the window at some workmen who were busily gutting a row of eighteenth-century houses. Slowly he turned towards her; a dimly quizzical look filtered into his glassy red eyes.

'Sorry?' he said.

'Your job,' said Melanie. 'Joanna will never tell me precisely what your job is.'

For years Brian had said that he was reading for the Bar. He'd been reading for the Bar since Joanna had known him. It was much better than saying one was a barrister, an assertion that could easily be checked by consulting a reference book that was publicly available. Joanna had never known Brian open a law book and no one had ever seen him in the vicinity of the Inns of Court. More recently he had claimed to be 'lecturing' at various unspecified institutions. Joanna almost admired the way he managed to avoid disclosing what his subject was supposed to be.

'I'm doing a bit of writing.'

This was new. Joanna was about to put down her coffee but remembered just in time that the side table had been sold.

'Anything published?'

'And I do a bit of lecturing.'

'How interesting. Where?'

'At some of the colleges here in London. I work on a more or less freelance basis.'

Brian stood up and walked over to the rear window in the hope that the sight of her host moving would allay Melanie's in-depth enquiry into his personal achievements.

'Did you meet Joanna at university?'

'No.'

Brian rubbed the window-pane and stared into his neighbour's garden. Joanna and he seldom saw Mrs Ferhurst, the old lady who lived next door to them, but occasionally a tyre or a bath tub would appear on her lawn, and once, in the middle of winter, they had been puzzled by the sight of three mattresses positioned neatly on the frozen grass.

Joanna began to hum irritably. She had told Melanie that she had met Brian at university, which was true; but it was so typical of Melanie to check up – and so predictable of Brian to lie pointlessly.

'But we didn't really get to know each other until we were at university,' said Joanna, glaring at Brian in a manner designed to show that she didn't want her reputation for veracity completely destroyed.

'Sometimes,' continued Brian, 'I feel that I've known Joanna for so long that we must have met in a previous existence.'

The glare fled from Joanna's face and was replaced by an expression of hideous bewilderment. Was he joking? Even she found it difficult to tell. As he stood there by the window, the clouds thinned perceptibly and his blotchy red face glistened in the improved light as if he had just rubbed ointment into his skin to prevent it from flaking,

'Were you studying the same subject?' asked Melanie indefatigably.

With the air of one so squashed by the weight of his own erudition as to be incapable of answering such a simple question, Brian looked at his books. Not only were they crammed into the home-made bookcase, they also peeped from unpacked cardboard boxes and were arranged in precarious piles beneath the only remaining table and on top of an unsaleable piano. The carpet had disappeared underneath layers of accumulated newspapers and magazines.

'You read French, didn't you, Joanna?' said Melanie, her tone implying that she was perfectly sure that Brian must have read a much less acceptable subject.

Brian merely averted his eyes from his bookshelves and once more began to stare listlessly at the garden. Joanna admitted to having read French.

'All my life I've wished that I had a university education,' said Melanie.

This was a regret that Melanie had never expressed once during the entire year that Joanna had known her. Obviously she intended to bring intolerable moral pleasure on Brian to give a detailed account of his life since the age of six. One

revelation on her part, she reasoned, should be enough to open
the floodgates at once.

Brian, however, appeared to have discovered something in
the garden. His lips parted in holy horror, his eyes bulged and
he raised his right arm slowly. Melanie and Joanna leaned
forward. Evidently he was not about to announce something
commonplace – such as the arrival of a rare bird not seen on
these shores for twenty-five years. No, clearly something
truly wonderful had settled itself amongst Mrs Ferhurst's
rubber tyres and dustbins. Just as Joanna was about to move
forward, Brian's mouth closed slowly, his index finger
shrivelled, and he began to shamble back to his beanbag, his
loose-fitting clothes enveloping him as if concealing a body
macerated with disappointment.

His hangover was no worse than usual; in fact, if he had not
somehow known that he was incapable of keeping even a cup
of coffee down, he might have suspected that it was not there
at all, just as one might dismiss the presence of a ghost in a
house one knows to be haunted. Joanna had already gone to
work but had omitted to bring the newspapers upstairs. It was
a little cold for a summer's morning and he put on his
dressing-gown. Although it was made from fine material, it
had a rough, penitential feel. His skin was always sensitive
nowadays. He opened the door and at once noticed that the
walls, the stairs and even the mat which lay beneath the letter
box had become strangely brittle. The more he looked at them
the more he became convinced that the moisture was being
sucked out of the house and out of the world. Soon only the
dried shells of all that had existed would remain. Brian shut the
door hurriedly. He was sweating and his dressing-gown had
come undone to reveal white, hairy skin and a withered
paunch. Don't be silly, don't be silly, he kept on repeating.
Breathing heavily and feeling sick, he made his way to the
bathroom. He grabbed the Princess Di mug, which Joanna
had bought in an uncharacteristic fit of interest in royal
weddings, and began to swirl cold water in it, again and again.

He switched the tap off and stared at the water until all the bubbles had gone; then tentatively he dabbed some liquid onto his lips and tongue, sipped a little cautiously and then took three greedy gulps. He put the mug down. The icy water was rushing into his stomach, competing with great pools of acid. He couldn't help but feel that he should be emitting a hissing noise and clouds of steam.

Restored at last, he went back into the sitting-room, stopped and listened. There was no sound except for the clatter of dishes being washed up in the flat below. He opened the door and stepped onto the landing. The smell of cat's urine came creeping up the stairs towards him. All over his body he could feel a thousand tiny muscles relaxing. Everything was as it should be. Reality had returned in the form of the morning newspaper and four buff-coloured envelopes, almost certainly bills.

Joanna walked gingerly across the room and from time to time looked down to make sure she wasn't leaving traces of anything unforgiveable on the expensive off-white carpet. Melanie's office was decorated in pale shades that complemented the pastel colours that she wore. Joanna found visiting her a trial. She always suspected that she might leave mysterious stains on the delicate fawn covers or send a cup of coffee hurtling over the vulnerable carpet.

Melanie was sitting down behind a desk which had nothing on it except for a modern telephone, white and smooth like a Brancusi sculpture, and a large purple form that was claiming the individed attention of Melanie and her expensive pen. Joanna was usually daunted by the tidiness of the office: how the gleaming tables supported nothing more than carefully arranged magazines and a couple of rubber plants. Everything was bright, uncluttered and smelt of efficiency and polish. Today, however, the sun was in and the whole place had a somewhat exhausted look.

'Ah,' said Melanie without looking up. 'Please sit down.'

'Thank you.'

On these occasions Joanna felt that they were aping the vapid courtesies of male business life; and indeed there was something about the way that Melanie ran the office that eschewed the feminine touch. Everything was sparkling and house-proud, but colour and life had been avoided. Joanna looked at the wastepaper bin. The one screwed up piece of paper that lay in it looked as if it had been positioned there to affirm that the bin was not a mere ornament.

'I did so enjoy yesterday,' said Melanie.

Joanna shifted uncomfortably. It had proved impossible to persuade Brian to touch any of the meal apart from the soup; this he had sipped tentatively, sweating a little. At one moment Joanna had thought that he was going to be sick, but after swallowing some water he had made a successful recovery.

'I'm glad it wasn't too awful. I do apologise for Brian. His conversation wasn't exactly animated.'

'That's all right,' said Melanie. 'It's drink, isn't it?'

'Yes.'

There was no point in denying it any longer. Now that she had a career of her own she hadn't wanted to disclose anything that might have affected her chances of promotion, but Melanie had invited her out to dinner so frequently and made such repeated requests to meet her husband that she had had no option but to ask her to the flat. Joanna had considered inviting her to a restaurant but the thought of trying to engineer Brian through an evening on alien territory had been enough to bring home such a scheme's lack of feasiblity. Instead she decided to spring the event on him unexpectedly in the hope of catching him sober.

'Has he been like this for long?'

'Several years. The doctors have warned him.'

The sun came out and the room glittered efficiently at Joanna, rebuking her for inviting Melanie to an unclean flat and introducing her to a hopeless, drunken Brian.

'I'm sorry, said Joanna. 'I should have warned you before-hand. He had been a little better recently.'

Melanie opened a drawer and took out a diary. There were

no pictures of smiling friends or relatives on her desk – just the modern telephone with its push buttons and smooth surfaces, the partially completed form and the two empty trays.

'I was wondering if you'd care to come to dinner. To my house.'

All their previous meetings had taken place on neutral ground, a small Italian restaurant which was only five minutes' walk from the office. They talked about business and Melanie always paid.

'Yes, I'd love to.'

'Thursday, eight o'clock,' said Melanie, beginning to write before Joanna had started to answer.

'I think so. I'll check with Brian.'

The sun fell on the well-scrubbed rubber plants and then blinked momentarily on Melanie's gold pen as it crossed the page. Melanie stood up and walked round to Joanna.

'I'm so sorry about your husband,' said Melanie, touching her officially on the arm. 'It must be terrible for you.'

'Thank you,' she murmured, 'thank you.'

'I'll look forward to Thursday.'

'Yes.'

When Joanna reached the door, she turned round sharply and looked, as quickly as she could, at the carpet. It was still there – had survived her presence unstained.

Day shone through the curtains, tinting the walls first umber and then fawn. Brian opened his eyes. A few corners of the room were still dark, but sugary grains of light were scattered on the ceiling and a patch of sun about the size of a gull's wing had settled on the pillow next to him. He closed his eyes. He could hear Joanna moving around the kitchen, muttering imprecations directed at an elusive frying-pan or a missing box of matches. She was always disorganised in the morning.

As he rolled onto what had been her side of the bed, the sun fluttered across his eyelids and fleetingly turned the world orange. He buried his head in her pillow. For three years they hadn't slept together. In the kitchen the kettle sighed and the sound of her footsteps hurrying across the tiles reached him. Soon he would hear sizzling and spitting. Even when he was a boy Brian had been unable to understand the institution of breakfast: why people gorged themselves before they had expended any energy. The smell of bacon crept under the door. Retching slightly, he hid under the sheets, until the smell of himself and the darkness comforted him and he was asleep.

Joanna slammed the door and hurried off down the road towards the tube and work. Although the sun was shining, a few drops of rain from a distant cloud skittered across the puddles left by the previous night's storm. As she quickened her pace she tried unsuccessfully to suppress the memory of the weekend. Brian had developed the habit of cleaning his teeth eight or nine times a day; it seemed that whenever she went past the bathroom he was in there, spitting and scrubbing, until, judging by the stains on the basin, his gums bled.

She reached the station, brushed past some purposeless-looking scaffolding and bought a ticket. Brick dust caught her throat, and she noticed that one of the escalators no longer worked. They had been improving the facilities for a year now.

As the remaining escalator descended, men with briefcases and tense eyes rattled past her. She tried to concentrate on the advertisements, but somewhere behind each poster, with its fragmented encomia extolling underpants or automobiles, Brian lurked, reeking of toothpaste and gin, unshaven and with no office to go to.

She walked onto the platform and stood as far away from the line as possible. The tiles were peeling off the wall and vandals had scribbled on the map of the Underground. When the train came in, it was full of businessmen and large African ladies. There was standing room only. As she pushed her way into the throng, she was exhorted to mind the gap.

'Mind the gap,' she kept on repeating as the train rushed her into the City. 'Mind the gap.'

*

At half-past eleven Brian woke up again and inched his way out of bed. Although the room was now light, the curtains were keeping out the worst of the glare. He sat on the edge of the bed and began to dress himself slowly, as if he were putting on his clothes for the first time after a long illness. He knew that if he stood up too quickly he would be sure to become giddy. There was still some water in the mug he always kept on his bedside table; he drank cautiously, straightened himself and made his way to the bathroom.

On the carpet there was some dried shaving foam speckled with tiny black hairs. The mirror was not over the basin. Joanna's clothes were soaking in milky bathwater, and the whole room smelt of detergent. He turned the cold tap on and began to hack at some hard white toothpaste which had formed like coral on the edge of the basin. When he was sure that the water was cold enough, he plunged his wrists underneath the tap. The shock swept through his system, banishing the sensation of faintness. From outside came the noise of traffic and someone playing a radio.

When he was fully dressed he locked the flat and went out. For the last month he had been taking a stroll every morning. As he walked down the road, light leapt incisively off little puddles left by the roadside and hurt his eyes. Far above him in a remote, ice-blue sky cirrus crystallised. Although the sun was overhead and the silver birch cast sharp shadows, he huddled himself into his sweater. Young couples, tanned and wearing short trousers and open necked shirts, ambled past. White buildings glared at him; he began to shiver and then sweat. Some fifteen yards in front of him there was a wooden bench sited beneath a blue dome of foliage, a spot that was both shady and warm. He felt himself moving towards it with difficulty, as if hindered by the hazy light. And then, at last, he was sitting down and gasping for air. Everything was shady and quiet: if he remained still he would be restored. Birds, secure in their trees, began to sing soothingly. He felt the sweat dry on his face and his breathing become more regular.

Irrelevantly the memory of a cross-country race returned: the hectic winter skies, the saliva angry on his hot skin, the pain in his chest that gradually faded into the rhythm of running; how he would spit and sweat until all the moisture was gone and he was blown like parchment over the giddying fields.

At six they left the office. Joanna noticed how tidy Melanie's car was: no old shopping bags, discarded sweaters or empty cigarette packets. The seats were comfortable and there was a strong smell of perfume. It was the first time that she had seen Melanie wear make-up.

As they made their way northwards rain began to fall. They peered myopically through the windscreen at the smudged streets and scurrying, blurred shoppers. Rain bounced violently off the bonnet, lashed the windows and rose in great clouds of spray. Conversation seemed dangerous. Melanie switched on the windscreen wipers and they sat watching the world appear and then vanish beneath a swirling sheet of glue.

At last the storm slackened and Melanie drove quickly through the suburbs until the reached a cul-de-sac studded with neat modern houses. The rain had stopped but the wind still flung sketchy gusts of water from the dripping conifers.

Inside, Melanie's house was highly polished and the furniture gleamed in spite of the grey, watery day.

'Sherry?' said Melanie.

'Thanks.'

Melanie had chosen warm colours for her home. Although the room in which they were sitting was sparsely decorated, it emitted none of the chill which Joanna associated with her host's passion for order. The smell of food preparing itself for consumption drifted in encouragingly. Joanna sipped the sherry and felt herself relax.

'Why did you marry Brian?'

Joanna smiled at Melanie's lack of a small talk. 'I'm not sure,' she said. 'I suppose it was because I thought he had a vision.'

'A vision?'

'I suppose it was childish really. He talked of art a lot and knew about Blake. Things like that.'

'And he was convincing?'

Night began to fall over the wet trees and the grey garden. They could hear the wind wrapping itself intimately around the house. A log fire was somehow ignited without the touch of a human hand. Joanna felt grateful for the warmth and the glass of sherry.

'I was a farmer's daughter,' said Melanie, as she laid the table and lit two white tall candles.

'I can't imagine you getting the cows in,' said Joanna.

Melanie laughed and then began to speak of a childhood ruled by the bells of school and church and of her early determination to escape from the country. 'I don't know why but I always hated it. The mud in our farmyard, the smell . . .'

Outside the rain dripped onto the patio. Joanna thought of all the little gardens with their immature shrubs and well-edged lawns lying tidily in the dark.

'Come and eat,' said Melanie, her face softer in the half-light. 'Wine?' Tiny sparks of light drowned as she poured claret into two elegant glasses.

'Thanks,' said Joanna, taking her place.

Flushes of warm light spread across the mahogany table. As they sipped their claret, Joanna found herself hating the scruffy existence that she had led for so long.

'What is the matter with Brian? No one drinks as much as he does without a reason.'

'I don't know,' said Joanna slowly. 'I suppose it is that he never saw the vision he proclaimed.'

'I'm sorry but I'm not quite with you,' said Melanie, looking puzzled.

'Well, he had this vision of life, of a pattern which he believed in. That was what was attractive about him.' Joanna couldn't see Melanie's face, just her bowed head. 'But after a while he found out it was just something he'd put together from books and things.' The sentence sounded awkward. She leant forward urgently and felt her elbow nudge a wine glass over. 'Oh dear . . .' There was a click and the room was full of harsh electric light. A lake of claret the shape of Africa lay there being absorbed into the carpet. 'I'm most terribly sorry.'

'That's all right,' said Melanie, disappearing into the kitchen.

'It was very clumsy of me,' Joanna heard herself confess. 'I do hope you can get it out.'

Melanie made a few worried dabs at the carpet and then sprinkled on some more salt. At length she stood up and stared at the stain. The empty shelves glinted at Joanna like bones that had been picked clean of flesh. How could she ever have talked of visions in this bookless room?

Melanie went out and then reappeared with the sweet course and a polite, forgiving expression. She switched out the lights and they began to talk again. The electric log fire irradiated its constant, unblinking warmth and from the kitchen came the distant purr of the central heating system adjusting itself. The conversation drifted. Joanna's replies became more and more perfunctory; she detected a hurt note in her host's voice and then silence descended once more as they watched the candles become stouter, curlicued with wax.

'This is most awfully kind of you,' said Joanna, aware of the way she always borrowed her mother's expressions when in difficulty.

'You mustn't be afraid to talk about your husband. You know it helps to talk.'

'Yes,' said Joanna.

The stain was still out there in the darkness, waiting for the lights to be turned on.

Just after midnight Melanie dropped Joanna at the flat. The storm had spent itself, the sky was surprisingly light, and the moon shone on pools of rainwater. As she walked up the path, Joanna breathed in the dustless air and felt refreshed. She opened her handbag and began to rummage around for the key. Then she took out her compact, lipstick, a cigarette lighter that didn't work, her cheque book, what she suspected was a letter from an old college friend and a packet of paper handkerchiefs. These she laid methodically on the doorstep and told herself not to panic. She angled her handbag in the light; it gaped back keylessly at her. She picked up a pebble and lobbed it at Brian's window. There was a sharp click. The window looked as impenetrable as the wall that surrounded it. Angrily she jammed her possessions back and with the flat of her hand hit the door hard, which at once swung open and quivered against the inside wall.

Joanna stood at the bottom of the stairs. Above her Brian snored scornfully. The smell of cat's urine, a legacy they had inherited from a previous owner and had been unable to extirpate, leapt at her from the carpet. She dropped the latch and ran upstairs.

From force of habit she paused on the landing and listened at Brian's door. She was always afraid that he would choke on his own vomit. Gently she turned the handle and went in. The room smelt only of gin and socks. Moonlight fell on the white sheets, and his open mouth lay drying on his face like blood. Several blankets were crumpled on the floor. She closed the door, and went back to her own room and, having flung off her clothes, got guiltily into bed without washing.

As she lay there everything became clear: the visits to the restaurants, the requests to visit the office after hours and the invitation to her home. And what annoyed Joanna was that when it had happened she could not have been less prepared. To think that she had still been worried about that stupid stain.

The journey back would stay with her. As they went out to the car, Joanna had heard the thunder rolling away and felt an unexpected tenderness for Melanie's, defeated face, ageing in the yellow lamp-light. Joanna had wanted to apologise – how stupid she had been to insist on being taken home at once – but she said nothing as Melanie had driven her through the empty, hissing streets.

Joanna was horribly awake and could still hear Brian's stertorous breathing. She turned over three times, sipped a little water from the mug on her bedside table and adjusted her pillow. But it was no good. She got out of bed and went back to Brian's room. In his drunken sleep he had thrown off the bedding and now lay there naked. The white sheets were crumpled on the floor like layers of discarded skin. He looked vulnerable – newly hatched. Naked too, she lay down beside him and passed her hands over his body. She could almost imagine him young and undamaged again, but for his open mouth – a resident wound.

She was there for hours. The ceiling paled with the approach of morning, and then the day came too, slowly plating his body with silver light – as if it were something that could be made valuable.

Brian wearing a pink shirt, sat silently on a reproduction Regency chair. The banished beanbags were in a friend's cellar. Now that the number of his books had been halved, sturdy new shelves bought and his cardboard boxes burnt, the carpet was entirely visible for the first time in years. It was dirty with newsprint but otherwise quite well preserved, having been adequately protected by discarded *Evening Standards* and *Guardians*.

'Daphne Hoskins was most impressed with your ideas,' said Melanie.

'I'm glad,' Joanna replied. She'd been working in the office for just over a year. Promotion had been rapid. She bustled into the kitchen.

'And how is the book going, Brian?' said Melanie.

Brian fingered the top button of his shirt. What book? What was the woman talking about? And then he remembered: it was a project that the man from the Rehabilitation Unit had suggested. Something to get stuck into.

'Oh, it's coming along,' he said, doing up the top button of hs shirt. He was sure that he was beginning to smell. It was easy to tell from the way that Melanie kept dabbing her long nose with what he imagined was a scented handkerchief.

'Almost time for lunch,' said Joanna, reappearing from the kitchen. She looked at Brian. He was sitting with his knees pressed tightly together and his arms crossed. His black slip-on shoes were lightly speckled with toothpaste. She noted with disgust that he had done up the top button of his shirt. He looked as if he were in an institution.

'I hope you haven't done anything special for me,' said Melanie, stubbing out her cigarette.

Joanna opened the window and Brian immediately got up and, like someone practising how to walk, made his way out of the room.

The women waited for the sound of vomiting, but instead there came the noise of drawers and cupboards being opened and shut. Then the door was pushed ajar so quietly that it occurred to Joanna that he might be trying to slip back into the room unnoticed.

'Are you all right?' she said.

He sidled in wearing a pale blue shirt that was slightly too large for him. In the past three months he had lost a lot of weight, more than ever it was a struggle to get him to eat anything.

'Have some soup,' said Melanie.

'Thanks,' said Brian.

He sat down and Joanna put a bowl in front of him. Scalding steam rose from it and he felt himself beginning to sweat. He picked up his spoon and stirred the soup perfunctorily. The steam rose even faster, great clouds of it billowing into the air. He could feel his neck being ringed with perspiration. In another minute he would start to smell again.

'This is one of Clarissa Davies-Horton's recipes,' said Joanna.

'Really,' replied Melanie. 'I liked her courgette and black-berry soup, although I believe that some found it rather tart.'

It was true that his shirt was not sticking to his chest, but on the other hand he was sure that if he leant backwards it would. His forehead was wet; soon the sweat would begin to trickle into his eyes. Melanie and Joanna were sipping their glasses of water. He knew that they drank wine when they went out. A reeking obstacle that prevented them from having a good time, that was all that he was.

'I'm sorry. Excuse me.'

They watched him go out.

'Why does Brian change his shirt every ten minutes?' asked Melanie.

'I don't know. Why does he brush his teeth fifteen times a day?'

They heard an anxious, high-pitched cry and then what sounded like the noise of the wardrobe toppling over.

'He's not getting any better?'

'I don't keep any booze in the house now and he hasn't got much money, so I thought he was drinking less. But the other day I came home and found him flat out in the kitchen. Why does he do it? I don't know – and there are days when I'm not sure that he does either.'

Brian came back into the room. He was wearing a beach shirt which had a Spanish guitar motif. Joanna had bought it as a joke ten years previously.

'Sorry,' he said and coughed.

He looked unsteadily around the room. Three of the windows were open and he was sure that only one had been open before.

'Do sit down, darling,' said Joanna. 'It's quite unnerving seeing you standing there.'

'Sorry.'

In a minute they would tell him to stop apologising. He sat down and picked up the soup spoon. In Aubrey's *Brief Lives* he had read an account of a man who believed that his perspiration was turning into flies. Perhaps he was as deluded as that man. He put down his soup spoon and sniffed carefully. The rich smell of his deodorant was still there, but there was no denying that underneath all the perfumes there was the rotting stench that was himself. He felt the vomit rising.

As she watched him being sick out of the window, Joanna noticed that his shirt was tucked in at the front but not at the back.

In the hotel garden the plum tree shed its yellow leaves and stained the path with purple fruit. They sat in a row on a wooden bench – Brian slightly apart from Melanie and Joanna

– and watched the tall cedars shiver in the chill light of autumn. On the table in front of them a large silver teapot was growing cold; their visit was safely outside licensing hours.

'Tea?' said Joanna.

'No thank you,' said Brian.

The garden was bordered by tall trees that muted the roar of the traffic. No housing was visible. They were alone except for an old man who was mowing the lawn. The growing season was almost over.

'I've booked the tickets,' said Melanie.

'What was that?' said Brian.

They looked at him as if surprised that he could still speak.

'We're going on holiday,' said Joanna.

For the first time he felt scared. He tried to remember the financial details about the flat and the mortgage but couldn't even recall where he had put the relevant papers.

'I've got a villa in Ibiza,' said Melanie. 'I thought that Joanna . . . and you . . . might care to come out for a nice sunny Christmas.'

'It's been a miserable summer and it's so kind of Melanie to offer.'

Brian reminded himself that five years ago when he had stopped feeling despair and felt nothing instead he had counted it as a great victory. But somehow he had always assumed that Joanna would stay to look after him and make sure that he could continue to feel nothing in safety.

'Don't look so worried. You're going too,' said Joanna.

'Got to get you out a bit,' said Melanie.

It was in just such a voice, Brian realised without amusement, that she had encouraged the hockey team and no doubt the basketball and lacrosse teams as well. Of course he couldn't bring himself to say that. He lacked the energy to be sour. Anyway she was the clear winner.

'I think I'll go for a stroll,' he said, turning away from them quickly.

The wind blew the yellow leaves across the lawn. From somewhere came the sound of children's voices. Brian tried to walk correctly, neither too quickly nor too slowly; his arms, he told himself, should not be kept too stiff but should swing very slightly like those of any normal person. He reached the edge of the lawn and found a gap in the hedge which he had not noticed before. Beyond it was a small, well-grassed area almost completely encircled by evergreens that acted as an effective wind brake. The hush was so absolute that he might almost have been underground, the tall trees and lucid blue sky nothing more than frescoes sparkling on stone. In the middle of the clearing a wooden ship rested on a raised platform. Although it was about the size of a small yacht, it did not look as if it had ever put to sea; instead it seemed to have been borrowed from a Walt Disney cartoon. It was painted in primary colours and its deck bristled with bogus black cannons. Suddenly two blond-haired boys, their skin dark in the weak sunlight of late September, rushed out of the bushes and swarmed effortlessly up the ladder and onto the deck. For a moment he felt himself utterly possessed by a stubborn, impossible longing to be with them on their boat. As he walked away, he heard their voices raised in ignorant happiness.

The gardener was locking up the mower. It would not be needed again for many months. A gust of wind carried the last leaves from the stark plum tree. Brian knew that Melanie was holding his wife's hand underneath the table. Still, he had a bottle tucked away under the dirty clothes in the laundry basket. Tonight he would take it to his bedroom and drink it just the way he liked: all by himself and in the dark.

Biographical Notes on the Authors

CECIL BONSTEIN was born in the East End of London. He was a first aid leader in the first blitz, then served in the RAF and was in Bengal during the famine. He later worked as a manager in British Telecom. Thirty years ago he failed to get into print, only trying again recently. He has had stories in *Acumen*, *Critical Quarterly*, *Iron* and *Panurge*.

WILLIAM BOYD was born in Ghana and educated at the universities of Nice, Glasgow and Oxford. His first novel, *A Good Man in Africa*, won the 1981 Whitbread Prize and the 1982 Somerset Maugham Award; his second, *An Ice-Cream War*, was winner of the 1982 John Llewellyn Rhys Prize and was short-listed for the 1982 Booker Prize. He is also the author of the novels *Stars and Bars* and *The New Confessions*, and *On the Yankee Station*, a collection of short stories.

JENNY DISKI was born in London in 1947, where she still lives with her daughter. She is the author of three novels, *Rainforest*, *Like Mother* and *Nothing Natural*.

JANICE GALLOWAY was born in Ayrshire. Her short stories have appeared in every major Scottish literary magazine and in anthologies. She recently adapted Radclyffe Hall's *Well of Loneliness* for theatre and her first novel, *The Trick is to Keep Breathing*, was published by *Polygon* earlier this year. She likes cities and lives in Glasgow.

JANE GARDAM, born n 1928 in Coatham, North Yorkshire, now lives in East Kent. She is a Whitbread award winner, and her novel *God on the Rocks* was a runner-up for the Booker Prize in 1978. She has written eight books for children and nine for adults, her most recent being a collection of stories, *Showing the Flag*.

NADINE GORDIMER was born and lives in South Africa. She has published nine novels, including *A Sport of Nature*, and seven collections of short stories. Her first collection of non-fiction, *The Essential Gesture*, was published in 1988. Among many literary awards she has won the Booker Prize for her novel *The Conservationist*.

ROBERT GROSSMITH was born in Dagenham, Essex in 1954. He moved to Stockholm, Sweden, in 1977, remaining there till 1984, teaching English as a Foreign Language and translating. He then did a doctorate on Vladimir Nabokov at the University of Keele. Since 1988 he has been unemployed, except for occasional EFL work. His first novel is published by Hamish Hamilton this autum.

RUSSELL HOBAN has lived in London since 1969. He has written fifty-seven books for children including the Frances stories and *The Mouse and his Child*. His most recent adult novels are *Riddley Walker*, *Pilgermann* and *The Medusa Frequency*.

DESMOND HOGAN is the author of two novels, *A Curious Street* (1984), and *A New Shirt* (1986), and two collections of short stories, *The Morning Thief* (1987) and *Lebanon Lodge* (1988). His *Collected Stories* were published in the USA in 1989, with an introduction by Louise Erdrich.

JANETTE TURNER HOSPITAL was born in Australia and now lives in Canada. Her novels include *The Ivory Swing* (1982), winner of the Canadian Seal First Novel Award; *Borderline* (1985), runner-up for the Australian National Book Award; and *Charades* (1989), which was shortlisted for the Miles Franklin and the National Book Council Awards.

ELIZABETH JOLLEY lives with her husband in Western Australia where she cultivates a small orchard and a goose farm. She wrote for twenty years before publishing her first novel and is now acclaimed as one of Australia's most challenging and entertaining writers.

GABRIEL JOSIPOVICI was born in Nice in 1940. He lived in Egypt from 1945 to 1956, when he came to the UK. He is part-time Professor of English in the School of European Studies at the University of Sussex, and has written eight novels, two volumes of stories, five critical books, and a number of his plays have been performed in London and Edinburgh and on the radio.

FRANCIS KING spent his childhood in India, and later travelled widely for the British Council. He now lives in London. His many novels include *Act of Darkness*, *The Woman Who Was God*, *Frozen Music*, *Voices in an Empty Room*, *The Needle*, *A Game of Patience*, *Flights* and *A Domestic Animal*. He has also written five volumes of short stories, one volume of poetry, a biography of E. M. Forster and two travel books.

HANIF KUREISHI was born in South London and studied philosophy at King's College, London. He has written plays and two films, *My Beautiful Launderette* and *Sammy and Rosie Get Laid*. His first novel, *The Buddha of Suburbia*, is published this year.

MOY MCCRORY was born in Liverpool to Irish-Catholic parents. She took a degree in art at Liverpool and Belfast, and is married with one child. She has published two collections of stories, *The Water's Edge* and *Bleeding Sinners*. Her first novel, *The Fading Shrine*, is published this year.

STEVE MCGIFFEN was born in Manchester in 1954, and lives in Whitby, North Yorkshire. He began writing in 1988. 'Geology' was his first published story. He has recently completed a novel.

ADAM MARS-JONES was born in London in 1954. His first book of fiction, *Lantern Lecture*, won the Somerset Maugham Award in 1981. Since then he has edited *Mae West is Dead*, a collection of lesbian and gay fiction, and co-written (with Edmund White) *The Darker Proof: Stories from a Crisis*. He reviews films for the *Independent*.

ALICE MUNRO is the author of a novel, *Lives of Girls and Women*, and of six collections of stories. Her stories are published in the *New Yorker* and the *Atlantic*. She and her husband live in Clinton, Ontario, near Lake Huron.

PHILIP OAKES has published poetry, four novels and three volumes of autobiography. He has written for films and television. He writes an out-of-town column for the *Independent on Sunday* and reviews crime fiction for the *Literary Review*.

DAVID PARK was born into a working-class Protestant family in Belfast and has spent most of his life living and working there. He is married and currently teaches in a small grammar school between Belfast and Downpatrick. His first book and collection of stories, *Oranges from Spain*, is published this summer.

FIONA FARRELL POOLE is a full-time teacher, part-time writer; she is keen to reverse the roles. She was winner of the IBM writers' award in 1989, and won the Mobil-New Zealand Dominion Short Story Award the previous year.

FREDERIC RAPHAEL was born in Chicago in 1931, and educated

at Charterhouse and St John's College, Cambridge. He has published numerous novels and collections of stories. He won the Royal Television Society's Writer of the Year Award for his series of plays, *The Glittering Prizes*, and an Oscar for the screenplay of *Darling*. His most recent novel, *After the War*, was published in 1989. Married, he lives in France and England.

D. J. TAYLOR was born in Norwich in 1960. He has published a novel, *Great Eastern Land* (1986), and a study of contemporary British fiction, *A Vain Conceit* (1989).

JONATHAN TREITEL was born in London in 1959. He has worked as a physicist in California and has a doctorate in philosophy of science from Stanford University. Bloomsbury are publishing his first novel *The Red Cabbage Café* in summer 1990.

CHARLES WILKINSON was born in Birmingham in 1950. He was educated at the universities of Lancaster and East Anglia and has recently completed an M. Phil. at Trinity College, Dublin. A collection of his poems was published by Iron Press in 1987, and a number of his stories have been published in the *London Magazine*. He now teaches in Hertfordshire.

Acknowledgements

'It Will Grow Again', copyright © Cecil Bonstein 1989, was first published in *Critical Quarterly* Volume 31 Number 2 and is reprinted by permission of the author.

'Transfigured Night', copyright © William Boyd 1989, was first published in *Granta* autumn 1989 and is reprinted by permission of the author and Stephen Durbridge.

'The Vanishing Princess or The Origins of Cubism', copyright © Jenny Diski 1989, was first published in *New Statesman & Society* 27 October 1989 and is reprinted by permission of the author, Curtis Brown & John Farquharson, 162–168 Regent Street, London W1R 5TB, and *New Statesman & Society*.

'After the Rains', copyright © Janice Galloway 1989, was first published in *Edinburgh Review* 82 Winter 1989, and is reprinted by permission of the author.

'Chinese Funeral', copyright © Jane Gardam 1990, was first broadcast on Radio 4 'Morning Story' on 3 January 1990 and is first printed here by permission of the author and David

Higham Associates Ltd, 5–8 Lower John Street, Golden Square, London W1R 4HA.

'Jump', by Nadine Gordimer copyright © Felix Licencing B.V. 1989 was first published in *Harpers* October 1989 and is reprinted by permission of the author and A. P. Watt Ltd, 20 John Street, London WC1N 2DL.

'Company', copyright © Robert Grossmith 1989, was first published in the *Spectator* 23/30 December 1989 and is reprinted by permission of the author and Anthony Sheil Associates Ltd, 43 Doughty Street, London WC1N 2LF.

'The Man with the Dagger', copyright © Russell Hoban 1989, was first published in *Granta* autumn 1989 and is reprinted by permission of the author and David Higham Associates Ltd, 5–8 Lower John Street, Golden Square, London W1R 4HA.

'An Affair', copyright © Desmond Hogan 1989, was first published in the *European Gay Review* March 1989 and is reprinted by permission of the author and Rogers, Coleridge & White, 20 Powis Mews, London W11 1JN.

'The Loss of Faith', copyright © Janette Turner Hospital 1989, was first published in *Prairie Schooner* Winter 1988/89 (under the title of 'Expatriate') and is reprinted by permission of the author and Vardey & Brunton Associates, 125 Moore Park Road, London SW6 4PS.

'The Goose Path', copyright © Elizabeth Jolley 1989, was first published in *Encounter* Magazine September/October 1989 and is reprinted by permission of the author and David Higham Associates Ltd, 5–8 Lower John Street, Golden Square, London W1R 4HA.

'Goldberg', copyright © Gabriel Josipovici 1989, was first published in *London Magazine* April/May 1989 and is reprinted by permission of the author and John Johnson Ltd, Clerkenwell House, 45–47 Clerkenwell Green, London EC1R 0HT.

'Vibrations', copyright © Francis King 1989, was first published in the *European Gay Review* March 1989 and is reprinted by permission of the author and A. M. Heath & Co Ltd, 79 St Martin's Lane, London WC2N 4AA.

'Esther', copyright © Hanif Kureishi 1989, was first published in the *Atlantic Monthly* May 1989 and is reprinted by permission of the author, Rogers, Coleridge & White, 20 Powis Mews, London W11 1JN and Faber and Faber Ltd.

'The Wrong Vocation', copyright © Moy McCrory 1989, was first published in *Critical Quarterly* vol. 31 no. 1 and is reprinted by permission of the author and Anthony Sheil Associates Ltd, 43 Doughty Street, London WC1N 2LF.

'Geology', copyright © Steve McGiffen 1989, was first published in *Stand* Magazine winter 1989/90 and is reprinted by permission of the author.

'Baby Clutch', copyright © Adam Mars-Jones 1989, was first published in *Granta* summer 1989 and is reprinted by permission of the author and Peters, Fraser & Dunlop, 5th Floor, The Chambers, Chelsea Harbour, Lots Road, London SW10 0XF.

'Goodness and Mercy', copyright © Alice Munro 1989, was first published in the *New Yorker* 20 March 1989 and is reprinted by permission of the author and Abner Stein, 10 Roland Gardens, London SW7 3PH.

'Arthur Seal and the Hand of Fate', copyright © Philip Oakes 1989, was first published in *Woman's Journal* July 1989 and is reprinted by permission of the author and Elaine Greene Ltd, 37 Goldhawk Road, London W12 8QQ.

'Oranges from Spain', copyright © David Park 1989, was first published in *Critical Quarterly* vol. 31 no. 2 and is reprinted by permission of the author and Anthony Sheil Associates Ltd, 43 Doughty Street, London WC1N 2LF.

'Skinny Louie', copyright © Fiona Farrell Poole, was first published in *New Zealand Listener* May 1990 and is reprinted by permission of the author and Glenys Bean Literary Agency, 15 Elizabeth Street, Freemasons Bay, Auckland, New Zealand.

'The Beverly Hills Snowman', copyright © Kola Investments 1989, was first published in the *Sunday Express Magazine* 24 December 1989 and is reprinted by permission of Frederic Raphael and A. P. Watt Ltd, 20 John Street, London WC1N 2DR.

'At Brackus's', copyright © D. J. Taylor 1989, was first published in *London Magazine* April/May 1989 and is reprinted by permission of the author.

'Shaking Hands with Theodor Herzl', copyright © Jonathan Treitel 1989, was first published in *London Magazine* February/March 1989 and is reprinted by permission of the author and A. P. Watt Ltd, 20 John Street, London WC1N 2DR.

'In the Dark', copyright © Charles Wilkinson 1989, was first published in *London Magazine* December 1989/January 1990 and is reprinted by permission of the author and Curtis Brown & John Farquharson, 162–168 Regent Street, London W1R 5TB.

We are most grateful to the editors of the publications in which the stories first appeared for permission to reprint them in this volume.